Vaneglory

by the same author

BELOVED SON

VANEGLORY

A Science Fiction Novel
by
GEORGE TURNER

FABER AND FABER
London · Boston

First published in 1981
by Faber and Faber Limited
3 Queen Square, London WC1N 3AU
Printed in Great Britain by
Willmer Brothers Limited
Rock Ferry, Merseyside
All rights reserved

British Library Cataloguing in Publication Data

Turner, George
Vaneglory
I. Title
823'.914[F]   PR6070.U71/

ISBN 0-571-11664-7

Our plesance here is all VANEGLORY;
This false world is bot transitory;
The flesh is brukle the Fend is sle.
Timor mortis conturbat me.

Art magicianis and astrologgis,
Rethoris, logicianis and theologgis,
Thame helpis no conclusionis sle.
Timor mortis conturbat me.

WILLIAM DUNBAR, "Lament for the Makaris"

For my friends in and from Glasgow. And if you demur that Donald's dialect is not always consistent, why, neither is yours—particularly among those of you who have, like Donald, knocked about the world and picked up bad habits from Sassenachs, Yanks and Ockers.

This novel was written with the assistance of a grant from the Literature Board of the Australia Council.

CONTENTS

The characters in this novel are creatures of the author's imagination and bear no relation to any person living or dead.

PART ONE

Glasgow, AD 1992 — And Time to be Going

A man's dying is more the survivors' affair than his own.
THOMAS MANN, *The Magic Mountain*

Maytime in Glasgow was never the season of troubadours, though roamin' in the gloamin' wi' a sonsy bit o' slap-an'-tickle was a Maytime side of life even as late as 1992. The other side was silent shipyards and bankrupt industry and sad jokes covering proud despair.

The grim city did not agonize alone in the final year of the Gone Time, when half the world starved, half shrank before the mutating plagues and none of it believed deep down that the end had begun. Glasgow was only one more among a dying many.

But it was there, in the shadow of planetary collapse, that an ancient side issue of history gathered impetus.

I

The transit house was only another nondescript city dwelling, deliberately so. They used it only for convenience, mostly during personality changes.

This afternoon two of them were there. Plus, of course, Willie tap-tapping in the cellar. They sat in the half-furnished parlour with the table and a manila folder between them.

The older man, who might have been forty, asked, "What do you do with him all day?"

"Prepare his meals. Refuse to answer questions. Make 'orrible threatening faces—like this—when he gets insistent."

"Relax! The wind might change. How does he react to menaces from a man six inches shorter and thirty pounds lighter?"

"Four inches and twenty pounds!" said the small man. "And don't forget I'm dynamite, I am!"

"Ho-hum, you're not bad, but is he incapable?"

The small man, who was perhaps five feet four, said seriously, "He isn't, but I know what this is all about while he hasn't a clue, and that undercuts his morale—what I've left him of it."

"You say he hasn't a clue, Giles, but he *must* know who we are and what we want and why."

Giles hesitated, leaving something unsaid. "I'm not allowed to question him. I got well carpeted for playing games with him at the pub."

"I heard; it wasn't bright of you. What does he do all day?"

Giles raised a finger for quiet, and faintly from the cellar came the staccato of the typewriter. "All day? Biography for a daily more hypothetical posterity?"

"Writing down what's happened to him. Looking for a pattern, to work out what and why."

"You believe that? All right, you believe it. Do you read the stuff?"

"Of course. I let him have the machine to see what he might come up with. When I took the first pages away he was mad angry, then he cooled off and started making a carbon for me! And, Bjorn, I'm not getting a damned clue out of it."

" 'Bjorn' was the Norway job. I'm Alastair here, Scottish accent and all when I'm at the shipyard."

Giles was interested. "I don't know yet what you're doing here; the shipyards closed down years ago."

"You've been away too long. A few workshops and dry docks waited for a miracle to reopen them, and along came the miracle, the monopole drive! Rocket propulsion obsolete overnight, star ships on the way! Mankind really in the sky and one beautiful, huge, orbital laboratory-factory being put together in the perfect place—a shipyard. Three hundred metres of precision engineering, to lift into space under her own power! Think of the fortunes it cost to build that Barnard's Star abortion in orbit! The thing's two years on her way and already a technical revolution out of date; she was the first but that's all she was. And when *Pride O' Clyde* lifts—these bloody Scots lay it on thick, don't they?—I'll be aboard as Chief Engineer."

Giles was no longer interested, "It isn't space ships the world needs."

"But we who have the genes need this one. We need to know what space will do to us, or perhaps for us. That will be my real job aboard, guinea-pigging for The Company."

"Company of bastards!"

The vehemence was unexpected, but Giles had always been an emotional problem. Alastair played it lightly. "Bitter, Giles? Seen too much too often? *Weltschmerz*?"

"No." He gestured at the floor. "Him." The typewriter muttered in its prison.

"Willy? For sanity's sake, Giles!"

"What we're doing to him is barbarous."

"*Barbarous!*"

"Don't waste outrage on me, Alastair. He had an accident, a car smash, three years ago, two years before I latched on to him. He's amnesiac."

Alastair's eyebrows rose, but not with sympathy. "Tough titty, as they say."

"Whatever he did, he doesn't know it. He's newborn. He shouldn't suffer for what somebody by the same name did."

Alastair thought before he spoke. "You can't afford revisionism."

"Revis—Commie lingo! Shit's what that is! The Company are bastards and I am human after all."

"Are you? And after all what? Well, perhaps you are and perhaps you aren't, but don't prattle about it to the old man. He'll strangle you on your own guts."

Giles said sullenly, "It's a sense of justice with me." He pushed at the folder. "Try reading the first pages."

Alastair riffled the sheets. "Writes a lot, doesn't he?" He glanced more keenly at Giles. "Is this what you got me here for?"

"I wanted a friend to read it. We used to be friends."

"How could we not be?"

It was a careless, meaningless response. Giles knew he should not have used the word. Company relationships did not accommodate easily to emotional concepts. As Alastair began to read Giles thought, We've become The Company again, and when that happens we cease to be people.

WILL'S TYPESCRIPT : There are a chair and a table and a bed and a miserable forty-watt globe to make up the lack of a window.

There is also Giles bringing food twice a day—reasonable food in a starving world—and making faces when I pump him but answering nothing. At first the grimaces were unnerving, for there is real ferocity in this little man, but a sense of humour undid him. He began improving the performance, producing something new each time, and by the third day we both knew it for a game.

(Alastair's mind twitched disgust. *For sanity's sake, Giles!* A *bloody game?*)

I could laugh if I didn't hate his guts and fear his powers.

He brings the *Scotsman* and I read it from front to back; its restrained language strives to put at arm's length the darkening chronicle of world decay. Energy crisis : the oil shortage forecast twenty years ago is a reality still unprepared for, the building of nuclear plants is impeded by the oil shortage, and our braggart Australian solar assemblies are too slow in production (thanks to greedy unions and incompetent government) to benefit even ourselves. War and threats of war : little wars smoking and the big, big war ready to rumble, with everybody veiling threats at peace talks and nobody with nerve to throw the first punch. Food crisis : the Far East starving to death under the frightened eyes of a once-gluttonous West now unable to feed half its own people, despair at mutated crops with built-in toxicity, a pointing of fingers at countries like Australia where the wheat and rice still grow, and a questioning of how they escape while other nations die.

Terrifying, but remote to a man staring at the four walls of a cellar.

On the fourth morning—*this* morning—he brought the typewriter and some quarto. I wouldn't let him see me ecstatic at the gift of something to do, so I thanked him with spite. "What should I write? My diary of the subterranean social whirl?"

For once he did not offer a gargoyle mask but looked as if he would like to say a word, even a friendly word, but could not. And went silently away.

Forbidden to speak to me? That would be pretty strange after all the formidable chatter that went on before he trapped me in his damned damp dungeon.

Forbidden by whom?

(The typing broke off and was resumed on a fresh page.)

At breakfast (godawful Scotch porridge—parritch!—with the tribal flavouring of salt because sugar cane is another of the crops mutating themselves into sludge) he picked up the sheets I typed yesterday and before I could protest took them away.

Why should he—or anybody—be interested?

An hour later, in an unscheduled visit, he brought carbon paper. For once he unbuttoned a little, proffered the sheets and grinned—and fleetingly my stomach turned over as once again he looked for a swift second the spitting image of Angus.

So I have a public! But nothing happens down here; I haven't even Bruce's spider to weave cheap philosophy.

"Meditation in a Glasgow Rat Pit, by a Trapped Rat"?

But why should I write for you, Giles, when I can write for me? Intensive recall may provide clues I have missed.

So . . .

It was at Glasgow Central that I realized something inexplicably wrong in my behaviour. Something subliminal was rising and insisting and my spirits were troubled as I trudged down that grey station. (That was a fortnight ago. The *Scotsman* reports, still with demented dignity, that Britain's trains no longer run. What's it like out there, Giles, with paralysis setting in?)

I looked around for the ramp down to Union Street—and can pinpoint that as the moment of the onset of psychic cold.

I had never been in Britain before, let alone Glasgow; I had no more knowledge of Union Street than of the lunar mountains; I hadn't consciously realized that the station is elevated above street level . . .

I am trying to recover the sudden consciousness of what had been only a twinge in the back of my mind—that I didn't know what I was doing in Glasgow or why I had left Australia.

Think of spending eight weeks securing passport and visa and battling for a seat on what turned out to be one of the last planes to leave Australia (the *Scotsman* says my whole country is now grounded for lack of fuel), touching down in London to go straight to Euston and book for Glasgow, and leaving the train in a strange city—to realize that you can't account rationally for your presence or for anything you have done in the past two months.

I am amnesiac, Giles. Waking, three years ago, without a past was a terror that could be understood and dealt with; I read books about it and came to terms. There is no coming to terms with the knowledge of having, zombie fashion, carried out a series of actions leading from nothing to nothing. And of never once having questioned the lack of meaning.

Try to imagine effect without cause. That is what I faced, in a strange country, with the centre of my mind a gulf of unreason into which I might topple and never reach bottom.

Mind dealt with it as a mind always does this side insanity: Lot of nonsense . . . momentary hiatus . . . tired and need a meal . . . It's a mighty machine, the mind; with that scatter of small thoughts it covered over a gap the size of my whole private universe and made it possible for me to carry on.

I lifted my bag, walked down to Union Street, then to Gallowgate Street, and found something familiar about Glasgow. This could have been a shopping centre in one of the more crowded Melbourne suburbs—medium-rise buildings, plate glass, shoppers, the rising grubbiness of a city when the overnight clean-up is wearing off. But not the *musty* grubbiness that stank when petrol was available and cars ran.

I walked east without questioning why I should prefer one direction to another—a mental placidity had set in—until I came to the Trongate and recognized at once the old tower straddling the footpath. "Tron" meant, in the old dialect, a market, so this had been . . .

The cold returned, and the terror of not knowing.

Had Angus, talking of Glasgow, told me of the Trongate? Had there been a photograph? He had spoken so much of "hame".

It was not good enough. I dropped the bag and leaned against the nearest wall, wits scattering.

And there, a fantasy unleashed, was Angus, leaning against a pillar of the Trongate and grinning at me.

But Angus was home, at his flat in Melbourne.

It was night there, and he in bed.

The gulf in my mind opened to swallow me.

On the edge of panic I saw that this was not Angus or even someone much like him. There was a vague resemblance; repressed fright and confusion had done the rest. He spoke to me. (If it had been with Angus's voice it might have broken me in pieces.)

How were you there, Giles, and just then? And waiting for me.

How?

Who are you, Giles, and what do you want with me?

3

Alastair looked up from the script. "How *did* you do it?"

"Easy. I left Australia on the same plane as he but travelled first class and stayed in my seat at the fuel stops; not that it would have mattered if he'd seen me, because I'd started the Giles persona. I caught the same train at Euston, left Glasgow Central ahead of him and kept him in view along Gallowgate until I saw he'd overrun his cue for the hotel. He was coming loose and needed a nudge."

"So you gave him a glimpse of Angus where Angus had no right to be. Dangerous."

"Necessary. Manipulation isn't like hypnotic conditioning; we'd been out of contact for two days, time enough for his certainties to soften, and he was coming into conflict with realities. A reinforcing dose of fantasy was needed." He tapped the sheets. "As he tells it, he was ready to burst wide open."

"What an unpleasant job yours must be."

"You mean it takes an unpleasant bastard to do it?"

"I mean that a certain heartlessness may have become our unacknowledged problem." Alastair seemed startled by his own thought. "But you aren't heartless, are you, Giles? That's what this cry-on-shoulder session is about, isn't it?"

"Cut bitching and read on."

"Very well, but I still think it was risky to flash Angus at him when he was close to disintegration."

"I could steady him in seconds."

"From hysteria to normal? In seconds?"

"You have your talent, I have mine. The dose of Angus made him more receptive when he realized it was a stranger; the defences went down to let Giles in."

4

WILL'S TYPESCRIPT: One day I'll be free of your cellar, Giles, and I'll hunt you down as sure as humanity's middle name is cruelty. I'm human, after all.

(Alastair glanced up, caught Giles's eye, and laughed.)

Do you know that when I saw you I nearly cried out, *Angus! For God's sake, Angus!*

You are both short and slender in the legs and muscular over thin bones, broadfaced under hair with a shallow wave and blue-eyed in a complexion that demands brown. It sounds definitive but in fact could fit a hundred men with no two alike.

You asked, "Air y' lost, mon?" in an accent as thick as your damned parritch, and I probably sounded like an idiot as I lied, "No, but I'm looking for a hotel."

"There's ainly yin in this pairt o' Gallowgate. Gang a wee bit back an' y'll find it on the ither side, Aussie."

That straightened me a little; I've always counted my accent fairly neutral. "Am I that obvious?"

You grinned with that slight baring of teeth I have become used to; there should be a doggy growl with it. You said, with that fine contempt the Brits shower on tourists while they scramble for their money, "Tae them wi' ears tae hear."

(I'm trying to render your speech, but of course it can't be done. I can reproduce dialect, syntax and elisions but not even Shavian phonetics could put on paper that underlying burr, like soft gears meshing, that makes you sound the sweet bloke you assuredly are not.)

As you spoke you held my eyes with a deliberation a fraction too blatant. I had a queer double feeling about that: that I should resent provocative staring but did not. Then you said, with insulting indifference, "Gang y'r way, laddie; it's the Rab Roy y'r seeking."

I had thought the Scots talked like that only in comic novels but, by God, you actually do. But what matters is that I crossed the road and looked for the Rob Roy. (It *was* what vaguely I had been seeking. Had Angus mentioned it? I can't remember.)

I wondered later about your stare. Hypnotism? But the hypnotized victim is not aware of the transition of states. There's more in it than meets the eye (joke?). Something had been done to me and I didn't mind. That's the point—that my brain noted the fact, and didn't mind.

("It *was* a risk."

"No. I can't have him totally at ease; there has to be an edge of unrest I can sharpen and direct if need be. That's a big part of manipulation, the setting up of balances. His 'mental quiet' is only a lid over the archetypal traits the operator works on."

"Mental judo?"

"In a way. You use the man's own mind against him.")

Everything in romantic Caledonia is named for Scott or Burns, an olde worlde touch for tourists, done on the understanding that any non-Scot is too bloody ignorant to have heard of more than Sir Wa'ter, Rabbie and the Hieland fling. Still, the Rob Roy turned out to be pleasant and quiet.

And suddenly I had nothing to do.

So I did what everyone does in another country: I went out and walked and gawped and saw practically nothing I couldn't have seen at home. I had forgotten that the kilt is not everyday wear south of the Highlands and felt cheated that the folk in the streets could as well have been the people next door in Melbourne. You Scots should be lined up and shot for all those technicolourful travel brochures.

At some stage I wandered round the back of the City Chambers and came unintentionally into George Square. Hear Angus, being homesick: *"You must hear 'Roamin' in the Gloamin'' sung by ten thoosand people in George Square at Hogmanay! It's rousin'!"* I'll bet it is. Not even for Angus would I listen to that stale whiff of Harry Lauder from ten thousand drunks while the New Year dissolves in slush underfoot.

However, I recognized the white marble cenotaph he was so proud of and the Scott column sitting like an expensive factory chimney in the middle of the square.

Think I'm bitching, Giles? I feel entitled to it.

All right, then—George Square is a pleasant place. What's more, I had a tiny adventure there. Perhaps I should keep it to myself. Or might it have significance enough to unlock your mousetrap mouth for a round buccaneering oath?

I met a girl there. For a passing moment I met a girl.

I walked down the grass bank into the centre where the seats are, under the perimeter of trees. And there was a real tam-o'-shanter on a pensioner type sunning himself in that pale glow you Scots call daylight! Planted for the tourist trade in case it recovers?

I watched a girl come round from the other side of the Scott column—a good-looking girl, twentyish, quietly dressed but immediately memorable for the beautiful swan throat of some modern Annie Laurie and huge, gentle blue eyes. I stared, and why not?

She returned the stare with the faintest of smiles, with not a hint of a come-on in it, then spoke and reduced me to bumbling.

"A tourist in Glasgow! I thought they kept you all in ferry boats on Loch Lomond."

She robbed it of insult by being so honestly and good-humouredly amused, but "tourist" made the Polaroid on my shoulder swell to the size of a suitcase and tied my tongue in knots. When the poor thing had loosened itself I muttered that

I was in Glasgow because an Australian friend had been born here. It was my first thought and seemed vaguely true.

"Australia?" There was a spark of special attention in her voice, a connection made in her mind. "A good land to escape to." Which was a curious thing to say when you think about it. "What's the lucky man's name?"

"Angus."

"Just Angus?"

"Maxwell."

"Ah." It meant something to her; she studied me with a closeness which had nothing to do with my status as eligible male. "When you see him," she said, "remember me to him."

Perhaps it was some Scottish in-joke, but she sounded genuine.

"What name shall I tell him?"

She hesitated. "Jeanie Deans."

So it was a joke. "Come off it, love. Even an ignorant colonial knows the heroine of *Midlothian*."

She nodded, not smiling. "She walked the length of Britain in bare feet, seeking mercy and justice. Tell him that, too."

She gave me no time for questions. She simply went away.

It was queer, queer.

Has it meaning, Giles? Did you know about it?

5

"*Did* you know, Giles?"

"I was the tam-o'-shanter, wearing face anonymous-in-a-crowd. I wasn't quite close enough to hear, but it's interesting that she identified him. They're well informed."

"They? Should I know the girl?"

"Maybe. She's a Dissident."

"Ohoh! Name?"

"Jeanie Deans will do as well as any. How long do our names last?"

"Was it an accidental meeting? The Disses wouldn't dare interfere—or would they?"

"This one just might."

"Would she know of this house?"

"Don't we all?"

Alastair exploded. "Elementary precaution, surely! Is no one tracking her?"

"I've a group of semi-crim slum rats on her trail."

"Crims!"

"They're effective and they're cheap. We haven't the numbers here to waste Company on gumshoeing."

"Have they located her?"

"Yes. It wasn't easy for them."

"Why?"

"She's my kind—a face-maker."

A premonitory anger on Giles's face cancelled Alastair's urge to a shrug of disgust. He liked Giles well enough as Giles, but like the rest of The Company he found the face-maker mutation repellent. However, he didn't want to antagonize Giles; the little man was plainly blowing up an emotional storm. He was overdue for rehandling.

Best to say nothing and return to the typescript.

6

Then it was ten to six and—unwarned but unsurprised—I knew what I was to do. There's no point in belabouring irrationality; it was built into my mental scene.

So I went back to the Rob Roy where, on the dot of six o'clock opening, the bar was filling, though beer production had ceased with the curtailing of transport to deliver it. Hotels were serving from surprising stocks of wines and spirits, but even at their extortionate prices the supply must have been measured in days.

I risked my accent on a nip of Scotch and got it—for two pounds. That's the sort of thing that signals the closeness of the breakdown point. I'm seeing it in retrospect; at the time I didn't believe more than any other that the utter collapse of our way of life was not only possible but inevitable—and only days away.

Turning from the bar I nearly dropped my glass when I looked straight into Angus's eyes. No mistaking the high cheekbones and the unusually thick and corded veins binding slender wrists to talons of hands.

Yet he stared through me, not seeing me, and smiled greeting to someone beyond. And it was not Angus's smile.

You, Giles, of course. That illusion twice in a few hours . . . I turned my back, needing a moment for mental balance, and it gave you the chance to do the unforgivable, to speak from behind me, directly into my ear—with Angus's voice.

"So you foond the Rab Roy, Aussie."

I turned very slowly, taking hold of my mind, but my inclination was to cut and run and it must have showed.

You said, but in your own voice, "Y'll no' mind me speakin' tae y'? A stranger needs acquaintance in a strange land."

Because I didn't see yet that this was cat-and-mouse and because my mind played the usual trick of deciding that the fault must lie with itself, I said, "I mistook you for somebody else, somebody who couldn't possibly be here."

You shrugged, "Lookalike's no' sae oncommon."

"Same size and shape and both Scots, but that's all. You don't look alike."

You raised your glass and said as if it were a toast, "Then let's hope he's a freend an' no' an enemy."

It was a damned peculiar thing to say but, perhaps out of bewilderment, I answered with one of those confidences you give only to the chance-met stranger who will never reappear to confront you with it.

I said, "He's the dearest friend I ever had."

It rocked you, Giles. Whatever you had expected, it was not that. For an instant you lost control of your game. Then you nodded as though some unspoken question had been answered and asked, "A freendship o' great trust?"

"Absolute." And with the word the first doubt of Angus entered my mind. Angus had gone to great lengths to establish that trust, almost courting me to turn instinctive liking into a bond of affection. And had succeeded.

"Why then," you said, "haud tae it; a mon needs such."

My disgraceful little doubt ran back into darkness; what link could Angus have with this reptilian little man?

You asked idly (save that nothing you said or did was idle), "An' what's the wee freend's name?"

"Angus."

"That's guid Scottish. I'm Giles."

I did not name myself in return; that may have been a last subconscious caution before all caution became useless. I said, "And that *isn't* good Scottish."

"Y' say no'? Well, we hae Saint Giles's Cathedral in Edinburgh. Will y' say that's no' Scottish?"

I could have said, *Giles is an English saint, a ring-in,* but you went on prying. "An' what brings y' tae Scotland?"

I was calming down. (Did you arrange that in some fashion that evades me?) I said, making it a good-humoured throw-away, "I don't know what brings me. I got my passport and took the first available plane, just like that."

You disagreed with the arrogance of a Scot taking no bloody nonsense from a tourist. "It wasna like that. There's no per-adventures; there's ainly reasons."

The cold closed in again. "Peradventures" was an Angus word and one that he always used a little wrongly, as if it meant meaningless actions, which is not quite correct. You also used it that little bit wrongly, Giles.

("Giles, Giles!"

"Laugh, you bastard. So I'm not perfect."

Alastair raised eyes to heaven. "I have lived to hear him admit it! Thank you, God.")

I suppose I was fighting back (against what?) when I asked sarcastically, "Predestination, you think?"

"Naething sae extreme. A kind o' detairminism, mair like. Perhaps the wee Angus influenced y'r will wi' hints an' bits o' memories an' sich."

A jigsaw fell into pattern. He *had* pushed, feeding flashes of history and snippets of folk oddity and moments of lyric memory, creating my desire to see, to make the leap across the world. My silly tongue yammered, "He did talk a lot. Burns and Bruce and Wallace. Fingal's Cave and Lochleven Castle in the lake and Rob Roy's hideout on Loch Lomond. And the Gow Chrom of old Perth—"

"Ay, romance, romance! An' recited 'Lochinvar', nae doot, an' told how Birnam Wood sneaked up on Dunsinane, or—" I can't forget the change in you here, from mockery to outright venom "—or gied y' a snatch o' Dunbar."

"He's not classical; he wouldn't know Dunbar."

"No' even *Timor mortis conturbat me?*"

With that doomladen line you settled solidly into the shape of an enemy, and one who gave not a damn that I knew it.

("What was the point of the Dunbar line? What was gained?"

"Nothing." He admitted unwillingly, "I was angry and confused. Something he said."

"What?"

"It's there to be seen. But I feel The Company has lost the capacity to see some things."

Alastair thought for a long moment before he continued reading.)

You said, practically laughing at me, "An' noo y'd better come wi' me. I hae room an' bed for y'."

I can call up courage for most situations but I'll look for a way out of one that makes no sense. I said, "You're out of your mind," and pushed past as if you were one of those clowns the world's bars are full of. But you grabbed my wrist and I hesitated because only a fool makes a scene where he doesn't know the local conventions.

"Y'll come, Willie," you said, "an' y'll be looked after."

I had *not* told my name, and nobody but Angus ever called me Willie. Always Will or Bill.

You meant to break my nerve and you did; I went for the door, shoving my way through protests. I looked back to see you following me unhurriedly, on your face a look of derision which gave sudden way to a blaze of anger so intense as to raise the sweat on me.

I think then that I broke blindly for the door. I know I stumbled on the footpath, fell full length to skin hands and elbows and turn a wrist in white pain, and came to my knees

27

gasping and shaking like some drunk overcome in the public street. There may have been passers-by but I was in no condition to notice anything more than that it was you who helped me to my feet, making friendly noises and taking the opportunity to twist my head so that you could look directly into my eyes.

"Y' must come hame, Willie," you said, for the benefit I suppose of onlookers, then snarled in my ear with no trace of Scotland in your English, "You've been babied enough. Now you'll do what you're told, Will Santley, under full control. Won't you?"

And of course I did, with outward calm, with on the surface of my mind a total trust in you. Also in my mind, deep down, a conflict twitching at my brain but refusing to be recognized.

I acted willingly but against my deeper will, docilely carrying on while a stifled part of me lodged useless and unintelligible objection. I recall vividly the walk from the Rob Roy to this cellar, my mind seizing avidly on surfaces, with everything inward suppressed.

Is this what is meant by "full control"?

We walked by way of the Clyde embankment and then through Glasgow Green. You talked the whole time. (Part of the mental misdirection process?) We covered a mile or more before we crossed a bridge out of the park to a run-down suburb. And finally we entered this house and came down the stairs.

You said, "Sleep, Willie," and shut the door. And I slept.

The thing that puzzles me and disturbs me most, a fortnight later, is the moment of inexplicable angry hatred on your face as you followed me from the bar.

7

Alastair threw down the typescript. "A bungle, Giles, on the grand scale. You're slipping. You said you were angry but this reads more like uncontrolled spite."

"I'm as good as ever I was. I was under pressure of guilt." Looking mulishly down at his hands, he did not see Alastair's raised eyebrows. "That's how guilt works; you take out your pain on the one betrayed, flog his stupidity to excuse your own double dealing. But it doesn't help."

Alastair understood that very well; importantly, Giles also understood it well enough to exercise self-control. The Company could not at this juncture rise to the extreme co-operative effort required for major rehandling of a member's psychological lesions. When the Santley affair was over, yes; they could not afford the loss of the unmatchable talent of a venomously revengeful Giles. Meanwhile . . .

"If it did, still you overreached yourself badly. Did Ancient Lights wring you out like a rag?"

"He was mild. I was lucky."

Damned lucky; he had escaped with little more than cautioning.

The old man had begun with the usual performance which should be comedy but never was.

"Which are you? Why are you here? What do you want?"

Memory, not senility, was the problem.

"I am Giles. Also Angus. You sent for me."

"Why? What have you done?"

"That has been reported to you." Consensus was that he be encouraged to *use* his memory, to force it until it disgorged.

"Aaaah." That was petulance at the prodding. For years they had urged him to submit to memory clearance but the old autocrat had used his prestige to argue the necessity of mental continuity. Indeed he had vast experience and factual knowledge, but Giles did not concede him so superior an intellect.

Silence dragged; the old devil would finish in a tantrum. Giles offered a small assistance. "You will have had the observer's report." (That so important an operation would be quietly monitored had gone clean out of his angry mind in the hotel.) "I came as soon as I had him settled."

Ancient Lights (and who had concocted that suitable but ridiculous name?) could conjure recollection of his earliest life in stupefying detail but new material needed time to take hold.

"Aaaah!" The same exhalation, but charged with success. "Your handling from Melbourne to Scotland was faultless."

First, Giles thought, the good news. "So why did you frighten seven devils out of him in that bar? His subconscious is now fully aware of being manoeuvred; any intrusion of paradox could break him. We don't want a schizophrenic unable to tell fact from nightmare or a catatonic to be excavated with psychological tools. Your usefulness is at test. Why did you do it?"

He had been prepared for summary discipline, not a searching out of motives. He said drearily, "He shamed me and I lost my temper."

"Shamed? Temper? *Arrogance!* You are a servant, a man under authority."

When reference to the King James version appeared it was as well to take care; when surrogate God sat in judgement (though they were atheist to the last man and woman) Giles's arrogance was poor stuff.

Recalling the moment of lost temper, he said rapidly, "I made the Giles-Angus switch to break his self-possession. He had to be routed to the transit house at once; it wasn't safe to leave him loose and beginning to work things out. It had to be forceful direction with no time for build-up."

Surrogate God said, with infinitely insulting patience, "In your small-boy argot, I was not born yesterday."

No, indeed. "He said . . ."

"Well, he said?"

"That Angus was the dearest friend he had ever had, spoke of him in terms of absolute trust."

"A technical triumph. And so?"

"That was enough."

"For whom? Explain."

So he was to eat dirt. "I have spent a year with Santley, attaching to myself all that is most decent in him. In order to bring about his destruction."

"What of that? It was the plan. *You* planned it."

So he had. And seen only the challenge, the subtlety, the intrigue, the game. So—sullenness and silence.

"Have you developed love for this man?"

That startled him. "Love!"

"Friendship is a form of love as selfishly irrational as the

30

sexual variety. It is an indulgence The Company cannot tolerate. An imbalance. A perversion."

He knew The Company's sterile, cold-blooded view only too well. They did not have close relationships even among themselves. Though some were different . . . How much did he really know of himself? It was hard to understand how, in the balance of loyalties and affections, love of the manipulative game could bring him to betray one for the other.

He said, with a feeling of burning his boats, "I'm dirty to my own touch. I took pride in conscious treachery."

It was received with mildness, with what might pass for understanding but was not. "You mustn't quote middle-class morality at me; it's a trap for good brains. This man is for judgement."

He risked greatly. "Pre-judged."

"That is not your business. Don't make a fool of yourself over morals, ethics, rights, wrongs. Keep him in fit condition to understand what's said to him."

He capitulated because against The Company he had never known how to argue. "I'll be careful with him."

Ancient Lights looked directly at him, meditating. His status had fallen; if another manipulator had been available he would have been taken off Santley at once. "And with yourself, I hope. Now go away."

He should have known from the start that the game had its price, that you can't create a bond without giving something to it, that for every action there is an equal reaction. So he had to live with himself and the knowledge that he could do nothing for Will now. Nor, if Will were indeed the enemy, could anybody else.

What might the old bastard have said had he tossed a return fragment of the King James version at him, the verse about forgiving seventy times seven? Even that towering self-sufficiency would scarcely have thundered back at him, "Thou shalt have no other gods before Me!"

He sketched the scene briefly for Alastair. "Now, a fortnight later, nothing's changed. We have to wait on Randal."

Randal was needed if Will's memory was to be probed beyond

31

his destructive accident, but he would not leave present charges until it suited him. Randal tended to ask why what had waited a year could not wait two or ten?

So he was shocked when Alastair told him, "Randal will see him tonight."

"Why wasn't I told?"

"You are being told now."

That put him in his place. Who and when did not matter, only what. Alastair looked down to the typescript but Giles reached across to take it from him. "The rest isn't relevant."

Alastair sighed and asked, "Are you in fact learning to love your enemy, Giles?"

"If you're talking Christian philosophy, no. I'm rediscovering fellow feeling."

"You've slipped on that slope before."

That roused him, and Alastair had done it deliberately. He asked aggressively, "What do you mean?" and knew immediately what had been meant. "That this has happened before—and that I've been dememorized of it?"

"Several times." *If only he knew it, we have played this scene so often.* "Your emotional states have always been troublesome." He added, "For you we also take away memory of the clearing, to leave no clues to distress you."

He thought well enough of Giles to pity him; the small man possessed an exquisite talent, but the gutter cunning that went with it could not match the cold attitudes of The Company. He was and would remain a tool, a miracle of virtuosity in the hands of entrepreneurs.

He said gently, "You're to be dememorized again when this affair is over. Emotional reasoning can be traumatic."

"I'll refuse processing."

"How, Giles?"

Nobody had ever said a successful No to The Company's Yes, but he could try. If he tried often enough he might at length succeed.

Alastair had, he supposed to himself, some sort of approval of Giles, but not enough to tolerate aberration. "I can't help you. Dememorization will."

"I want to remember. To remember the ruthlessness."

Alastair suggested mildly, "Call it 'practicality'," and stood. It was time to leave before irrational argument was forced on him.

"Inhumanity."

"That's a question not finally settled; you may be right. If you are, what can any Willie or Wilhelmina mean to you?"

He made his exit in the consciousness of a smart line smartly delivered.

8

It was easily said, later, that the complications and conversations of that night left Giles in the right frame of mind to be inexcusably careless. Giles-Angus, the face-maker and manipulator who had said that there are no peradventures (he had checked the word after reading Will's comment), knew that the carelessness had been ordained.

After the event he had no doubt that the tiny diversion had been self-arranged in the depths of his mind.

Poor little subconscious trying to raise impossible ransom for peace of mind . . .

When Alastair had gone he prepared the routine tasteless meal for himself and Will (wondering the while what enormities had required more than one dememorization to quiet his howling spirit: betrayal upon betrayal, as The Company's smiler with a knife?). Meat, a very little, he could obtain two or three times a week by devious means; across the world cattle died as fodders mutated, turned toxic and rotted. Tonight: a square of tough goatflesh from the Highlands where genetic plague had not yet taken full hold—a few vegetables grown in The Company's hidden hydroponic tanks (but who could police water if that should be the infiltrating agent?)—a slice of something like bread, nearly unobtainable wheat stretched with ersatz flour—a smear of hoarded jam for luxury when butter, lard and margarine had vanished from a couponed, queueing market. Plus a huge pot of tea, sugarless and milkless. Tea, mysteriously, resisted blight. (British to the last, said the sad wags.)

33

No *Scotsman* for Will tonight; the presses were dead. Their last announcement had been of their own demise as oil and power were cut completely. Had the paper lived it would have contained only reports of food rioting, the final silence of industry, the terrifying diminuendo of electronic communication across the planet and the curious air of waiting, neither apathy nor total despair, in the streets and the countryside. And the rising tide of raging suspicion against his precious Australia as presumptive originator and death-master of the blight.

Willie, with his daily consumption of censored news, fractional reports and confused inventions of half-understood happenings overseas, had no idea of the size of his world's disaster. The piece by piece description of the breakdown of the planetary machine could never convey the shattered panorama of the truth. The slowing, still complaining but basically optimistic world he had left a fortnight ago no longer existed.

Did it matter? He might never see it.

Balancing the tray on one hand, he opened the cellar door and nudged it wider with his foot. Then—

Always at this point, *always*, he paused outside the doorframe and made sure that Will was in his view. While he could catch the man's eye he was safe from any attack less final than an act of that God in whom he did not believe.

This evening he had a passing thought that he had forgotten the salt and pepper shakers—and looked down at the tray. (No peradventures, he told himself later, with perverse satisfaction.)

Will's first kick flung the tray in his face.

The second took him in the kneecap with outrageous agony. As he buckled forward, blind with pain, clenched fists clubbed the back of his neck and his throat was driven on to Will's rising knee.

His Company metabolism had its limits; it could not operate instantaneously. He was semi-paralysed and unconscious when he struck the floor.

Will had not counted on success; he had been deadly afraid of the powers that struck without impact and restricted without leash. He had kicked out, head averted from the undefeatable eyes, because he needed to demonstrate to himself that he yet possessed free will. The effort mattered, not the outcome.

Having looked no further than the action, he was caught in a paralysis of impulse.

In stillness he contemplated Giles supine, crumpled but breathing after a blow to the vertebrae that would have killed many men, face to the light, revealed in detail, as the tight cheek muscles relaxed and the skin over the jaw slackened, softening the grimness. At the corners of the eyes the pattern of crow's-feet altered and the lids tightened; the eyebrows arched and a vertical furrow vanished from the smoothing forehead; the lips thinned minutely as the mouth widened; the prominent ears flattened against a skull whose scalp crept forward in a reshaping of the hairline; the narrow nostrils flared as the full tip of the nose sharpened and curved slightly down; the square maxillaries retreated and lifted the cheekbones into prominence.

Angus lay at his feet.

With his mind beaten into acclimatization with the grotesque and the bizarre, Will found the transformation not unlogical so much as difficult, to be thought at rather than wondered at.

One man was two men. Or two were one.

When control was relaxed, Angus, it seemed, was the real man, the original, the friend who had conned, tricked, abused and imprisoned him.

That hurt; it would have hurt so much less had Angus been the mask, the one who did not exist. Hating a real Giles was easy; hating the remembered Angus was not.

He roused to the thought that he was not as surprised as he should be, that in fact he simply contemplated in a mental blank and it was time to move on.

He did what seemed obvious, still without planning after his unlooked-for victory: he dragged Angus further into the cellar, locked him in and went up the stairs.

In minutes he knew there was no one else in the house.

At the front door he blinked at daylight; by his watch it was not quite eight, so the long twilight would not set in for another hour or so.

What to do, where to go?

With thought stirring at last he turned back into the house, returned to the cellar and unlocked the door. Angus, whoever and whatever he was, should not be left in a locked room to starve.

Back at the front door he looked about irresolutely, then stepped into the street of ancient factories and dwellings blackened with the grime of Glasgow's age.

10

In a quarter of a mile he could see only three people—two men half a block away towards the western end and, a hundred yards in the other direction and across the street, a girl. So close to the central city, even in a slum, there should be more people about.

His unease was assailed by stillness and silence.

He listened, thought uncertainly that he caught a murmur of crowd voices far off and began slowly to understand.

The news columns of past weeks crowded his mind in a dense, cumulative statement of the reality his private angers had relegated and passed by.

While he tapped out complaint in a cellar the city had run down and stopped.

Not only the city. The idiot planet had discovered what "energy crisis" finally meant.

He walked northward, where he thought the river lay, trying to think in a situation which offered little his ignorance could use.

Giles did not rob me; I have money. I am decently clean— Giles (ANGUS!)—provided for that. I am not hungry; not yet. I have wallet, passport, plane ticket.

36

If he reached London, would there be a plane for catching? In this stillness he thought not; the very voicelessness spoke of immobility.

What, then?

There would be pursuit, but not yet; Angus would not be capable for hours.

(In fact Angus was already stirring, thinking that what had happened was his own doing, examining a temptation to let the fugitive have his head in a changed world that would take more than a moment's getting used to, examining the knowledge that he could not risk further error, examining the possibilities and making decisions but not hurrying to implement them. The Company rarely hurried; there rarely seemed need for it.)

After such handling, however, they would not easily let go of the fugitive. And Will knew it. How, then, to hide?

For a beginning he could only keep moving and remember to catch no man's eye. Others might share Angus's talent.

Thinking it, he caught the eye of the girl he had noticed so alone in the street. It was as easy as that; sooner or later, without intention, you looked someone in the face.

Looking quickly away, he yet saw from the corner of his eye her half-gesture, the slight shrug of disappointment.

Prostitute? In a residential street? Unlikely, but circumstances had altered. In a dying, starving city anything would be available for money—or, more likely, for food. He risked another glance, seeing nothing attractive, only a grubby blonde, slouching, stockingless in plain skirt and blouse. Poor little bitch. Guiltily, aware of £200 in his pocket but knowing he might need every penny, he hurried on and saw the river a short block ahead.

The people whose distant murmur he had heard were there. It looked as though all the people were there, standing in groups or milling aimlessly along the river walk.

Frighteningly, it had already come to this, that they either stayed inside or congregated in the natural public places. Hide or huddle.

He could afford no part in their dilemmas. His remembrance was plain, of coming this way under Giles's compulsion, of a bridge at this street's end crossing the Clyde and entering a park. He searched his mind for a name and found it—Glasgow Green. The greater part of it lay on high plateau above the river, ideal for the detection of pursuit, whereas if he kept to the streets every corner and doorway could trap him.

He crossed the bridge and climbed to the high level.

Here were people indeed, in their hundreds. The broad lawns were arenas of noise, of futile gatherings and meetings. Listening momentarily at one group clotted around a speaker, he made nothing of the thick, Glaswegian tirade; Giles-Angus spoke purest English by comparison. Not that the theme of every mouth would be any but money, food, government irresponsibility, transport. The rest would be the undertone of fear that these were no longer the things that mattered, formless fear of a future rushing on collapse not of inanition or the battering of barbarians at the gates, but of simple running out of the means of subsistence.

He followed the main path, paralleling the river, through the shouting and fumbling of a culture in process of dissolution.

Twenty yards ahead of him a man stepped from the grass on to the path, moving in the same direction but looking over his shoulder, seeking something or someone behind Will, back towards the bridge. He was tall, perhaps in middle thirties, big in the rawboned, fleshless style, workman-nondescript in dress and general appearance.

Will watched him covertly, fearing anything at his back. When for a moment the man faced his front Will looked behind but saw only park and preoccupied people. He turned about to find the other toe-and-heeling backwards, staring downhill, and thought the gaze passed across him. Unseeing?

He would have felt safer if he could have seen to whom the antics were addressed. Or would he? Giles-Angus had mercilessly eroded his self-possession.

Ahead of him he saw the Queen Victoria fountain with its stone fripperies of the past. It was time to ask direction to the London Road, where a few commercial vehicles might still be moving south. Wishfully . . .

The rawboned man halted his fore-and-aft dance and made a short signalling gesture. It could have nothing to do with Will; the man had not so much as glanced directly at him.

He walked backwards all the time now, gesticulating obscurely and finally waving a plain signing-off. His backing took him to the iron railing round the fountain, where he rested, still watching beyond Will's shoulder.

Will would have passed within a yard of him if the man had not leaned out and with an inordinate reach taken him by the elbow to swing him round and bellow, "Y're the yin that accosted my sister!"

Reflexively Will moved with the swing to drive his elbow into the unguarded belly—and missed badly as the other stepped a quick pace beside and behind him, whipped round to place a knee in his back and pushed him solidly into the railing. The iron upright took him under the breastbone, hurting vilely.

The rawboned man shouted, "There's bastards think in puir times any lass is free game but y'll no' claw my sister!"

Caught in the oldest of traps, Will flung himself back, expecting a fist at his head or a boot in the crotch. There would be no help from bystanders who would be more likely to help lynch him. With a wild swing only half thrown he found both hands grasped and forced behind him up to the shoulders. The rawboned man was fast and much stronger than he looked and he leaned heavily, bending Will back over the railing.

And muttered, "All's for appearance, laddie. Be easy; you'll take no hairm." And howled, "An' what do y' say the noo, y' molestin' bastard!"

The performance was well judged; passers-by gave them a wide berth but were ready for entertainment. The rawboned man shook him and it hurt. "Make it look guid, laddie! We canna tell who's watchin' an' you're no' helpin'."

Close at hand a girl's voice called, urgent and a little frightened, "No, no, Donald! That's not the man!"

Donald allowed surprise. "Y' say no'?"

"Let him go, Donald! You're making a spectacle of us all."

"Sister" spoke London English. Careless.

Donald murmured, "Easy the noo," and released him with a show of embarrassment and apology. "Man I canna say—"

Will paid him no attention. The scene had been played to let the girl catch up with them. And of course she was the grubby blonde, now brown-haired. A blonde strand curled from the

39

zipper of her handbag. Her neck had slimmed to the Annie Laurie throat he remembered from George Square; he thought her face settled a trifle more as he watched.

"Another one," he said.

She breathed, "Not so loud," and joined Donald in a duet of apology and explanation long enough to let the disappointed bystanders move on. Then, "I'm sorry but we had to get to you quickly. They'll be after you."

Donald capped absurdity. "We're rescuin' you."

Will could imagine nothing to say to that.

The girl asked hurriedly, "The little one—did you kill him?"

"Knocked him out."

"You should have killed him! It wouldn't be easy but for your own sake you should have." She was annoyed with him, in a small way, as if he had forgotten to pick up the meat for dinner. "He's the dangerous one."

Donald hissed at her, "Would you hae the whole o' Glesca knowin'?" He took Will's hand like one still in the throes of apology. "Walk quietly wi' us. Will you do that?"

Will took his time. They were impatient but did not hurry him. Giles had enemies it seemed, and he, Will, was a bone between dogs. And if Giles needed killing . . . a shocked residue of affection revolted.

"If I don't, you'll force me?"

The girl shook her head. "You can risk it alone if you won't be helped."

Donald said urgently, "A freend, even in unco' shape, is no' to be havered over."

"I want to get back to Australia." In his own ears it was the cry of a lost small boy.

"You canna. Nothing flies." He made it factual, final, not with the dark art of Giles but through his serenity. Facts existed and one accepted them.

Will, fallen between antagonists, might as well take one choice as the other. And they might turn out an improvement on Giles.

He walked with them down the path to the Clyde embankment gate.

"What would stop you forcing me? You have the crawling flesh; doesn't the evil eye go with it?"

She merely looked irritated. Donald said, "Those are no' simple things an' no' for careless talk in public."

They passed the gate and left the Green behind them.

"Where are we going?"

Her impatience broke. "Do you know Glasgow? Would you be wiser if I told you?"

Donald scarcely moved his lips to say, "Bishopbriggs. That's aboot six miles frae here. Can you ride a bike? You'll need to."

"Yes. What's there?"

"Safe lodgin'."

The far side of the street was the frayed eastern edge of the central city, a shambles of empty shop fronts and silent warehouses. There were few people in sight; they were clustered in the park, gathering strength against spiritual nightfall.

Donald said, "Wait here," crossed the road, vanished down a lane and in minutes reappeared, riding a bicycle and leading another. He handed the second machine to Will. "Yours, laddie." With one arm and not much effort he lifted the girl on to the handlebars of the other. "Follow close."

Will said, "Six miles is a long dink."

"Dink?"

The girl spoke with venomous restraint. "Australian! He means you carrying me on the handlebars. For sanity's sake, get going."

"Six miles is no' so far, Aussie. Hae you money?"

"Some."

"It's no guid. Last week it could buy you a meal but this week the world is grindin' doon an' you mun hae coupons for food—an' maybe still get none. Hae you coupons?"

"How could I have?"

"Aye, how? So dinna pedal off doon the London Road thinkin' you'll ootdistance me wi' the lass ridin' high. You'll starve if you try it. I know ways o' gettin' food withoot coupons, but you dinna."

Will said nothing.

Donald smiled suddenly with the openness of one who offered friendship and asked trust, as though he had only given some sane advice. Which, probably, he had. And so, back home, had Angus's smiles asked and promised.

Pedalling uphill, away from the river, Will thought this must surely be the damnedest rescue operation since the passing of high bikes.

II

Committed to a definite course, even if without knowing what course, he was able to shift his attention from himself and take some proper notice of the scene. At once he sensed how little he had gleaned from a newspaper struggling with ineffectual language to tell the last and biggest story.

Their way took them through the big north-eastern residential sector of the city, and at the end of the day the city was drawing its shutters against a longer night than its uneasy spirit could guess. A few were abroad, a few corners carried small arguing groups, but liveliness had retreated. The sheer emptiness of the roads, carless and truckless and bearing only little clusters of cyclists heartening each other against a heartless future, mocked and threatened.

The stillness gripped until he realized it as not yet the final stillness but the absence of the undertones of a city. Quench the bass *obbligato* of traffic and industry, and the sounds that are left—voices, footsteps, creakings and slitherings—drip into a bowl of silence.

The blunt facts—energy depletion, transport stoppage, food shortage, poverty, suspicion, violence—coalesced in a creeping apprehension. In the warm evening he shivered in a fear of disaster incalculable in the simple terms of life and beyond confrontation by the mind.

His generation had matured in a declining culture, aware of the downhill run but never thinking, *It can end in my time.* Science, politics and brute force had shored up the culture while between them they destroyed its foundations; day-to-day living had bred acceptance of day-to-day changes without seeing them as short, quick topplings down. For every crier of doom there had been a prophet of paradise, and paradise is easier to accept.

42

Men and women, himself included, had smiled their day-to-day smiles as though the smiling could not end. And that soon. While Will Santley wrote spiteful nonsense in a cellar it *had* ended. Without his noticing.

In a primitive need for closeness he drew alongside Donald to say, foolishly enough, "The whole city is dead!"

"Och ay, an' a' cities."

The girl smiled mockery. "Moping indoors while civilization ended! You missed the fun."

She could not see the contempt on Donald's face. Will asked, "Fun?"

"The imperishable spirit of man realizing that what it had refused to know was snapping at its throat. And then, oh, the tears and the screeching, the blaming and the pleading, the rioting in the streets and the shooting of the mobs—shooting, with no over-the-heads nonsense."

If this was her pleasure, she was mad.

Donald said sharply, "Shut up, bitch!"

She replied calmly, "He might as well learn."

"No' frae lips o' spite an' contempt. He has eyes to use." He asked Will, "What do you see?"

"Bicycles. And lightless houses."

"Power's gone, 'cept for essentials; nane for hooses. No petrol save for food transports—an' they runnin' wi' armed guards. There's few other vehicles; ambulances, police, army maybe. What else?"

"Men in the streets. Some men, that is. Not doing anything. Like pictures of the old depression eras."

"Only by talkin' in the streets can they learn anything, sharin' scraps o' news. No papers print an' the radio tells what government lets it tell—for forty minutes a day. If you have a battery set, that is. But in the street you can pick up a whisper whaur there's food for stealin'—for your bairns an' your woman."

Will looked about. "But where are the women?"

"Their men keep them in the hoose."

Jeanie Deans laughed without humour. "We've shed a hundred thousand years in a week, gone back to proper division of labour—hunter and bedwarmer."

"You don't feel unsafe in the streets?"

"I don't feel unsafe anywhere." She meant it as calmly as if it were not idiot arrogance.

Donald said—not explaining the girl's certainty, rather ignoring it—"The streets are quiet the noo but last week she knew better than to show. You'll ha' read o' bluid runnin' in the streets in novels. Well, it ran here, in this road an' in gutters across the planet."

"But it stopped?"

"It *was* stopped. Do you no' see the armbands?"

He had seen them casually, as part of the ambience; now he observed that of the men in sight perhaps half wore a red cloth brassard. They walked the footpath, dressed as others dressed, with the brassard for uniform and a sombre alertness for distinction.

"Vigilantes. A sort o' scratch polis—or volunteer peace corps—an' a few plain thugs. But they keep the streets safe. To a point."

"With guns?"

Jeanie laughed. "You're a simple man. Guns! The government had its fears and had its underground minute men ready—armed with sonics. Tiny ones, hand size." He hadn't known the sonic generators existed as hand weapons; they were heavy, lumbering military units. "They destroy eardrums, burst blood vessels, cause convulsions. They can kill and the minute men don't waste time on low-energy settings. When trouble starts, people die. There's not much trouble."

Donald said, "Still, you'll see the vigilantes walk three together an' each three stays in sight o' three mair. There's no love for them."

"What do they think they're preserving?"

Donald approved. "Your brain's workin' the noo; that was a proper question."

"You have an answer?"

"They're presairvin' peace until things settle doon as before an' life gangs on again like last year—they think. They're seein' the end o' the world but they dinna believe it yet. Do you believe it, laddie?"

44

Will said gravely, needing relief from the insupportable, "Aye, Donald laddie; I see it's sair true."

Donald was offended. "You shouldna mock the guid Scots!"

12

The house in Bishopbriggs was large, Edwardian and solid; the garden had, at any rate until recently, been well kept.

"Yours?" Will asked.

"Leased," the girl said shortly and, while Donald walked the bikes round to the back of the house, opened the front door. In the dim passage he waited for her to switch on the light.

She urged him forward. "Straight ahead to the kitchen. Hasn't it hit you yet that there's no power for light? Or oil for lamps, or candles to give a glimmer? What there is the government hoards."

She began to chatter a little in the sanctuary of "home". "But we have a wind turbine on the roof and a generator in the cellar and some contraband oil, so we'll have light when—"

The light came on.

She turned to run, but men moved from the side rooms before and behind them.

She froze into calm. One of them shoved her, and Will allowed himself to be herded after her; it was ceasing to matter who pushed and pulled at him.

In the kitchen a shabby, lank, unshaven animal with foul teeth and a bald scalp fringed with absurdly long back hair shook its head in sadness. "Aye, we foond the oil an' the wee genny. It waur verra selfish o' y' tae hoard sae." The accent was thicker than Giles at his worst.

The back door of the kitchen opened and a semi-conscious Donald was flung half-across the room, bleeding from scalp and face. An overweight thug with a bike chain followed him in, complaining, "Yon's a strang bastard," as Donald collapsed to his knees and slowly flat on his face.

Chain at the ready, he rolled Donald over with his foot and would have searched him if the animal had not hissed, "Dinna touch him mair! The wee mon may no' like it; we dinna ken wha this bastard is."

Donald stirred and grunted. The animal said, "Watch but dinna hairt him!" He gestured to Will and the girl. "Sit doon an' bide."

There were kitchen chairs. They sat. She asked, "What are we waiting for?"

"The wee mon."

Will recalled that the Scottish "wee" can be meaningless, non-descriptive, a decoration.

Donald rolled to his hands and knees. The bike chain stirred and the two from the passage moved closer. They were the dregs of any city the world over—sharp but unclean, evil but empty. Only the animal was totally animal; the kitchen was disgusting for his presence. He grinned at Will with startling brown stumps. "The wee mon'll hae a word wi' you, I'm thinkin'. Y' near killt him."

So his "wee" *was* descriptive. "Angus? Giles?"

Donald clawed upright and rested against the wall with his face in his hands. The sharp thugs watched him.

"Angus? Giles? What's a name the noo?"

Donald clutched at his stomach, bending forward in pain.

The animal hissed, "Did y' hae tae kick his guts in? Wasna' the bike chain eneuch f'r y'?"

The other was sour. "No' eneuch f'r him. I tellt y' he's a strang bastard."

Without preamble, without reason, the girl shrieked in violent panic, "Donald! They'll kill me! Help me!"

With all their eyes on her Donald straightened in a curiously reflex movement, with a sonic gun in his hand, and killed three men in three seconds.

The sidespill of the beam pierced Will's head like a silent bellow so close to the ear that it stabbed and agonized. He had not imagined what the terrible thing was like; the suddenness of blood spurting from the noses, ears and mouths of slaughtered men was a fresh frightfulness for the world. What shatterings took place within he could not guess, but they died at once.

The animal sat down quickly on the nearest chair and raised

his hands, eyes on the gun, perhaps conceiving that, since he lived, a hostage or information was required, and grinned sickly at Will. "Y' hae the richt freends."

Will looked dazedly from the dead men to the girl, who looked *satisfied*. She showed no reaction from fear because she had not feared; she had simply jerked Donald into action—just as Angus had sometimes done with himself.

She said matter-of-factly, "Donald's a vigilante, but he'd have been lynched in the street if he'd worn the brassard alone."

Donald's sudden activity had cost him pain; leaning on the wall he ordered dully, "Frisk that shit for weapons."

While Will did so and found nothing he said, "My heid aches," and Jeanie rummaged some form of analgesic from a drawer and began to clean the blood from him. He asked the animal, "Who're you?"

"Murdo Munro. What's it tae y'?" He was one who recovered quickly.

Will said, "You're Giles's man !"

"I dae a job f'r a wee mon."

Jeanie said over her shoulder. "Of course it's Giles, if that's his name of the moment. He always uses the town scum for his dirty work."

"Scum" did not perceptibly outrage Murdo Munro.

Will asked the girl, "Now your rescue's come apart do we run or wait for Giles to take me back?"

"Wait. Now you're in the open I have bargaining power."

So, among the dead, they waited.

After a while she said, "You might as well shoot the other one, Donald."

"No." Will saw that he avoided her eye. Her lips thinned but she did not press him.

He spoke suddenly to Will. "Aussie, I'm no' a killer unless I must be. If the lassie is in danger I can kill. Then I canna help myself because she has the compulsion on me. But there's no danger here needs killin'."

The girl smiled lightly, as if she could afford to overlook minor rebellion.

Will looked quickly away from her glance.

"Dinna fear her eye, Aussie. It takes weeks o' cunnin' to

build the compulsion, an' I think it's the wee Giles will hae the eye on you. If so, he has you, body an' soul."

From the back door Angus said, without accent, "His body is perishable and we fear his soul is already sold."

Jeanie gasped in surprise and desperation, "Donald!"

"She wants you to turn your gun on me, Donald." He came into the room, walking stiffly.

"I ken it, but she's in no danger frae you, I think. I see nothin' to kill for."

Angus surveyed the bodies on the floor, appraised Donald's cuts and abrasions. "I feel fortunate for that."

Donald continued as if he had not spoken, "This gun can hairt sair withoot killin'. So noo we will a' sit at the table—Jeanie in front o' me an' you, wee man, opposite where you can watch her an' she watch you. The Aussie will sit behind you where you canna catch his eye. The scum can sit anywhere so lang as we can a' see it."

Angus laughed aloud. "I could do with a few like you."

"Maybe. Move!" As they hesitated, "Do you want me to prove the hairt?"

They sorted themselves on to chairs.

"Maybe we'll hae some answers."

Angus settled himself. "Are you entitled to answers? I don't know you."

"I'm Donald Baird. Are you wiser for that?"

"Call me Angus—and be no wiser for that. As for answers, what are you to little Jeanie here, who scatters messages about justice and mercy?"

Donald did not reply but fixed his eyes on the back of the girl's head with, in them, a mixture of emotions Will could not read, save that love was not among them.

Angus said, "Perhaps I can tell you. You're meat, Donald, picked up when meat's needed and put down when her blood cools. She's always kept a muscular bedboy or two. At other times you're errand boy or strongarm man or breadwinner or whatever style of jump-when-I-whistle she happens to need."

She could have killed then without thought of justice or mercy.

Donald's face was totally blank. Will thought, *It's true . . .*

48

sex on demand, unable to refuse or run ... and the degradation of knowing what you do. What a hatred!

Angus asked, "Do you want to be free of her?"

She snapped, "You're mine, Donald!" but he took her by the nape and she could not turn to stare at him. There was, Will saw, a physical compulsion working in the man, a conditioned reflex making his body also an enemy in the struggle not to act when she demanded. But he could fight when his gaze was free.

Angus smiled and she shuddered. Donald asked, "You can do it?"

"With time and patience. But I don't know what can be done for you, Will. It may have gone too far." For a brooding moment he seemed to forget them all. "Everything too far. But it may yet be possible to turn my talents outwards, to be of some use in the world."

This obscurity made sense of a kind to Jeanie who spat, literally spat, and jeered, "Forgive me for I have sinned! From the expert in betrayal!"

Will was concerned with his own obscurities, not theirs. "What has gone too far? Why am I here?"

Not Angus but Jeanie rushed in with impatience, "You're Will Santley, aren't you? If you aren't, there's no sense in it. So how can you not—" She studied Will's face, seeking truth where there was only puzzlement. After a while she said, "He's amnesiac, isn't he? Or has he been cleared? He really doesn't know!" Her angry eyes seared Angus's unwilling nod. "And still you'll—Oh, you unbelievable bastards!"

The small man's voice was desolate. "We are. It's our ideas that need clearing, not our memories." He shook his head violently and changed direction. "Murdo! You did a good job. Now get out."

The animal scampered for the door, self-control vanishing at the thought of freedom.

"Murdo!" He stopped dead. "If I hear talk outside of what has happened here tonight, I'll blame you for it. And kill you. And you know I'll do it."

"I ken it." He nodded at the dead. "What o' them?" It was

49

the question of a cautious businessman; he had no feeling for them.

"Nothing. It's time this house was closed down, and who'll worry over a few dead in a world growing thick with them?"

Murdo Munro slipped back to his rat's nest and never knew he had dipped his dirty hands in history.

"Now!" Angus said comfortably, and left no doubt who dominated the room; the sonic gun was not a factor with him. There was more to Angus than trickery and treachery.

"What shall we do with your Donald, Jeanie Deans? Something we must do because I read him as a man not to be threatened. He can't be allowed knowledge."

"What knowledge? An' why no'?"

"If you know too much you'll have to be killed."

It was not a threat but a statement, an explanation.

"Ah." Donald thought about it. "You are armed?"

"Oh, yes!" A knife appeared in Angus's hand and buried itself deep in the woodwork by Donald's head. "Fast reflexes. I could kill you faster than you can use that gun."

"You shouldna chance it. Will, see what mair weaponry he carries."

Angus stood and raised his arms. "I'm clean."

With hands he tried to keep from shaking, Will made sure that this was true.

Jeanie said idly, "He could kill you as easily unarmed; this is vaudeville, a calming for worse things. But he's right, Donald, that I must let you go. Permanently. Get out and keep silent while you don't know enough to be a nuisance."

Angus sat down.

Donald picked phrases. "I'm no' scared o' words, an' I need to ken what's doin' here, what you baith are an' yon Aussie withoot a memory. I'll trust mysel to get oot alive. It's worth a risk to scrape the bottom o' this."

Angus was practical and chilling. "The risk is certain death; if I wanted to save you then, I couldn't. Convince him, Jeanie. Hasn't he served you well? Given meat for your itch? Admit the debt and send him away!"

She shrugged. "You heard me free him, but he can be stubborn. And the sonic might get you first."

50

Will thought, *She doesn't give a damn. She can enthral another tomorrow. Total power brings total hedonism brings total selfishness.*

He was surprised to hear Angus ask, "Don't you care what happens to him?"

"Should I? Would you?"

"I would."

"Oh, yes, *Forgive me for I have sinned.* Your moral wallow."

"How long have you had him?"

"In reason's name, do you think I keep count?"

Donald cried out with rending force, "Ten bluidy years! Time oot o' mind!"

Safe from her eyes he could erupt in anger and despair, but the servitude was deeply rooted in psychic trickery. Will saw him torn. But ten years! She looked no more than twenty-three or -four.

Angus asked, "How old is she, Donald?"

Her face hardened in contempt.

Donald shrank a little on himself. "She doesna alter. But some lassies haud the years well. Maybe she's thairty-five."

"More than that, Donald."

"I'll no' hae that." Will wouldn't have it either, but Angus and Jeanie remained silent. "I ken there's operations." He sounded desperate. "The doctors work miracles. They say." He ran down, not believing that either.

"No doctors, Donald. No miracles."

"Are you talkin' o' witchcraft? I'm no hieland clown scared o' his fey grannie."

"No witchcraft. See, you have just encountered the edge of knowledge. What do you think might be the secrets in hiding?" Suddenly he pleaded, "Please go, Donald."

"So far an' no mair? You mean well but I'll take my chance. An' killin' me may no' be that easy. An' I think yon Aussie could do wi' yin on his side."

Will came out of a half trance of incomprehension. "And what's for me? You don't imprison a man just to kill him later."

Jeanie showed a faint, impatient pity. "Don't you understand

51

that they want something from you first? *Then* they'll kill you."

He felt quite alone in the universe.

She said more gently, "Has nobody told you that they want what is buried in your lost memory? Angus, what sort of monsters have you all become?"

Angus's face was a study in spiritual anguish

Caught between brute world and fantasy, Will asked incredulously, "Angus, you didn't trap me all the way to Scotland just to kill me?"

Angus shuddered. Jeanie breathed, "But he did, he did. Now he's suffering but it's too late. He's the eternal pawn who always suffers when the meanings become clear."

The front-door bell, an old spring-winder, shrieked and subsided in rusty whirring.

13

Donald became wolfishly expectant; any happenings might be turned to advantage.

Angus's face cleared and he shook his head. "My friends. I sent for them as soon as I knew where you were bringing Will." He grinned for a coming impudence. "It would help if you answer the door, Donald. If I leave the room Will might run— and where could he run to save into trouble?"

"Your problem; you solve it."

The bell shrieked and ground down again.

Angus urged in his own fashion. "It may be too late to protect you, but I'll try. Now, let them in—please."

Donald leaned across the table as though he might read behind Angus's eyes, nodded shortly and left the room. Jeanie called derisively after him, "He'd promise Christ the Devil for an altar boy if it suited his need."

They waited, with Jeanie watching Angus in a tense and excited wondering.

They heard the latch and she breathed sharply in.

There were voices.

Then footsteps.

She hissed, near to tears, "He didn't do it."

Do what? Will wondered—and remembered the gun.

Angus was contemptuous, not of Donald's failure but of her singlemindedness. "He hasn't a killer's heart and it would have gained him nothing. Where's the profit in killing one to avoid killing another?"

Donald called, "There's just the yin come in but there's another outside."

From the threshold a short, plump, bearded and angry man glared at Angus. "You sent a first-urgency message. It had better be justified!"

"It is. Will! This is Doctor Randal Cooke, who we hope will locate your forgotten past."

Will asked unsteadily, "What sort of doctor? Psychiatrist? Hypnotist?"

Cooke said, without bothering to look at him. "Mr Cooke, Angus. I am a surgeon."

For Will all the fresh fears fell apart in an old terror that had been drilled into him. "You don't understand!" His voice broke, squeaking; he tried again in a frightened croak. "If you try to relieve the pressure it will kill me. Then you'll get nothing."

His protest died under Cooke's glance of unbelief. The surgeon turned on Angus.

"Is this the patient? Where did this rot about pressure come from? Is he amnesiac or has your treatment made an idiot of him? I warn you, Angus, I'm not to be knitted into your game-playing." He faced Jeanie with animosity. "What's this bitch doing here? I know of her. Dissident! All sentiment and no damned sense." Donald he looked over with irritable evil. "Who's this? Another Diss? And why is the room an abbatoir? Can't you work, Angus, without carnage among bystanders?"

"Which question first? His name is Donald and he's Jeanie's newly ex-sex object. She's here because she poked her nose into our affairs. Donald did the butchering—under compulsion. Yes, I can work—"

Cooke's furious eyes were on Donald. "Sex object? A norm?"

"I'm afraid so."

53

"He'll have to be killed. See what you've done to this helpless man, you selfish woman—"

He broke off at Angus's chuckle and bridled with fresh rage at the sonic gun pointed at his throat.

Angus intervened. "Put it away, Donald. I've said you'll live and I mean it."

Cooke's anger vanished like an artifice whose purpose has run out. "Been making promises, have you?" He took Murdo's vacated chair. "What's happened, Angus? The unexpected? Are you out of your depth?"

"Not yet. Will, tell about your amnesia."

Will was silent but for the tiny sound of his trembling.

Donald came in unexpectedly. "Will, this talk o' deein' is still talk. Tell, if it'll shed light on a black business."

Angus asked, "May I turn round, Willie? I can calm you."

"No. I don't trust you. Or this doctor. Why should I?"

"It might make sense o' a' this haverin'."

Donald had his powers, human powers; Will capitulated.

"My skull was fractured in a car accident. That's what they told me. I don't remember the smash or anything before it. There's a splinter of bone pressing, and a clot."

Cooke bellowed, "God and Satan hear him! Keep talking, naive and boneheaded clot!"

"The doctor said relieving the pressure would cause a haemorrhage. I'd be dead or a vegetable."

Cooke gave vent to exasperated hilarity. "Young man, if your brain were riddled with cactus spines and squeezed between Angus's hungry jaws and clotted with gobs of Glasgow porridge, there would still be no reason why it couldn't be relieved without danger to yourself. What doctor was this? A horse doctor with docking shears? Angus, did you swallow this nonsense?"

"Not being a bloody physician, I had no choice. The doctor's name was David. Edwin David."

"Never heard of him. A quack. Man, why didn't you go to a reputable public hospital?"

Will protested that it had been a public hospital.

"David was your specialist? And told you that rubbish?"

Jeanie said, "I know of him."

54

"Another Dissident? Lying to the patient to block pursuit of his inconvenient memories?"

Angus said, "If that's so, it raises more problems. What else do you know about him, Jeanie?"

"He's a genetic surgeon."

Cooke bawled at her, "Don't be a fool, girl! I know the record of every genetic surgeon alive."

"Including the Gangoil staff?" To Donald and Will the name meant nothing but the other two were shocked.

Angus said, "Since Gangoil is an Australian government genetic-research laboratory, location unknown, the proper deduction is that Will's mind holds something Gangoil wants hidden. Perhaps it was this David he told secrets to."

Cooke stood. "Then we also shall know them. Tonight. I have an ambulance outside, one vehicle that can run the streets without being burned or bombed. We can leave at once."

Angus whipped round with cat speed and caught Will's eye before he could turn his head. "Be calm, Willie. I've promised to do what I can and I keep my promises. Believe that no harm will come to you."

Cooke snorted and Jeanie raised despairing eyes as Will's tension subsided visibly.

Donald winced, seeing from the outside what had so often been done to himself. He said with unconcealed savagery, "I second the promise."

Jeanie tried to catch his glance but he avoided her; she hadn't Angus's flashing reflexes. "Donald, you go no further with us! Stay behind, out of it."

Cooke asked, "What does he know?"

"Nothing that matters."

"Why should I believe you?"

The sonic gun moved round the circle. "I'm no' leaving a man to be killed for a gabble o' double talk."

Cooke lost his temper again—or pretended to. "Angus! Kill that fool!"

The gun looked at his throat. He stared as if he saw and heard the impossible as Angus said, "Don't try it, Randal; you aren't fast enough. I could take it but I don't intend to. He's good for Will; let him come."

Cooke made an abrupt, sweeping gesture, denying responsibility for the irrational. As if no contretemps existed he asked Jeanie, "Is this David one of us?"

"I know only his name and profession."

Cooke cursed but Angus said, "Either he's a Diss or the Disses are using him. They've stolen a march and we should move to Australia to investigate. But how can we manage that now?"

Jeanie asked, "Is the unbeatable Angus defeated by a transport shortage?" He did not miss the secretive smile as she turned away, had no doubt that she had more to give when it suited her.

Cooke pointed a foot.

"What about these?"

"They'll be collected during the night." Murdo would leave the bodies to rot, but keeping the peace demanded that Cooke's instinct for asepsis be placated.

Angus stayed close to Will as they left, knowing that his calming order plastered bluntly over the apprehension of death had been a stretching of his capacities; a slight tipping of balances could drop a screaming lunatic on to his hands, a man lost in a schizophrenic gap between realities.

Outside, the end of the long twilight glimmered towards night. The ambulance waited in the drive. A young, dark driver whom Cooke addressed as Carlo opened the rear doors for them; they sat on the bunks and were shut in. In seconds the car moved off.

Will, awash in inordinate calm, saw idly that Donald sat with his back carefully turned from Jeanie, trusting her not at all, and he listened with only mild interest when she spoke.

"I can tell you a little but it won't help. I know nothing of Gangoil save that David is there. I don't know him as Company; perhaps he's a new one. I first heard of him when a message came that Angus was closing in on someone named Santley in Melbourne and that this should be stopped. Then we heard that Santley had booked a flight for Britain and the word was that he mustn't fall into Randal's hands for brain search. About that time your people trapped Ronnie and Helen and cleared their minds, leaving me as the only active Dissident in Britain.

It was just chance that I spotted Angus playing private eye in a tam-o-shanter in George Square and realized who the solitary Australian must be. I trailed him to the transit house but couldn't do anything until he walked out through the front door; our rescue was spur of the moment, arranged by signs. I'm only sorry it hasn't succeeded."

"It took a pretty complex sign language to do that," Angus said. "It makes me wonder what you've been using him for besides the obvious."

Cooke ploughed over his curiosity. "Not helpful, but we have Santley, and the Dissidents have not. Yes, Angus, you'll have to go back to Australia and trace this David. I'll talk to Smith about it."

"Talk to him about a plane while you're at it; that should be quite a conversation." Cooke scowled but Angus watched Jeanie with thoughtful eyes.

Out of his Angus-bred serenity Will asked, as he might have asked about the weather, "What sort of secret needs murder to protect it?"

"Ours," Cooke said.

"The Dissidents don't think so." But in defeat she sounded only petulant.

Cooke gave a sour parody of Ancient Lights. " 'When I was a child I thought as a child . . .' "

14

The trip seemed excruciatingly long. Will's flattened emotions deemed his situation marginally improved. Donald was potentially friend and supporter, the peculiar Jeanie seemed in some measure his partisan, but Angus's championship seemed based on obscure personal needs. Wearing Angus's face, he had the unScottish voice of a stranger and his loyalties were split in finicking divisions of what he would countenance and what he would not. The web of goodwill and illwill would be perplexing, if he could care sufficiently . . .

The truck slowed, turned, bucked across a gutter, rolled a short distance and stopped. Carlo jumped out, then swore at them. "Get that ceiling light out! Looting's been stopped but we don't want to have to fight off inquisitive strays."

He was another with nearly accentless English, which did not match his Italianate name and appearance.

They piled out. Cloud obscured the stars; the moon had not risen; it was black dark at last.

"It'll rain," Carlo said cheerlessly. "The path's just here. Single file and hand on shoulder and we won't break ankles in potholes." They sorted themselves into line. "Ready?"

From the rear Donald said, "No. Where are we?"

Carlo muttered, "For Christ's sake!"

Cooke answered with ice in his voice. "At the Clydebank shipyards because I must operate here. It is not possible to requisition a hospital theatre for a patient who has not entered through Casualty or to dismiss an inquisitive theatre staff because I do not appreciate their presence. Just as I am not permitted to dismiss you, Donald Quixote, little as I appreciate yours. May we go about our business?"

Carlo asked, "Do you want that Scottish bastard taken out?"

A grin rippled in Angus's voice. "Donald carries a sonic gun." He seemed to approve of Donald, irrespective of loyalties.

"Shit!" The driver took himself and his bravado into the darkness and they stumbled and swore after him. Rusting hinges creaked as they moved through a gate. A voice, low down, called, "Randal?" and Cooke answered, "Here, Alastair."

"Steps," Carlo said, and they felt downwards. "Break your fucking neck, Donald Gunman."

At the bottom they were on concrete; a dimmed torch gave direction; a door opened in a looming surface and they passed inside. It closed and a light came on.

Alastair, fairheaded and bony, confronted them. "I can't use many lights; I'm on storage batteries."

The room was about a hundred feet long and as wide, regimented in rows of drafting tables with chairs and drawing-boards, with prim little areas of clerical record-and-file. Only the globe by the door was lit but the shadows did not hide tables overturned, fixtures smashed, the contents of filing cabinets torn and strewn.

Vandalism had hit hard in the treasure troves of hastily

58

closed down industrial complexes, the holiday of barbarism before an equally barbaric orderliness supervened.

Will heard Alastair say something he did not catch, save for the word "dusting", followed by, "It's a life and death world for us as much as them perhaps."

What news he had given had an electrifying effect on the Company personnel. Angus made a small, despairing sound and asked, "Where?"

"London and the whole south."

"Dusted! But who would do it?"

Alastair said with concern but with the same lack of urgency which seemed to characterize The Company when they were not actually in purposive motion, "Who knows? Unmarked, automated rockets at a hundred thousand feet. We don't know the rad count yet or the size of the area dusted; we only know it has begun. They won't stop at London. It's time to be going, if there's a means of going anywhere."

They looked to Cooke as if for decision. Perhaps he possessed intellectual or professional eminence; if so, he took his time.

Will felt his arm clasped. "Maybe your time is no' yet."

"Is he talking about radioactive dusting? A war?" A tingle of interest suggested he should *care*.

"Aye. You've been oot o' touch while the world spun itsel' silly, but we've all been waitin' for the first blow."

"I had newspapers. It seemed remote."

"Ay. Endin's always seem far off but noo London is deein'."

"Why London? Why not Moscow, Peking, America, even Australia?"

"Any Britisher could ha' told you we'd be the first target in a big war. Britain's the store, the fuellin' ground, the aircraft carrier for invasion or defence. Askin' destruction! London's a beginnin'; Liverpool tomorrow maybe. An' then Glesca. We're deid, Willie, if we stay."

Cooke heard him. "You're dead, Donald Quixote, but not Santley, I think. He'll survive anything short of dismemberment—if we don't kill him ourselves." He thrust his face into Will's. "You know that, don't you?"

Whatever reaction he sought, he was disappointed. Will said,

59

with demented placidity, "If you mean that you or anyone can survive high-level radiation, you're mad."

Angus assured wearily, "He's genuine, Randal; he doesn't know what you're talking about. So why not get on with it? We need the facts, whether the world goes to the hell it's made for itself or not."

"Indeed why not? Is the X-ray set up?"

Carlo told him. "In the rec room."

"Enough power, Alastair?"

"If you aren't wasteful."

"Eight or ten exposures. And the autoclave."

"Enough." He gestured through the dimness, "That way," and went ahead to turn on the recreation-room lights; behind him they threaded through litter and destruction.

The X-ray had been set up by a billiard table, with beside it an autoclave, a small table with towels and auto-sterilizing swabs and a larger one with kidney dishes and a glitter of instruments. A cabinet in transparent plastic displayed pre-sterilized gowns, masks and gloves.

Donald breathed, "Dear Jesus!" as the reality of surgery penetrated. Will, safe in repression, observed without feeling. Cooke inspected his instruments and nodded to Carlo, who gathered them into the autoclave and switched it on, smoothly becoming assistant and nurse.

Cooke said, "The blather about lethal pressures and impossible operations makes me suspect we'll not need them, so we'll not scrub up, nurse, until we must. Now, Santley, where do the headaches strike?"

The surprise question gained him no more than before; there *were* frequent headaches. Will indicated an area at the base of his skull. Cooke glared and referred to Angus, who looked intrigued.

"You've had him under control for a year. Could another hypnotist be using him simultaneously?"

"I don't know; I'm not a hypnotist."

"Then can two manipulators, or whatever your vanity claims for its expertise, control one subject?"

"Not without collaboration; paradoxes of instruction would drive him insane. If you're asking could someone else impose a programme which would not interfere with mine, a simple programme like having headaches return on the kind of cues encountered often but irregularly in daily life—such as a striking clock or the sight of red hair—yes. If such programming was done while he was in hospital—it would have to be a solid job, tantamount to imprinting—he could be released with a certainty of recurrence over several years. And my manipulation, on a different level, probably wouldn't conflict with it. The idea of the imprint would be to keep the seriousness of his condition before his mind—" He paused, working it out. "If it's not pressure or lesion—if it's a memory block, that is, the headaches would be signals automatically reinforcing the block. Very ingenious. It would take a good operator."

"Who could do it?"

"I could."

"Spare me. Who among the Dissidents?"

"Our little maneater here might, but I doubt it."

Jeanie said, "I haven't been in Australia."

"If we have one there I haven't heard of him. But I don't know every one."

"I suppose not. So, it's on to the table with you, Santley! We'll see what these pressures amount to."

Some remnant of volition mumbled in the back of Will's mind, counselling refusal, and he climbed on to the table while he thought about it.

Within twenty minutes they knew that his amnesia was not caused by clot, splintered bone or any physical impairment—that his skull had never suffered fracture.

His memory was not suppressed by damage but, in Company fashion, rerouted into synaptic isolation. The Company had, they told him, its own methods of reversing Company work—but the necessary team was not immediately available. He remained a problem.

15

Carlo began packing instruments. The Company absorbed the finding placidly; their concern was the problem itself. Will felt himself to be a jigsaw piece, his humanity unimportant, when Alastair asked, "Is he in fact Santley? The poor bastard's just a set-up. But for what?"

Carlo looked up to ask, "Are you saying David has slipped us a fake and passed the real one on? Where to?"

"Gangoil. Assume that the real Santley is Company, a new one we haven't contacted. Gangoil would want to discover whether his—" he glanced at Donald and altered the sentence "—capacities can be transferred to others."

Jeanie said with casual spite, "That's what Dissidence is about: we want it done, The Company doesn't. If he's a substitute, The Company has brought an innocent here to die in its private war."

Angus snapped at her, "Do you feel virtuous by default? He may be the real Santley and all our reasoning askew. We must attempt Australia, if only to save his life." He asked pointedly, "Mustn't we, Jeanie?"

"If your talents include walking on water."

But he was sure of her. "Let's have your suggestion."

"Why should I save your skins?"

"Because you preach justice and mercy for Will. Come on, girl, it's too late for bargaining. Have you an Australian contact?"

She studied Will for a long moment before she said, "Helen gave me an emergency signal code, but with communications going silent everywhere it may be too late. If a satellite still operates it might be tried."

Carlo stopped packing. "Communications is my job. There is one, just one. But how do I persuade Control to let me make a private call when power's doled out by the milliwatt? Only official urgents go out now."

Impossible—until Donald called, "Jeanie!", instinctively dropping his eyes. "If the call could be made, what then?"

"I would ask for an orbiter to be sent."

The demand was breathtaking.

"An' get it?"

"If I could persuade Gangoil that we are worth their trouble. The place seems to have enormous influence."

Cooke almost spat. "Gangoil! Do you both plan to sell us out?"

"Are you a saleable commodity? If they have a real Santley, their work is three years in progress." She smiled acidly. "If you want to persuade them to drop their research, this might be your chance. *If* they'll accept you."

Carlo interrupted, "First arrange for a roomful of clerks and operators to permit the call."

Donald asked, "How many's a roomful?"

"At the orbiter port, seven. And a vigilante guard."

"I'm a vigilante. I'll deal wi' the guard."

"Donald Quixote indeed! And can you deal with the staff?"

"Can *you* work the transmitter?"

"It's my job."

Donald showed the gun. "On low power, it stuns."

Carlo eyed it sourly but said, "It's a chance. It's as well you didn't break your fucking neck."

Donald rested a hand on Will's shoulder. "I'll no' be helpin' for love. I'm buyin' passage to Australia for Will an' me."

Again, with a decision wanted, they looked to Cooke. "If he serves The Company and that's his fee, pay it. The escapade is yours but I must get back to the hospital. Not that I can do much about malnutrition, and that's becoming the major problem. Take me there, Carlo, then you'll want the ambulance for your melodrama, I suppose. Keep me informed, Alastair."

Carlo followed him out, wheeling the X-ray pack.

With one thing decided, Angus began at once on another.

"Sit down, Willie."

Will sat. "What now?"

"You've had enough sedation; you may need quick responses before the night is out. Look me in the eye. Come on, man, the eye doesn't do anything; it's only a signal to ready your reactions. Look!"

Will looked. Angus said, with intensity, "Your emotions and your self-determination are repressed because I ordered it. The order is cancelled. You may do as you please."

Will shook from head to foot as reined-in tensions flooded his mind; he would have fallen from the chair if Angus had not held him.

Through whimpering minutes, like a machine shuddering to a standstill, the animal fear of insanity and death dissipated.

Donald watched in revolted fascination. "An' you can get him back his past?"

"That won't be easy, with another operator's cues to be located and cancelled, but it can be done." He added quietly, "Then I'll want someone to do it to me."

Alastair warned, "For your own sake, Angus, don't," and took an involuntary pace back from the face of a suffering demon.

"I need to know. I need punishment." He made it sound a normal need, to be sought and accepted, but below his voice the spirit ached.

Some day, Will thought through clearing mists, he might begin to understand. Hatred, wearied by contradictions, receded into incomprehension; the man in torment was a third person, neither Angus nor Giles.

As Carlo picked up his final load Donald called after him, "Bring back a nurse's cape frae the hospital! A red yin."

Carlo nodded understanding but Will's tired mind puzzled and gave it up without asking. Weeks of pent-up strain assaulted his labouring brain and, flat on the cement floor, he slept.

It seemed no time at all but was almost one o'clock when he woke to the metallic crash of Carlo tipping guns out of a briefcase. He saw Donald toss the red cape to Jeanie, who took it with a mock curtsey for the implication of women's work and set about making vigilante armbands. In a drafting table drawer she found a razor blade and a few pins, some pieces of thread, a length of thin string, a nail which would make needle holes—and was competently in business.

Donald vetoed the guns. "No vigilante carries firearms an' a man wi' a sonic will cut you down at sight o' yin. An' a sonic is faster because you need no' be so accurate. Noo, Carlo, show us the transmitter layoot."

Carlo found drawing paper amongst the litter.

"The orbiter-port staff know me as a technician, which will help us get close. Orbiter schedule was never more than one a day, so the administration block is small." He sketched quickly.

64

"Offices and flight lounge on the ground floor; Communications on the first and Flight Control above them. No flights now, so only Communications is manned."

Alastair said, "There'll be soldiers."

"No. Government never trusts its armed forces in troubled times; organized manpower can be dangerous. They use minute men and keep the army out of the way. Minute men are more loosely organized, less self-sufficient. Right, Donald?"

"We protect oor ain."

"There are twelve vigilantes in two shifts of six, three on the runway side and three in the front area. The six off shift will be sleeping in the flight lounge. We'll have to put them out of action. Donald?"

"Ay; we've no' the numbers to post guards over them. An' we want their sonics."

"How do we get them?"

"Is the ootside o' the buildin' lit?"

"No. Power's conserved. A forty-watt globe over the door can be lit if needed, but that's all."

"We must get them to light it so we can see to knock 'em doon. Leave other plannin' till we see the groond."

Carlo glanced round, catching eyes. "I suppose we're agreed Donald should handle the attack?"

There had been no discussion; there was no dissent.

"Meanin' that I'm the ainly yin can use the sonic an' no' make a clumsy killer o' mysel. Also I ken the passwords for the night. Ay, I'll lead, but Carlo must take over in the radio room."

"Of course. You don't need to point that out."

Donald considered him sombrely. "Does your flummery include brains that do withoot ordinary discussion?"

"The Company have worked together for—for a great number of years; we don't need much talk between ourselves."

"You're young for 'a great number o' years' an' so's Jeanie. An' maybe the wee Angus an' a'. Eh, Will?"

Angus cut him off. "What we are matters less now than what we do. Who will wear the brassards?"

"Mysel an' Will an' Alastair. But you, Angus—Jeanie says you're fast but are you strang?"

"Not as strong as you, but enough. And faster."

"Then you can haunt the dark while we get the guards into the light, a sort o' invisible resairve. But I'll no' hae men killed; we want their sonics, no' their lives. I want no karate madmen breakin' harmless necks."

"You're no killer; nor am I."

"Guid, for I'll no' hae it."

"And Jeanie?"

"Will stay in the dark wi' you until she's needed to talk to this Gangoil. Watch her!"

"She needs us as much as we need her."

"I dinna trust her."

"We know her better. You'll have no killing and I'll have no revenging yourself on her."

"I dinna follow the fine points o' your loyalties."

"Do you think," Alastair asked, "that we could keep to the business in hand? It will be dawn in two hours."

"We'll leave noo. I'll ride in front wi' you, Carlo; I hae questions. Noo let's awa' withoot waitin' to think o' things to go wrang, an' then fear to move at a'."

16

When they quitted the ambulance only the faintest luminescence of water told Will they were on the river bank. Carlo removed the engine rotor; they had no manpower to guard against plunderers.

Donald drew them together. "Jeanie, if they gie you this orbiter craft, how lang for it to get here?"

"Two, three days perhaps. How can I tell? If they send one they'll take who suits them, not necessarily all of us. I can only argue."

"An' I'll lay you've a bluidy right argument ready. We canna haud men at gunpoint like hijackers for twa-three days so we send oor message an' get oot. Back to Bishopbriggs. Hae you a message ready?"

"Yes."

Carlo said, "We can't bring the orbiter here. The staff have access to guns and grenades; they might be able to ground it or take it over for themselves. Jeanie should direct them to land at the regular airfield at Abbotsinch; the runway is long enough for rocket take-off. They'll get no landing instructions because the place is deserted, so if we ask for an ETA it will be up to us to be there on time." He added, "Tonight's affair must seem inexplicable to staff and vigilantes. I'll be recognized, but that won't matter unless I'm caught. I won't be."

Moving up the bank to the edge of the airfield they saw the control block no more than a hundred yards away, barely visible, humped black on black.

Carlo breathed, "The door's dead centre. Three guards this side; three on the runway."

They discarded caution now; noise was required to bring the guards into the open. Donald, Will and Alastair, wearing brassards, marched Carlo between them directly towards the control block, behaving as an escort. Behind them Angus and Jeanie moved through the dark.

They were within yards of the building when a voice, disembodied in night, said quietly, "Halt there, Clydebank."

Donald answered "Strathclyde," and was told, "Bide still an' identify yersels."

"We're frae the Infirmary an' we're escortin' a man o' yours, Carlo de Luca. He's to relieve a man wha's wife is ailin' an' askin' for him."

"Sae? Speak up there, Carlo!"

"Here, Andy. It's Phil's missus is sick."

The vigilante's voice had receded steadily towards the door. The forty-watt globe bloomed yellow, strong enough to fall on their armbands and show Carlo's face. And on the silent forms of two other guards with weapons drawn.

The commander holstered his sonic. "A' richt, lads; they're oors."

The group gathered at the door. As the commander turned to open it Donald brought up his gun and laid the three unconscious before they could begin to move against him.

Alastair whispered, "The others have come from the far side. May have heard the challenge."

Will had heard nothing, nor apparently had Donald, but confirmation came in a voice asking. "Wha's wi' y', Andy?"

Donald answered without hesitation, "I'm no' Andy; it's him I'm lookin' for. We're Infirmary detachment an' we're escortin' ain o' your boys—Carlo."

"Why did Andy no' see y'?" The voice came closer. "Wha's that on the groond?" He cried harshly, "Get y'r bluidy haunds up! That's Andy!"

He commenced another gasping syllable that died in a soft scrabbling and thudding and someone else groaned in the dark.

Angus and Jeanie came into the light, the girl wincing and clutching her hand. Angus said, "Use the sonic, Donald. Make sure they stay out."

Donald slipped into the shadows and reappeared with three more sonics. "They'll keep an hour or twa. How did you dae it?"

"We heard them and got behind them. With their silhouettes against the light it was easy."

Jeanie wrung her fingers. "Mine called out. It's years since I used force on anyone."

Always time for the casual comment, Will thought; strength resided in their ability to remain unruffled. He said, grudgingly, "None of us heard them except Alastair."

Carlo said, "I did, but Alastair spoke first."

Donald grunted, "Mair bluidy tricks."

"Don't look for miracles," Angus told him. "Your senses haven't been trained; ours have. How do we move now?"

"Carlo first to halt suspicion. But first, this." He distributed the vigilantes' sonics around the group, tucking the odd one into his own belt. "You must no' fire these. Cover, menace, but dinna fire! They're tricky, an' you can kill withoot meanin' tae, so you must no' fire at a'. I'll turn on the yin that shoots an' teach him what's meant by agony. Noo, in wi' you, Carlo."

Luck found them four of the off-duty guards asleep in the lounge, and low-energy beams at the side of the neck shifted them into paralysis without waking. The other two, playing cards in an office, had no chance.

"They're workin' men," Donald said regretfully. "They dinna understan' the needs o' violence an' vigilance."

"You seem to," Angus suggested.

68

"I ha' been a maircenary soldier."

"No credit to you."

"An' when I came to ken that, I stopped. Are there no mair, Carlo?"

"Only staff now, on shift upstairs."

"Then it's up wi' us."

They removed their shoes for quiet on the cement steps and carried the extra guns awkwardly in their belts. Carlo led them down the corridor to the door marked "Transmitter Staff Only" and entered casually.

Somebody said "Carlo! What are you doing here?" and simultaneously he stepped sideways from the door, letting the others race past him.

In the immediate uproar one girl acted with unexpected reflex to fling a heavy filing spike at Donald's head. He ducked and snapped a beam at her feet. She screamed and fell, clutching her ankle.

Sight of the guns brought the room to silence.

Donald said conversationally. "The lass is sair but no' damaged. If nane interferes we'll do oor business an' get oot wi' hairt to nane." The thickened accent betrayed his tension.

A small, shirtsleeved man, with a snarl to match his pug face, demanded, "What the hell is this, Carlo?"

"Banditry, sir. We must make a satellite call which you wouldn't approve and which you're not to hear. So you will all move into the corridor while this lady and I make our contact. In the corridor you will remain silent. Sonic guns trained on you will ensure it."

The staff filed silently outside, carrying the lamed girl who compressed her lips against the pain of muscular cramp. They went patiently as if, Will surmised, these last days had sown apathy in them and life had become one meaningless damned thing after another. Nothing short of animal violence was worth resentment.

He waited thirty-five minutes with a gun he must not use trained on people who pointedly ignored him.

When Carlo and Jeanie came out she said briefly, "Two days."

Carlo grimaced. "We were lucky. They were difficult."

Donald asked, "Tapes cleared, records burned?"

69

"Nothing to give us away."

"Then let's gang hame." He smiled genially on the staff. "I apologize for oor actions but withoot real regret."

Mutinous silence followed them down the stairs.

In the lounge Donald insisted on leaving the sonics behind for their owners because "A vigilante withoot his weapon is meat for lynchin'."

It lacked minutes to dawn as they stepped over the unconscious bodies at the door and made for the ambulance. The cloud cover had lifted and a huge and bloody moon hung over the river.

Donald hugged Will's shoulders. "Twa days! We could be oot o' here before Glesca goes the way o' London."

He was premature. The ambulance had barely moved when its radio told them that a station in the south still called.

A newsman doing his job because nothing else remained to do reported the dusting of central England and Wales.

In the waning voice of an underpowered station the real world rushed in. Their triumphant raid shrank to a skirmish on an anthill.

17

They huddled, but not together, each into himself. For Will they were revealed in a dark but revealing light. *They know each other, depend closely on each other, but have no love to bind them. The Company is no fellowship. Each stands finally alone. Whatever they are is not worth being. I am not one of them.*

Only Jeanie put out a hand for comfort, but not to her own. Habit turned her to Donald and a sharp withdrawal, reminding her that she had dried that fount of comfort long ago.

Will forgot them all as a faraway man's voice spoke of the death of England and his own ending.

"London died last night. The funeral is not yet but death was delivered; there is only the waiting. Tonight Birmingham and Coventry were dusted, and Bristol and Cardiff and a thousand towns and villages whose names will fade as the network of communication thins and breaks for good. I speak from Birmingham but I don't know how much longer the diesel plant can run. Across the city all lights are out except the light of fires; final night has set in. This is death and we know it—time to think of last things. The output of the dust has been measured; within a few hours the average radiation dose will approach two hundred rads for every man, woman and child—and will continue to rise, for there is no avoiding death that seeps through chinks and crevices in dust and through material barriers in silent swords. The dosage will become insufferably high, but we will be dead—all of us—before we discover how great the cumulative dose may be. I am told that cockroaches may survive us, having a great natural resistance. Could *they* be the next masters of the world? It seems a poor return for what we have been and done, however mistakenly or ineptly, but perhaps that is what is meant by survival of the fittest."

He won't feel pain yet. In a day or two, lassitude and nausea. Pain later. It's no way to die; bombs could be quick and clean.

"Last night, from London, we spoke of marauders coming over at great height, but we were guessing. They did not 'come over', they came *down*, vertically down in power dives at speeds beyond interception. From where? Who knows? From a waiting sleep in some quiet orbit beyond the satellite bands? From a base on the Moon whose empty face could hide a thousand bases? We don't know, as we don't know whose hand delivers them. Or why. We cannot so much as put a name to our destroyer. As if a name matters now."

There can be no reaction to the razing of a culture, the dissolution of so many centuries of error and achievement. Tears later; not yet.

"Great destruction is great spectacle, so the scene has its beauty. The carriers come down from out there; our instruments detect them but we cannot see them and at such approach-speeds we cannot hear them—at first. Announcement of their arrival is a burst of barking cracks, for all the world like the firing of an old Bofors gun, each accompanied by the brilliant flash of a carrier splitting open, like a puffball scattering spore to a waiting wind. The eyes recover from the flashes in time for the ears to be assaulted, as the sound of their coming catches up with the moment and the sky is alive with their screaming down. While the ears recoil the eyes see what the puffballs have scattered—a blue haze, palely shining, that spreads and spreads across the sky until its dispersion is so fine that it seems to have disappeared. But it is there, dropping silently down. Soon the radiation counters tell us it is here and rise to insane chattering as the invisible cloak folds around the shoulders of us all. Now we turn them off because they have nothing more to say that is worth hearing."

I balance between promised life and promised death without knowing who I am or what I have been. Do I die the less if a world dies with me? What must I feel? Later, perhaps . . .

In the closed universe of the ambulance they kept the stillness of observers of revealed hellfire.

18

Will turned to Donald, who rested as still as the others but with a hard face over his thoughts, showing none of their apprehension of apocalypse.

Strongminded this one, but at bottom a romantic optimist.

The stone face spoke. "Twa days may no' be enough, Will. We must watch opportunity."

A larger practicality supervened in Jeanie's voice, holding for once the warmth promised by her gentle face, a regret and farewell as she pronounced a death sentence.

"Too late for watching, Donald. Gangoil will take only Company, and only six of us. Alastair, Carlo, Cooke, Angus, the old man—and myself."

Donald tapped Will's shoulder. "There's a point where The Company balks at payin' an uncomfortable debt."

"Not The Company, Gangoil." Her tone hardened. "They want us for what we are, for study. You are of no use to them, Donald. And Will they want dead."

Will suffered a surge of shock, not fear but outrage at having survived from moment to moment in an ambience of death to have his life threatened again by his own people in his own country. But Angus forestalled the fury on his tongue.

"He'll not be killed while I say he'll not. Gangoil is nothing to me and if The Company tries to override me it will have on its hands such a dissidence as it never dreamed of."

She asked with laughter, "Must somebody give up a seat for Will?"

"Two seats—Will and Donald. We do pay our debts."

Alastair said, "I don't think you'll bring it off, Angus, but that's between you and your peculiar conscience. Just the same, why *should* he die at Gangoil's say-so?"

Angus insisted, "He won't," but she spoke across him. "He said it and meant it. He wouldn't listen to argument."

"Who wouldn't?"

"Doctor David."

"Will's doctor!"

"I suppose so; it's an unusual surname, and the news that we have Will shook him badly. I'd say he was frightened."

Angus and Alastair asked together, "Of what?"

She spread her hands. "I was pleading, not probing, but if Angus wants to save the sacrificial victim at the eleventh hour he'll need to find a way of substituting David. I think that would be the price."

"And why not?" Angus asked. "It's a fair price and maybe a suitable exchange." Massaging his neck and shoulders, he dismissed the matter in the way of The Company when their shorthand conception of discussion was completed, and changed the subject. "I'm stiffening up. You did a job, Willie; I need sleep."

He should, Will thought, have needed at least a neck brace.

Alastair returned talk to essentials. "When's rendezvous?"

"Friday. We're to be at Abbotsinch at midnight and wait."

"Good." He used the intercom to speak to Carlo in the driving cabin. "Please drop me at the shipyard."

"Very well, but why?"

"I work there. I am building a ship."

"For the sake of sense, Alastair! There mightn't even be a bloody Scotland by next week."

"That may be, but I'll continue until I'm certain there's no more can be done."

He cut off the microphone.

Jeanie stared. "Angus was always unbalanced. Now you join him."

"You are dedicated to your dissidence and yourself, and I, in the face of all facts, to tomorrow."

When Alastair left them at the shipyard Donald raised a hand in half salute. "There's a Company man I can a'most understand, but—" his voice lifted for mockery "—what is The Company? In the face o' such history as is in the makin' it may be no mair than an idea in its own heid." He nudged Will. "We'll pry truth oot o' 'em yet, but I doot it'll prove matter worth killin' for in a deein' world."

"So do I," Angus said, "but I'm too tired to argue."

He closed his eyes and his face loosened in lines of pain. Will was not sure that he had in fact intended to kill the man, but any normal neck should have broken. The thought trailed off in a half sleep that persisted until the ambulance drew into the drive of the house in Bishopbriggs. He woke to hear Donald jumping to the gravel and saw fleetingly a glint of light on his drawn sonic. Jeanie prevented his sleepy attempt to follow. "Let him check. There are thieves everywhere—not looters, just simple good men with hungry children, ready with violence they hadn't known was in them."

He sat still. *Where's the end? Caves and scavenging?*

Donald came back. "Nane's been here." He shook a comatose Angus who gasped with pain as he straightened his back. Carlo came from the cabin saying, "I'll have to stay with you now."

"Och ay; you'll hae been reported by your boss. Put the ambulance in the garage."

"It should go back."

"We'll need it. Yin less at the hospital is no matter; they can commandeer hearses an' swish limousines an' gie a few drivers work to haud their brains in place while they still can."

They went to the kitchen. When Carlo came from the garage he encountered, in dawn light, three corpses like wax dummies and the air already tainted.

Donald lifted one at the shoulders. "Stiff as a board. Take him under the knees, Will, an' we'll get them oot o' here before they stink. We hadna intended comin' back."

74

Will did as he was told, head averted from the blood-black face and burst veins.

Jeanie bent to the second. "Give me a hand, Carlo."

Blood, dried over clothing and floor and walls, did not move her, and Carlo was something of a nurse, familiar with death. Will was not; he could only try to ignore his revolted stomach.

They laid the dead in the woodshed, under the old coke bags.

Angus had not offered to help them and now he caved in, crumpling on his bones as though emptied of shape and strength, and muttering, "Where's a bed?"

Donald took his arm. "Through here." Angus shook him off, cursing quietly. "I'm lamed awhile, not a cripple! Just show me!" He went, limping and bent.

Donald jerked his head at Carlo, who nodded and followed. When he came back he asked, "What did you use on him, Will? Four feet of lead pipe?"

"My hands, clubbed. And I kicked him in the knee."

"The knee's nothing; the bruise is nearly clear. But the other—two vertebrae displaced and possibly cracked. He has carried on through a lot of pain."

"I don't care if he's maimed for life."

Carlo found that worth a chuckle. "Angus? By you? Not a chance."

"Not even with cracked vertebrae?"

"They'll heal. He'll sleep for twenty-four hours and wake in fair condition."

Donald stared. "Withoot doctorin'?"

"Without."

"Mair strangeness."

"It will have to stay that way until we gather a consensus group. Even Jeanie's dissidence wouldn't let her brief you without consensus."

She agreed. "We aren't individually free. But you are, Donald; you needn't keep your back turned. That's over."

"Till your need calls for yin mair sairvice!"

"No. I promise it."

It sounded as though he spat.

She said tightly, "For so long as you have before the world kills you, you will be your own man."

He said nothing to a contemptible placebo.

Carlo coughed, like an intruder. "You can believe her. She won't break a promise given before a Company witness."

"You're an uncouth people; how should I believe?"

"Because your value now is as a free agent who can think and act quickly. It no longer pays to interfere with you."

Donald was still for a long time. At last he said, "Yes," and turned round. "I see that's how it could be."

He looked straight at her.

Will doubted that he could have found the courage; his experience had been a pale thing beside Donald's shackled years. He saw Jeanie try to smile and fail and turn away in a defeat more convincing than a world of promises.

Carlo said, "Get some sleep. I'll keep watch, though I think there's little need."

"I'm no' tired. I can take the first four hours."

"I can stay awake about five days if need be. So can Angus when he's well. Uncouth people, as you say. Put Will to bed before he keels over."

19

Through the next night, Thursday, Britain was without news. If dust fell, moving through the northern shires towards the Scottish border, only those under the fall knew of it.

On Friday night, with four hours to go, Carlo asked the unbearable: "If the orbiter doesn't come?"

"Then we take to the Hielands. It's hard livin' there but it's withoot toxins—so far. Maybe the dust willna come."

"The crofters wouldn't welcome us."

"We hae the means to fight an' haud what we take until we could run oor own farms. We'd live."

Angus, fitter but sardonic with a lingering ache, said, "Take? Would you kill for food?"

"I wouldna, but folk could be made to share. It would be poor eatin' for a season but we'd live to grow oor own. Would you kill to eat?"

"I don't think so."

"What sort o' answer's that? If you must eat to live, then you can starve, an' starvation doesna heal like a cracked neck. How long does it take to starve?"

"Longer for me than you."

"You'll hibernate, perhaps?" The irritable joke hit a mark; tiny tensions betrayed alertness. "Like bluidy reptiles in holes?"

Will asked tiredly, "What are you people? Little green men in disguise?" Sarcasm covered a real suspicion.

When none of them replied Donald said, "I hae thought it but wouldna risk bein' laughed at."

Jeanie shook her head, not laughing. "Neither green nor disguised."

"But no' like us. Alien."

"So is an albino or a mongoloid idiot or a genius."

"That's evasion."

"It's all you get, until consensus."

Will said, "I just hope the damned orbiter comes. Without it knowledge won't be much comfort."

At nine o'clock Carlo took the ambulance to collect Alastair, Cooke and the old man, Ancient Lights—whose name, it appeared when he arrived, was John Smith.

He surveyed Will with a lively professional interest and Donald with the approval of one who had heard good reports of a promising colt, but paid no attention to their puzzlement.

All they had heard had pointed to senility or fragile age, but Ancient Lights was surely no more than twenty, easily the youngest of The Company. Yet, and yet . . . in speech and attitude he wore permanently an agelessness defying definition. He was one more unexpectedness for which questions would bring no answers.

In any case, Carlo caught all ears with an unexpectedness of his own.

"Alastair intends to stay in Glasgow."

Alastair looked as though he expected opposition but Smith seemed approving and Jeanie to be disgusted.

Angus laughed to see Will and Donald jerk to expectant calculation. "These two want to know what will happen to Alastair if Glasgow is dusted, but they don't want to risk his deciding to take that vacant seat. Do you, Donald, Willie?"

Donald grinned without shame but Will flushed and side-stepped. "Don't call me Willie. You aren't that Angus; he never existed."

"Very well—Will. But he exists and that's a source of pain. As for Alastair, he'll be safe."

"Stored food," Alastair explained. "With famine on the way, the government laid in underground stores at key works, counting on an interval of panic and a return to normal. If looters don't find it I'll eat for several years. I'll stay with the *Pride* as long as need be." As if their lack of understanding condemned him he cried out, "I'm her maker! She's mine! There'll be revival but there'll also be pillage and destruction before the world settles, and she'll need guarding. Come the dust, there'll be no shortage of guns for collecting."

"But a shortage o' folk to use 'em on. Och ay, you've a lover's reasons, but the laddie in Birmingham spoke o' a killin' dose."

"The storage vaults will protect me through the worst of it, but even on the surface I would live."

Smith said sharply, "Be quiet!"

His youth dissolved in an unchallengeable authority. He dominated, took them up and squeezed them with his will. And relaxed again as if a spring had flexed and snapped back.

Jeanie murmured, "He shouldn't stay. It's sentiment."

Cooke spoke disinterestedly. "He knows his mind. That young man, Santley or whoever he may be, has been harshly treated and should have Alastair's seat."

Smith said with great good humour, "The one they want murdered? That's our business, not theirs. You see, we are not done with you, young man. It has been suggested that you are a substituted dummy; we must have the facts from this David." He dismissed Will as a consideration dealt with. "Now, you, Mr Baird. What do we do with you?"

Donald asked, "Did your mother no' teach you manners? You may rule this brood o' monkeyshines, but no' me."

Smith's aura of testy command faded, switched off, Will thought, with mountebank precision. "I am too accustomed to giving orders; I ask your pardon." For an extraordinary moment he lost grip on what he said and began again with a hint of desperation. "My name is—Smith. Yes, John Smith. It is easily remembered. You, Mr—" He dried up altogether.

Since none of The Company seemed prepared to prompt him, Donald said, "You ken I'm Donald Baird. You said it a minute since."

"Yes, it had slipped my mind. Somewhere—" He continued briskly, "The Company owes you a debt."

"I bargained my brains an' my gun for twa seats on the orbiter. Yin's gone; I am owed the other."

Angus said firmly, "I guaranteed the bargain."

Smith pursed his lips. "Did you indeed, Giles-Angus? Whose seat did you promise?"

"Mine—if I'm pushed to it."

Smith smiled like a good-tempered hanging judge. "You could hardly offer another's. What do you think of that, Donald Baird? Greater love hath no man, and so on. Or has Giles-Angus bragged himself into a corner he must now stay in?"

"I dinna ken aboot stayin' in it. Will has no love for him an' may be right, but I think Angus is a guid man when he does what he wishes instead o' what he must. So I think he's driven wi' guilt to promise mair than's possible."

"I know all that. Do you refuse the seat?"

"I'll no' take his. He meant well."

Angus said, "I promised it; you earned it. Like Alastair, I'll live."

Smith ignored him. "Who offers Mr Baird a seat?"

"Nane. When the bargain was made I didna ken a' the circumstances. Nor did any 'til the satellite call was made."

"And I thought Highlanders were the romantics! Do you know what radiation poisoning is like?"

"I ken it's no' a decent death."

Jeanie cried out, "Stop it, Donald! He's playing with you."

"Ay, I recognize the cat to my moose. Should I beg? Maybe the dust willna fa' on Glesca, but if it were fallin' this minute I'd no' beg for what is mine an' bargained for."

"Not you, Donald. He wants *me* to beg."

Smith's lips thinned and Will saw his enjoyment of baiting a Dissident. *Power tends to corrupt* ... "You who call yourself

Jeanie Deans and talk, I'm told, of justice and mercy—do you plead for your seat?"

She did not face him but her "No !" was strong.

"And so?"

"Donald, he means that I took ten years from you and must not be responsible for denying you more."

Donald's face became totally bland. "Are you offerin' me your seat?"

Twice humiliated, she snapped, "I offer nothing. He means me to stay. The seat is yours."

"An' if I refuse?"

Smith said to the air, "Now we embark on a situation of idiot comedy."

He misunderstood; Donald's attention was on the girl. For a volcanic moment his face took on hatred, a flare of rage beyond simple vengeance, that blazed and went out. They were all brought to tension, expecting violence.

But he said on a long exhalation, "But I'm no' refusin'. I'll sit in your place an' take joy in it. No' for the ten years but for the knowin' what you did an' still doin' it. For makin' me your prostitute an' givin' only compulsion in return. For that ! You hae the need for men. It can be a sad itch in a woman. It'll be puir livin' for you in dead Glesca, wi' you wanderin' among corpses—in heat."

She answered nothing at all but spoke to Smith as though Donald did not exist. "This is not discipline for discipline's sake, I hope. Is there something to be done here?"

"Most surely there is." Smith, with penance established, went brightly on the new tack. "It's an opportunity we must not miss, with you and Alastair on the spot to attend to it. You must search Britain for radiation immunes. Among fifty million people they will show up simply by staying alive—if they exist. We must prepare a search pattern . . . Whose house is this? Where can we move for discussion?"

Jeanie said, "There is a sitting-room." Leading them out, she posed for a moment with head raised and fingers caressing the swan throat. "Cuddle your hatred, Donald; it's a poor thing, you'll find. There'll be a future for me—and good men in it."

She went and Donald brooded vengefully after her. "If there are immune folk, Angus, they'll be your kind?"

"Of course, but that wasn't what she meant."

Smith shot from the passage like a rampaging demon. "You dare, Angus! You dare hint!"

Will heard in the little man a rebellion, sullen and determined. "Perhaps our ideas are due for rethinking."

Smith's fury vanished; turned on, turned off. So *deliberate; so more or less than human.* He said from some cold and impregnable authority, "Be most careful, Angus," and went out on a waft of dark threat.

Carlo said, almost sadly, "You might as well have declared yourself Dissident, Angus."

"I declared it in my heart a week ago."

And that seemed to be the end of it. Donald muttered to Will, "If the wee man dropped a clue I didna pick it up."

20

At eleven they left for Abbotsinch. In almost empty streets scattered trios of red brassards made still a forlorn pretence at guarding a world without end. Glasgow had burrowed within, where the thickness of a cupboard door might be additional armour against wrath to come; those with cellars were the aristocrats of the damned.

Donald and Angus sat in front with Alastair driving, wearing brassards because the two Company men could produce the spectrum of Glasgow accents, from alderman to guttersnipe, if halted and called on. Alastair and Jeanie were to keep the vehicle when the others had gone; to Donald's query about petrol, Alastair owned that his stores held more than canned food.

In the lightless night Donald surprised the other two with a rarely emotional account of what he had learned in the streets during the day—of whole suburbs of families sealing their homes with blankets, clothing, mounds of earth, even paper pasted over cracks and airholes, not admitting the uselessness because there was always the miraculous chance . . . the chance that tomorrow might dawn as usual, that the blue pestilence might be exhausted. They had prayed last night and it had not come . . .

They looked at him with a sympathy he felt to be false; they were of another kind, concerned but with a different concern.

They passed fires, isolated as yet, but spreading. If fire brigades still existed, the members looked after their own.

Not until they crossed the Clyde and turned into the Paisley Road were they able to look back across the water to see the whole heart of Glasgow blazing beyond the highrise towers.

"That's Sauchiehall Street, burnin' frae end to end." He burst out, "Wha'd burn their own city? Why?"

Carlo said coolly, "Nobody. Accident. With no one to put it out a lighted match is a disaster. For all we can tell, half the world is burning."

They arrived at the deserted airport with a sense of having driven through a side corridor of death.

Alastair said, "To the loading end of the runway, I think," and drove on to the tarmac. "The Australians won't know this field; they'll land from the open end."

They began to lay out beside the tarmac material brought and stacked during the days of waiting—paper, cartons, split crates and boxes, anything burnable and enough of it to form a flare-path a hundred yards long. Short, skimpy, but hopefully enough. They had also a drum containing the last of the house's generator fuel and odd cans of oil from Donald's cellar workshop.

When it was done they could only wait. Nobody spoke much; The Company seemed to have little to say to each other when immediate action was not in view.

Donald stayed apart, his back to them all. Will approached him, saw tears and retreated from the small horror of armour pierced.

Angus also waited alone, moving his shoulders in a pain-relieving exercise Carlo had devised for him; the wonder was that he could move them at all. Will, for all his distrust of the man, had a question that disturbed him. "What could Smith have done if Jeanie had refused to stay behind?"

82

"He probably would have required me to put her out of action—physically—until we had gone."

"And you would have done it?"

"She owed life to Donald."

After such matter-of-factness he felt able to pursue an idea that haunted. "Are you The Company's executioner?"

The answer was peculiar: "I think I have been; I'm not sure. I'll not be yours."

Then the world's end came a brutality closer.

In the east, not far away, three whipcracks split the sky like a triplet of the old anti-aircraft guns. Three yellow flashes spat instantly across the night. Three centres of blue haze remained, sparkling and swelling in widening discs, growing paler and dimmer until in a few breaths they too merged with the black sky.

In the new darkness the sound of the projectiles screamed down from invisible heights, overtaking the burst containers. In the city the dust fell.

Angus bellowed, "Donald! Will! Into the building!"

He took their arms and rushed with them into the administration block. "It won't be much protection but it may damp the dosage until we get to Australia."

Donald gasped protest as he ran. "Dosin' is cumulative."

"So it makes sense to avoid direct contact as long as possible." They ran into the flight lounge and stopped there. Angus explained, "If we can hold below a reasonable exposure the Gangoil people may be able to treat you—this is not Hiroshima time, when you could only wait to die."

"Gangoil doesna want Will or me."

"Gangoil doesn't know what it's getting. Keep still tongues and we'll deal with it."

Three giant cracks sounded directly over the airfield. The yellow flashes were blinding in the windows. The edge of the blue cloud floated into the frame of the window.

Donald said, "Death comes in a pretty shape."

Will fought to control his shivering. "Doesn't anything frighten you?"

"Ay. Yon wee man scares the shit oot o' me."

Angus was amused. "Still?"

83

"I'm a Scot an' no' an educated yin. I laugh at superstition but at the bottom o' my mind there's things common sense willna shift. I fear nae man, Angus, but my flesh crawls for an ee that commands wi' a glance an' a life that lives when it should dee." Beyond the window the blue cloud faded quickly, but he was watching the movement on the ground. "An' I think Gangoil's men are here."

An aircraft swept in across the river, its wingtip lights alone in the sky, at tremendous speed though decelerating from its sub-orbital leap around the curve of the world.

At the end of the strip the little makeshift flarepath sprang alight. From the air it must have been a poor glimmer against burning Glasgow but out here, past the city's edge, it would be observed as a lonely dart of fire.

The orbiter completed two screaming circles, miles wide, before it had slowed sufficiently to make a pass down the runway, unleashing a battery of searchlights along the approach. On the third pass it fired retro-rockets that jerked it violently in mid-air while drogue parachutes opened like medusae pursuing it in flight. It touched down on the extreme end of the barely adequate runway, bounced and touched again, fired a last retro-blast that would have incinerated anything in its path, overran the tarmac and the burning flares and came to a jolting rest just short of crashing into the building. Automatically the drogues cut themselves loose as they collapsed.

Angus urged, "Out! You'll have to take your chance with the dust now."

As they ran the ambulance passed them, heading away from the field. Jeanie and Alastair had not waited for a complication of farewells.

Will had seen orbiters only in newscasts. The reality was a stub-winged raindrop powered by ramjets for manoeuvrability and a rocket engine to boost it through and over the atmosphere for free trajectory to its point of re-entry. It was a military craft, ruinously expensive to run; that Gangoil should command one at need argued vast influence.

It seemed huge for a small payload but he knew that most of its bulk was fuel storage and combustion ways.

A window slid open and a flat Australian voice ordered, "Stand still while I count. Five. Should be six."

Will had not noticed one missing; with a feeling of more unreality he heard Smith in placid explanation. "The medical situation here has altered since we spoke to Gangoil. Doctor Cooke has decided to stay with his people."

Angus's expression seemed to approve this useless decision. What could one man do among a million and a half who would die though a hundred Cookes stayed? Observe and learn? The Company had cold enough blood for it.

The Australian grumbled, "They won't like this."

"The doctors and biologists will like it well enough when they understand the reasons."

"Your worry!" The hatch fell suddenly outwards on a floor-level hinge, extended itself, split and became a ladder. Two men in flying suits climbed down to stretch and stamp their feet. "Bonny Scotland's a bloody cold hole by the feel of it." The pilot's voice altered to moody questioning, "Who's burning the city? Who's the enemy? Have you found out?"

"No."

"The same all over—nobody knows. Like a plague without a carrier. Did you know there's neutron bombing in America and Russia?"

"We've had no news for days. Who began it all?"

"Began!" It was a cry of desolation. "It happened. I suppose somebody pushed the first button, but who'll ever know when there's only rubble to sift? People are starving and dying for no reason. They don't care who began it; they only want to know where the end is."

The co-pilot was calmer. "There's not much damage in Australia. We'll get our turn but for now it's quiet—by comparison, that is. What were those flashes we saw coming in? And something like blue gas?"

"You saw that?" Smith's tone was fireside chatty. "Haven't you heard about the radioactive dusting?"

At first his meaning eluded them; RD had been a theoretical hazard, a ploy of the backroom boys, not seen in action. Then their reaction was unambiguous—a swift backing away gathering itself for escape up the ladder.

Smith raised his voice only a little. "There's nowhere to run. Your ship was contaminated before you landed and you are now. As are we. We must hope that advanced treatments are available in Gangoil."

The habit of authority had some effect. The pilot examined his hands as if he expected immediate eruption and sloughing; the other scratched uneasily at exposed skin and said, "They can treat it. What's the dose rate?"

Smith lied, "Not too high, but we'd best leave without delay. We should experience no serious deterioration—for a day or two."

The pilot's grimace was only half successful. "By then we'll be in hospital or in trouble. Get inside. But you can't take those suitcases—mass–fuel ratio matters when juice is issued by the cupful."

"Inside" was the cargo compartment, bare, windowless and without seats or handholds. Thick cellular mattressing had been fastened to the walls, floor and ceiling; it would be needed at take-off.

The co-pilot gave advice. "Stand for take-off—against the rear wall. And I mean stand, not sit. We go almost straight up when the rockets blow; if you're folded up the acceleration can lock you into cramps and break bones. So stand until we flatten for trajectory."

The rear wall was barely wide enough to take them crowded abreast. As the co-pilot withdrew, the cargo hatch closed and sealed itself and the lights went out. Cargo needs no light to see by.

Angus complained to the darkness, "This will give my neck buggery," and with the words the ramjets shrieked up the scale, the orbiter shuddered and hurtled forward with bludgeoning force. With the first boost it lifted its nose and literally leapt from the tarmac. The major rocket system came in with a deafening yell and tossed the craft through the stratosphere and into the arc of its free flight.

Angus grunted once and was silent. Acceleration pressure vanished as the yell muted to a snoring hull vibration, then ceased altogether.

The hours passed in immense boredom. The Company men made no conversation, apparently felt no need of sound as a weapon against darkness. They were formidably self-sufficient.

Will called up the conversations of the past two days at Bishopbriggs and retrieved the continuing impression that they spoke at rather than with each other, that in their few moments of personal interaction each accepted or rejected comment and argument but remained himself apart, in some personal sense uninvolved.

If this isolation were the sum of their mysterious "difference", who would want it? He could not take seriously the idea that he might be one of them . . .

Donald said as if he had homed on the thought, "If Will is ain o' your kind—" and stopped.

Smith said, "If, indeed," with profound disinterest and Will's "I'm not" was spluttered indignation.

Carlo said, "You have no way of knowing until certain things happen. Or don't happen."

Angus prompted, "What's your 'if', Donald?"

"That your Company is split; there's a secret—which I'm no' guessin' at—that some would keep an' some would tell. Jeanie says this David is Dissident, so maybe it was David told your secret somewhere an' no' Will. An' Will knew it, so David took awa' his memory, an' noo he wants him deid because he fears Angus has gied him his memory back as he said he could. Maybe you've been lookin' to kill the wrang man."

Smith was testy. "Do you think we haven't considered that?"

"Then there's the revairse—that Jeanie is wrang an' Will's the Dissident, no' David. An' so David wiped his mind to prevent him tellin' your secret. An' so there's still nothin' to kill for."

Angus interrupted, "What matters is that Will is in danger no matter which way the probabilities spin—and I would like to have your sonic gun in my hand, Donald, when we land at Gangoil. May I have it?"

"Why, Angus? I'm no' welcome at Gangoil, so I may be the yin needin' a weapon."

"You also are my responsibility, and I have better reflexes than you. You know that."

"Ay."

"I can see better, hear more keenly and react faster than you. I can see, hear and smell attack and strike back while you are making up your mind. The first moments at Gangoil may be crucial. Will you lend me the gun?"

Smith complained, "For the sake of all our sanities, give him the damned gun. He'll pester till he gets it."

Donald said, "He has reason. Take it, Angus."

Feeling and fumbling in the darkness the exchange was made. "You ken the settin's. Thumbstud full forward for full power. Once safety's off squeeze the trigger aboot twa seconds an' anythin' for four to five yards in front o' you will dee. So be careful."

After that they were quiet, until the retro-rockets fired without warning and the hull vibrated and their black box tilted its nose down towards atmosphere.

It was just possible to speak over the bellowing outside. Carlo told them, "We should land about seven in the evening if I have local time figured correctly. In the southern autumn it will be dark."

An invisible intercom crackled through the wall padding and the pilot's voice bawled indistinctly, "Landing in six minutes. Spread your backs against the *forward* bulkhead for landing. Can you hear me?"

Carlo bellowed, "YES, WE HEAR YOU!" and supposed it was enough because the pilot did not call again.

The long descent was gentler than the take-off until the final burst of retro-rockets pinned them like flies to the padding. With another huge jerk the drogues gripped air. The orbiter touched and rebounded, touched and rolled to a jarring halt.

They steadied themselves in the dark, each readying his nerve in his own fashion.

The cargo hatch freed itself with a wet sucking sound and

swung back. The light came on. The co-pilot faced them, with a gun.

"Come out of there one at a time, with two yards between. Go down the ladder and line up on the strip where the guards tell you." He was not hostile but meant to be obeyed. "Get moving!"

In less than a minute they stood in line (ordered by an official voice, owner unseen but barking a fine military style) in the brilliant light from a cluster of mobile standards at the edge of the strip. They were almost blind beyond the circle of light but knew there were soldiers, two of them faintly visible as shapes with carbines loosely pointed.

A sharp little wind bit at fingers and ears. The night was mountain cold.

From the darkness the official voice informed with energy but little interest, "You will not be kept waiting. Doctor David is on his way."

A fresh voice called from further back, "I am here," and a shadowy David became visible at the far rim of light, his face still indistinguishable. "I'm told you have been exposed to radiation. You will receive immediate treatment."

He took a step forward, revealing his face, and at the same moment caught sight of Will. The recognition seemed to unnerve him.

Angus muttered something raging and incomprehensible as fragments of the Gangoil puzzle fell into place.

David and Will might have been brothers, much of an age, much of a build, not amazingly alike but sufficiently so to raise new lines of speculation and confusion.

The scientist yelled with unlooked-for, terrified desperation, "That man—Santley—on the end of the line! Shoot him!"

The two partly visible soldiers turned their heads, looking for instruction. The unseen officer said, "I can't allow that, sir. I can place him under guard for you."

David was shrill and uncontrolled. "He was to be killed in Scotland! It was a condition of their coming!"

"I can't permit execution on your say-so, Doctor."

"Can't you, by God!"

He was at screaming pitch and had his own gun. He came

running into the circle of light, shooting with the hysterical wildness of the novice.

Angus snatched at the sonic and crouched reflexively as invisible guards whipped warning shots past his head.

The movement occupied a lethal fraction of a second. David's second bullet, with idiot's luck, took Will over the left ear and tore the side of his skull open. He was dead before he began to topple.

Angus's animal howl of grief and self-loathing was lost in the silent, bursting sidespill of the beam at full power as it took David in the mouth at two paces and burst his head apart in red spray.

The soldiers, experiencing the hand-sonic for the first time, were momentarily stunned by the inaudible pressures.

Angus bellowed, "Run!" and grabbed at Donald, dragging him back and away. He knew that Smith and Carlo, wounded or whole, could look after themselves.

They were in the darkness as the first random shots came after them and they kept running into the night. "Stay with me, Donald. Don't lose touch."

The shooting stopped for lack of targets.

Angus slowed to a walk, whispering, "Be very quiet and keep moving. Now they've seen what a sonic can do they won't search in the dark—I hope. They'll fear we all have them."

They reached the edge of the landing field and stumbled on rougher ground. Behind them a black mass of mountain rose against stars; before them half the heavens hung in a cold void; low down and far away were scattered, tiny lights which might be far windows. They were on a mountain plateau, high up.

"We'll keep going down. There'll be bush for hiding by day when they set helicopters after us."

Donald stopped abruptly and stood a moment, thinking. As Angus turned to him he said, "Gang your way, Angus, but I must gang back if I'm to live."

Angus came close, peering.

"We stood in the open while the dust fell an' my claes will be riddled wi' the stuff. The dose has been buildin' a' the hours since we left Glesca, an' I've nae powers to heal my poisoned bluid."

Angus squatted down with his hands clubbed at his eyes, like a savage keening over his dead. "I forgot, Donald. Believe me, I forgot." He dropped his hands. "I lost Will and couldn't stand to lose another. I have long experience but I'm not a clever man; I move when I should wait and hesitate when I should move. So Will's dead. Go back and take your chance, Donald—kill or cure. They can't all be devils."

Without a moon it was not easy to see his face. It may have been a subtlety of shadows that made it a mask of mourning.

"Here—your gun."

"Keep it. In minutes I'll be safe or deid but you'll hae a world to fool or fight."

"Thank you."

"Gang quickly the noo."

"I'll come back as far as I can with you. If you come safely through we'll meet again. Bank on it. I have debts to pay."

They went slowly back to the circle of light still shining on emptiness before the deserted orbiter. Both bodies had been removed; only black blood marked the ground. Angus held back in the darkness, gun ready.

Donald called out, not too certainly, "Hello there!" and stepped hesitantly into the light. A startled voice yelled, "There's one!" and Donald snapped to face the sound, hands rising above his head.

Perhaps he moved too suddenly or perhaps they feared the unfamiliar and terrible gun or too many nerves were strung—perhaps all of these. Of the six rattling shots, two took him in the chest and one squarely in the throat, to lodge in his spine. He fell and did not move.

The officer came running, furious, and shouting blame at men who edged into sight, unsure of right and wrong in what they had done. A rifleman turned the body over and said, "He's dead, sir."

Angus felt for the thumbstud, tempted to kill. Then the officer inspected Donald's body more closely and he heard him order that the man—he did not say "corpse"—be taken to (and here he thought he heard correctly) the "storage bank".

He lowered the gun.

If Donald lived, and if he understood the significance of

Gangoil rightly, more could be done for him here than by all the talents of The Company. He waited, ears alert for any movement near him, until orderlies brought a stretcher, examined the wounds, conferred briefly and took Donald away.

The lights went out. He was alone on the mountain and this was the end of all his defiance and cleverness and planning.

He said softly, "I'll be seeing you. There'll still be some sort of world."

He turned his back on Gangoil and moved silently downhill.

He thought briefly of Smith and Carlo, without concern; survival was their heritage. He would not miss their companionship; neither he nor they had much of that to give each other. Save for occasional projects or when consensus was needed, meetings were rarely sought. There were many, absorbed in their affairs throughout the world, whose paths had not crossed in centuries.

INTERLUDE

One Man's View of Social Change

Excerpted from "The Lindley Memoir"
(Melbourne Town Historical Source Documents)

From Notebook 1: While we in *Columbus* circled Barnard's Star in a forty-two-year ignorance of history, the planet collapsed. The power complexes and monolithic states crumbled as a devastated food supply brought technology to a standstill and centuries of accomplishment to barbarism. It's said that there was little overt warfare; starvation doesn't maintain battle stations. Plague and a terrible philosophy of survival murdered world population to a tenth of its voracious swarm.

Then the crop mutations died out, staple foods reappeared and the Reconstruction began. A new world rose in precipitate flight from a nightmarish yesterday. It was an unsure and shaken world, terrified of its disastrous past—and of the revelation of brutish selfishness which had eliminated the useless old to create a muddled paradise for the young.

It was this world to which our innocence came home in 2032, and our homecoming lifted the lid from Pandora's box of lethal memories.*

From Notebook 4: Campion's threat to have me brainwashed (as we once called it) or mentally restabilized (as the mentally automated psychlinicians term the process) was never carried out, and the most abominable scare of my life passed me by for the most politically stupid of reasons.

Religiously devious Parker and pragmatic Campion held very different views of the future development of the Australian State, and Parker's opportunist snatching of the Cathedral Rally from under Campion's nose shattered a powerful combination. Campion's foolish injection of rampant religiosity into a political gathering, followed by Parker's grabbing that particular ball and running with it, developed into public snarling, a division of adherents and an eruption of street brawls which finally brought intervention from Security.

* The return of *Columbus* was narrated in *Beloved Son.*

95

This was the joke their bungling deserved. The basic strategy of that Rally had been the undermining of Security's authority! Once they disturbed the peace and left a few fanatics dead in the gutters—and one contender, Parker, controlled the only useful public order corps, the Civil Police—Security muzzled both with a single directive.

My personal good fortune lay in being rescued from Campion by the new Security Commissioner (the Beckett who was to meet so grotesque an end) who extended protection and hired me as a civilian employee of Security. No one dared touch a Security man.

From Notebook 5: Unrest died for one side's lack of a leader when Campion was killed in an aircrash. It was openly said that Parker engineered the crash to remove a political rival but, since Parker's police conducted the investigation (it was a local matter in which Security could not intervene), the open saying achieved nothing.

The change that was by then becoming apparent in Parker convinces me that he was every whit capable of removing a man who obstructed his messianic need. What had been latent became plain. The religious devotion which had seemed a curious growth in the mind of that impermeable man developed into a public pursuit of zeal. His already stiff personality became inflexible and dangerous. He degenerated from a man respected to a man feared.

Ibid: My greatest humiliation in the twenty-first century was the discovery of how much you children of the Reconstruction detested we "vicious" survivors of the earlier civilization.

"Gone Timers" you called us, and it was a curse.

To Parker and Campion I was valuable, treated with affability, even deference, until they conceived that they could do without my horrifying (but eagerly sought) political advice from the great age of corrupt politicians. Once I was no longer an agent of the leaders the smiles vanished from a thousand faces around me and I learned what the brave new century really thought of its forefathers.

It was blind vanity that had allowed me to accept the mask

as reality through all the first months. Once my protection had vanished and I became a working man without status, these ideal-crammed youngsters gave me the treatment a Jew might have expected in Hitler's Germany.

Beckett, thank heaven, never pretended to be a friend; he had a use for me and the good manners to be cordial.

Columbus went back into space without me (the Epsilon Eridani trip), leaving me the only twentieth-century "revenant", except for a couple of Gangoil senilities who stayed sensibly inside their mountain. I spent a lonely and humbling time as the live symbol of a world's disgust.

PART TWO

Melbourne Town AD 2037 — The Art of the Man on the Spot

A decision is the action an executive must take when he has information so incomplete that the answer does not suggest itself.

ARTHUR WILLIAM RADFORD, *Time*, 25 February 1957

I

A moment before waking . . . darkness and realization of the self . . . the affirmation of existence . . . I *am*. Thought heaves into action, taking up the burden of intelligence for the day. Feeling begins.

It began with intimations of residual tensions in nostrils and anus, calling up a notion of the orifices of his body having been plugged, as for death, and of the plugs having been only recently removed.

He opened his eyes with difficulty, as if he forced rusty shutters. Shapes bent dimly over him. He saw as if through very dark glasses and would have removed them if his wrists had not been fastened down. As were his ankles.

He bellowed with terror then in a voice that cracked and howled in a confined space—a cupboard or a coffin. The dim figures seemed to hear and gesticulate.

Warm air blew round him from unseen nozzles, as if he were being dried after immersion.

He made an effort at calm. Connect, only connect! Life to death to life . . .

He was Will Santley and he had been shot.

He remembered the man with his own face, shooting wildly. Perhaps he had not been badly hurt. But, oh yes, he had!

A cover slid aside, allowing more light to enter. Four white figures leaned over him. He seemed to be in a large space with a warm atmosphere. The support under him moved abruptly, carried him up and sideways, abstracted itself from beneath him and deposited him on a soft surface. The ties at wrists and ankles dropped away.

An Australian voice with familiar, flat vowels asked, "Do your eyes ache? Can you stand the light?"

He was in a hospital. Naturally. He had been shot.

Movement seemed heavy and slow, but he removed the dark glasses and blinked at walls and ceiling. *Bright* white. He tried to sit up and was told, "Take it easy. You've had isometric massage but your muscles have been out of use."

Indeed, yes; he could have sworn the joints creaked. He settled back. "I'll try in a minute." His voice rattled, not pacing itself properly.

"Wait!" At the prick he turned his head stiffly to see the plunger go home. Relaxation then. Perhaps an analgesic also. Invigoration followed quickly. This time it was easy to sit upright.

"That's better. That's *good*!" Bedside manner.

He felt his hand, his shoulders, looked down his body and saw only clear skin. "But I was shot!" He fingered his ribs, "Here," his stomach, "and here."

The doctor touched his left temple. "Here also, but that was dealt with long ago, along with your radiation sickness. You should be in excellent condition."

"I should?" He turned to see the speaker more clearly. "You're the bastard that shot me!"

The man's face, like his own after a fashion, in fact surprisingly like the one he knew from his shaving mirror but more mobile and expressive, told a whole story of negation in jerks and flickers.

"That was another Doctor David. My—" he hesitated slightly "—my father. He also was—er, shot—immediately afterwards. Badly. He died irrevocably."

Irrevocably? Comment on the implication was not possible; he concentrated on present things.

He sat on the padded surface of one half of a structure about eight feet square. The other half was a sunken bath with unfamiliar fixtures in its walls and a transparent carapace which had been moved aside. He had been in that. This place—was it the fabulous Gangoil? Had they taken him in after first shooting him?

His bath was one of many; orderly rows of them stretched down perspectives before, beside and behind.

He swung his legs down and stood, staggering slightly, well enough but rusted with disuse. The men, in surgical gowns but without masks, observed him, letting him find his legs, not offering to help.

His brain, he thought, had also rusted. One obvious question!
"If your father shot me how is it that you are his double—and
the same age?"

"A coincidence of timing," Doctor David said diffidently.
"It happened some forty-five years ago."

"Ah." he sat down, not absorbing it. "You're not serious?"

"Oh, yes. You have been under retarded metabolism for forty-
five years. You have aged no more than two years."

Retarded met— . . . the process they had used in that star
ship to make the voyage of lightyears possible?

He said hoarsely, "Mirror!"

One was handed to him by a man with an English voice, who
said, "We all ask that, don't we?"

No ageing. He had been about thirty-three (a guess, un-
provable) and he now seemed even younger and clearer skinned.
He essayed a half-hysterical little joke. "It does you good—a
cup of tea, an aspro and a long lie down."

One behind him asked, in an authoritative accent, "What
was an aspro?"

It was true, then : some simple things had been forgotten.

"A headache pill. Am I scarred anywhere?"

David tut-tutted, "No! We don't *sew* wounds; we regrow
the whole area."

Silly, out-of-date Will! "Why was I shot?"

David reacted despairingly. "We hoped *you* could tell *us*."

"Didn't Deadshot Daddy tell you? No, he couldn't."

"I was not born until three years after his death, from
cryo-preserved tissue, some of it denatured. There is more to
cloning than the simple cell surgery and transplantation and
DNA activation your geneticists played with; I am lucky to
be alive. So are you. With half your head blown away, only
Gangoil then possessed the techniques to heal you."

Cloning was no miracle to Will; it had been in the air for
a generation before his death. "I knew he wanted me dead—"

The authoritative voice said, "You did?" and the English
one warned, "Please, Simon! Later."

"—but not why. So why have I been healed and kept?"

"Because we also did not know why, and in order to obtain,

perhaps, the answers you do not appear to have. Who are you, what are you, why were you brought here?"

This was as unreal as those conversations with The Company only yesterday, forty-five years ago.

"Who: I'm not sure; I'm amnesiac. What: Nothing special that I know of, though there seem to be other opinions. I'm here because the others brought me. Ask them."

At the far end of the huge room a figure came into view, short and broad, carrying a package bearer-fashion on its head, skittering between the baths like something on spider feet. As it came close his stomach turned light and cold. It was about four feet tall, in a shapeless smock that swept the floor. Its face was a plain disc of flesh with a mouth, two holes that might represent a nose but no ears or eyes that he could see.

It pattered to within touching distance of David, halted and waited. He took the bundle from its head and dropped it beside Will. "Your clothes. They have been carefully preserved and seem in good condition." He patted the thing absently on its bald skull and said, "Thank you, Rosie."

In some manner it heard and skittered away. David said, "Your time would have seen nothing like Rosie."

Will muttered, "Why do you let it live?"

"Why not? She's not unhappy. We would eliminate her if she did not enjoy living. In general terms she is a failed experiment, but not to the point of summary disposal."

The prim tone was firmly holier-than-thou.

"Experiment!" He did not hide contempt.

David pursed disapproving lips. "Whatever you are, you aren't a scientist." That closed the subject of Rosie; the next was menacing. "We will have to subject you to some pretty rigorous questioning over the next few days." He spoke as if Will's co-operation was not in doubt.

Will asked sharply, "What do you mean by 'rigorous'?"

David became acerbic. "You owe us your life. Surely a few answers are small payment. I know that some portion of your brain was destroyed in the violence at your arrival and that though the area has been regrown there will be some memory loss. We have to hope the loss is not crucial."

The English voice said, "He was wondering if you contemplated torture."

David was shocked. "In Gangoil! What a disgusting age yours must have been!"

Will said, "Your clone-father was a killer; why shouldn't you be? I'll tell you what I can, but I was just a chip in the game they played."

"Chip?"

The English voice explained, with a smile in the tone, "A gambling token. Gangoil hasn't learned the simple pleasures, Mr Revenant. But who played the game?"

"They called themselves The Company."

"Who did?"

"If I knew I'd say. Ask Angus. There were five of us in the orbiter and three were Company."

"Three escaped. We hold one other, a sandy-haired man."

"Donald! He's not Company. You said 'escaped'?"

"They ran and did not come back. Perhaps there was too much shooting to make a stay worth while." That was very dry, stage English. The speaker was fair and thin, perhaps forty plus. He was sunburned, as was the younger and sturdier companion standing with him—the authoritative Simon. The contrast with the other pair was extreme; David and his aide had the pallor of burrow dwellers.

"My name is Lindley," the Englishman said. "I was a psychiatrist in what these Reconstruction brats call the Gone Time. Since most of my work has been taken over by computers I am reduced to odd-jobbing for a living—a sort of senior tea-boy to the Security forces."

His companion seemed uncertain how much was satire, how much genuine. "What is your name?"

"Will Santley. I think."

"Think? A total amnesia?"

"Yes." Perhaps these psychiatrists could . . .

Simon asked, "Would you be a Melbourne Town man? You called it only 'Melbourne', didn't you?"

"As far as I know, I am. And we did."

Simon wrote on a pad. "We'll see if there's any record of you. Odd files keep turning up in odd places. Go ahead, Jim."

Lindley asked David, "Why not get the other one out?" but David seemed unwilling. "Why the hesitation? Have you been up to something?"

David had, in a half-hearted fashion. "Ah—a few years ago I became curious about this couple who don't belong with the experimental bath subjects, so I wakened one for questioning. The other one." He gestured at the bath on Will's right. "He was incomprehensible."

Will said, "I'll bet he was," and went to peer through the carapace of the bath while David continued his complaint.

"I couldn't follow more than a word or two of his talk; it sounded like broken English spoken through a throat defect."

Through the heavily tinted glass Will could see, sunk in a greenish fluid, tubes at his nose, eyes under dark spectacles, hair floating like weed in the liquid, Donald in sleep. *All that's left of my world.* It was a lonely thought.

He said affectionately, "It was Glasgow Scottish—a mixture of a whole stew of dialects with local idioms and a throaty burr that made everything sound foreign."

Lindley said raucously, "Och ay, laddie, an' wha's for usquebaugh the noo?" They stared but nobody laughed. "All right, I know it wasn't very good, but we'll understand each other. Get him out, Doctor David."

"He's dangerous." David had had his fill of yesterday's barbarians. "He became violent."

"Why?"

"Frustration, I suppose. He understood me but not I him."

"In his day dialects were common and his ears were attuned to variations, but you in your rabbit warren have never heard any but Australian speech. Which was not thought one of the world's finest. What happened?"

"He became threatening; we used a narco dart and bundled him back into slow met." David pretended no heroism. "He was obviously a strong and active man and I had no reason to think the other might not be as bad. I left it at that. It was only curiosity on my part; there was no urgency to investigate them." He added resentfully, "There was never urgency in Gangoil until that pestilential Parker came here. Now it's do

106

this and do that and stop the other and begin something new. I suppose *he* has a finger in this?"

"No." Lindley did not elaborate. "Just revive this man, please. He'll be all right among people who understand him. And you might as well put your clothes on Mr Might-Be-Santley; you're back in the real world. Such as it is."

Revival was an automated process, a cycle of eighty minutes, most of them occupied with electronic massage and isometric exercise after injections directly into the major muscles. Motors whirred; telltales winked; smart sallies and withdrawals went on among syringes under the green liquid.

Simon watched with interest, asking questions. Lindley muttered to Will, "Simon remembers data and collates it—in his head; he's a top man at his profession."

"Which is?"

"A sort of diplomat-cum-policeman. I think he'd rather explain it himself."

"And you're his tea-boy?"

"A sour joke. He calls me his Special Assistant."

"Did you come here the same way—through these baths?"

"Partly. I was a psychiatrist aboard *Columbus*. Do you remember that?"

"The star ship? It started for—Barnard's Star, wasn't it?—a couple of years before the—the end."

"Yes."

"You skipped years. The time-dilation effect."

"Plus months in the slow chambers. I came home to find England dusted to death." He frowned with an inward anger. "I try not to think about Britain but there's always something to recall it. Now you—in sound and colour."

"I was there. I saw it happen."

"It wasn't your home." He turned from Will, depressed and out of temper, and walked moodily down the room.

Simon said softly, "Like a good psychiatrist, Doctor Lindley despised patriotism until he found himself with nothing to be patriotic about. Don't ask too many questions yet; this time is so far from yours that the answers may be meaningless. And I think your friend is ready to move."

The words were friendly but the tone was tight; Will felt

that if politeness were peeled away there might be revealed a repressed distaste. Unbalanced, he turned instinctively to Donald.

The bands at the Scot's wrists and ankles snapped back into the padding and his hands went to the glasses.

"Will, lad! I saw you dee wi' your heid torn open!"

"Second chance!"

"Ay, I was killed too, I think. They woke me an' a fulish man said . . ." For a moment they were lost in wonder at life and death and the conjuring tricks of time passed.

Donald said, "My thrapple's creakin'," and David approached with a hypodermic. "What this?"

"It's all right. A stimulant. I've had it."

David made the injection nervously and jumped when Donald said, "At least I hae an intairpreter this time aroond."

Lindley came sauntering back to say, "They'll need food in their bellies. I always did."

David bridled at unprofessional interference but Simon spoke with authority. "Feed them at once if they need it. Get this man's clothes if you have them; find him some if you haven't. I want a room where Doctor Lindley and I can question them privately."

He stripped off the surgical gown and threw it aside. He loomed in the white world, neck to foot in black and silver, tight-fitting and sleek. A *pretty* uniform, Will thought; chorus-boy stuff. But there was nothing operetta-romantic about the face and manner of the man taking charge; here was authority without need to assert it.

David threw a tantrum—protested that the patients were his, were Gangoil's over four and a half decades, that as Director of Gangoil he had right to full information—

Simon asked patiently, "Do you know why these men were brought here?"

"You know I do not. Nobody knows."

"Then I think that an activity so secret that nobody knows its nature is too important to be left to scientists. If it turns out that they belong within your research ambit, you will be notified."

In the silence, Donald said with mock awe, "Holy Jesus!"

Simon, taken off balance, asked warily, "Are you some manner of Cultist?" and flushed at Lindley's smothered snort of laughter. "Apparently I've said something foolish." He turned to Will. "You see how the simplest communication has its problems."

2

Most of the administrative work of the Melbourne Town Civil Police was carried on by civilian staff, and the Chief Clerk, having neither rank nor uniform, was a man to be watched by those with both. He had the trust of Controller Parker—as far as anyone had the trust of that opaque man—to the point where he acted for him occasionally in confidential matters; he was responsible also for the compilation and preliminary assessment of reports bearing on promotion and posting. So he had little authority but formidable power.

His privileges—such as easy access to the Controller and the confidential files—were significant. A minor one, in his view, was the privacy of a personal office; it was not so much minor as laughable when measured against the ability of the Surveillance Section to bug anything that squeaked between Melbourne Town and its administrative limit at the Murray River. He knew his conversations and calls were monitored by technical personnel; his closeness to Parker made his lightest word gold-precious as a hint where promotion opportunities lay or where rapid change of course was indicated before an advancing Parker storm.

Since he believed that a man born with a talent for intrigue should keep it sharpened, he took pleasure in defusing and diverting the small plots he saw hatching out of his private reports. This involved, as a first line of defence, some caution in communication.

So it was simple habit which, when the vidcom purred for his attention, caused him to press the *Scramble* before answering. Random scrambling would delay Surveillance about eight hours while they back-tracked through the electronic jungle, giving him time to plug loopholes.

The screened face of Doctor David brought no joy. As a fine biologist but a muddling administrator, David ran a Gangoil which survived his Directorship on impetus and habit; his problems bore always the scars of hasty decision and tardy regret. As he lived in a condition of outraged sensitivity, the present eruption was unexceptional.

"Where is Parker? I asked for Controller Parker!"

"He's out of the Complex."

"Out!" Typically, simple hazards occurred to him too late.

"He doesn't waste time at his desk; he keeps me for that."

"Please find him! I need his advice urgently. The matter—" His excitement ran down and presumably out at his toes; he feared the Chief Clerk only less than he feared Parker. He feared most people Out There. Beyond the womb of Gangoil there was neither certainty nor civilization.

"You could explain your problem to me, Doctor."

"Yes. Perhaps." He asked with desperate calm, "What authority has Australasian Security in Gangoil?"

"None." The Chief Clerk needled gently, "Unless you are up to something that Security feels has planetwide implications." He raised shocked eyebrows. "You aren't, are you?"

David had no sense of humour at all. "I? I? How? You know our research is totally dominated by the Melbourne Town Medical Board."

The Chief Clerk remembered a detail. "Security also has the right to sequester films, recordings, documents and artefacts of historical value. There can't be much of that stuff left since the archival rat pack went through your cellars. You should know all this."

"But I do not know what authority Beckett has to order revivifications!"

"Offhand, none." Beckett himself, indeed! "There may be circumstances whereunder the bodies could be classified as historical artefacts." Interesting, interesting; it paid to keep an eye on Security when its motives were unclear.

"Nonsense! He is here with the detestable Lindley and a horde of Techs with psycho-translation equipment—"

"With what?"

"Now what have I said?"

110

"I don't know. Let me think."

Psychiatrist Lindley, psycho-translator par excellence. *And* Beckett in person. Big business! He asked, "Are they hacking at those poor bloody telepaths again?" *That* could be interpreted as having global implications, but he didn't believe it; the telepath scare had long been defused. "I thought that line was discontinued."

"It is. They are not interested in the research subjects at all. We have two old sleepers from the Gone Time—"

"*Be quiet!*" He didn't believe, either, in the thought that had crossed his mind to cut David off in a vocal reflex. To the affronted face he said, "Make no complaint to Beckett—or to anyone else. Controller Parker will be most interested." The name would frighten David into complicity. "I will vid back in ten minutes. From a public call centre," he added for listening ears and spinning recorder filaments.

In this ethically confused culture the most private mode of making a call was through a public centre. The data bank sub-unit would record the conversation but it would be lost among millions of others, recoverable only by someone who knew beforehand what he sought and how to identify it for the search unit. Both Parker and his Chief Clerk used public centres regularly.

A block away from the Complex he punched the Gangoil code, asked for David and heard him paged through the mountain maze until a voice said, "He's here somewhere," and the screen held on a blank white wall. David came, scowling but resigned.

"Scramble!" The biologist did so. "Who did they want revived if they weren't interested in grotesques?"

David did not regard his rehandlings as grotesques. He replied with futile dignity that these were two unknown, unrecorded, uninteresting men who had been in slow met since the Gone Time, and who had been flown in from Britain in early days for some forgotten reason...

He bent closer to the screen. The Clerk seemed to be in shock. "Are you ill?"

"No!" The explosive syllable was an outcry of some meaningless kind. "Who are they?"

"I have said they are unrecorded."

"If you revived them surely you *made* some record. Their names, man!"

David poured frustration at the screen. "I asked nothing! I was permitted to ask nothing! Between Parker's hooligans and Security's louts I have no authority in my own laboratories! The men were removed from my jurisdiction without so much as by your leave. If it matters, one of them is Will someone-or-other and the other is a half-articulate barbarian from some area of old Britain—"

He was alone with a darkened screen. A cut connection was as much manners as he had learned to expect from the world outside Gangoil.

In Melbourne Town, Angus leaned for a moment with his head against the blanked screen. He could not remember when last he had allowed himself tears.

He had never seriously entertained the possibility that two so shattered men could be preserved alive.

3

The room assigned them by a sulking David was empty of furniture save for tables and chairs. That was changed quickly. Black-clad figures—junior figures, less ornate than Simon—appeared, driving small trolleys loaded with sectioned equipment to be assembled against the walls and plugged into impossibly tiny batteries. They were all young men, in late teens, working with trained speed.

"Recording gear," Lindley said. He alone wore civilian clothing—plain khaki shirt and slacks and soft brown shoes.

Simon smiled with his skindeep lightness. "The Gone Time had nothing like this."

"Och ay, nae doot we'll be wonderin' like loobies at your baubles an' trade goods."

"I don't quite follow, but I think you are not impressed. Like Doctor David, I am lost with variant English."

"Bluidy foreigner!" Donald said cheerfully.

Simon hesitated, found a smile. "A reverse usage?" So the amiable insult still had a place in social exchange.

Last came helmets like hair dryers, connected to panels by hanks of fine leads. One fitted the back of each chair, on a flexible arm. The silent workmen left, except one older Tech whose silver chevrons probably indicated seniority or specialization. He leaned on the wall, waiting.

Lindley said "Tech Sanders,"—and Tech Sanders straightened slightly—"is this room bugged?"

"Not any longer, Doctor. It has been disinfected."

Lindley nodded. "Let's sit."

As they did so, Simon said suddenly, "My name is Simon Beckett. I am the Security Commissioner for the Australasian Sector." He had an air of reciting a hurriedly prepared speech. "Our conception of discipline and protocol these days is different from yours, Doctor Lindley tells me; we try not to impose forms of thought or behaviour. You should not be formal with me unless circumstances make it advisable, any more than are my Techs and Specialists in off-duty hours."

He was plainly conscious of a gap unbridged.

Lindley explained, "It's a difficult idea, that people behave efficiently, courteously, thoughtfully, generously because it gets results. In five years I haven't become accustomed to it. The Commissioner—Simon—is saying that you should be at ease with him and other officials. But he is not sure what will put you at ease."

Will said, "Explanations."

"And we need them from you, too, so please be patient. For the time being accept that a new culture, which you won't easily understand, has risen on the rubble of the old, that it is highly technological in senses different from those you are used to and that we will ease you into it as gently as possible. My own induction was violent and regrettable; we will do better by you."

Will waved at the helmets and the metered panels, his manner blunt. "Meanwhile, this."

"Better than weeks of routine questioning."

"Do we have a choice?"

Lindley said flatly, "No. You'll come to no harm."

"So you say."

Donald reached to shake his arm. "Laddie, if we had a choice we'd hae no way o' knowin' how to make it."

Beckett showed surprise, as at unlooked-for intelligence, and tried again. "Security is an organization of stateless men. On induction, in late childhood, we lose nationality and are trained to be—" he hesitated "—what we are. We have great responsibilities; you might say we guard the peace of the world. We are not universally popular but we are tolerated because so far we have been successful."

Will grunted, "The Gunboat Commander apologizes for being top dog among the unruly natives."

"I don't understand the reference or your resentment."

Donald said sharply, "Yesterday is forty-five years awa', Will, an' you canna gang hame. This is his day an' we must listen. So we're listenin', Simon."

"Thank you. There are eight Commissioners of various areas who are responsible to a World Council. Although they are members of the Council the Commissioners may not vote on their own decisions. Otherwise there is no form of seniority in the Council; all are responsible to all of the others. Which can be most discomforting for the Councillor detected in error or poor judgement. Membership means that I am one of the most senior men in the world. That I have made myself personally involved in your revivification may give you some idea of the priority attached to it."

"Attached by whom? The Council?"

"For the moment, by myself. I am the man on the spot; I *am* the Council."

They digested their implied importance—and Simon's—in silence until Donald said, "It's no' a bad start to hae friends at the top. Eh, Will?"

"Yes? My last weeks were spent where I couldn't refuse an answer if I wanted to and ended in being shot to pieces by a maniac on a mountain top. Now, more of the same? What do you expect? Backslapping and laughter?"

The Commissioner looked enquiringly at Lindley, who said drily, "The torture, sensory deprivation and psychiatric trickery that you knew are crude, stupid and unproductive against

114

today's methods. We have drugs to make you tell secrets you didn't know you possessed—and a combination of visual illusion, drugs and psychoelectronics called 'deep question' which will very nearly interrogate one brain cell at a time. One thing you can't do in this year of disgrace, two thousand and thirty-seven, is keep a secret somebody else wants. As a fact of life you can't love it, but you must learn it." He went on more gently, "Last resorts are used only at the last. Simon would rather you aided willingly; that way neither side suffers trauma. Don't be a wasted hero, Will."

Donald raised a hand to the waiting helmet. "Will's no' bein' heroic; he's bein' afraid. An' I'm no' so brave mysel wi this waitin' to claw my heid. Recordin', you say, but I'd be happier knowin' what it does."

"It detects the electrical discharges of your thinking brain, records them on a sensitized filament and reassembles them as thought for transmission to another mind."

That was more than they had bargained for. Donald was suddenly helpless, a hielan' chiel apprehending magic, but Will stirred out of his sullenness. "Electronic telepathy? There was something—Bombers?"

"In the 1970s," Lindley agreed, "the United States air arm experimented with computers which could read the patterns of a crewman's brain and act on his mental orders more accurately than any manual control. I used the great-great-grandson of that computer on *Columbus*, where we called it Mentascript. This is a hundred times more sophisticated."

Will objected, but without combativeness, "All brains don't think in the same terms and symbols."

"And so translation is necessary, from the personal thought mode to universal symbols and arbitrary glyphs on filament. Translation is a highly specialized profession."

"Yours?"

"Mine."

Will studied the consoles and the helmets, and Lindley saw his man hooked, *wanting* the experience. "What do I do?"

"Just run through the events which led to your being shot. It will be confused at first, but I'll ask questions until we find a suitable start point; then you tell it silently in your mind.

The most complex stories can be unloaded in minutes once the parameters are set. It's clearing the ground that takes time. Tech Sanders!"

"Yes, Doctor?"

"This is the linkage: Santley will transmit. I will receive and you will record my symbolic translation. Baird and the Commissioner will receive the translation through me."

Sanders repeated the instructions as he set the board.

Beckett said wrily, "If I tried to receive direct it would be like swimming in a mental stew."

Donald smiled because it seemed somebody must, but he did not quite believe so much official affability.

Lindley waited for Sanders's nod. "Have you a start point, Will?"

"I think so. Melbourne before I went to Scotland."

"Start recording."

Sanders placed his head under a monitoring helmet at the control console; the faintest of whirrings was the only sign that the filament rolled.

The reception was dreamlike save that the impressions were sharp and colourful; touch, smell and taste were represented directly; words formed in the mind without sound but with the illusion of sound.

The first few minutes, however, were chaotic, incomprehensible until Will learned to let thought run rather than try to direct it. Then it seemed remarkably simple.

It was Lindley now who floundered in a mental entanglement outside his experience. Smooth transmission had scarcely begun when he called a halt and leaned forward out of his helmet radius, to sit with eyes closed, breathing hard.

"I don't know what your Giles's coercive technique was, but there's nothing like it in psychological theory."

"It didna feel the way you hae it."

"You've had the experience also?"

"That I hae; you'll come to it in the tale."

"Then you'll be able to check my interpretation."

Will said, "It wasn't confusing in reality, except when the . . . the subconscious, I suppose . . . tried to break through."

"But your memory holds all the repressed material as well

as the active imprint and I'm getting an indigestible slug of mutually exclusive feeling and intention." He thought for a while. "I can only relax completely and hope my mind will not reject the unacceptable."

After the fourth attempt Beckett suggested setting a computer to unscramble the superimposed images and fringe patterns.

"Not while the data banks can be milked by remote control. What we have here isn't for public scrutiny."

Donald tasted an old sourness. *Politics; gameplayers.*

After an excruciating hour he agreed that Lindley had "caught the feel" of it.

The final recording was taken in twelve minutes, ending abruptly with Will's death—a simple cessation and a bare flicker of darkness before the Gangoil awakening.

Donald completed the tale verbally in a few sentences but received only half their attention.

Each, in his own way, was immersed in the wonder of having experienced—not watched but experienced—another's death. Without pain to explode the mind there was nothing to it.

Nothing at all.

Fast.

Sudden.

Dead.

4

He lifted his head. *Tears pay no debts; I won't fail them again.* He stayed in the refuge of the call booth while his shaken brain recovered . . . and at once informed him that the emotional outbreak had been irrational.

They who had been in the hands of death were safe in the grip of Security; it was he now who was under threat as never before in a stupendously long life of chance and risk.

Danger did not awe him; he had skills and experience and a talent for deadly games, but the instinctive sentiment for Will and Donald disturbed him. No, not Will—Donald. He owed Will a debt for ill-treatment and had developed some closeness

117

to him in the manipulation of trust but Will was not in fact a likeable man, something of a dull dog, self-centred and not improved by psychic interference.

Then why Donald? A good man as human beings went, but Angus had few short-life friends and viewed them with distancing pity for their impermanence.

Donald, then, as representative of something?

Of Scotland? That was just a random idea.

Random?

The Scottish connection fell into his mind too neatly for comfort, too closely to that other Scottish reminiscence which came on him, in moments of abstraction, as a stirring in the deep dark. Dememorization was failing after too long without Company contact and support; the process, once started, could erode stability. A buried Angus of old schemes and treacheries was rising to the light, and this was no time for personal hells to break surface.

Deliberately, with a practised repression, he put the thought by and focused on immediate danger. The brain whose value had always been its coolness under pressure rather than special acuteness set itself to map its plight.

Lindley with a psycho-translator meant that Beckett would soon know all Will and Donald could tell him. So, how long might he remain undetected and what could he do? Not long and not much. The translator was a Security instrument, absolutely restricted, but the Civil Police had data on it. He knew, for instance, that visual presentations on the filament were not definitive; the chances were against Will's or Donald's portrait memories, filtered through the relay of Lindley's brain, being accurate enough to identify him immediately.

He had perhaps one day before inevitable capture.

Then the Gangoil genetecists and the Town psychlinicians would be at him like wolves, tearing his mind and body in an explosion of research. He would be probed and mapped, questioned and deep questioned, sampled and catalogued and physically and psychologically tested to the edge of destruction. With such biological gold at the rainbow's end there would be no thoughts of him as a human being.

Well, in his heart he did not consider himself one.

Carlo and John Smith—bloody old infuriating but dependable Ancient Lights—where are you now?

They had disappeared without trace from the mountain, melting into the crumbling nation; he had seen and heard nothing of them since. He suspected that as the transport lines reopened they would have made for Europe and secret entry into irradiated Britain where no one would locate them while they waited on the emergence of a new world.

Alastair, man of his word, would be in Glasgow still, watching over his obsolete ship . . .

Scotland.

Now there, all unnoticed, lay a constructive idea.

He went out into the autumn sunshine with a bright new tension in him, something absent through the years of the Reconstruction—the sense of contest, the pitting of wits, the snatching of opportunity, the alarms and subtleties and manoeuvrings and shocks. Whether hunter or prey, he played to win, for the game's sake rather than because The Company wanted this or that.

For it had occurred to him that in one bizarre aspect Donald was possibly unique on the planet. There could be move and countermove in that knowledge when the hunt closed in.

5

Sanders, the Tech, removed his helmet and pronounced the filament sharp and clear.

"Breathe a word of it," Beckett told him, "and I'll feed you to the psychlinics. This material is not merely restricted, it doesn't exist. And since you are now too well informed for your own good, you will act as my personal aide until this investigation is completed—and be personally responsible for the comfort and safety of these two gentlemen. You will attend all briefings and discussions."

"Yes, sir." Sanders did not seem surprised.

The team is being picked, Donald thought. But the light approach was so brittle—fantasy, murder, mystery, destruction and not a hair turned. However slipshod Security's protocol, its mental training was superb.

Beckett said, "Now we'll work out what we really know about this affair. Sit down somewhere, Corey."

Corey. One of the in-group now. The appointment, so big it smelt of promotion, had been in mind all along, only produced now with off-the-cuff insouciance. The Commissioner's kind was familiar to an old mercenary; the negligent spontaneity could be devious and deep and dangerous.

Sanders sat on the tray of one of the consoles, looking very fresh and young. Twenty-two or -three, Donald estimated, and the staggeringly senior Commissioner no more than in mid-thirties. It used to be said that the world was for the young; that elderly complaint had come home to roost.

"Go on, Corey; it's your story."

Sanders spoke to the point but without the flatness of official reportage: "Gangoil had a military guard once. You two met it. The soldiers dispersed when government foundered and nobody in a starving world would feed them, and they abandoned their useless records and heavy junk to the Gangoil store rooms. When Gangoil was opened up about five years ago by a civil policeman named Parker, Security obtained custody of the stuff for historical research. As a trained archivist I supervised some of the cataloguing and we turned up, among the orderly-room reports, the private diary of a Major Thoms. He was in charge of the guard detail that killed you both, and it was he who insisted that you be revived and treated in order to discover what had caused David's panic and death. My guess is that by the time you were in shape, he and his command had vanished in the general breakdown. Then Gangoil shut itself in and you were forgotten. However, there was a thing in Thoms's account that brought me up short. I showed it to Jim Lindley because he's our authority on the Gone Time, and he showed it to Simon."

The easy "Simon" shocked Donald's old-soldier sense of fitness; there should be limits to tolerance.

Sanders unfolded a sheet of paper. "It's about the weapon that killed David. And it's graphic. Listen: 'The thing was activated at a range of about two yards. There was no flash, no visible projection, only a sort of non-sound like a sidespill of one of these new sound-cannon, the silent bellow effect. I hope David died instantly. His head *swelled,* while blood spurted from every orifice and then *through* the flesh, which seemed to reach its limit of strain and open up in strips as if exploded from within. His brain flushed out through the nasal cavities, spraying in whitish tatters and I heard his skull splinter in a dozen snappings of bone. He was irrecoverable, *destroyed* down to the base of the throat.' "

He put the paper away. "At least we know now where the things are. We thought the old sonic cannon a barbarous thing, not worth study, but the hand weapon is another matter. *Thousands* of them—your vigilante issue, Donald—in the wrong hands ..." He let it lie.

"It's no' a weapon for bairns, but Angus was ragin' an' hadna the proper skill. It can be gently used."

Will said, "All the batteries will be harmless by now. Drained and corroded."

"Those are no' torch batteries, lad! They're solid-state pieces, ceramic coated; they may leak charge in time but no' corrode. An' they can be recharged frae the hoose electric."

Lindley translated, "From a domestic power source. So the Scottish guns are probably still usable, but they are where nobody is likely to get at them for a few decades."

Beckett parted his lips to speak, changed his mind, then spoke after all. Donald thought that what he said was not what he had first intended.

"It's time we looked at some of those dusted areas. The excuse that the world has been too busy to sort its garbage won't hold for ever. Meanwhile, we came here to pinpoint a gun and have hunted down a miracle."

He leaned back in his chair until he could place his feet on the corner of the table, smiled at the white ceiling and rocked gently as he numbered the attributes of the miracle.

"People who can control the muscular structure of their faces. A mental manipulation new to our psychology. Superfast reflexes. Immunity to radiation damage. A hint of hibernation. Probably other characteristics we haven't spotted. Am I quite mad? Corroboration, Donald?"

121

"I saw these things wi' Will, an' before him."

"So take to the hills! Supermen are among us!"

"The Company is no' a joke."

Behind Beckett's bonhomie lurked contempt, whether for The Company or for the opinions of Gone Time revenants was obscure. "Agreed! Agreed! But we'll get nowhere with mouths hanging open in awe. After the witching and warlocking achieved in Gangoil we possibly take more easily to biological fantasy than you do. So, putting our brains to work, note first that it's a very mixed bag of talents we've spotted. Why should a hypnotist, for want of a better word, need to hibernate, or a radiation-immune develop a natural disguise faculty? What's the connection?"

Lindley said, "In evolutionary terms, they are all survival traits."

Beckett brought his feet back to the floor. "So they are! So they are! Go on."

"In psychological terms these could be the most successful, least resistable, most dangerous animals on earth."

Beckett was thoughtful. "Angus displayed fast natural healing, didn't he? Hard to kill."

The next step was a long one.

Donald gave the lead, harshly, "Jeanie!"

"The lady who didn't age in ten years. Comment, someone?"

Will shivered. "A feeling about them." He groped for expression. "While we waited for the dust to come north they talked about the opportunity it created for immunity research, as though slaughter was something to use, not a disaster to be lived through if we could. Donald and I waited for the end of the world but they waited on an interesting new interruption."

Sanders asked, "To what?"

Donald cried, "Could you no' hear it in the translation? Interruption to their bluidy self-centred livin'! A nuisance, but it would pass, it would pass! They were like folk wha'd seen empires rise an' fa' an' needna concern themsels over another wee disaster. They had only to wait!" His eyes dared them to laugh. "They didna care because they are no' men whose time runs oot at seventy. That's my feelin' an' Will's too."

They had been half prepared for it but it needed digesting.

Sanders began quietly to dismantle the equipment, taking it apart into neat blocks for loading on the trolleys.

Beckett asked, like one refusing to be impressed, "Am I to assume that these three, uh, *foreigners* are still with us, looking much as they did before the Collapse?"

Sanders said over his shoulder, "I think I've seen Angus somewhere."

"Don't be hasty. Translator portraits are chancy."

"I know—but someone, somewhere."

Donald said, "Doctor Lindley's vairsion o' Angus's face wasna true to my memory."

Lindley supported him. "We all see colours, angles, spatial relationships differently; emotional attitudes affect vision. Donald's Angus is not Will's and my Angus is Will's filtered through my rationalization. But I agree with Corey that there's a nagging familiarity."

Beckett decided, "We assume him alive and nearby. Has he kept that disgusting gun? Will he use it if pushed too far?"

"I think you'll no' push Angus so easy. An' I'd trust him wi' the gun before thousands o' others."

"The human race thanks you for your support. We'll ask the data banks to sort him out. The average height has increased considerably in two healthy generations, so there won't be many men in the Town less than five and a half feet high. If he's near we'll have him."

"An' when you hae him, what?"

"Offhand, I don't damned well know, but it's better Security should have him than some other parties. He'll be a world problem, along with his Glasgow friends. Corey, drop the packaging and call the work detail to finish it. Find David. Tell him I'm taking Santley and Baird to the Town and that our visit is restricted information until I tell him otherwise—which may be never. Frighten him. I don't want him gossiping his fool head off on the vidcom."

Corey went out and Beckett fell into a trance of thought. When he returned to the moment he said, "What had they against you, Will? Would you like your amnesia probed to find out?"

"If you intend it I've no choice."

"Prickly, aren't you? The world isn't all coercion and disgust." There was no missing the undertone of contempt as he added, "A twentieth-century man mightn't be able to make much of it."

He fell quiet again. When the work detail came for the equipment he looked blindly through the activity to ask of nobody in particular, "How long do the bastards live?"

Moving away from the others, he was in a private world. Lindley, sensitive to the unspoken, crossed to him to say softly, "There need be no limit genetically."

Beckett focused slowly, said, "There has to be a limit."

"Because eternity is unimaginable? An eternity of creeping boredom surely is. Or an eternity of watching all you love age and die."

"Yes, but a thousand years might have its attractions." He laughed with an uncharacteristic slyness and shook Lindley's arm. "Tell me, old Doctor Sour-apple, that you'd refuse a thousand years."

Lindley said steadily, "I'd think twice before I accepted it." Beckett laughed, not believing, and Lindley knew he would not be understood. "In physiological terms, extended life may imply an inability to die when death might be needed. Or preferred. Self-destruction is difficult for the sane."

It was as well in Beckett not to alienate the revenants before they were milked dry, but with Lindley he did not bother to hide the distaste the man was fully aware of.

"Preferred? I thought your century bred adventurers."

6

When Civil Police Controller Parker found himself in a position of strength by virtue of being, however fortuitously, in a specific place when a specifically relevant incident took place, he credited neither accident nor coincidence, but the just hand of God.

(His confidence was no joke; a Melbourne Town dominated by Cultists felt that God so often worked in His Mysterious Way to Parker's advantage that some reciprocal arrangement with the Will Of Heaven was not easily discounted. Non-

Cultists, a noisy and not too popular minority, made no secret of their opinion that the Controller's God was as narrow-minded as Parker and used similar methods.)

So he did not consider the central event of this afternoon a favour of blind chance, or make any song and dance of thanking God for His providence; he was accustomed to their smoothly combined operation.

Luck, accident or coincidence, what happened was this:

In Gangoil, Senior Tech Corey Sanders warned Doctor David against mention of the Commissioner's visit and activities. David, having already talked far too much to the Chief Clerk of Civil Police, heard him with stunned fright (which Sanders interpreted as flustered resentment) and at the first chance raced to the vidcom to beg Angus's silence.

Angus was no longer in his office; he was walking the Town streets, scanning his shaky future and the outcome of actions now in planning.

Parker, returning to his office from a snap inspection tour of the police Complex, heard the vidcom buzz in his Chief Clerk's office and wondered peripherally why it was not answered. He did not expect Angus to be permanently chained to his desk . . . still, he was one who liked his command neat and ready.

He took the call.

A frantic David was explaining that Angus must treat his previous call as something that had not happened when his eyes caught up with his desperate tongue and dismay silenced him.

Parker asked, "What call?"

David knew better than to disobey a Security order, even an order of doubtful legality, under pressure from Parker or anyone else.

Parker repeated, "What call?" while considering what interest Angus might have in Gangoil—or vice versa.

David found his wits. "I'm not at liberty to say."

"You can tell my Chief Clerk but not me? What call?"

David was silent.

"Doctor David, it is my business to be well informed, so I

know that the Security Commissioner went to Gangoil this morning. Has he told you to keep your mouth shut?"

Tracking Security movements was a routine precaution, the rest a reasonable assumption which David's distress said was spot-on. Parker shook his head in a sympathy as grim as a threat. "Outside your profession, Doctor, you're a helpless ass. You've already been indiscreet to my Chief Clerk and want to save your hide. Am I right?"

David's montage of resentment and misery was proof that the transgressor builds his own hell.

"Well, your hide is safe. No mention will be made."

He cut the connection, went to his own office and leafed through his trays for Angus's memo on David and the Security visit. There was none. There should have been one.

He had Angus paged and was told that Mr Thomson had left the building an hour before, destination unknown.

"Find him. Don't bring him back here; I just want to know where he is." On second thoughts he said, "Whatever he is engaged on, don't disturb him. Simply report his whereabouts."

Personal com-units in wired uniforms flashed messages through the Town; the Controller was upset and Angus was for it.

It took half an hour to track him to an unlikely refuge; a bored patrolman recalled seeing him enter the cathedral.

Angus had gone to church.

Parker pursed his lips, smoothed his uniform, glanced at the polish of his shoes, set his cap regulation-straight and left the Complex at about the same time that Beckett's party left Gangoil.

Emergence from the white corridors to the Bogong High Plain took the Gone Timers by surprise. They had noted the absence of windows but had not realized that they were inside the mountain rather than on it.

At five thousand feet a different and cleaner air blew across pasture; there was incongruity in the grazing cattle in autumn sunlight while men tortured nature deep below their hooves. An island of innocence in the violence of history.

Donald turned completely round, absorbing vastness and the

spread of the valley at the mountain's foot, its entrances vanishing in haze. The eternal Scot, who never in his heart leaves home and holds some of himself puritan-safe against the world, sniffed the air to smell only wet earth.

"It needs the scent o' heather."

Will laughed. "He thinks that's a compliment." Then suddenly, "I've been here before."

"You were killed here."

"Before that."

"When?" Lindley made it casual.

"I don't know." He tried, eyes blind with effort. "No. *Déjà vu*, maybe."

"Or a beginning."

Whichever, it was a flash, and gone.

The waiting flyer took their curiosity. Short, narrow, streamlined and wingless, it seemed unengined and unpowered until Lindley pointed out the tiny jets, gimbal-mounted, no larger than flashlights. "Monopole jets. The monopole was lost until we brought *Columbus* back from Barnard's Star. Now the world uses them."

They embarked without comment—miraculous novelties were already the norm, beyond exclamation—but Donald's eyes held the horizon. "I want to see all this country."

Beckett said shortly, "Some day. Not yet."

A second flyer, with the handling detail and equipment, was airborne, hovering. Like a lift rising, they moved beside it. The two craft turned their noses in vibrationless quiet to the southwest, paused as though they sighted on a target, then went into an acceleration that held punishingly steady. In a few minutes the pressure relaxed as the power was cut, and Will, at his window, saw the little portside jet somersault like a tumbling toy. Instantly deceleration began.

Air distance to the Town was about 150 miles. Eight minutes after leaving the High Plain they circled over Melbourne Town as Will called out his shock and loss.

His city was gone. Of the octopus that had enwrapped the bay and spread inland to the mountains only a dispersed network of streets remained on the south bank of the Yarra, a loose growth of buildings and parks like a table-top model of a country town.

"What happened?" He turned from the window, begging. "Was it the war? I *lived* here!" He caught at Lindley, shaken by the brutality of change. "There were three million people!"

For him only weeks had passed since he walked the streets of metropolis, huge, immutable.

Lindley freed himself gently. "That would now be the population of the whole country. The fighting war didn't hit hard here—a few bombs in the silly days when the sky apparently exploded at random—but there were famine and disease and worse things."

"A city doesn't vanish!"

Beckett spoke harshly, for the quick kill. "They tore it down for its copper and glass and piping, its stoves and baths and tiles and bricks; they had a world to build and no factories or power to make the things to build with. All over the planet the monster cities came down. What use were they? Once the sewerage failed they were plague traps."

But the grey rubble of broken concrete and twisted steel and powdered brick, edged and pocked with green where the bush crept back to the land stolen two centuries before, all neatly boxed by a few black strips of roadway thriftily preserved, was beyond his acceptance.

Lindley said, "Donald told you, you can't go home again. It isn't there any longer."

Donald made a quick, bitter sound. "They'll no' hae torn Glesca doon. There'd ha' been nane alive to do it."

The flyer came to a mid-air halt. The jets rotated smartly through a quarter circle and dropped the machine vertically into the courtyard of Security HQ in St Kilda Road.

Lindley lingered only to see that Sanders had taken charge of Will and Donald before he headed for the basement and the Archival Research Section's data bank and terminals.

At his call for a free console a Tech operator raised a hand. "I can give you eleven minutes before my next booking."

"Good enough. I want an Identity and Information search, Australia-wide, dates prior to 1992. Subject, William Santley,

S-A-N-T-L-E-Y, age in 1992 approximately thirty, but not certain. Hospitalized 1989, discharged as amnesiac. Attending doctor, a genetic surgeon named David, D-A-V-I-D. I want birthdate, education, profession, criminal record if any, illnesses physical and mental. And relatives, if any. How long?"

The operator began keying the board from his notes. "Depends on how many false trails. Two to six minutes. If any record at all, that is. A lot of the paperwork of the period was destroyed one way and another. It may require separate collateral searches."

"Census archives in Canberra is pretty solid."

The board lit up in series. "Who's authorizing this?"

"I think the Commissioner will approve it as a research expense."

"It's your neck."

Information that once might have taken him weeks to obtain, if it could have been obtained at all in the bureaucratic haze, came so quickly that it seemed impossible for Will ever to have had an identity problem.

The man's name *was* Santley, changed by deed poll while in hospital, from—David.

The relationship was not unexpected.

Birthdate . . . Lindley's hackles rose. Yet, why not? The Company had suspected it.

Children . . .

He considered that line for several minutes. It was an extraordinary item of information and not a comfortable one.

The operator asked, "Finished with the terminal?"

"Yes, thanks."

"Got what you wanted?"

"Yes." *More than I dreamed of.* He thought again about the things he now knew and hypothesized, and said, "I'm not so sure after all that the Commissioner will approve this search. Book it to me personally."

"Your money!" said the Tech as he altered the record.

My risk also. If you'd killed him in the first place, Angus, this mess would never have surfaced.

Angus had no interest in God but an affection for cathedrals.

In his need for thought he had taken to the parks and streets and wandered as far as Princes Bridge. Across the river, at the edge of the rubble of the old city, stood the cathedral, preserved, according to legend, as a historical and cultural monument but more probably because it contained little of use for the building of the new Melbourne Town.

It had been worth a reprieve. Tracing with love the slender exaltation of grey-gold spires, he speculated on what religious glory might mean to Parker. The teachings had never stayed the man's hand where mercy was inadvisable, or intellectual honesty denied him an argument when expediency nudged. It was highly probable that he had engineered the air crash which had killed Campion, the ex-Security Commissioner, when their public relationship became strained. The jealous god had a jealous servant; the gentle Jesus must find cold lodging in that arctic mind.

Angus had never understood religion except as a political irritant and a basis for cloudy philosophies. *Living a step or two further from eternity, I am less impressed by it.*

He crossed the bridge and entered the cathedral, empty of worshippers at this hour. Five in the afternoon till six-thirty was the fashionable time for being seen publicly practising one's politico-religious affiliations.

He had long ago decided that Christian morality was laughable when it was not disgusting, that Buddhist mysticism offered only virtue as its own reward in a vacuum, that the Islamic Paradise was uncivilized and that the most benevolent of gods could not stomach the more primitive religions. If forced to a choice he might have plumped for the materialism of the Hindus, who could treat an unsatisfactory god to a round of ill-bred oaths and take their business next door to one more genially bribable to heed an adherent's requirements; the West had always had mistily foolish ideas about the no-nonsense Hindus.

Still, devotee or dupe, man had found inner marvels to express in stone and stained glass and carved wood.

He walked the length of the nave between the huge pillars and sat down on the steps of the choir.

The Gothic cathedrals had been, of all man's buildings, the

closest to ecstasy. But he remembered the Parthenon in centuries before fools had used it for a powder magazine, and in earlier years when the colours had not withered from the friezes. And the gorgeous and gaudy but finally soulless temple at Ephesus. And back, further back . . .

His mind rocked between past and near-past to settle on that clouded fragment of a scene which lately had visited too often. It had nothing to do with religion but much to do with guilt and expiation. Or so he feared.

The large room was indistinct. The hall of a manor house, the public room of a large inn? An argument raged in silence he could not pierce. There were soldiers but as in a dream he could not distinguish them properly. One, very young (he was sure of that though the face was blurred), leaned against a table, relaxed but seeking with genial insistence to impose his will.

He himself was off to one side, whispering to a—general?— who leaned to listen and question and frown.

Without reason he was horrified, frightened, and came to full consciousness with a deliberate bursting of bonds, rejecting the scene and the burden of unknown guilt.

It was no dream; it was memory The Company had taken from him; it was reforming. Each time he saw with greater clarity, finer detail; the moment was not distant when he would know what had been taken from him. And why.

Atheism did not preclude belief in a self-built hell.

This time he had seen that the young man wore tartan trews. He did not know all the complex range of clan tartans but he had recognized Royal Stuart. And an odd impression lingered of a horse race . . . a connection with a horse race.

Steeplechase, hurdle, Epsom, flat, hunter, Derby, plate . . . Derby? The English Derby? How?

Black shoes halted a step away from his eyes, grey Police trousers knife-edge neat above them.

"And what is a damned heretic doing in the house of God?"

Only Parker would say "heretic" and mean it, where another would settle for "pagan" and a deprecating smile.

"I come here often."

"I know."

"You have me tailed? Why?"

Angus could risk more than most, but Parker took a moment making up his mind to accept bluntness. "I don't, but my patrolmen observe that an atheist haunts the cathedral in less crowded hours and the word passes." He found the light touch difficult with a man who sat and gazed up at him where another would have stood. "Some feel it unseemly that I employ a heretic while I occupy a prominent position in the church."

"You don't really occupy any position in the church except that of parishioner, do you? A very powerful parishioner, of course. Are you about to sack me?"

Parker sat on the step beside him; he did it badly, having no gift of camaraderie. He wanted something. He said with finicking accuracy, "Not yet. Do you imagine I would?"

"If there was advantage in it."

"You favour brutal honesty."

"Mightn't God approve of an *honest* heretic?"

Parker stiffened. "I appreciate candour but not outright irreligion within the walls."

"Sorry."

"You aren't." Angus glanced at him and waited. "If I sacked you, you might defect."

Oho! Talkative David? "To whom? Have you enemies?"

"Power lives among enemies, within the gates as well as without." Without change of pace he asked, "What did Beckett and Lindley do in Gangoil this morning?"

"I don't know."

He noted with amusement that Parker could not control a tiny eagerness as he closed on the prey. "You did not report the call from David."

"Was it worth a report?"

"Security business is always worth it. Report now."

"David wanted to know Security's right of search and general interference in Gangoil. I quoted the statute."

"Only that?"

"Nothing more."

"It should have been reported."

Angus reflected that he had counted on a day's grace to slip through Security's fingers, but a questing Parker could be as dangerous. He asked, without finesse, "To what end?"

"Beckett doesn't give personal attention to trivia."

True. Nothing for it now but crude attack. "What do you know that I don't?"

Impudence brought a result. "You forget yourself, Mr Thomson."

The man radiated chill, but that was not enough. Angus wanted the glare of anger and slipping control, but Parker stared ahead at the great south doors as if his displeasure might shock them open.

He had gone too far now to stop. He said, "Ah, come off it, Harold," a familiarity offensive enough to bring explosion, and laid his hand on the Controller's wrist.

Parker loathed intimate touch, any touch. He flinched away and his head swung in affront.

Placidly Angus caught and held his gaze.

Throughout the Town he had prepared men and women of useful position against the day when manipulation might be needed, they unaware of the coercive command implanted but never activated. Parker had been among the earliest. It had been a snatching of invisible hostages to fortune.

Parker's anger vanished.

That was as it should be.

What happened next was not.

Parker asked, "What causes that tic in your left eye? I've noticed it before."

Angus's shock came close to losing him his grip of the encounter and of a situation he would have sworn could not occur. The twitch of the eyelid was the signal which set the controlling stare apart from a chance crossing of gazes, the order which took hold of areas of the man's conscious mind and cut them from areas of volition. That Parker had observed it was unprecedented and dismaying. Control here might be a fragile and doubtful operation.

He was badly unsettled but said dismissively, "A nervous affliction. Not important. What did Beckett do at Gangoil?"

Nothing for it, with control so infirm, but to dig like a frantic tyro and watch out for the unexpected.

Parker responded, properly, conversationally, "He told David his visit was not to be mentioned, to anybody."

"Is that all? It isn't much?"

"It may be a great deal."

Already the voice displayed disturbing overtones of inward puzzlement. The man was aware, so soon, of conflict between intention and behaviour. Here were strong individuality and powerful urges. And, almost with the formation of the thought in Angus's mind, he proved it.

When Angus asked, "Why should this interest you so much?" he answered with the sharpness of full self-possession, "That's my damned business, Mr Thomson!"

No one had ever broken coercion so quickly. Less than a minute, Angus thought, with a sense of power repulsed and toppling. But calm was his supreme possession; he said smoothly, "I didn't mean to pry."

"The devil you didn't! You said—asked—" Parker trailed into uncertainty and stood up. Like any subject returning to awareness he was not sure what had happened and what had not, but he was troubled in mind, and Angus knew that a troubled Parker would seek reasons and answers.

Parker said abruptly, "Come back to the office. There's work I want cleared up tonight," and set off down the nave.

He had come in a pick-up van, and drove Angus back to the Complex with him. On the way he detailed the work to be done, all unurgent, invented without even the compliment of subtlety to keep Angus under his eye while—

While what? Angus wondered, no longer able to regard the Controller with sardonic contempt.

7

Beckett's office was large, bleak and austere save for a single late-blooming white rose in a cut-glass vase on his desk. To Lindley even the rose nodded with reserve in such surroundings.

Beckett asked, "Are they settling in?" and Lindley answered that they were; if Beckett assumed that he had spent his time assisting Sanders with the quartering of the revenants, well and good.

Beckett's interest was perfunctory; his mind was on higher game. "Set up a data check for men below five-foot-six in the Town and winnow out those fitting Angus's apparent age range and general description. There won't be many. Corey can have your people look them over unobtrusively in the morning."

My people. That rates them exactly on the scale of expendability. "And if they spot him?"

"Inform me. No one else! Take no other action. And now book terminal time for a background check on Santley—birth, family, work history, anything you can get—and put a Class 1 block on the data channel if it looks at all evocative. I don't want others at him yet."

"I'll do that." The deceit flowed with all the serenity of innocence. If detected he could still recover with a little wriggling, but he had not yet decided what he would do; that must depend on Beckett. He put out a testing tendril. "I've a feeling we should take no action on this business. Bury it; leave The Company alone. Forget them and they won't bother anybody."

Beckett studied him speculatively and said at last, "Don't be a fool."

Lindley pushed a little. "The Company doesn't want exposure. My guess is that's the real reason Angus killed David—he didn't want a geneticist peering at Company DNA and chasing a paradisal dream the world is better without."

That might even be right, though now he did not believe it; what he needed was a glimpse of truth from Beckett.

The Commissioner loosened the upper section of the tailored overall and (having given himself, Lindley decided, a quarter minute for thought) pointed out that a discovery once made will inevitably be made again. The matter had come to light *now* and now was the time to deal with it. "Besides, I want that murderous gun before it is used, or found and copied by some nationalist group with more ambition than ethic. Angus has it, so we'll find Angus."

Given the generally anti-violent philosophy of the time it was reasonable, but it was not enough. A further push was needed. "Shall I do a transcript of the filament for your initial report?"

"To World Council? Of course."

"It can be ready by morning."

"It isn't urgent." Of Lindley's dissenting silence he asked, "Do you think it is? I'll report when we've done all possible checks *and* located Angus. As yet we have only uncorroborated fantasy."

Technically true, not wholly true. He would have protested if Beckett had not continued with a breaking of reticence that told him his probing was understood. "It has to be genetic, doesn't it? Not a sport or a freak but something Gangoil can unravel. Once the gene pattern is established and the modifications to cells and organs, Gangoil can decide on practicable physical adaptations for the already naturally born. It needn't be a matter for sperm and ovum alterations having to wait on a new generation. I'd say the immunological systems come into it and the hypothalamus. And virus dormancy. Wouldn't you?"

He was at his most genial, tossing ideas for catch and return. And, under the geniality, most urgent.

... *more ambition than ethics*, Lindley thought, and answered, "It isn't my field."

The brown eyes narrowed. "Come, Jim! In your day 'psychiatrist' indicated medical training as well, didn't it? You must know the general geriatric data—just as I do, without the training."

"It's too specialized for broad spectrum practice."

"But Gangoil's field is the whole of biology. It should be possible to get fast results once an experimental animal is made available."

"Angus?"

"Probably the nearest."

Not the nearest, and now I'm surely not telling you. "Angus may not be easy to handle. In any case, Security doesn't control Gangoil."

"Special conditions can be invoked."

The tone of the exchange had altered and it seemed that Beckett had thought far ahead. Well, slow wits did not rise to

Commissionerships, and now it appeared that he had thought further yet, some little way into Lindley's state of mind.

"We won't talk of suppressing knowledge, Jim, or of burying dangerous ideas. You came to grief once before when you meddled with policy in a world you didn't understand—and don't yet understand as well as you think. I saved you then by interference where Security had no real right, just as it has no right in Gangoil. Must I spell it out?"*

The threat was the final error, the revealing voice of the Beckett behind the mask, the voice of authority and power and the corruption that waits with them.

"No need." No need at all; his mind was made up.

When he left Beckett's office he went directly to a Directory terminal and located Angus Thomson's home address.

Like Sanders he had recognized familiarity in Will's visualization. Despite optical and psychological distortions Corey also might have made the connection had he possessed the one additional piece of information which had bridged the gap for Lindley and laid the real face over the pictured one. Corey did not know that the Chief Clerk of Civil Police, the shortish, cheerful Mr Thomson, far from Will's menacing cynic and who occasionally assisted with local information, was named Angus.

That done, he took Beckett's sensible advice to block the Santley data channel. The Tech operator took the information out of circuit without argument. Nobody argued with a Beckett authorization.

Parker's rage grew with repression until he prayed that blind fury should not lead him into misjudgement, haste and error. He prayed at his desk, without words, offering up his anger, and perhaps God heard; he achieved a modicum of serenity. No longer apprehensive of misjudgement, haste and error, he sent for the Officer of Detectives.

"Mr Thomson is to be covered night and day. Complete cover—activities, contacts, vid calls. Report to me verbally am and pm, with no written or taped record."

The Officer repeated diffidently, "Mr Thomson?"

"Surprised? So am I. Keep the investigation between your

* Lindley's previous history is related in *Beloved Son*.

tail-squad, yourself and me. If Angus is alerted I'll fire you; if word leaks to the rest of the Force I'll have you for dereliction of duty. Get on with it."

Then he sat still, deciding what had happened to him. His brain, perceptions, will had been interfered with. The touched hand had been offence; what followed had been sacrilege, for the Will and the Soul are one and the property of God. God would deal with His own, but for the profanation of the body there would be a profane reckoning.

He could not account for what had happened, for his mind being dragged in opposing directions and capitulating to the wrong force, as if tongue and body were machinery operated from outside of himself. Something Angus had done—but what?—showed him to be responsible. Also he had asked questions beyond his province, had insisted, pried.

Hypnotism? Hypnotic techniques, too undependable, had lapsed; the psychlinicians achieved mind control by separating areas of consciousness with subtly moving diagrams. Nevertheless he called for a terminal connection and had an encyclopedia essay displayed on the vidcom hookup. Nothing. What had been done to him did not fit the data on hypnosis.

For the present he would have to rely on the tail-squad. The surveillance would be operative by now. He went to Angus's office and told him to go home. "Other matters have come up. There's no hurry for that stuff now."

In the intensity of his anger he could only gaze past the intolerable man's ear and leave the room before he was tempted to violence.

Angus tidied his desk. Whatever Parker intended was in motion and now he was wanted out of the way. Probably a total tail had been ordered.

"And so?" he asked softly of the air. He let the tip of his nose curve downwards and slicked his ears flat against his skull. It was a game he hadn't played in all the years since Giles bedevilled poor Will. If he were tailed he would make pursuit a nightmare for the pursuers.

8

With arrival at HQ Will and Donald had changed from items of concentrated interest to objects for disposition.

Lindley had called, "I'll see you shortly," as he disappeared through a side door. Beckett might have forgotten them entirely as he swung up the steps, stiff and black and slender, without a word.

Sanders said with service smartness, "This way!" and led through corridors where brilliantly coloured and varied civilian dress jostled black uniforms and khaki fatigues in a crowded busyness. No one gave them more than a passing glance; their dated clothing could cause little comment where personal preferences denied any form of generally accepted fashion. They mounted stairs to a quieter floor and finally passed a RESIDENT BLOCK sign into a zone of empty passageways.

The room Sanders opened to them was stark.

"Two beds." There were none in sight. "We haven't proper quarters for guests but you'll be comfortable."

So they were, once he had explained the operation of the fittings. Furniture folded or fitted flush into the walls and many of the controls were not obviously visible; from beds to vidcoms it was unobtrusively complete.

Donald said, "A sar'n't-major's dream o' barracks. Inspection-proof."

The comment passed over Sanders's head. He seemed preoccupied and anxious to get away, so much so that Will offered an ironic, "Sorry we're keeping you."

Sanders accepted rebuke stolidly. "We're not uninterested in you but you've become secondary to the problems you brought with you. We bought a load of trouble with curiosity about an old gun." There was no useful answer to that. "If there's nothing you need I'll leave you until dinner."

And he did.

Alone, they had little to say to each other; the whole experience beggared comment.

Will lay moodily on his bed but Donald prowled the apartment, loving the gadgetry, varying the window glass from clear to opaque to black with pressure on the frame, making the lights blaze or soften by passing a hand over invisibly sensitized wall areas and regulating the bookrack and reading screen by vocal command. The washroom and shower space were playgrounds of vanishing faucets, draughts of warm and cold air and puffs of soap and scented spray.

His playing scraped Will's nerves. "For Christ's sake, what's so 'braw' and 'bonny'? We're prisoners, not bloody guests! We're here to do as we're told and pretend to like it. Don't think they won't skin us like rabbits if they feel that'll bring results!"

"Then until the skinnin' starts I'll keep my heid screwed straight an' take some pleasure in sma' things."

He leaned against the window frame and the sunlight winked in and out.

"Dear Jesus, but will you stop it!"

Donald reduced the light to a golden glow. "Your mind's had a maulin' frae the wee Angus; try to be easier. They'll no' hairm us; it's Angus they'll be after."

"I hope they find him and take him apart. Slowly."

"D'you hate so? Maybe you've reason, but through him you came through a' the bad years in sleep."

"By accident, not good will. If I'd never known him I'd have lived my life in my own town among my own people."

"A short life, laddie."

"They didn't all die."

"Did they no'?" Donald came to sit on the edge of the bed, hard faced. "You walked the corridors o' this place an' saw what I saw. How many were mair than thirty years old? Three in four were barely twenty. We're old men here. Where did the others gang? 'Famine an' plague,' says Lindley, 'an' worse things.' What worse things? Livin' in Melbourne you'd ha' been a deid man, however it happened. As for the wee Angus, he's a braw little bastard an' I hope he runs rings roond that Beckett. Dinna be fuled by Beckett's easy way; he's no' a friendly man. But if you see Angus, trust him. He's no' your enemy any mair."

Will sat up. "Trust nobody! They want the long life! They think they can dig extra years out of Angus by genetic scanning, and perhaps they can. And that will be the end of our world. You know what men will do for money or power? That will be loveplay compared with the actions of idiots who'd sell their souls for ten extra years of life and condemn a nation to death for a hundred. What do you think they'll do for eternity?"

"No sane man would want to live for aye."

"Offer it and watch their sanity fade! These Becketts and Davids and bright young worldbuilders will take what they want—and it will be the end of them. You don't get a thousand years or a hundred without paying for them."

"You're gettin' worked up."

"Am I? What do you think the whole stinking Glasgow business was about, except that the Dissidents wanted to declare themselves and The Company wanted their existence kept secret? The Company was right."

"You canna be sure o' that."

"I am." Will frowned. "It came to me." Whitefaced, he muttered, "It is so."

"You had a flash o' memory on the mountain an' noo maybe another. If it's comin' back you may soon get the whole o' it."

Will lay back, shaking. "I don't give a damn what happened. I want to live and die in peace. I don't want to know."

9

Angus visited an off-shift workshop before he left the Complex and used an illegal instrument, of whose existence he should have been unaware, to check his clothing. He was not bugged. Until he reached the street he kept a distance between himself and others, enough to prevent attachment of a filament beacon. If he were tailed it would be the hard way, by sweating manpower. Also, night had fallen; the tail's task would be marginally more difficult.

He decided to walk the two miles to his apartment, by the beach road, if only to force cursing plainclothesmen to dog him step by step. In fact he detected no tail—but Parker did not use incompetents.

His flat overlooked the bay in what had been St Kilda (where in the Gone Time Will had subjected him to endless boredom of pier fishing while he established control). His three rooms were a profligate allowance for a single man in a culture which stressed communal living. Austerity was a legacy from the last century's squandering but Parker, who understood privilege and perquisite as psychological hooks, had pulled strings for him; Angus, who understood Parker, had no hesitation in double-crossing a benefactor who would throw him to the psychlinicians the moment expediency suggested a profit.

If he had taken the bus he might have failed to see Lindley across the street, leaning on the esplanade railing, elaborately not watching the door of the apartment block. Instinct suggested complication, perhaps danger, but it would have been foolish not to discover what the psychiatrist wanted, whatever Parker's suspicions might make of the meeting.

"Doctor Lindley! Studying the hive dweller in his habitat?"

"No, Giles. I was comparing the habitat with the highrise tenements of old Glasgow."

It was an onslaught, detection ahead of time. Lindley must be Beckett's messenger.

He turned to lean his elbows on the railing, back to the road and observers. "Turn and keep your mouth to the sea. I'm under surveillance but it will take them a while to move round in front of us." He did not doubt they were there.

Before them the ground dropped steeply to the seawall and the beach; they looked over black and moonless water to the hanging stars.

"What does Beckett want?"

"He didn't send me. He hasn't spotted you."

But Lindley had. Strange. "Then what do *you* want?"

"To warn you. Get out of Australia."

A friend? Stranger and stranger. "Good advice but hard to follow."

His acute hearing caught them at last, two of them, padding round the slope fifty yards away, trusting to darkness. He turned slightly to keep his back to them and their directional micro-phones, but it was no place to linger.

"Listen! They're closing in. Wait for five minutes after I leave you, then stroll off through Albert Park to where Campion's lakeside camp used to be. I'll meet you there."

It was Lindley now who asked, "What do you want?"

"Word with Beckett." He saw it as the only decision, one The Company might never forgive, but inevitable.

Seeing Lindley ready to object he turned with a casual wave and crossed the road. Lindley curbed argument to act an in-different, "See you."

Angus went straight to his apartment, activated the lounge-room light, opened a window overlooking the backyard games courts and leaned on the sill, a blameless citizen enjoying the autumn night. And listening. After three minutes he detected the man in the shadow of the sports store-shed, when he shifted his weight and scraped gravel.

It was total cover. He had humiliated Parker beyond bearing, invaded him where he fancied himself commander of his unity of will, mind and spirit. And been caught at it. So now Parker would have him for dissection of motive and method, with expenditure of resources no object.

But not tonight.

He moved to the bathroom and opaqued the window to blackout level before he turned on the light. Let them pry at the lounge, scratching at stillness and silence.

He closed his eyes to make the first changes, concentrating on the *feeling* of muscles contracted into fresh positions which must remain unchanged for hours, perhaps days. He could judge maintenance of the mask only by the feel of it. He com-menced a basic face, allowing the scalp to recede and furrow the neck while the hairline rose—a slightly ageing effect. He raised the outer ends of his eyebrows, tightening the upper eyelids, altering the angles of the crow's-foot lines.

With the pattern of stresses fixed he looked into the mirror, then experimentally flattened his ears to the skull and hollowed his cheeks. The effect was suitably thin-faced but mildly diabolical. Too noticeable.

He dropped the eyebrows to a square line and opened up the

nostrils to aboriginoid flanges. The effect was notably coarse; a person of no distinction. Suggestion of a sagging chin, lower lip heavy, mouth pouting and narrow . . . not every touch was essential but it was his boast that the secret of a successful persona lay in attention to detail.

Appearance from the back—the back is as recognizable as the face—was a difficulty never satisfactorily solved. Gait, set of shoulders, swing of arms he could handle, but these were not enough. He did not like artificial aids, which could be total betrayal in a tight corner, but a wig might for once be justified—something long and flat to accentuate the apparent length of the face and change the shape of the head from the rear.

His hands, with their heavy blue veins, he could not alter; there are no malleable muscles in the backs of them. The best he could do was keep them out of sight. He chose a long-sleeved shirt, vertically striped to narrow the breadth of the chest, and tight trousers to narrow him a little further.

He tested walks until he found a loose gait which felt in character: manual worker, unclassified.

All this occupied less than ten minutes.

He collected small items from hiding places. The sheath and knife he strapped to his right forearm above the wrist, and flexed the fingers a time or two to be sure the blade dropped smoothly into them.

He assembled the pieces of the sonic gun and charged the matchbox-sized battery from the service lead. After forty-five years it should function; he had kept it clean and lubricated and the power stud was the only moving part. It fitted snugly into the shoulder holster he had made for it.

There remained only the jester's touch to get him out of the flat undetected.

He returned to the loungeroom and used the remote control to black out the window. To worry watchers further he laid an adhesive film over the pane and peeled it off, leaving an asymmetrical, faintly glittering snail-track tracery on the glass. The presence of a laser scatter to defeat listeners should drive them frantic.

With an illegal and very sensitive olfactometer he located the clear paint of two microphone patches on the ceiling, so fresh that the needle jumped rather than quivered. He had been sure of their presence and they had been applied within the hour. For that clumsiness Parker earned a parting flick on the raw.

Like all but the newest of Police recruits he had a jammer (also illegal) for protection against house bugging. He placed it on the table in plain sight and beside it his identification and employment papers. To be apprehended with Angus's documents would be a worse error than having none.

Then he rapped snappily on the door panels and called, "Wait a minute. Who is it?" He rapped again, then opened the door and treated the microphones to a surprised intake of breath followed by, "Commissioner Beckett! Why—come in, sir."

Then he switched on the jammer. In the Police Complex, he hoped, a furious Parker ached with speculation on a meeting quite unanticipated. Treachery, no doubt; treachery most foul!

He stepped into the corridor and within yards fell into familiarity with his new stride; by the time he left the building he was fully in character, a manual type of no special consequence, leaving after presumably visiting a friend.

Across the road two grey uniforms leaned where Lindley had leant, one with a subvocal transmitter clinging to his throat. Uniforms so soon! Parker had loosed the hounds instantly; he was not to get out of the block. No? They looked casually at him as he turned his face to the light to let them see his uninteresting innocence.

He set off rapidly for Albert Park, anxious to know what Lindley offered or threatened.

On the run, with that old exhilaration which had to be choked back, he embraced the game: Angus with his capacities against the powers of the human world.

Free though he was, a tiny thing happened as he hurried, not so much an incident as a passage of thought while he coursed round the west end of the lake to where Lindley should be waiting. With his mind swinging at random, the idea surfaced that he had used this persona before.

Creating the face, he had thought it an original; now he felt it was based on one used in the past. Unconscious repetition could scarcely be avoided, but when and where?

He shut out the question, not risking unwanted memories; he knew better than any psychiatrist how the mind could thresh when old torments were stirred.

Even so . . . he suffered a flash of himself in a similar long wig, but one curled at the ends, talking with—reasoning, arguing with—General Murray. The name came easily this time, but who the devil *was* the man?

He forced his attention to the present.

Before him the moon rose, orange-gold on the horizon, and beside him the lake sparkled in answer; the air was heady and heavy with damp grass and the tang of the near sea. A moth glimmered on pale wings in the moonlight.

There was more peace here than the world deserved—or was likely to find. Without hurry he drew the sonic gun, set it for medium power and pressed the firing stud.

The moth swelled, broke, exploded in shining dust.

The gun worked perfectly.

Parker's fury, embracing injury and insult, left no room for incredulity. If Beckett clandestinely in Thomson's apartment was a violation of inter-service ethics, the jammer was insolence, a thumb-to-nose announcement that any crudity would serve. Beckett would regret that.

He radioed local patrolmen to surround the block and sped into his own action. "Three men! Armed! At the double!"

He was away like the wind while the Duty Officer found men and chased them after him to the pick-up van. Parker drove with a frigid efficiency of corner-cutting and brutalization of traffic that shook the nerves of the patrolmen, who thought they knew the limits of his singlemindedness.

At the apartment block he swept up to the two watching the door.

"Have you seen Thomson?"

"He hasn't come out."

"Or Commissioner Beckett?"

That merely puzzled them.

"Come with me!"

At Angus's door he hammered and kicked without reply. He

146

drew his gun and a shocked patrolman cried, "If the Commissioner's there—"

"Then God help him," Parker said and blew the lock out.

On the table the jammer glittered as brightly as a laugh. Parker clutched at the discarded personal documents, recognizing them through shaking anger as a farewell jeer.

He activated Angus's vidcom and punched the Security number. "Get me the Commissioner!"

The Security Tech, almost inviolable in his uniform, allowed himself a raised eyebrow at the raging tone. "The Commissioner has gone off duty for the night, Controller."

So the Commissioner was from home. For proof: "Get him!"

The Tech stiffened. "I'll see if I can get him—sir."

He wouldn't get him; timing would convict Beckett.

Unbelievably, Beckett was there, lounging in pyjamas and unimpressed by urgency. "Trouble, Controller? Earthquake, invasion, plague?"

Parker crackled ice. "A matter of protocol."

"At this hour? Are you serious?"

"Since you chose to interview my Chief Clerk without first notifying me, damned serious."

"Who?"

"I said: my Chief Clerk."

"That insolent little man who does incognito duties for you when you need to bend laws you might otherwise uphold? I haven't seen him."

Parker knew precisely how little authority Security could exercise in a matter of local administration. "I have a voice filament to say you're lying."

And in the irrecoverable instant realized that the filament said nothing so definite.

Beckett asked courteously, "Have you checked with the practical jokers in your Technical Section?" and cut the link.

Under the eyes of his stunned men Parker steadied to the understanding that he raged against the edges of a Security operation he was not to be permitted to observe.

Then Security, or World Council itself if need be, would learn better than to turn Parker's trusted servant against him.

He recognized that in the flow of anger he had omitted the

obvious: he had not sought out the record of the trusted servant's confession with Gangoil. Somewhere in that would lie the clue to Beckett's interest.

Beckett, in the wreckage of a peaceful night, could think of nothing connecting him with Thomson, whom he knew offhandedly. If he hadn't been so irritated by the man's manner he might have sorted out the foolishness with him.

As he mulled it over, the face of the insolent little man crossed gently with Lindley's projection of Angus.

Insolently, he hadn't even changed his name!

At the core of astonishment was the realization that not until now had he fully credited The Company's existence. His brain had accepted and evaluated the evidence but the depths of nerves and consciousness had not; the slenderness of credibility had not permitted him to believe that the promise of a long tomorrow was a true promise.

In the vidcom call of a demented fanatic the promise had been dropped into his hands.

He shuddered between elation and horror of the unknown as the possibilities opened before him. Where he had hoped with a counterfeit belief, he *knew*.

10

In the shadow of the boatshed Lindley's determinations faded to uneasy tension. Angus was not terrible in confrontation but the terrible was in him; in cooling blood Lindley was afraid of this animal who was more than or not quite a man. He had lost the impetus of his starting out.

Angus came, wearing his own face (with the muscular-memory pattern on instant call), and his first words held latent menace. "Are my lads safe and well?"

While a nervous Lindley affirmed that they were, the professional in him heard and filed a hard, possessive note in the question.

The next query was practical. "Can you get me to Beckett?"

"Yes, but I don't advise it."

"Why?"

"I think he'll ship you to Gangoil and keep you there until every organ of your body is scanned and understood."

Angus said with unexpected gentleness, "Your voice is trembling. Be easy. The Company looks after its friends."

"You smell of the supernatural."

Angus chuckled. "Brimstone? No, we're on the whole very ordinary people, more peaceable than your own bloody-minded breed though less hypocritical about the so-called right to life." (Paradox? Let Lindley chew on it.) "Has World Council instructed Beckett to put me in Gangoil?"

"World Council hasn't heard of you. Beckett wants conclusive evidence before he reports, a wrapped-up case. Including a wrapped-up Angus."

"Reasonable."

"Rubbish. He's seen the sparkle on the fountain of youth and there'll be no report until he's bathed in it."

Angus spat. Lindley saw him tremble and thought it was anger, but what he heard was contempt. "What does he hope for? Does he think my spleen can be mashed for an immortality serum or centuries of life granted by some DNA juggling?"

"He's nobody's fool. He knows longevity involves a perfected immunological system and perhaps hypothalamic change. Stimulate one and reprogramme the other—and maybe add a millennium to life. Given you to study, Gangoil will devise the techniques."

Angus seemed amused rather than perturbed. "You could be right. We've made no studies of ourselves; the laboratory techniques weren't available until Gangoil started up. And we aren't scientists by inclination. But you think a handful of years is enough to seduce a World Councillor, a man indoctrinated from boyhood to the service of mankind without consideration of self? Why, so do I."

"The short view of life is filled with desperations you wouldn't be able to guess at."

"So?" Angus pushed his face close. "Don't you also want to live for ever? Or even another thousand years?"

"No!" He thought that he at least half believed it. "This world can't take sudden longevity. I don't mean overpopulation

149

and shrinking resources—there's no *psychological* ability to cope with an indefinite span. Every idea, custom, belief, taboo, every relationship and conception of responsibility would have to be rethought, reorganized, redirected. Our whole lives, our laws, our desires, our simplest needs are predicted on a limited life; remove death and the result will be the removal of all inhibition—schism, blood and misery."

Angus was fascinated. "You've really thought about it!"

"Since this afternoon I've thought about little else."

"Of the other possibility also? That Beckett could keep the whole matter under his hat and create an elite of the undying, selected by himself?"

"That would be far worse." In a useless gesture of wariness Lindley stepped away from Angus. "The best thing would be that all of you, Company and Dissident, were found and killed. There must be ways of killing you."

Angus's low laugh was genuine. "Many, but they aren't the answer. Once, pinbrains used to advocate killing off all the sexual deviants, not seeing that generation after generation the killing would never end. We too are continually being born, so our existence has to be faced and an accommodation found. In this data-bank world we can't hide by creating a fresh persona or moving to another country; your data banks mean that you have to acknowledge us, live with us or deal with us. Like most of us I'd prefer to remain unknown, but how long would I last in this guise or any other?"

He took a pace into the moonlight to display the face of a stranger.

Lindley studied him with a hissing of breath. "Not long. Aside from census, as soon as you tried to get a job or rent a room or board a transworld transport . . ."

"So it's best I see Beckett and talk sense to him. Only World Council has the organization to decide how to face up to The Company, and I can reach them through him."

"You'll get nowhere. You have centuries as a birthright; you don't understand the temptation."

"Probably not." Angus was quizzical. "You seem to feel you can resist it."

"I don't know. I suppose I'd want to be one of the elite. Nobody can be trusted."

"So you'll use me to bring down Beckett if you can, eh? And then think about the good of humanity?"

If it was a shot in the dark, it homed. Best to face it. "So I care more for myself than for humanity; that's what genetic viability is all about. But you're right about bringing down Beckett—or anyone else who wants the prize in his own pocket."

"Can I bet you have a more personal reason? Beckett saved you from Campion's psychlinicians, didn't he? And the proud man never forgives a favour done him! Now to hell with philosophy and get me Beckett."

"You'll regret it."

Angus spelt out his need. "My people, all over the world, must be found and alerted; that requires huge resources. If I take a chance on Security, which has the resources, I don't know how I'll come out of it but I *will* come out. I'm on the run but I'm not defenceless; I'm bloody hard to take and harder to hold. So let's get to Beckett."

They moved towards St Kilda Road, Angus stepping out in anticipation of action. He asked abruptly, "Did Beckett bring my boys to Melbourne Town?"

"They're here." Lindley put out a hand to restrain his haste, disturbed again by the possessive tone. "You say *my boys* as I might say *my puppies*."

Angus was amused. "Is that what you hear?"

"I can understand you feeling above the herd, but longevity only marks a difference in kind, not necessarily in quality."

"Don't be so damned sure of that. But Will and Donald are owed something; I hope to pay it."

"Good doggies! Here are your bones!"

"Don't make too much of it. Did you ever own a dog?"

"I raised Great Danes in England."

"Loved them?"

What is the nature of attachment to a dog? Lindley shrugged and was honest. "Very much."

"I love my boys."

A gap of incommunication opened. The cool statement of the nature of the chasm between them brought a decision to

Lindley, to withhold what he knew about Will, information private to him alone and which would involve Angus intensely. Aware of playing a double game and keeping faith with none, he was not certain how the knowledge could be used, but it was crucial knowledge which might buy his safety from both sides.

Lindley did not consider that he owed the reconstructed world any debt. It had, in ways mostly brutal, stripped him of friends, culture, self-respect and all familiar things, leaving him his life because he was a useful anachronism, a psychiatrist actually trained in those techniques which today were programmed into diagnostic machines. His loyalty was to himself.

Like any psychiatrist, he walked in the same shadows of self-deceit as his patients.

As they neared the barracks he was about to suggest that Angus revert to his own features, to save explanation to Beckett, when he saw that the autumn night strollers on St Kilda Road were seeded with the faces of patrolmen in plain clothes. He muttered an alarm to Angus, who asked, "Where's this Angus they're looking for?"

Angus was happy with the scurry his baiting of Parker had roused. Passing a patrolman who saw him every day he murmured, "God's good night, Brother," and the Police Cultist answered with grave courtesy, "Yeshua's blessing!"

At the barracks Lindley announced to the unseen beam of the robot gatekeeper, "Private guest. Mr Giles Campbell, for the Commissioner."

Angus wondered at the choice of alias—"Campbell" had its place in the emerging recall of tartans and General Murray.

As they crossed the courtyard, "Do you want to see your boys?"

He smiled bleakly. "To pat their heads and inspect their coats? No. Business first."

The lounges and corridors were empty; the building was quiet.

"I see Security keeps office hours."

"Security works overtime only when the sky is falling. The measure of its success is that it looked like working itself out

152

of a job—until this afternoon." He threw open a door. "My quarters."

It was a barely adequate bedsittingroom, spartanly fitted, though Angus knew the walls concealed additional furnishings; Lindley, whatever his status, was accorded nothing special in accommodation. He wondered did the psychiatrist see himself as Beckett's dog? Because he was, he was. But unloved.

Lindley punched Beckett's suite number and the Commissioner's face appeared in the small vidcom by his bed.

"I've news."

"The hell you have! Parker?"

"No. Why Parker?"

"He called up to feed me some rancid insults about interference with his Chief Clerk."

"Which you denied?"

"On my dignity."

"Prepare to plead guilty. I have the man with me, asking to see you."

Beckett reacted violently; his voice became harsh, choked, stiff. "What does he want?"

"Asylum." A side glance showed him Angus, out of screen range, listening like an analyst to a tape.

Beckett relaxed. "You know who he is?"

Lindley said carefully, "I have realized it."

Beckett pondered, said at last, "The private office."

"Now?"

"Yes. And—Jim! Where is the gun?"

Angus motioned Lindley aside and held the gun to the screen. "This?"

"Yes. Show your face." Angus fronted the screen. "Who—? Yes—of course." Angus loosened his cheeks and nose and twitched his ears like a clown. Beckett gasped a taut, excited laughter. "Extraordinary. Now, please give that damnable gun to Doctor Lindley, then he'll bring you to me."

Angus surrendered it without argument; it was not a weapon he would use from choice. Lindley placed it in a small wall safe while Beckett's eyes followed him from the screen.

"Now, please allow Doctor Lindley to search you. The Santley record showed that you carry a concealed knife."

Angus slipped the blade into his palm, held it up, then gave it to Lindley. "If it will make you feel better."

He was no suppliant.

II

Beckett pulled a dressing gown over his pyjamas; he favoured the informal touch. On his own ground he feared no man, even an unarmed Angus—but he would have a gun in reach.

Considering gambits and possibilities, he called Sanders, who came to the screen from a shower, water running in his eyes, tousled and unlike the efficient young Tech who meant to rise fast in the service. *And what does he think about The Company?* It could be important to discover how his aide viewed youth, health and a long tomorrow. To be attended to as soon as possible.

"Place Red One on standby." Sanders received the instruction without overt surprise; Red One was Beckett's personal flyer. "And four armed escorts; there may be a prisoner. Give them gas pistols."

That was unusual and Sanders was no slouch. "*That* prisoner? You've located him?"

"Yes. Cancel the search procedure."

He cut the link.

In the private office he cleared everything from his desk but the white rose in a cut-glass vase, salvaged from a museum, his private testimony to the existence of a world outside the service.

He had barely had time to assume the Councillor's mask—cool, unimpressed by the bizarre—when Angus entered with Lindley at his elbow. He had reverted to his Thomson features—his own.

Beckett waved silently at a chair but Angus marched to the desk and leaned across it to upset preparations: "You know what I am. I've a fair idea what you are. We don't have to spar for openings."

Beckett changed his tactics with the speed of thought, barked,

"Sit down!" snatched the gun from his lap and levelled it at Angus's face.

Angus shook his head, sighing, "Don't be nitwitted, man." But he sat in the chair at the left corner of the desk and glanced from the Commissioner to his white rose as if they told something about each other.

Beckett gestured and Lindley took the chair at the other corner. Eyes never leaving Angus, Beckett played a dance of fingers on the miniature console on the inner edge of the desk.

For the briefest of instants they were in total darkness, not the simple darkness of an unlighted room but the absolute blackness of the interior of a sphere which neither sound nor radiation could penetrate. Angus had never experienced an energy blind but he realized what had happened and thought that sensory deprivation must be like this vanishment of the universe—but he had long ago ceased to be awed by conjurers or scientists. He had decided not to disarm Beckett yet when a light flashed from the desk, powered by a tiny nuclear "battery" in its base.

The wall of immaterial darkness curved over and round them and under their feet, appearing impossibly solid, its lower edge cutting below the floor. Lamplight touching the inner blackness was absorbed; its energy, like the contained heat of their bodies, would return to the generator below the floor, but would represent only a fraction of the staggering cost of propagation.

Angus assessed Beckett without rancour, wondering how long the man could maintain this ultra-expensive privacy, disregarding the foolish gun. Lindley's biased reading of the Commissioner was probably close to truth, though a corrupt Security officer was nearly a contradiction in terms. But the finer the balance the swifter the fall, and for a Beckett presumably pierced by the pettiness of three-score-and-ten the prize of corruption must be, in human terms, incalculable. Lindley just might see reasonably straight but others—and the idealists could be the least logical—found temptations and pitfalls only molehills they would strongmindedly surmount. Like experimenters with heroin.

But probability was not a judgement; Beckett must have his

155

chance. He said amicably, "It's possible to kill me with a bullet, but you must know exactly where to place it."

Beckett spoke at Lindley without shifting his gaze. "We don't want him dead, Jim, only manageable. A bullet in any joint should be enough for a day or so. Now, Mr Thomson, what do you want?"

"Protection."

"Against psychiatrists, geneticists and the power-hungry? Also to throw your problem in the lap of World Council as the only organization with global influence."

"Yes."

Beckett lowered the muzzle. "The stomach. Difficult to miss, very painful and distracting, however miraculous the healing powers. I think you are about to explain to me that for psychological powers and demographic reasons mankind is not ready for the problems of extended span. I agree."

And Angus said nothing.

"So you have decided that World Council must take you and your Company under its wing, making all the difficult decisions and enforcing them—for your protection."

The disadvantage of a powerful indoctrination, Angus thought, is that a man has to argue himself out of it while not believing a word of his thesis.

Beckett continued, "I don't like that solution. With capabilities like yours running loose, within a decade The Company would rule the planet. The Council would be the perfect tool for your operations. You have a comment?"

Beckett knew how to formulate a hangman's argument, Angus conceded; he said, "I hadn't thought of it. Nor would The Company. We dabbled at times in shaping history but only left ends worse than the beginnings. We're not tempted to run the world; it's a job for paranoiacs."

Shaping history . . . With extraordinary force the vision of himself at Murray's ear flashed in his mind and he knew this time something of what he had said to the general, with vivid recall: *The French will not come. I am only now from France and have the word from Lewis's self.* It was then that he had worn the long wig whose ends curved inward to the neck, and

156

then that he had played his last hand at the game of changing history, and damned himself to his own contempt . . .

Beckett's voice shattered the picture, raw, suspicious. "Are you ill? He's fainting."

Through nausea he heard Lindley say, "I doubt if he could," and struggled for equilibrium.

The gun still pointed, but the Commissioner's eyes were thoughtful. "Vulnerable. In some way vulnerable. You can be managed, little man."

"Not by you, I think." He said, firmly now, "You have in the end no option but to refer me to the Council."

"Not so." Beckett shot a glance at Lindley, a bare flicker of attention away from Angus and back again. "Jim, are you recording this?"

"Of course." Recording of blinded consultations was routine, essential for reference and affirmation. He had pressed the stud on his watch as soon as the darkness closed in; under the rim the filament ran steadily.

The gun, Angus noted, had begun a minute weaving, not enough yet to tell Beckett that his grip was beginning to cramp on the butt and his muscles to react against strain. Human beings suffered severe limitations.

Beckett said, "Lay the watch on the desk. And leave us alone."

Lindley unclipped the instrument and laid it down. He stepped through the blind, allowing Angus to observe the fact of a man walking through an apparently solid wall. And to observe the confidence that did not even bother to warn its dog to keep a still tongue.

He turned back to Beckett and the gun, considering the distance, the developing tremor, the chances, and said, "Now for the real talk, with the witness out of the way. But he didn't shut the recorder off."

Beckett, with his eyes on Angus, felt across the desk with his free hand, but the desk was wide and long and when his groping fingers touched the watch they nudged it further away. With a soft thud it fell to the carpet. Beckett could not risk trying to retrieve it.

Angus was philosophical. "Never mind; the evidence can be

157

erased later. When do we leave for Gangoil? That would be the idea, wouldn't it?"

"That depends on yourself. I have some questions, which you might as well answer honestly. We can drug, psych or deep question truth out of you."

That was less certain than Beckett imagined. However: "Understood. You want to know what your biological expectations might turn out to be."

Beckett's smile had not varied; it was there and he had forgotten it. The concentration behind the mask must by now be a diamond point of intensity. Latently paranoid? But aren't we all, given the needed illusion?

"Yes," Beckett said, making his death certain.

After that Angus answered questions cheerfully and truthfully while he watched muscular control falter as inner tensions froze the grip on the gun. These philosophically tough but basically peaceful people simply were not used to handling weapons seriously, and he had no intention of getting hurt.

Lindley did not leave the office. The sphere of the blind occupied less than a quarter of the room; he sat down to wait out the end of talk behind the darkness.

No doubt Angus argued while Beckett gave himself wholly away. Unholy compromise might be possible but he did not believe Angus could talk the man out of his enchantment; he did believe that Beckett would have Angus in Gangoil tonight. From the deserted administration floor they could spirit a shot man to a summoned flyer and in Gangoil the flexible powers of a Commissioner would easily rouse means of coercing David.

His own situation as potential witness and/or suppressor of knowledge was precarious; he would have to convince Beckett—

Into his scenario walked Corey Sanders shouting, "What the hell's going on here?"

A godsend, a witness; not every mouth could be stopped even by Beckett. "Simon and Angus in there."

"*That* Angus?" Sanders sucked at his lip. "Something's happened downstairs, but I don't know—" He meant that a subordinate doesn't invade a blind without extreme reason. "I've been trying to vid him for ten minutes past."

With a solid *thunk* something ripped splinters from the door frame, ricocheted and thudded into the cement wall.

Lindley gasped, "Beckett's shot him!" before he grasped that this could not be so.

Sanders reached automatically for his gun, but he was in house dress and weaponless. He had a young man's courage; he stepped through the black wall.

Half a minute later he showed his face through the blind, like a mask on a black screen, to say tightly, "Come here."

To what? Beckett had missed his shot and was not likely to have been allowed another. Lindley was tempted to run and keep running. But to where?

He stepped through.

Beckett was dying in his chair, a hand fallen to the desktop, his smile a rictus of surprised disbelief, his throat cut and blood spurting. Blood covered his robe, the carpet, the desk and the white rose. It mingled and flowed with the water from the smashed vase whose edged fragment had cut his life out. It splashed and soaked Angus, who held Beckett's gun on Sanders. One long, glass sliver lay in the dying man's lap, where Angus had dropped it.

If Sanders had been shocked, he had recovered; he was thoughtful and calm, even curious.

"Why did you do it?"

As they watched, Beckett died.

Angus said, "You couldn't have saved him. It was necessary. He was dangerous."

"To you?"

"And you. And Doctor Lindley here, and the world. He had a secret and wanted it to himself."

Lindley said, "Tech Sanders knows who you are."

Angus cried furiously, "And how many more? Have you yammered like magpies? Haven't you the brains for silence?"

"Corey was the filament monitor. No others, Angus."

Sanders said, "Forget that for the time; there are other things happening—" and stopped. He breathed deeply once and took command. "You can put that gun down; I know enough not to take chances."

Angus grinned savagely and laid it on the desk; in a race

159

for possession he would get the first shot off while Sanders still reached for it.

Sanders gestured at Beckett. "This first: gun or no gun, I am in charge now. I was his aide and am man on the spot. Now, the facts?"

"He tried to shoot me. I took the gun from him and cut his throat."

They could not avoid the still-astonished eyes, the lips parted to protest. Lindley cursed under his breath and closed the lids firmly over the dead stare.

Angus said, "I was born with speed inbuilt."

Sanders nodded. "I understand that. He had no chance. It was murder."

"Execution."

"That requires proof, agreement, law."

"Proof? On the floor, by your feet."

Lindley picked up his watch, wiped blood from it on a clean area of carpet, saw that it was still recording and switched off.

Angus asked, "Can that thing play back?"

A moment later his own voice addressed Beckett, the tone tiny but clear. "You know what I am. I've a fair idea ..."

Sanders listened, stone-faced.

Lindley stopped it at the sound of the shot, shaken by the recital of naked greed. He had expected circumlocution, self justification, specious argument, not animal grasping. He knew now what the breaking of a life's indoctrination sounded like: hysteria. For Sanders it must be the hearing of his world-creed trampled and smashed. But the Tech remained impassive.

Angus would have argued his case but Sanders gestured him to silence with authority. Angus shut up, for once approving Security's man-on-the-spot practice; this one seemed the right man.

Sanders said, "You have a case but you aren't the judge; others will decide, but not yet. You want to argue—for secrecy and long consideration, I'd think—before World Council. That's sense. But again, not yet. There's a new urgency, a question of what to do about Controller Parker."

Angus said, "He knows nothing."

"Don't depend on it. He has your friends, Santley and Baird. That's why I was trying to vid the Commissioner."

He had thrown a bomb and knew it, but if Lindley was shocked, Angus seemed shattered with an almost animal grief.

Sanders knew better than to stop for shock and emotion; he hurried on his facts. "Parker sent a squad of greybacks to pick them up as unregistered aliens of undeclared presence in the country, having no data-bank records. Census and identity are his province; we couldn't block his legal right without taking him into confidence, which was unthinkable without Beckett's permission. And he was unreachable. We had to let them go." There was huge anger in him, restrained because angry actions are only failings; he attempted a looser speech as if it might feed back relaxation. "Parker hasn't access to translators but he can command the psychlinics and you know what he'll do with that helpless pair. And if he and his damned Cultists get a whiff of lives extended like their biblical patriarchs' it'll take more than their God of mercy to hold them back. We need an excuse to recover them before that grey-minded man smells the facts."

Angus had only useless desperation. "Parker! Parker with my boys!"

Lindley squirmed. *I wiped the record; I gave him Santley.*

"I don't know," Sanders said, "how Parker was aware of their existence, let alone their whereabouts. Gangoil was under order of silence."

Angus said dully, "David had talked—to me—before you shut him up. Parker will have found the conversation and pressured him. Ask the right questions and David's face answers through a shut mouth."

Sanders did not waste himself on recrimination. "That greyback bastard doesn't know what he has there; he just wanted to counter coup against Beckett by whipping them from under his nose. Now he'll take them apart to see why we wanted them. That's where I begin to be afraid."

Angus cut across him in an extraordinary, embarrassing abasement. "I played a stupid joke on Parker without seeing where it might lead." He reached blindly for Lindley's hand and some of the psychiatrist's awe of him dropped away. *Master*

161

seeks comfort from dog, he thought as Angus struggled with unexpected truths. "I am not a clever operator. I am nothing very much in The Company, a play-actor and sometimes an executioner. Millennia give you knowledge but not intelligence; that's something else. I do some things well but in the end there are regrets and torments that have to be wiped out of my mind before they drive me out of it!"

Lindley slipped his hand free, leaving the man staring at empty fingers as if they had betrayed him.

Sanders had not missed a word or gesture but he said roughly, "Whatever you're talking about will have to wait. I want those men out of Parker's reach and there's no time to wait for a new Commissioner to take over."

Angus muttered, "He's easily enough killed." It was a statement, indifferent to implications.

Sanders snarled at him, "You're less than a not-clever man; you're an idiot. Will it help your Company to come on the world stage in a continuing bloodbath?"

Angus was himself again. "I know more of Parker than you ever could. If he smells longevity you'll have to kill him—or The Company will have to do it for you, in self-protection."

Sanders made a sound of civilized disgust, and Angus let loose on him. "Your snot-nosed ethical society exists in a world of peace and good will that's scared shitless of having nearly wiped itself out and bows to World Council as if it had special revelation! You've never seen human beings with a great greed in their eyes but you'll see it if you don't act to keep The Company under wraps—and act bloody fast. You can lose your precious world again by being afraid to dirty your ethical hands in preserving it."

Sanders turned to Lindley, who nodded, and back to Angus. "He agrees with you. Nevertheless we will do as *I* say and we will do it before questions are asked about the persistence of this blind. The nuclear battery under the floor is draining energy at three hundred dollars a minute and the auditors will cry havoc. But Angus is our difficulty because the gate-robot will know he is here."

"It doesn't know." Lindley explained how he had brought Angus into the barracks.

Sanders said, "That's our first piece of luck," and showed that he knew how to use it. "That makes it possible for Angus to leave the barracks as Campbell and return as Thomson with an appointment with Beckett. I'll write him a Private Visit card. Then he can go to your apartment and switch back to Campbell. Angus, can you make these changes quickly?"

"Twenty seconds."

"Good. As soon as you're back here we can query this blind, discover the body and start a hunt after killer Angus who has unaccountably disappeared. At that point I will have to notify World Council; they should send a new Commissioner within hours. Meanwhile we'll think how to tackle Parker. I'm assuming you'll work with us, Angus; it's to your advantage."

"In this plan, yes. Later, we'll see."

"I suppose that will have to satisfy me. Be careful when you're outside. Parker will have a tight net out for you if he thinks you're here."

"He has anyway. Now to business." He snapped his fingers, called "Abracadabra, hey presto!" and held their starstruck attention for the transformation from Thomson into Campbell. It was an anticlimax when he rolled up his trouser leg to produce the wig he had snapped to his calf with a rubber band.

As he combed it out he asked Lindley, "What made you choose Campbell for my alias?"

"Chance, an association of ideas. I once knew an Argyll family of Thomsons who are—were—a branch of Clan Campbell."

Angus smoothed the wig into position. "Thomsons are Campbells? Perhaps I knew it at some time."

Lindley laughed shortly. "The man who forgot being a Campbell was never a Scot."

Angus said slowly, "I'm not a Scot. Campbells—there was Glencoe, wasn't there? But that was earlier."

"Earlier than what?"

"Than the rising, the Forty-five." A grey apprehension crept into his face. He asked, knowing he should not, but driven, "Who was General Murray?"

"Who?" Lindley took his arm. "You'd better sit down. You're ill."

"Ill? I'm frightened." He stumbled backwards to the chair and sat heavily. "Who was he?"

"No friend of the Campbells, at any rate."

"Who was he?"

"If it's so important, he was Prince Charles Stuart's senior general, the one who turned back at Derby when another march might have won his man the throne of England."

Angus gazed at him with shocked eyes and said between a howl and a whisper, "I turned Murray back. And then there was Culloden." A mask melting and flowing, his face lost cohesion and shape as he forgot everything but ancient guilt. "The bodies of the highlanders lay four and five deep at Culloden, slaughtered like penned rats. I did that." He slid forward from the chair, clutching at Sanders who backed instinctively from the incomprehensible; into his puzzled face Angus spat bitterness: "You brats deny history because you have none." He drew himself upright, pondering, with a blank gaze that had forgotten Sanders already, and began a silent, intolerable weeping. From a deep place he inhabited alone he said, "I lied to Murray. The French would have come. Lewis was waiting on the news."

With the mask dispersed it was an empty, gutted Angus who fell like a log, with only silence in his rigid, gaping mouth. His head curved forward and his knees rose to his chest in the spasm of total retreat to a past so distant that no memory or pain could follow him.

The black sphere, like a bubble outside space and time, held them in still astonishment.

Lindley came professionally to life, bending over him and trying fruitlessly to unlock his arms. He felt the muscles of upper arm and thigh and shook his head in sullen surprise, then with difficulty turned him on his back to examine his open eyes.

"He's conscious." He made it sound like an insult to good sense.

Sanders asked shakily, "What is this?"

"The ultimate classic catatonia; the impossible hundred per cent case. It's a wonder the cramps don't break his bones." He turned a bewildered face. "I triggered it. I don't know how."

Sanders bent over him. "This is psychological? A clinic job?" His experience encompassed nothing like it.

"Not your style of clinic; preventive manipulation and pharmacology has lost sight of these cases. A withdrawal as savage as this is bloody near impenetrable. He may well pull out of it in time or his peculiar metabolism may keep him a live vegetable."

Sanders was less interested in Angus than in the difficulties multiplying by the minute, but Lindley was thinking what he might attempt. The limbs might respond to relaxants—selective drugging might help if the relevant brain area could be located—a touch of slow met and revival might be worth trying ... even shock, that confession of failure, as a last resort.

Sanders was saying, "This wrecks planning. We'll have to get him down to your room and hope we aren't seen." He thought no further for the moment; the future must develop on opportunity. "If we're seen I'll do the explaining." He picked Angus up like a parcel. "When was all the prince and general stuff? Gone Time?"

"Nearly three hundred years ago."

"Hell!"

"He has solved one of history's minor quibbles, but that's not all of it. It symbolizes something else, repressed into forgetfulness."

Sanders shrugged and stepped through the blind with his burden.

Luck held. Duty postings worked on the operation floors; off-duty and standby ranks were in the recreation areas or on leave; administration was deserted. They met nobody.

Sanders laid Angus on Lindley's bed and let frustration show. "He's wearing the wrong damned face; he must stay hidden."

"Here?"

"For a while, a few hours. Then what?" He added fretfully, "I hoped to use him tonight."

"For what?"

Surprisingly, Sanders blushed with a young man's self-consciousness. "Adventure stuff. Is that gun here somewhere?"

"The sonic pistol is in my safe."

"Leave it there. I wanted him to wear the Campbell face to

165

raid the Complex and collect Santley and Baird at gunpoint. At three in the morning there'd be only half a dozen standby patrolmen about and he knows the place well enough to avoid them. There'd have been only suspicion to connect the raid with Security and he'd have brought it off like a party game."

If the Glasgow caper meant anything, he probably would have. "We may have to do it without him."

"No! We can't have Security openly kidnapping. Parker would have us on civil charges and convict on all of them."

"Santley can't be left there."

"He must while I notify GHQ, which doesn't favour interference with civil units." He eyed Lindley with suspicion. "Why do you say Santley rather than both of them?"

"Because a lifelong check on him told me who he is."

"Brother to the original David?"

"No. What would you guess for his age?"

"Early thirties."

"Discounting the Gangoil years in slow met, he's sixty-eight. Born in 1924."

Sanders breathed out hard. "Another one."

"He doesn't know that because the knowledge was removed with the rest of his memory—removed, if the Glasgow story is to make sense, by the original David. Who was his son."

"His son killed him? He must have been another of them."

"Not necessarily. The gene structure would be complex; a single recessive could nullify the whole pattern. But if David was Company, so is his clone, the present David."

"Parker could get him, too. As soon as he starts back-checking Santley—"

"I've had the data wiped into Reserve."

"Then he'll wonder why it's blocked and bring in the psych-squad to break the amnesia."

"So we must have him back. Tonight. Baird, too, if possible."

Sanders sat on the bed, observing the locked-in Angus morosely. "How?"

"We may be able to pull a legal trick on Parker, and we have someone who might do it."

In the corridor outside an intervox came to demanding life,

166

paging. "Me, damn them!" Sanders activated the vidcom. "Sanders!"

A harassed operator said, "We have been unable to raise the Commissioner since your last attempt thirty-eight minutes ago. A messenger has just reported that a blind is operating in the private office. Do you know why?"

"No, I don't. As his aide, should I investigate? I can't enter a blind without good reason."

"The reason is eleven thousand dollars worth of power. He may have been taken ill."

"I'll see to it." He cut the link. "The luck's run out and here we go, half cocked. I'll be tied up for the rest of the night so you'll have to see your plan through alone. I hope it's a good one."

As simply as that he was gone, and Lindley knew how it felt to be Security's "man on the spot". But he was not a Security man, and prey to self doubt. His idea had not been outlined, let alone discussed, and Sanders's trust was a compliment he could live without.

Then he thought, reasonably, that it could and should be discussed with the person who must carry it out, and he punched Alice White's internal vidcode.

With the luck that follows drunks and fumblers she was off-duty and in the building and answered at once.

Sanders performed his pantomime of discovering carnage, killing the blind and yelling blue murder, and girded himself for inevitable departmental battles.

The most senior Tech took over as acting-Commissioner and at once pointed out that murder, as a civil crime, was a matter for Parker's detectives.

Sanders fought that quite correct decision to a standstill, claiming the top secrecy of Beckett's current project and remaining firm in refusal (as aide now automatically in charge of the project) to discuss it with anyone save GHQ; it involved, he said, the two who were already in Parker's hands and it was essential that their importance be not realized by any civil authority.

By sheer mulishness he carried his point; he had sweated

apprehension that trained civil detectives would expose his double dealing in minutes, for the procedures of criminal detection were as arcane to him as were Security's convoluted jugglings to the Police.

Over the issue of communication with GHQ, infighting became intense. He insisted on his right, as sole holder of classified information, to encode and transmit the message. The acting-Commissioner capitulated because he had no option but to believe Sanders's insistence that the message would be incomplete without the information he refused to divulge. But he capitulated snarling.

Sanders, his mind unpleasantly pinned to a murderer bone-rigid on a bed upstairs, thanked his luck and ran for Communications.

The message itself, coded, scrambled and transmitted by untappable laser relay through a com-satellite, was fairly brief. He made a blunt statement of murder, requested a new Commissioner at the earliest moment, stressed and restressed the need for secrecy and ended with a deliberately titillating statement of the reason for it. "Project in progress: investigation of confirmed—repeat confirmed—human mutations displaying potentially lethal capacities. Data known only to self and Lindley."

Watching the half-second quiver of a needle which told him his message had gone out in a single compact bundle, a super-hieroglyph, he had the desperate feeling that he was trying to run the planet and not necessarily doing it well.

Through all of this threaded the uproar about finger prints. These, clear as engravings on the splintered glass, were identified by a call to Census Data. But the gate-robot's record showed that Angus Thomson had never in his life passed the watchdog eye of Security HQ. Theories proliferated; consensus was that entrance and exit could only have been effected from the air, while common sense objected that no craft could hover so low without being detected. Personnel were mustered for a search wherein every level and sector was invaded simultaneously.

Since Lindley searched his own room and area, this produced

only a conspiratorial smile from Alice White, fascinated by the inside view of Security playing against itself.

She was honey-blonde, in her mid-twenties, not particularly good looking but good enough, and more intelligent than a preference for listening let show. Like most of her generation she was a strong girl, with what Lindley saw as a generosity of figure which would in his century have been thought better for a little trimming here, and here—and there.

If she sometimes looked older than her years, she had known traumatic suffering, an experience unusual for the young in their overprotected ambience. Lindley had played his part in that and contributed his peck of twentieth-century social psychology to her rehabilitation. If she never had thanked him for it, he knew why and was not hurt; their moment of confused emotion could never be repeated.*

She wore the Security uniform with a touch of severity; she had been a civilian clerk with the service when Lindley first met her, now she was an inducted servicewoman specializing in international law. A severe façade, he thought, to keep straying male hands at bay, but didn't believe it; Alice, he surmised, had her moments.

They were very practical moments as she surveyed Angus.

"Do you say he is actually conscious?"

"He is not *unconscious*, but all his observation is turned upon himself and all his psychic energy is devoted to rejection of reality. Or perhaps of himself."

"The world is too much for him?"

"I suspect he feels unworthy of the world."

"Wouldn't you have to be at bottom terribly vain to feel like that?"

"That's very perceptive of you."

Aghast at the power of the mind, she said, to ward off awe, "With his mouth open he looks like a fish."

"He's screaming."

She shivered. "And only he can hear him? Yet that poor little thing killed Beckett."

"Please make a habit of not mentioning such knowledge, even

* Recounted in *Beloved Son*.

169

between ourselves. I've told you enough to let you know what's happening if Parker tries to bulldoze you but not why we must have these men, because that would jolt the wits out of you. And that is not an insult."

He had Sanders paged and in moments obtained the screened face of a man seeing the night through on nerve and split-second decisions. "Can you spare a few minutes up here, Corey? I'm sending our girl off to Parker shortly."

"*Girl!* Against Parker?"

"Why not? They aren't going to fight it out on the floor. She's ideal for the job."

"If you say so. I'd better know what you're doing. Ten minutes."

It was twenty minutes, but he came. Alice said, "I'll tell you quickly what we plan."

His ragged, distraught look eased as he listened. "It could work; it just could. Jim, what have you told her?"

"Enough to cover operational accidents; not the big thing."

Sanders said, "Open your mouth to anyone but us two, Alice, and I'll have your head for a paperweight." He was too tired; the geniality came out badly, like a promise.

She behaved as if it had not been said and he left without further talk.

She nodded at the bed. "I wouldn't care to be in Corey's shoes if that one is discovered."

Or in mine. Lindley said, "It's time you got going."

12

At one in the morning Parker was alert and waiting. By two o'clock he had begun to think Security would not move, that his action had thrown the masters into an unmagisterial spin.

Locating Angus's Gangoil conversations for playback had been a lengthy, fiddling business but rewarding in the sign-posting of a mystery. Subsequent mental thuggery against David, whose discretion had collapsed under the impression that all was known, had yielded only further puzzles. Parker yearned for that translator filament; psychlinicians might take a week to get half as much by routine methods. The minor question of resemblance between Santley and David seemed peripheral.

He could not hazard a guess as to what he had stumbled on, but Santley's memory block would make justification for his prying. The Reserve block on the man's lifeline data was only an irritation; Security had moved fast there but the blue-black booklet on Parker's desk would hold them at arm's length. It was a quite powerful item of antiquarianism.

He was not interested in the unintelligible Scot save as a possible exchange item—after he had been taught some sense about the use of indiscriminate violence.

By two-thirty he had decided that Security was afraid of tipping its hidden hand, and so could not move at all. At ten to three he was informed that a Security Specialist waited to serve a Sequestration Warrant.

"His name?"

"Hers—Alice White."

"Do we know her?"

"She's in law; rights of aliens and such."

He thought there was something more; the name rang a faint bell. "Tell her to wait. Do a lifeline check."

It took three minutes to land on his desk. Reading, he smiled for the first time that night. She was Lindley's ex-bedmate of the riots of 2032—and Lindley had been reported with Angus in St Kilda before he disappeared. So he had no doubt now where to look for Angus. Where that insolent double dealer fitted the jigsaw was not apparent, but he had wisely run for protection.

"Send her in."

He did not approve of women in service jobs—*they distract good men*—and this one improved nothing by bouncing up to his desk, confident and demanding.

"I've come for Baird and Santley." She added, with a professional brightness, "I didn't expect to find you here at this hour."

"But I've been expecting you, or one like you."

He waved for her to sit if she wished and she did so, squaring her briefcase neatly on her knees. "That's excellent, Controller.

171

If we understand each other's positions there need be less argument."

Quick bitch! "Or more."

"I have Sequestration Warrants." She laid them on the desk. "Security claims the custody of these men as stateless persons. No national government has jurisdiction over them."

He flicked them over. "Unsigned."

"I'll sign them if you wish—as complainant to unlawful detention of wards of Security."

Smart bitch, too. "You haven't had time to raise a ward order."

"One will be raised by morning. We may as well act as though it exists, because it will."

But, he thought, she did not wish to sign unless she must; she did not want documentary evidence of Security interference in his hands. A weakness to be exploited. He said, "I'm prepared to discuss the men—as separate cases."

"Very well." She affected casualness but he was not deluded; he had struck at a point of unpreparedness. "Baird", she said, "is a Scottish national."

The easy one first, eh? "Scotland doesn't exist. It was dusted off; it is one of the areas World Council designated non-countries. He has refugee status only, and that is a Civil Police affair."

Her smile undermined his certainty "That's a common mis-apprehension. No region was ever designated a non-country; the term is 'unadministered area'." She quoted the statute and section. "That Scotland is uninhabited is a temporary con-dition." She added for sweet bitchery's sake, "You can't be expected to be *au fait* with the details of international law, but the man remains a Scottish national requiring temporary settlement, and therefore Security's responsibility."

He would not make a fool of himself by checking that; she would not dare be other than right. He had learned a phrase from Lindley in the old days when they had been on speaking terms: *You win some, you lose some*. Quite. He said, "It's a lot of fuss to make over a fossil."

"A historically priceless survival. May I see him now?"

Without warning he shot her an offer. "I'll trade him for Angus."

"What have you to trade with? Nothing. And who is Angus?"

Good, he admitted; very good indeed, but the seeing eye was not deceived. He knew, and she knew, that he had spotted Angus's bolthole.

He sent for Donald, who came escorted by four patrolmen with drawn guns. He had been treated with coagulants and sterile patches but not otherwise cleaned up. One eye was nearly closed and his mouth swollen and cut; he limped slightly; his trousers were rubbed and streaked with dirt and his jacket torn at one pocket. He was not subdued; if anything, he strutted a little.

Alice was shocked; Security personnel saw little of the realities of Police work. "How did this happen?"

Parker snorted and Donald informed her, in the soft but clogging accent she had been warned against and could barely follow, "I tripped on the polis officer's boot an' bruised mysel in twenty-three separate pairts."

It fell flat; the standing jest of a century of police lockups had not survived the Collapse.

Parker growled, "He tried to escape custody. He put three of my men in Casualty and one in splints with a broken leg. It's a trained butcher you're laying claim to."

She could not repress a glitter of interest in the man. There were aspects of frankly sexual glamour about the Gone Time which knowledge of its degradation and brutality could not suppress, and she could not envisage the techniques whereby one man might work so much havoc on trained patrolmen, but the drama of one against many always called for admiration ...

He did not look a brute, more a good-natured larrikin if such were possible. When she told him, "I'm taking you back to Security barracks," he answered, "Thank you," and no more, accepting a further turn in the vaudeville of happenings.

Parker reminded, "There are assault charges pending."

She shocked him by snapping, "Don't be such a damned fool! You know there's more at stake than a civil disturbance

173

writ; your whole attitude betrays it. Press charges if you must; Security will deliver him to the court when required."

The outburst was an error, to be paid for; she should have observed diplomacy while his patrolmen were present, but he absorbed insult impassively. To Donald he said coldly, "You're free to go."

Donald hovered. "I dinna hae my bearin's." To their incomprehension he offered in his pedantic clear English, "I do not know my way."

Alice smiled at him and he smiled back as though split lips and bruises were routine. "Find your way to the street and wait for me."

"I'll do that, lassie." His eyes summed her; he said softly, "Sonsy!" aware that she would not know the word, and marched off without a glance for Parker.

Parker had missed nothing. "A character," he commented drily. Donald would be remembered and she also for having responded, however fractionally, to the admiration of a Gone Time savage.

She said determinedly, "Now, Santley."

"I'm holding Santley." He fingered the blue-black booklet.

"His origins are unknown and until a provenance is established he is Security's responsibility."

"His origins may be doubtful but a provenance has been established. There is documentary evidence."

That seemed scarcely possible and she could not hide the instant of shock. However—"May I see the documents?"

"There is only one." He shook the booklet at her. "In the Gone Time there were no central data accumulations as we know them and individuals carried personal identification. This is called a 'Passport'. It seems to be some sort of travel approval and it was in Santley's inner pocket. Here!"

He held it out to her, spread at the second page. She could not doubt its genuineness; the elaborate layout in two languages, perforated code number, heavily watermarked paper and worn appearance could not have been designed and fabricated in less than a day. She had never seen the man but there was a photograph of someone of the correct age group—and wearing a tie, a forgotten dress accessory of the era.

Description, she read, and under it: *Name*, WILLIAM
SANTLEY—*Place and Date of Birth, Unrecorded*. (He had
changed his name by something called "deed poll", hadn't he?
From David. Or had the change been made without benefit of
formality and records faked in some way? That was a common-
place in old stories.) *Height, 172 cm* and so on. It had been
issued in 1992.

"Place of birth not recorded. Effectively stateless."

"Not so." He reached out and turned the page. There it
was: *National Status*, AUSTRALIAN CITIZEN.

"My man, I think."

She had no argument; she had lost the one who mattered to
Lindley and Sanders to an idiot document which only an
irrational past could have spawned. She said as steadily as she
could, "Security will, nevertheless, wish to interview this man.
I will present the relevant documents within the hour."

Parker retrieved the passport. "That is not possible."

"The protocol is clear. Security has right of access—"

"If the man is available for interview."

"Why shouldn't he be?" She leapt at the obvious. "Has he
been harmed?" *Give me a hint, just a hint, of police violence . . .*

"Not here or in this time. In his own day he suffered an
injury resulting in amnesia. Since data-registration requires
lifeline details, which seem to have been removed from the
banks, the alternative is to treat his amnesia."

"But not at this hour of the morning."

"Why not?" he asked, making a gaping ass of her. "Surgical
treatment is under way. Be content with your barbarian Scot;
he seems to have an eye for a female figure and the language
should be easily learned. Goodnight, Specialist White."

He began to sort papers on his desk.

She could only pass over the insult and ask—without hope,
knowing he need not tell her—"Which hospital is he in?"

He turned his sharp profile to show the grin at its least
pleasant. "He is under psycho-operative process and will not be
available for several days."

Through Lindley's window seeped a pale promise of dawn. He
had extruded chairs for them and perched himself on the foot

of the bed where Angus lay coiled as he had been seven hours before. Only shallow breathing said he lived.

Sanders had sent Alice to bed, unkindly, with no explanations and little praise. She had gone off in fury, frigidly disciplined and polite.

Sanders and Lindley, edgy on two stiff whiskies each, were falling into recrimination. Sanders blamed Lindley for the loss of Will and would continue to blame him while the pressures of deception made him unreasonable. The Gone Timer knew about passports, should have considered the document and planned round it—

Donald winked his good eye at Lindley for comfort and sipped neat whisky while he waited for the air to cool.

Lindley protested that had there been no passport Parker would have found other means. Finding the block on Santley's lifeline data would have told him he was on to something big, and he'd risk much for an armlock on Security.

Sanders said furiously, "And by morning he'll have it. Then where will we be?"

Donald held his glass to the dawn light and squinted through it. "As Will himsel might say it: Up shit creek."

"Your friend's in dangerous hands. Don't you care?"

"I care but I'll no' waste my brain in greetin'."

Lindley translated, "Weeping."

"He hasn't the face for it." Donald became a fresh focus for frustration. "You don't seem surprised that he's one of them."

"No' greatly; there had to be a reason for the a'mighty fash in Glesca, an' I think I'm past surprisin'. What's done is done an' that Parker's the yin to watch. What will he do the noo?" The accent was thick; he was more concerned than he allowed.

"He'll race to the cathedral to tell God about it."

"A kirk man? That's no' guid where there's mair power than feelin'. His kind will tell God what's expected o' Him, then tell himsel that God agrees."

Sanders pushed his glass away; he could not risk exacerbating weariness. "That means he'll grab for long life when he finds out about it. Didn't some old biblical bird live to nine hundred or so? That will make his justification—a return to the old biblical tradition."

Lindley said, "That's Old Testament. The Cults all teach from the Gospels. And Parker's not a hypocrite."

"You're joking!"

"He *believes* in God, whatever his private version of deity may be. He'll lie and misrepresent in the name of God, but it *will be* in the name of God and what he thinks God will approve of."

"So what is his God likely to tell him?"

"Only God knows."

"So what do we do? Wait and see? How can we?"

"We must. Don't get yourself in any deeper, Corey. As it is, when the new Commissioner arrives you'll be lucky to escape with a whole skin. Harbouring a killer won't sit well, however you argue it."

Donald interrupted calmly, "Your killer moved."

Lindley bent over Angus. Perhaps he had moved, very slightly. He inspected the eyes and fancied change, a softening of the stone glare. He felt the muscles at thigh and upper arm. They were soft, resting, not clenched.

"He's coming out of it." He breathed a great relief, took the right hand and gently opened the fingers; they remained open.

The eyelids flickered and the man shuddered from head to foot.

Lindley straightened his legs from the foetal position and turned him on his back. With a sigh he relaxed completely.

Awareness returned slowly, in stretchings and inarticulate sounds, but in time he looked at the world and saw it.

"Donald." It was a purr of satisfaction.

"An' how's my wee Methuselah?"

He whispered, "You talk too much. You mustn't tell the world." He said more loudly, "I said we'd meet again."

"Ay, you did."

His face was drawn with exhaustion; for a moment he seemed to sleep, but asked with closed lids, "What happened to me?"

To Lindley the question sounded perfunctory, as if he knew and wanted confirmation. Yet a peripheral amnesia was not unlikely. "You suffered what I can only call a catatonic fit.

177

I couldn't treat it; I had to hope you would come out of it naturally."

"And naturally I did." He opened eyes that leered slyly. "A metabolism geared to survival learns to do without doctors." He asked Donald, "Where's Will?"

Lindley said quickly, "Resting. He's being prepared for memory probe." It was probably the truth, and the question gave him opportunity to seek a reaction which a weary Angus might not be able to conceal. "We know he's one of your kind."

Angus only looked wearily pensive and asked, "But what kind? We're all different." He roused to throw a mocking snippet of information. "It isn't a general mutation. Nothing so simple. A whole group of syndromes, no two matching." Then it appeared he had reached a conclusion of his own. "The Company was right about Will. But nobody knew him."

Lindley caught his meaning. "A new one, perhaps. He's only sixty-eight years old."

"A baby. Yet somebody must have known." His voice strengthened. "*That bloody Jeanie.* Lying bitch! Playing the Dissident hand right through to Doomsday! But who was David? That's the puzzle."

"He was Will's son."

Angus laughed aloud, shaking his head. "Oh no, no, no!" It was the complete contradiction of superior knowledge. "Twin maybe but not son. Not ever son."

He closed his eyes and was instantly asleep.

Sanders looked thoughtfully down on Angus and back to Lindley. "Where did you get those data?"

"From the banks."

"Retrieval or processing?"

"Both. The information was assembled from several sources and correlated."

"The basic sources would be twentieth-century official records —humanly acquired, humanly written and filed."

"Yes."

"Add programming errors and faulty recording leading to processing foulups and fantasy could be produced. Angus knows something more; I'll back him to be right."

"He could be." Lindley's admission was sulky; his knowledge

of retrieval and processing was minimal but he should have thought of these things.

Sanders pursued, "What did Beckett think?"

"I didn't tell him."

Sanders studied him as he had studied Angus, his eyes accusing Lindley of monumental stupidity. "What were you doing? Trying to hold a card up your sleeve?"

"Something like that."

"You realize I'll have to tell the new Commissioner? They're sending Ferendija."

"Then my pedigree will damn me anyway. He's known for an old-style chauvinist: anybody born before the Collapse is a cultural error and should be made to pay for it."

Will was not under surgery although at the whiff of a really determined *habeas corpus* from Security he could within minutes have been under an excellent facsimile thereof. He was under interrogation. Not severe interrogation, just the preliminary heart-to-heart, the sighting shots before selective pressures were applied.

Preliminaries were all the confused and furious Will needed for the opening of a spillway of speech.

The psychlinician (not the same word as the dated "psychiatrist", but covering expertise in electronics, statistical analysis and the reading of electro-cerebral printouts), having been summoned from sleep, was in no mood for fantasy.

As far as he could determine, the sullen and vengefully talkative man was not insane or prone to hallucination and had no discernible reason to assault his intelligence with a torrent of archetypal folklore about little monsters who lived for ever, changed shape at will, froze with the evil eye and were physically invulnerable. He was impressed by Will's motive for co-operation, expressed with force whenever he implied doubt: "I don't give a fuck what you believe or whether you're the Police, Security or the Royal Society of Shitlickers. You all want the story and you all get the same story and why the hell should I care whether you like it or wipe your arses on it? I've had a gutful of the lot of you."

The psychlinician used a mild form of sensory detector

179

without shaking the impression of truth, then took a chance with a truth drug so powerful it frightened him. He concluded that, whatever experiences the fantasist had actually undergone, he believed his version to be truth and insisted that Security also believed it. Security, of course, had the advantage of a translator, which might reveal a very different angle of subconscious vision.

He couldn't accept it; there had to be a simple explanation; let Parker worry it out.

Parker listened to his report with his customary blankness and asked, "What do you think?"

"Illusion or delusion, but he believes it and says Security does too."

"You don't?"

"No."

"Break his amnesia. Find out what caused it, why David shot him, where he comes from, everything. Use surgeons if need be; I'll cover you with the proper permits. Keep your mouth tight shut and report to nobody but myself."

The psychlinician recalled a last detail. "He seems to think that his Angus bogey is running loose in Australia."

Parker's face was a study in malice. "Yes. Angus with the evil eye."

The psychlinician escaped, half convinced that if an evil eye existed, Parker had that moment developed it.

In a culture wherein information could be had for the effort of framing a question correctly, data terminals were as common as vidcoms. A result of this was diminution of the capacity for awe. With endless wonders available at buttonpush the teenager was accustomed to them and his elder unimpressed. In Parker's pragmatic mind surprise had long been voided in simple acceptance. His response to the hints of super-characteristics was, after the first tension, cool. It was finally a question: Is this feasible?

He began with the simple-language encyclopedia banks. After the usual false starts (framing questions to penetrate a blank area in one's knowledge is not easy) these gave him directions to explore and keywords for triggering specific information. Then he essayed more specialized queries.

Hypnosis he had already discarded and shape-changing led

only to dead ends of folklore, but extended life spans made an astonishing field. He had not dreamed how much was already known of the biological requirements for prolonged life. The idea was thoroughly rational, given more investigation of the immune systems, the hormonal functions and the meaning of the word "ageing".

There could be truth in Santley's fairy tale. Security thought there was.

God surely worked in a mysterious way. He, Harold Parker, had stolen Santley on a whim of hurt pride (privately he could admit it), and God, watching, had lifted him up on to a high mountain to show him all the Kingdoms of Time.

He began to plan.

Security would be busy concocting justification for recovering his Santley, so Security must be taken out of play.

This was no wild or impractical dream but an end which could be achieved by constitutional means. Only five years ago the thing had nearly been done, but the impulse had died in a splitting of objectives. It was time to revive those days.

He considered the tools to hand. The Bishops and their chapters would be useless; they sought text rather than pretext, the right rather than the outright.

The Missioners? No; they would argue means in a quibbling of internal jealousies.

The Circle of Acolytes? He had no love for those brash young people, barely out of their social-preparation years, who split scriptural hairs with vigour and uproar and whose girls and men alike occasionally broke each others' bones in the name of intellectual give and take. His patrolmen loathed them, because the common tolerance of the young who would rule tomorrow's fair world made it unwise to deal violently with their violence, and sullenly urged their suppression.

It could only be the hand of God, moving still in that mysterious way, which had restrained him from breaking them before this, for plainly they were a power reserved for his use.

He gave orders for several of the more prominent Acolyte hotheads to be brought to him in the morning, whether they liked it or not. He slept well for what was left of the night.

13

The new Commissioner flew in from Hawaii GHQ after a thirty-hour series of debates on aspects which had not yet occurred to Sanders. A side effect of this delay was the addition of a new factor to the equation of activities: by the time he arrived the Circle of Acolytes was in full cry in the streets.

The intercontinental flyer touched down at the old Essendon airfield and was met by acting-Commissioner Senior Tech Edwards, whose greeting was amputated before formality's mouth was properly open.

"Is Sanders with you?"

"Yes, sir."

"I want him. And a two-man vehicle. He can drive me to your HQ."

"Yes, sir."

"Are you acting-C?"

"Yes, sir."

"Continue so until I take over. That may not be for several days."

"Yes, sir."

Edwards felt that his side of the conversation lacked sparkle.

Sanders drove slowly, as the Commissioner had instructed; it was to be an introductory session, a summing up.

The new man was shortish, stocky and dark, speaking excellent English with a mild accent Sanders could not place. He was old for a Security man, probably in his forties, which was fairly old for anyone of this day. He would have been born on the brink of the Collapse years, when child mortality by plague and starvation had reached towards a hundred per cent and only the extravagantly fittest survived.

"My name is Ferendija. I am the second-ranking Commissioner of the service."

Sanders knew that his message had not been underestimated. This man was one of the nexus who had selected and trained the children who became Security, a Slav who had survived not only his deadly era but a childhood among the intractable Mediterranean Vendetta States. His presence meant that World Council was alert and alarmed.

"Now, Tech Sanders, who knows that Beckett is dead?"

"Only HQ personnel, sir."

"Sure of that?"

"As far as can be. We gave the newscasts the story that a replacement Commissioner was coming in to allow Beckett to be withdrawn for special assignment."

"Good. Who killed him?"

"A mutant named Thomson."

"Why?"

Sanders said evenly, "Because Beckett wanted to live for ever."

"Indeed!" Ferendija turned his head to examine the Tech's expression. "Was that a good reason?"

"Under the circumstances, I think so."

"The hell you do!"

"Yes, sir. The hell I *do*!"

Ferendija appreciated a man who knew his mind. "So the mutation of your message would be a longevity trait?"

"Longevity is one trait."

"One!" He smiled genially to cover a feeling of being swallowed alive. "And you *don't* wish to live for ever?"

"No. There could be disadvantages we don't know of yet. I suspect there are."

With extreme self-denial Ferendija bypassed the lure of bizarre gossip. "How many know of this alleged mutation?"

"Doctor Lindley, myself and two revenants. And it isn't alleged, it's real."

"Revenants? Does that mean Gangoil is involved?"

"Very much."

"God's guts!" Not the expletive of a Cultist. "We should have shut that place down." That was simple railing; Gangoil could ignore Security so long as no Ethic was transgressed. Standover men like Beckett might force entry and terrorize David but could do little officially. "Revenants!"

Sanders kept quiet. Twentieth-century leavings made a touchy subject with Ferendija's generation. *Venomous* was a word for their attitude—and, after all, they had suffered the devastated years . . .

The Commissioner said, "I don't know what questions to ask."

"A suggestion, sir: Filament and tape records contain most of what we know. It could help to study those before proceeding."

Ferendija brooded: *His first major takeover; he wants to feel trusted and important.* "A useful thought. Thank you."

From the car he contemplated morosely the dereliction of what had been the western suburbs, the stock scene of any great city where structures had been gutted for their useful materials and the remainder left to weather and rot. Half a century might pass before the planet found time to halt its frenzied scramble towards stability long enough to clear away the debris of its downfall.

At the city's heart one huge mass remained intact near the northern entry. He asked what it was.

"The Gone Time Public Library, sir."

"It's an eyesore."

"But an important library—sir."

A touch of offended pride? "That saucer dome is an architectural error of tact, and the world is full of libraries."

"Not of libraries with Australian historical documents and records."

Ferendija laughed. "Australian born?"

"Yes, sir."

"And proud of it, eh? For two and half decades Security nibbles chauvinism to its necessary death, and still you are patriots! History, indeed! This country existed only long enough to throw up a virility-folklore, an incomprehensible electoral system and an atrocious accent." He peered slyly. "You don't needle easily? Good, but you Australians are too big for your small boots and very much a nuisance. Five years ago you unearthed Gangoil and suborned a Commissioner from his loyalty; you produced those pitiful neo-telepaths to frighten the daylights out of the world, then followed with a rash of Cultism which even the Orthodox Kremliners watch with suspicion. Now you give us a murdered Commissioner and a mutant strain that lives for ever."

"For centuries, at any rate."

"You have become a troublesome people that Security will eventually have to do something about."

They had passed through the heart of the demolished area and were approaching the cathedral.

"If I slow down a little more," Sanders suggested, "you'll see Australians proposing to do something about Security."

"Are you trying to score off me? Slow down—stop!"

A crowd had gathered round the steps of the west porch and spilled along the lawns but had left the footpath clear. (Donald would have wondered, but it was Ethical that a gathering should not obstruct others; training in manners and consideration was strict—until a flashpoint was reached.) There were a hundred or so listening to the determined young girl on the top step, mostly older teenagers but with a sprinkling of parental types. It was, by Town standards, a large audience for a street speech and it seemed an attentive one.

The girl spoke seriously but conversationally and seemed to be easily heard. Ferendija snapped the window down.

"—giveth and the Lord taketh away. That's the text, isn't it? Well, the Lord gave us Security while we grew from chaos but it's time for Security to return to the Lord who gave it. We don't need nursemaiding against our errors. We *do* need to make the mistakes of inexperience without Nanny Tech kissing our butts to make them better every time we slip. Under Security we don't know what a real and working world is like!"

The quiet voice, unamplified, sounded directly into Ferendija's ears, as if she stood beside him. Incredulous and affronted, he said, "She's using a sound screen!"

The diaphanous thing was barely visible, a few points of light floating in the shadowy porch.

The girl saw the black vehicle with its ensign of enfolding wings and fell silent. Slowly she lifted her hand, pointing, straightening the arm like a spear for launching. It was well judged, well done. Heads turned, a hundred heads in contemplation of the black car.

185

She dropped her arm and said loudly, "*But*—" The heads turned back to her. She had technique.

"But," she insisted, "we can be free of Security! If the *people* tell Security it must leave Melbourne Town—leave Australia—it must go! That is the Great Ethic which Security itself devised so that it could never become dictatorship or tyranny. We, the *people*—"

Ferendija closed the window. "Bloody demagogue! The same old cry." Sanders headed the car for Princes Bridge. "Where would she get a sound screen?"

"From Security, the Prime Minister's Technical Section or the Civil Police."

"Security, no. PM wouldn't risk it. The Police?"

"Are also Australians and mostly Cultists. And what Police force, anywhere, loves Security?"

Ferendija felt he approved of this young upstart who had casually taken on a planet-sized problem. "Assuming this is Police-incited, is it a new thing?"

"As of yesterday. This is not an isolated meeting; there are dozens, everywhere. It's orchestrated."

"And it's likely that the Police are behind them?"

"With Controller Parker nothing is unlikely."

"Oh, that one!" He knew of Parker—who did not?—who had had his share of the world newscast bands during the neotelepath affair of '32. His mouth twisted in angry distaste. "Is this connected with our main concern?"

"I'm afraid so, sir. And I mean, afraid."

"It might teach them a lesson," Ferendija said, being deliberately provocative, "if we take them at their word and get out."

"Or teach us one—that they can do well without us."

"Are you trying to shock me?"

"Being realistic, sir."

"Still, you shock me. I'm not used to hearing Security talk sense about its own ultimate unimportance."

That shocked Sanders.

Ferendija took over the private office, called for a cup of tea, drank it, asked half a dozen questions and began work.

"Get me Lindley and his records and have translator gear brought."

He let them fidget while he experienced the Gangoil filament twice without comment, then again in bursts, questioning Lindley until he felt he understood it thoroughly. "Now the sound tape. Under blind, I think."

The darkness flicked round them; the lamp came on.

He heard the interview three times. At the sounds of death his lips twitched and he became thoughtful.

He said, "Security has been accused of programming common human reactions out of its servicemen; so much for that lie. I didn't like the man but I never detected such greed in him or the fear of death so starkly. Hearing makes a wound in a life's work."

Lindley tried not to look wise after the event. Sanders waited on judgement, which came in unexpected form.

"After two days, Tech Sanders, do you still feel that you were right to protect your Commissioner's murderer?"

"Yes, sir."

"So. Doctor Lindley?" Not that he cared what a Gone Timer thought, but he might need the man.

"Surely."

"And was Thomson right to kill him?"

Lindley said, "For Angus it was self defence."

"Don't cavil. Sanders?"

"He was right."

"Murder not excessive?"

"He was man on the spot for the world. He made his decision and acted on it."

"You stand by that?"

"Yes, sir."

"Then I'll stand by you when the storm breaks. Which it will. What has happened since?"

Sanders told him and the near edge of the storm broke at once. "Dear Cultist Christ, were you out of your mind? You let that policeman get away with blatant kidnapping!"

"The inter-service relationship——"

Ferendija used a raging Slavic phrase for the relationship, and stormed on. "Are you one of the programmed, the brainwashed, the mentally straitjacketed? One of the reasons why Security is outliving its usefulness?"

Lindley interfered. "You're being unreasonable."

"Shut your impotent Gone Time trap!" Nevertheless he took notice, continued more calmly, "You should have gone after him—recovered them by force—in the street if necessary. You could have pleaded confusion, anything to gain time to find a way to hold them legally. Surely you thought of it."

Sanders admitted unwillingly, "Yes."

"But didn't do it. Blame's pointless; it's an old story. You were tugged by the balance of authorities, the Ethic, the conventions of administrative action, your own ideas of right and wrong and the knowledge that every decision must be imperfect. No one envies the man on the spot."

Lindley said, "At least he took some action where others might have frozen in indecision."

Ferendija shut him up. "Watch your own defence, Doctor Lindley! Your Gone Time deviousness in concealing the data-bank information was less than reputable."

Sanders tried. "His reasons were better than you may think. Doctor Lindley's history—"

"I know his history. Yesterday is dead; his actions are today's." He changed tack. "That woman—Specialist White—it was a mistake to keep her ignorant. Curiosity loosens tongues; she will ask revealing questions of the wrong people. So bring her up to date and give her a job to let her think she's trusted with responsibility. Invent one. Importance will keep her mouth shut."

Needing a messenger, he fixed on the humiliated Lindley. "Now bring the Scot here."

Stepping through the blind shook Donald's self-possession more than anything so far in the new world. Once inside he poked at the black surface, absorbed and wondering.

Ferendija, reared in impatience with the old world, did not want to waste time on this peripheral figure, but there could be a role for him. He said without preamble, "I understand you are some kind of professional thug."

Donald considered the unearned insult as he turned from

the fascinating blackness; he could do as well for openers.

"Ah was a maircenary sojer." He allowed accent and dialect full holiday, cheered by an approving glint in Lindley's eye. "That's yin kin' o' fechtin', but Ah dae weel eneuch at t'ither kind." He touched his discoloured eye. "It took six o' the braw polis buckies tae gie me this'n."

Ferendija was able to take the general meaning, coldly. "It's no commendation; we don't favour violence as a way of life."

Donald was prepared to modify accent and vocabulary for a man who was willing to try, but not his attitude. "Do you take credit for that? I've seen that you hae mair stinkin' methods to haund than simple beatin's."

Ferendija retreated, wisely, from a guttersnipe exchange. "If we find each other barbaric, so be it. But there's a question: How can you earn your keep in this world? At this moment it means, of what use are you to me?"

"For use against my grain, nane at a'. Unless you want a tool turnin' in your haund."

The obsolete idioms were baffling. Lindley explained while the Commissioner concealed annoyance at the savage's advantage of understanding. He ignored the taunt. "I'm told you've seen little of Melbourne Town."

"A glimpse frae the air."

"Then we must let you out to become acquainted with the new century and its people."

Donald smiled at him, as one old double dealer to another. "Oot in the streets you'll use me to keep the attention o' freend Parker while you make your moves elsewhere. Och ay, but if I break a law in innocence an' he feels I might benefit frae the speerin' o' his heidshrinkers—what then?"

Ferendija came to mental attention; he had underestimated badly. "It won't happen. You will be protected night and day."

"That's as guid as sayin' I'm bait."

No use denying. "Safe bait. However, you're not property and I can't force you. What else useful can you do?"

"Many a thing, but I'm takin' your job—for money." Ferendija's eyes widened. "You hae ca'ed me professional, so what's the pay?"

Lindley laughed outright. "What's the going price of guinea pigs?"

Sanders, amused but practical and thinking better of Donald than Ferendija ever could, suggested, "Put him in uniform. Parker won't dare touch him but he'll break his patrolmen's hearts tracking his movements. Hire him as a Specialist Tech in, uh, exotic combat methods. How about that, Donald?"

"Why no'? It's food an' bed an' pocketmoney."

It was a good idea and Ferendija was constrained to hide his distaste for the thought of a Gone Timer in an honourable uniform; even the comparatively civilized Lindley was a continuing offence. "Very well. Tech Sanders will see to your induction and outfitting. You can begin your sightseeing in the morning. Please leave us now."

Sanders said to Donald, "Wait in the corridor," and when the Scot was gone turned to Ferendija. "I've moved among Gone Timers—Doctor Lindley and a few others—since *Columbus* came home. They're people, like us."

Responsibility, Lindley thought, had developed an aggressive streak in Sanders; few would have sailed so close to insulting one of the most powerful men in the world. But perhaps he did not understand the personal relationships within Security as well as he thought because Ferendija, after a momentary bleakness, accepted it.

"I may be unreasonable, but I have been reared in revulsion of them from birth. I can't accept them as equals. I am frank about it, Doctor Lindley."

"You may as well be. I have no illusions about my second-class social status in the eyes of contemporaries. In my day we had the same problem with Negroes."

Ferendija did not understand. "Was there something peculiar about your Negroes? I know several of them—fine men. What do you mean?"

"We were brought up to consider them socially and culturally inferior, and refused to see evidence that they were not. So they lived second-class lives they did not deserve."

"I take your point—with difficulty—but I cannot annul my reactions simply by realizing that I should. This Scot, for instance—"

"Probably despises you as ill-mannered and ill-bred."
He left no doubt of the pleasure he took in saying it.

A simmering Donald told Angus what had occurred. "But I'd agree to maist anything that gets me oot in the sun."

"What's his name?"

"The mannerless bastard didna say. He doesna waste civilities on Gone Timers."

Angus had wondered when and how Donald would have his nose rubbed in this aspect of social truth. "In this dedicated new world, Donald, nobody liked Gone Timers. You are the wreckers of their planet, which is fair judgement. You are also bloodthirsty, treacherous, ecologically stupid and paranoid. Again fair judgements, in terms of history."

"An' they are nane o' these?"

"You'll find out. Their faults are yours, inverted, twisted and decorated with face-savers. Your generation said 'morally wrong' when it meant 'don't rock the boat' and 'the historical solution' when a barefaced doublecross was coming up. Today they say 'for preservation of the culture' and mean 'stop that or we'll throw you to the psychs'; 'ethically impossible' is double talk for 'you won't con me into doing the decent thing'. This lot are subconsciously frightened that if the restraints of the Ethic are released they'll discover themselves the same monsters as their despised grandfathers."

"Yet the newscast says the Tooners are cryin' for the chance to risk it. There's street meetin's."

"I sense Parker stirring a diversion there. Don't give him an excuse to re-arrest you; he's the original arch-bastard, with God's approval."

"So? I think the Commissioner would hae me taken in so he can show his muscle snatchin' me back."

Angus grimaced. "That's a rough game, but you said he promised protection."

"Ay."

"Security keeps its promises."

"Like The Company?"

Angus glanced sharply and fell silent.

Donald said, "I'm on edge. I didna mean hairt."

"You did, and I might as well face it that The Company is finished." He announced dissolution with thoughtfulness rather than regret. "There'll be no room for us once the news of our existence leaks out."

To Donald this was an unthought-of aspect. "After thousands o' years?" The pointless protest fired an instant's flash of the vastness of what Angus had said. To him it must seem that eternity had displayed an ending, time itself begun to grind down to his elimination. "Yet I think you'll no' be so easily got rid o'."

Angus for once did not rise to optimism. "You'll find a way."

The "you", defining his classification and position, stung with its announcement that the Angus of Donald's private reality did not observe Donald as part of his. Any more than did the damned Commissioner. He saw, disconcertingly, that he was cast away on an alien planet.

Angus continued, "You must find a way, if only to justify your millions of years of evolution. Or be pushed off the board by a handful of genetic errors."

Then Lindley put his head round the door to summon him to the private office.

"Hail to the new master! He won't care much for me, either."

"You'll no' blame him for thinkin' o' Beckett wi' a cut thrapple."

Left alone, Donald had thoughts of his own, unconnected with an Angus who needed no one else to worry over his safety. Lindley would have been interested and a little alarmed, since the man had met only one woman in Melbourne Town, to hear him say appreciatively to a blank wall, "Sonsy!"

Angus was not awed by Ferendija's career and reputation. To him, Security was only another stop-gap preservation of a status quo eternally unbalanced by the same powers as were marshalled for its equilibrium ; it would go the way of all attempts at regulation—Marxism, Victorian morality, religious persecution, dictatorship—as inner change rendered it obsolete.

Still, he must pay this ephemeral man of authority respect. It rankled that his intriguer's cunning was mostly applied experience, that these seventy-year mayflies were on average more intelligent than he. Forgetting it had lost Will to Parker.

What did the man see with his unimpressionable gaze? A freak? A specimen? Or just a damned nuisance?

Ferendija said, "That would be the Campbell face; you couldn't risk your own in barracks," and fell silent.

What he saw was a man so ordinary that the melodramatic structure around him fell apart and common sense took hold. That the man had dangerous talents was acceptable—so did thousands of the otherwise normal—and Santley's filament recorded impressions he believed to be true, but Santley had been in the grip of imposed illusions . . . there was no need to fantasize Flying Dutchmen and Wandering Jews. Basically, here was a twentieth-century guttersnipe, preserved by means needing investigation, with all his century's potential for disaster.

When he was ready he asked, casually but attacking the myth at its heart, "How old are you?"

The answer was flippantly unexpected, "I don't know."

A trickster's reply. Well, an imposter would suit very well, resolving problems at a stroke. But the man continued talking, and talking froth.

"There's a mnemonic overload; only useful memories persist. That is, those we use most. We discard a lot you might think valuable, but to us an assimilated past is disposable. I don't retain much before Akhnaton."

Patter. Mystification. "And who was Akhnaton?"

"An Egyptian ruler some three millennia back. A promising culture was smothering under priestly authority and we fed him concepts of monotheism to help break their hold. But it came to nothing."

Uncheckable, of course, though the ruler had probably existed. "I'm not seeking armchair chat." Angus smiled thinly back at him. "I'd say you're about thirty-five."

"You can't believe me? Do you want only expectable answers?" He explained insultingly, as to a child, "Donald Baird knew me forty-five years ago, and Gangoil can prove that I've never been in a slow met bath. Set your doubt grappling with that."

193

Ferendija had to face the fact that his emotions rather than his intelligence rejected the problems incarnate in Angus. The sheer size of the emotional assumptions implied in the acceptance of a limitless continuity . . .

He might as well accept what he could not otherwise explain, but he said, conceding nothing openly, "Grotesqueries don't change the fact that you must be judged as a killer." The smile became impudence; the man derided him. *But carefully, carefully; he can be dangerous.* He asked a pivotal question, "How many of you are there?"

"I don't know that either. I'm aware of about forty but there must be many more around the world." He counted on his fingers. "I'm here; three, possibly five, should be in Glasgow; Will and David must be counted as possibles until further information comes in, and the others might be anywhere, minding their business. Parker's God may know how many but it's unlikely that anyone else does."

It was a quiet bomb, a deliberate expansion of the limits of the enigma, and he seemed to enjoy it. "We aren't a secret society of ancients meeting stealthily to discuss the hidden history of the ages. We do know a few exotic secrets but they're shatteringly unimportant, and we meet only in temporary groups when there's something to be done in concert. Actually we live ordinary little lives, keeping out of sight, preventing the neighbours becoming suspicious and avoiding each other."

Ferendija looked to Lindley for understanding and saw him as amused as the damned Thomson. "Avoiding? Why?"

Angus laughed. Lindley suggested, "After several thousand years they're fed to the teeth of each other. One thing they don't give a damn about is who is what or where."

"How should we? What interest remains in someone I've known for thirty lifetimes? Loose groups keep in touch because matters affecting us all have to be passed on, but it's like those cell organizations where one member only knows the identity of just one member of another cell for essential contact. There may be scores of cells, even hundreds, but I doubt that. If they don't want to be found they'll take some winkling out. Years! But you'll have to do it, won't you?"

The mockery ground at Ferendija's self esteem; he said harshly, "We can't give years to it."

"That you can't. And there's worse to come. What of all those not old enough yet to have realized their destiny? It's a natural mutation—Randal Cooke says a group of mutations —rare but inevitable. The larger the world's population the more genetic variation there is in each breeding cycle—and it was well over six billions when the Collapse came. Many will be just beginning to realize something is not normal with them."

Ferendija watched the limits of the problem expand wildly, and Lindley pushed them a little further: "They can't even recognize each other as kin. If The Company couldn't identify Will as a long-liver, how will we find them?"

Ferendija stared at him with black hatred.

Angus explained, "We can only locate newcomers by becoming aware of their cover-up tactics and then checking on them for a generation or so. We miss some for centuries. Nobody knows where or how many."

"But you have a central group, The Company."

"A term of convenience. Any group with a project calls itself The Company until the job is finished."

Ferendija protested, with a sense of outrage, "You slip under every rationalization!"

"Our rationality isn't yours."

"I realize it." He asked bitterly, "If I ask you about The Company and Santley, will I understand the answer?"

"Oh, yes—and it can do no harm now." But it wasn't so simple; he had to consider how to present it. "We are a menace to short-lived men and they to us. In early years some of us capitalized their talents as shamans, oracles, what you will, but they only raised the enmity of what you might call the human professionals; they were too good, and none of us can regrow after having his brains splashed on a rock or being eaten by some believer in transfer magic. In time we realized that our first duty to ourselves was to keep out of sight. But the computer age has pinned the world down in data banks; changing names and locations won't hide us much longer; we'll be picked up as census anomalies."

They might bluff individual banks, Ferendija knew, but not the planetary network. *Good.*

"Then the rise of molecular biology was a catastrophe. With gene manipulation practicable, we knew that the first one of us isolated by the computers would be handed to the geneticists —and man's next big survival test would begin." He added, almost idly, "We've never given human beings credit for sense or restraint before temptation, and we aren't wrong, are we, now?"

The Commissioner thought of Beckett and writhed.

"A dissident faction formed, arguing that the human psyche *could* withstand the shock of extended life, that we would in any case be unmasked soon and should put ourselves under the protection of a responsible power. The rest of us didn't believe a responsible power existed; any power of that day would have turned us into laboratory rats, with greed for life calling the hypodermic shots. The Disses wouldn't act without general agreement; even in feud we observed that much discipline, and there the matter might have rested if we hadn't got a report that someone in Australia had talked to a geneticist. A specific man, Will Santley, was pinpointed and I was sent out to bring him to Glasgow; it had to be Glasgow because he was amnesiac and our only brain specialist, Randal Cooke, was with the Glasgow Royal Infirmary and refused to leave his post."

"Discipline, you said!" Ferendija was contemptuous. "Don't your individuals have a sense of responsibility to their kind?"

"That? Yes, when it's needed, but there was no need to push Randal. Our perspectives are millennial; we knew that if the Australians had knowledge, whoever held it would sit on it until he had the whole game tied up—who wouldn't?—so a year for preparing and moving Will was neither here nor there. Then, as it turned out, I came out here and collected Will just in time to see the world structure of unbalanced power and wrecked ecology go down in ruin almost overnight. Any urgency was out of our hands for ever. It's your urgency now, to protect your world against the effects of knowledge of our existence. It could be the one action justifying Security's existence before everyone finally gets sick of you. As part of it I want my people protected."

196

The demand, so casually thrown in, poised Ferendija between rage and despair; he was in no position to commit the world to promises. Seeing another aspect of future fearsomeness, he asked with real dread, "Do you breed true?"

"True to what? We're various. Randal says each of us is unique, having only a few factors in common. More troubles, eh, Commissioner?" He let the question hang in an atmosphere heavy with resentments before he pointed the obvious. "If we bred true we'd have overrun the planet before your history got a toehold. We don't breed at all. Our chromosomes don't take with normal humans, which is expectable, and it seems our individual variations prevent cross-fertilization of our own kind. That's why Randal thinks we're a whole slew of kinds pivoting on the non-ageing factor."

If Ferendija was relieved, Angus still had no joy for him. "It won't help. Gangoil will bypass the laws of heredity and biological brilliance will leave you in a deeper hole than ever." He looked to Lindley. "So David was not Will's son."

Lindley considered chance in an infinite spacetime and was not convinced; but he held his peace.

Ferendija remarked that the fact rendered Jeanie's treatment of Donald the more objectionable.

Angus made an immemorial gesture. "It's all in the point of view, and fornication is one of the few enduring pleasures. The only unusual thing is the time she'll hang on to one that suits her. But it isn't our couplings you have to worry over because Nature's on your side—so far. Only so far. Beware the magicians of Gangoil!"

The jeer penetrated Ferendija's frustration. *Gangoil must be quietly immobilized.*

The thought brought decision. He fumbled at the desk console. The blind vanished; sunlight poured in.

He said, with choking malice, "Leave me alone!" and forgot them. As they left he was already staring into the light, seeing that quarantining of Gangoil might be linked with other actions . . . a plan of campaign began to form.

The simple answer is that they can be killed . . . "brains splashed on a rock" or fire, acid, beheading . . . irreversible deaths. Gangoil can learn to identify them at birth by DNA sequences as damning as fingerprints . . . each generation of men to seek out and destroy an endless enemy . . .

Contemplating an eternity of protective murder, his mind revolted. His own generation had committed the demi-genocide, the killing of the old and the useless in the famine years of the new century, that the new young might live to rebuild the world—and had not recovered from the memory. They had preserved the race but in their deep hearts had never found forgiveness. The second generation was guiltless but tainted, "born in sin" as the Cultists had it, giving meaning to that ancient triviality.

There must be means other than murder.

If there were they evaded him, but he did not want to face the trauma of another legacy of bloodletting. His own generation knew too much about blood-guilt.

For the present, he must see to it that Parker's interference did not end in public revelation and disaster.

And here a mercenary soldier might earn his professional fee! Spiteful chauvinism added uncontrollably, *And die in earning it. "Who lives by the sword",* as the Cultists have it . . . *Lindley, too . . . the Gone Timers could pay their debt to the present.*

The plan was there, full-blown. It remained only to act before he allowed himself to be sickened by the consciousness of his own meanness of spirit.

He sent for Sanders.

"I'm told the Circle of Acolytes are a violent lot."

Sanders answered cautiously, "They fight among themselves, mostly over questions of dogma and interpretation." He had never been out of Australia and was unsure of European attitudes to physical conflict; he thought they considered it undignified, which was for adults true enough, but in Australia much allowance was made for youth into the early twenties. He thought best to add, "They're a high-spirited bunch."

"Don't they clash with non-Cultists?"

"Why should they? The non-Cs aren't interested in them."

"So they have no natural enemies? Not even among people who disapprove of their present anti-Security campaign?"

"Older folk disapprove but they can't interfere without

breaking Ethic. Youngsters are inclined to side with the Acolytes because they're new and active."

"They're Parker's weapon. I want them silenced."

Sanders said uneasily, "They stay within legal right."

"I want them silenced." To Sanders's blankness he added, "Violence may be used. Not, of course, by Security."

"A street confrontation of some kind?" That was an unrelishable crudity. "But with whom?"

"You should know the possibilities of your Town."

Sanders offered a suggestion so outrageous that, happily, Ferendija would see the project as impossible, and drop it. "The junior street gangs might do it, for kicks."

Ferendija permitted himself to be shocked. "Juniors? I wouldn't care to be held responsible for that." Then he said, meditatively, "Still, it would be a salutory experience for the Acolytes." His still gaze pierced the Tech's shocked disbelief.

Sanders backtracked. "It's not possible. It would cause ethical outrage. There would be questions in Parliament."

"There surely would—if Security were seen to have had a hand in it. Perhaps you can think of something else?"

Their glances held. Sanders recognized his unspoken orders and knew they never would be spoken; he was alone with the operation, trapped by his own tongue. His understanding of high policy and World Councillors came of age in the space between Ferendija's last word and his next.

"When time and place are set, let me know. Then we'll plan what is to happen under cover of uproar. I intend to flush Controller Parker from his unholy burrow."

Sanders heard him out with impassive and helpless anger.

The Commissioner gave orders now, safe and uncontroversial orders. "For that I'll need Thomson. He can't stay hidden with Lindley for ever, so hire him as a civilian aide, personal to myself. Use the persona name—Giles Campbell—and face, of course, and let him be seen familiarly round the barracks."

"He'll need biographical background and some explanation of his employment."

"Why, then, provide them!"

He had sympathy for the departing Sanders, learning political action from a man he would never trust again. He did not wish to know how Sanders would stir the kids into action without betraying them all, but it would be done and his conscience would hold him to ransom for it. But the stakes were immense.

14

Ferendija himself supervised Alice White's session with the recordings and she thought he seemed satisfied with her responses. The translator filament was a seamy exposition of the Gone Time intrigues she had been reared to despise and fear, but Beckett's murder was more terrible because it had happened in her time, to a man she had known, at this same desk from which she heard Angus in cool reproof as he cut a throat: *"Even for my kind there can be unexpected endings."*

She was chilled again by Ferendija's flat summation: "There's no point in querying that little man's motives; Beckett had become a complication best removed."

She wanted to cry out, "It isn't a game!" but saw with cold fright that only a gamesman's attitudes could absorb and withstand such events. When he asked, "And what would *you* give for an extra thousand years?" she shuddered and could not answer. His chuckle told her that was enough.

He seemed satisfied that she understood the necessity of silence. She was not so shocked as not to realize, when he told her she was to educate Donald in this century's style and conventions, that the work was designed to confine her contacts to the small group of the aware while providing company for the pressure of an intolerable secret.

Less satisfactorily, she must make the best of Donald. In the Police Complex, swaggering in his cuts and bruises and speaking a purring brogue, he had struck at her sexual response; she had been instantly attracted, animal to animal, and knew why the infamous Jeanie had tied him to her.

But that he was a Gone Timer could not be forgotten. In the pitiless squalor of his provenance the climate of the time could only reject him.

She had forgotten such provenance once, just once, with Jim Lindley, under circumstances of strain and fear she would not willingly recall and the inhibition was now more powerful because of it. It could never happen again.

Awareness of this new male might nag below the surface of rejection, but one was aware of many men without racing into copulation at the flick of an arousal. She could bear with Scottish Donald—as an assignment.

But as an assignment he infuriated her in his refusal to be impressed by her pride of culture. He was insensitive, obtuse, the quintessential Gone Timer.

In cold contemplation of the rubble at the heart of Old Melbourne he said, "At least in Australia the people didna dee in heaps," and she thought *Damn his meaningless Glasgow*. Until she realized that death from the night sky was not yet a week in his past, that he *knew* what she had only at second hand. Catching herself in error did not improve her tolerance.

Of the cathedral he confided that he was not worshipfully inclined after a too-strict presbyterian upbringing (*whatever that meant*), and that if he had heard aright they had preserved religion for all the wrong reasons.

She guided him sulkily down the hillside lawns to the main streets of the Town, supposing drearily that a man of the great canyon-cities could be only bored by these quiet thoroughfares; but here he was observant and curious. (Of course, he had been some kind of soldier—a dirty word in post-Collapse vocabulary —and she knew vaguely that such persons had been trained to alert observation, to make themselves more disgustingly dangerous.)

But she chafed at his inability to fathom the obvious principles of daily dress, where uniforms—such as overalls or slacks-and-shirt—were worn for productive service ("What you called 'working hours', as if they were unpleasant") and that leisure clothes were *decorative*, designed to the wearer's pleasure, often designed *by* the wearer, with nobody wanting to copy another . . . Photographs in historical files showed Gone Time streets whose dense crowds were monotonously similar, as though they wore service dress the whole time—

"Ay, by day. But after dark the lads an' lassies were like hummin' birds."

"Why after dark?" she wanted to know, and listened while he explained an incomprehensible system whereby work was done mostly in daylight hours on a basis of so many hours a week under rigidly controlled conditions. When she pointed out to him the sensible conception of industrial labour being performed at the most *useful* time under optimum *personal* conditions, he argued that this could only lead to underpriced labour or overpriced products. They abandoned the subject in mutual incomprehension.

She became city-proud when he acclaimed the lawns and gardens at the corners of every city block and the avenues of trees, until he remarked that the flocks of bicycles made the Town look like a Glasgow suburb in the fuelless days just before the Collapse. When she told him that all transport was controlled by Government agencies he noted the fact, darkly, as essential to the police state.

So he had to explain "police state" and drew an outburst against his comparison of a sane and simple system with his dead culture of secret surveillance. To which he remarked that what he had already seen left him feeling "you're still no' far ahead o' the savages when the skin's peeled back."

Unable to allow herself tears of rage in uniform on a public street, she did the next worst thing and treated passers by to the sight of a Security Specialist slapping the face of a uniformed Tech who unhesitatingly slapped back and growled, "Behave yoursel the noo!"

Close by, somebody laughed venomously. "The nursemaids tell us how to behave, but who tells them?"

He did not catch the point of that but Alice said quickly, "Away from here! Across the road!"

She was too late. The mocker called, "How secure is Security? The *people* can topple it."

Donald halted, startled by sound which seemed to originate at his ear, yet with nobody close. Alice, recognizing a sound screen, which might be anywhere in its semi-invisibility, urged, "Please! Before they collect a crowd."

He started after her, bewildered, and automatically took her arm to assist her across the traffic lanes. She shook free, furiously, nerves and urgency recognizing only the Gone Time barbarian, and hissed at him to stop pawing her in the street.

He did not know that a minor courtesy had vanished from the code and she had never heard of it.

He muttered savagely, "You'll no' be thinkin' I'm tryin' to court such a ragin' bitch!" (But the idea had not been far back in his mind.)

White-faced and scrabbling for self-control she gasped, "In here," and darted into a café.

At a side table she tapped distractedly at Coffee, Milk and Sugar buttons. Donald said nothing at all and she was too upset for speech, but when the coffee decanted from a spout that clicked fussy measurements (he stared at it as an offence to decent living) she snapped a wall switch and the small sounds of the café melted indistinguishably into a low crackle.

His refusal to show surprise or ask a question forced her to explain. "A privacy scrambler. Only someone actually at the table can hear what we say. So I can say—" and it bid fair to choke her "—I beg your pardon."

She thought she had done it pretty well until he said, "If you think I'll do the same, I willna. I'll no' hae my face slapped in the street by any woman thinkin' her sex will save her the return."

She asked helplessly. "What has sex to do with it?" and had to wait while he considered changed relationships between the sexes and finally grumbled that if she did it with her eyes open, no apology was required of him.

"Of course there isn't. I was foolish, but you were so damned rude. We are not savages and you—" She stopped on the edge of worse.

He finished for her, "An' I am no' the man to tell you beautiful folk you're no' really so bluidy wonderfu'."

She sipped coffee, searching for a reply that was neither petty nor downright mean. "You don't have to be so contemptuous. This is a young world and we started with nothing."

"You started wi' all history behind you an' the signs are that you learned no' a damned thing frae it."

She said tiredly, "Oh, go to hell."

A young man hovering by the table leaned insolently into

the privacy zone to ask, "May I share?" and kissed Alice lightly on the cheek. "How's life, Alice lovey?"

He was in his twenties, dressed in brilliant green shorts with a red sash. For all Donald could tell it might be a work uniform, though he thought not. One thing he was sure of was that the light impudence was skin deep; it might be second nature but it was not the man.

Alice shook her head. "It's not the time for you to be with us, Joe."

He winked at Donald and said, "But I'm sure it *is*. Not for your sweet sake, Alice-me-love; you can take care of yourself in this rat's nest but Mr Baird might be tempted into all too successful action against those Acolyte boyos outside. Eh, Mr Revenant?"

"Maybe, but I dinna ken your name or face."

" 'Dinna ken'! Fantastic! But I know your name and face and so does all Melbourne Town after this morning's newscast. Instant fame!"

"I've no' been photographed or interviewed."

"Oh, you have, you have!"

"Is the man daft, Miss White?"

"No. He's a very senior cryogenics engineer in Data Storage. He paid for his degree studies by community service as a dining-room attendant at the Security barracks, so he knows the Techs, has a political background and probably has information he has no right to." She added unwillingly, "Perhaps we ought to listen."

Donald surveyed him coolly. "If you're a freend, I can use yin. Sit doon an' tell me aboot the newscast."

"Floating lenses and lip-read lasers on remote control. They picked you up the moment you left the barracks. You were in the flash items before you hit midtown."

"But why?"

"You're news, man! Security snatches mysterious Scot from Gangoil! Why, but why? Why does this revenant interest International Security?"

"Only Security could ha' told the story."

Joe leaned close. "My conclusion, too! And why? To make you known: to cause questions to be asked; to attract attention." A firmer nature peered briefly from his eyes. "You're bait."

"I ken that."

Joe sat back, puzzled. "The hell you do!"

Donald patted his uniform lapels. "This protects me."

Joe stiffened. "Put not your trust in princes, Donald Baird."

"You ken the Book? You're Cultist?"

Joe shuddered. "Their God forbid! The more literate bits get around. I'm telling you not to trust Security. I worked for them and I know them. And Alice knows them. Eh, love?"

She was mutely uncomfortable.

"Then is Security no' the conscience o' the world, above reproach?"

"Of *this* world, perhaps; but you don't belong to this world."

"Meanin'?"

"That to Security—and to most of the planet—twentieth-century people are a madness that can only cause disaster where they reappear. You're human, which entitles you to stay alive if you can, but not Security, or the whole world, by and large, will give more than a sigh of relief if you drop dead."

Donald stirred his coffee until long after the sugar was dissolved, ignoring the impertinence of Joe's eyes assessing his humiliation. Finally he dropped the spoon and faced Alice.

"I was wrang, Miss White. I apologize for touchin' your airm. The pig begs pardon o' his swineherd."

She shrank. "That's cruel!"

Joe refused comfort. "Whose was the first cruelty, lovey? Not the pig's, I'll bet. Now he *knows* what world he's in and what his chances are as bait in Security's fishbowl."

She cried out, close to tears, "What can I do? He can't understand how we're taught, how we feel. He *can't*."

"Quite so, but a wise old paranoid once told me that shame for your own feelings is the first crack in conditioning."

Donald came belatedly to see that her prejudice had been the target and he only the bludgeon callously used. It was a comfortless tactic but probably effective in a jackhammer fashion.

Joe's gambit was not completed. "Donald, what goes for the first generation and for indoctrinated service-folk doesn't necessarily hold for the younger brackets. You may find friends at need." He pressed the coffee buttons. "I, for instance, regard Jim Lindley as a friend." The spout clicked and measured and presented a cup. "Grey-guts Parker and the Cultist snivellers would grind you to a pulp to feed their ideas, but we non-Cultists don't like what those Acolyte boyos are up to in the streets today. So you will find friends—as soon as I have drunk my coffee and we move outside."

An alerted Alice read deeper into his meaning than Donald. "I'll call HQ." A tiny microphone spike emerged from a pocket-slit over her breast, but before she could speak Joe's finger made a bar across her lips.

"No, lovey. Take a lesson from your Scottish friend. Not even a surprised eyebrow from him. This move has to go through, brawl and all."

She was suspicious. "You've been co-opted?"

"Let's say there's an element of orchestration."

"I don't like it; I saw street brawls during the *Columbus* riots."

Donald read her as unafraid but filled with distaste. For overt violence? He could not plumb the *mores* of this age. He understood Joe, however, alive with politics below his lightness, and asked at a venture, "Hae you an instruction for me?"

Joe was delighted. "He's quick, Allie! Root out all that indoctrination and grab this one, girl! He's class." She burned with embarrassment but he was intent on Donald. "The message is: Keep your back to a shop doorway for a bolthole and wait for a small man with a gift for you."

Donald inclined his head, acknowledging.

"You know what it means, Donald boyo? I don't." He patted with a friendly hand, coaxing. "Come on; fair exchange! I've spent the morning rounding up boyos who can fight; I should be told something. No?" He withdrew his hand. "So be it—blind service to a blind ideal."

"If you live lang enough to ken what this is a' about—you'll wish you hadna." He asked directly, "Am I to be taken?"

"Double-crossed and fed to Parker? I doubt it but I don't know. The Police will surely interfere and they won't look on you with love; the story's leaked out of what you did to some of them the other night. May I give advice? The extreme martial arts have become legendary and most of us feel they should stay that way. Don't be more violent than you must."

"Och ay."

The small man must be Angus, possibly more of a physical handful than himself when the going was bad. The gift? He wished he knew, but with Angus present he would feel better able to cope with these parties who picked up sides as though a world crisis could be handled like a neighbourhood football match.

"An' whit aboot the lassie?"

Joe, rising to leave, did not catch his meaning. Alice, quicker to follow now, was touched despite herself. "I'll be safe. You look after yourself."

"A street brawl's no place for you."

Joe understood and was amused. "Chivalry, no less? Is that really twentieth century? You're the ball in this game; they won't touch Alice." He switched off the scrambler. "Well, let's get it over. And please, Donald, don't break any necks in your professional enthusiasm. The revenants can't afford that much unpopularity."

They stepped into the street.

15

It was late morning on an avenue of small shops. Donald had noted the absence of large establishments; there were no department stores, only small-town shops and arcade markets; big stores were of the Gone Time, perhaps, and by definition contemptible. Small was beautiful.

A voice said with spiteful distinctness, directly into his right ear, "Revenant shit!"

He swung about, casting, but no one was near enough to have said it; there were only a dozen people within twenty yards of him. In their faces was recognition (*the damned newscast*) and no sympathy; each had heard as clearly as he—and he was the known target.

In the eyes of the younger ones he saw the watchfulness of the involved. A waiting enemy was within touch of him and the unseen speaker had pinpointed him for the street to home on.

A new voice addressed his other ear. "It's wearing a black-beetle uniform! Our nursemaids have sunk low, brothers!"

"Sound screens at both ends," Joe said. "They've boxed in the block, so it's all going to happen right here."

A girl, sturdy and muscular like the rest of the loved generation but younger than most of them, no more than seventeen, called out, "The beetle's got a friend and it's Cryo Joey! A Gone Time connoisseur! Hobnobbing with the cold-store meat, Joey?"

Joe commented quietly, "That's the Acolytes' prime stirrer. Where she is, the game's on. Watch it, boyo."

She was a type familiar from the Gorbals to the Bowery but better educated. Donald was more interested in some street movements commanding his tactical appreciation. "Whit noo?"

"Hard to say. We don't know what they're after."

The older people, those in their thirties and late twenties, were melting into the shops as if they knew what was to come and wanted no part in it. Yet the numbers in the street did not diminish, merely grew younger with reinforcements from the stores and arcades. The soldier in him approved the way they waited, down the length of the footpath, in groups, at intervals of a chain or so. However he moved he would face a group prepared to take up whatever harassment was planned. Remembering orders, he noted the nearest doorways and then, to test the situation and perhaps force an error, walked up to the stirrer and asked gently, "Whit's your name, lassie?"

"Trouble," she said, with a side glance for applause.

"An' whit's gained by insultin' a stranger?"

"Hygiene. There's revenant shit on our street."

The strategy was plain. He matched it cheerfully. "An' plenty o' upstart young shit to match the auld, eh?"

The watchers moved closer. He saw that the dazzle of clothing styles had a thing in common: each wore a narrow cummerbund with, on the left hip, a white circle with a cross of Saint George. So the Acolytes did not fear identification when they broke the public peace. The loved young, he gathered, could get away with almost anything.

What was to come, came quickly.

The girl spat in his face.

He held his blow as Joe bellowed, "Don't touch her!"

"No fear. She wants it. It means there's polis waitin' nearby."

The girl had not moved; she watched him, head cocked.

He had forgotten Alice, who stepped beside him and slipped a hand under his lapel. Something clicked minutely.

"I've activated your uniform; that makes you a total recording battery. If she throws herself at you and claims you attacked her it won't work, because you are transmitting the pictures to HQ."

She stepped back, move completed. "Trouble" snapped her a glance of fury.

To sharpen her bafflement Donald took a long step towards her, bringing them breast to breast.

Puzzled, she stood her ground, but darted a questing look beyond him. Someone passed a silent message, for she contorted her face in fear, cringed away and raised her arms to ward a blow. His cameras were turned neatly against him. Somewhere a news-lens would be watching . . .

Behind him a voice asked, "Is the Tech molesting you, Miss? I can make an off-duty arrest."

Donald cursed himself for missing the plainclothes gambit while she cried out in fright and appeal, acting it out to the finish.

The plainclothesman, sashed and circled and crossed like the rest, put a hand on Donald's arm. "I must ask you to come with me, sir."

The old formula was a breath of home, but Donald was far from home and did not know what he could safely do.

He was saved the decision. An appalling human racket broke from the twin sound screens, engulfing the area in acoustic bedlam, an audial montage of grunts and yells, of words and curses and the sick sound of beaten flesh.

The Acolytes froze, not understanding. Then they did understand, but too late, and commenced to run towards the ends of the block.

A very young voice, soprano-cracked, screeched out of a screen, "We've got the bastards!"

They'd got the speakers, presumably, for the screens went

dead. "My boyos," Joe said happily. "Your man should be along soon."

What happened left Donald speechless, oblivious of the hand still resting on his sleeve and the patrolman petrified in a shock as great as his own.

Joe's striking force of "boyos" was a flash flood of the Town's younger teenagers, a racing wave of kids between thirteen and fifteen and not all of them boys. And they were armed. They poured down the road and footpaths in two yelling, demonic blocks, one from each end, herding the demoralized Acolytes between them. Their herdsman's goads were bikechains, quarter-staves and belt buckles.

The Acolytes greeted the rush with a horror as inexplicable as the attack itself. They made no attempt to fight back, little to defend themselves; most retreated uncertainly into the shop doorways and presumably to escape by rear exits, as though no alternative was feasible.

The screeching ferocity of the kids covered at first the circumstance that few of the Acolytes were actually struck. While they retreated, weapons whistled round their heads with more menace than danger and only those whom obstinacy or confusion led to hold their ground were seriously struck. And those were beaten with a will. What blood there was flowed freely but in general the kids herded their prey like game beaters, unopposed. They knew what they did, Donald mused; they had been briefed.

Nothing was clarified by Alice's gasp, "No, Joe, no! You shouldn't have done this!"

"Trouble" had stood still, either stupidly determined or incapable of decision, but she grasped what had happened and Donald could not tell whether her rasping, "Holy Yeshua!" was invocation or anathema.

The plainclothesman gave a long sigh and released Donald's arm. The Scot peered at him, "Will you no' take me in, polisman?"

The plainclothesman cursed him and hit out. He was inexpert but fast and the blow connected with the half-healed eye.

Donald staggered, said, "I maun hae somethin' for my pairt in this," and knocked him five yards and unconscious.

During his few seconds of action a new element entered the frenzy. Behind the kids, racing from both ends of the block and hemming them in, came grey-uniformed Police, formidable but caught napping, too late and too few to deal with an already successful riot. And apparently unarmed.

They confined themselves to grabbing the kids and passing them to the rear, roughly but without real violence; they were struck and did not strike back but only isolated and disarmed the yelling brats. Beyond astonishment, Donald thought the Police argued, practically pleaded with the young animals.

Joe had vanished. His area of footpath was cleared now of all but Alice, near to tears with an incomprehensible anger, and "Trouble" muttering a monotonous, "Oh, shit, shit, shit!"

He nudged her. "It's time you ganged hame."

She squealed with a last miserable defiance, "Fuck off!"

"Fuck off yoursel," he told her and tossed her through the nearest doorway. She did not come back.

Fifty yards away, Angus, with the Campbell face, fought through the press of patrolmen and battling larrikins, hitting and elbowing without favour. Behind him Lindley, sour-tempered and a little ludicrous, struggled with an ungainly brown paper parcel.

Donald placed his back to the doorway and said to Alice, "You shouldna stay mair. You could be hairt."

"I can't leave; I'm in uniform."

He marvelled but did not argue, and asked, "Why do the polis no' plaster the wee bastards?"

"Strike them?" She was horrified.

So Gone Time barbarism had betrayed him again. Just the same, "Ay; a few split heids'll stop 'em."

"These are children!"

Lindley had told him that the brats were the sacred cows of the period, the beautiful generation, the heirs of tomorrow. He thought of it while one of them, twenty yards away, opened a patrolman's face with a belt buckle. He said with utter contempt, "You're raisin' bluidy savages."

She blazed at him. "You're stupid and ignorant and primitive! Do you compare these with the filthy muggers and teen killers of your day? Can you measure street scum of the slum-cities against healthy children passing rite of passage?"

The gap between centuries yawned. "A rite, is it? Then some wee brain has plumbed the use o' it."

Angus broke through in a flurry of ungentle chops to Police and brats alike (Alice screamed something horrified and unintelligible) and came running with Lindley stumbling after. He bellowed, "Inside!" and pushed Donald into the shop, a grocery store. 'Straight through!"

Donald held back. "The lass. Alice."

"Forget her. Hurry!"

Lindley panted, "She's safe. Get going, man."

He had a final glimpse of her listening with an incredulous expression to a suddenly materialized Joe. She listened as if his words explained much and she liked none of it.

Because he had no way of knowing right action from wrong he let them urge and shove him while a frantic counterhand bleated for explanation. They raced him through a small dwelling behind the shop, where a woman shrieked and a child burst into tears, into a back lane and through another house and shop into a street a block distant from the dying sound of conflict.

A van waited, a large merchandise transport, enclosed, which moved off as soon as they bundled in at the rear.

Angus was in high spirits, enjoying an escapade. "Off with the uniform. Double quick! You can't wear it for this job. We have to pretend Security isn't in it."

Argument would only delay, and solve nothing; Donald stripped and Lindley's torn-open parcel disgorged shirt and shorts and daywear shoes.

"What noo?"

"This." Angus thrust cool and familiar metal into his hand, and with something like affection he stroked the sonic gun. "Is it fu' charged?"

"Yes, so it's best that you have it. I could make mistakes; no one must be killed or even badly damaged."

"Och ay." He buckled the shoulder holster inside his shirt. "What's the job?"

Lindley said disgustedly, "Brave boys in heroic action. Us!"

Angus bubbled with impudence to come. "This is barbarians' day out. Three-quarters of the police are tied up with those horrible kids of Joe's—"

"You know him? You arranged this?"

Lindley said, "I did. Poor Corey didn't know how to do it and didn't want to know. The Acolytes made their arrangements to trouble you—Joe and I rearranged them. The point is that there is now only a handful of uniformed men in the Complex; the rest are civilian staff in separate areas. We'll never get a better chance."

Angus thumped his ribs. "We're going to pull Will out."

A mercenary's pragmatism: if it has a plus chance of succeeding, try it; if minus, don't. Angus's excitement was not a good omen, a poor approach to an action. Raiding the Complex was an unlikely move but if Angus, who had worked there, thought it practicable, then it might be—high spirits or no. Still, "I dinna like it. How many's a handfu' o' polis?"

"Maybe twenty."

"Too bluidy many."

"Mostly night shifters, asleep."

"Better. An' the rest?"

"Back there battling the brats."

Lindley broke in. "Donald's thinking of our old police forces, thousands strong, but there's little major crime in this society; the psychlinicians see to that. The total force of the Town is less than eighty men and just now heavily committed."

The van stopped and the unseen driver knocked on the partition. "Last stop," Angus said. "We're one block from the Complex; this is the last chance for talk. When you were here the other night, Donald, did you notice the Checkpoint Office?"

"The glass box at the gate? I saw it."

"There will be one man in it. Can you stun him through the glass?"

The question hid complexities Angus could not realize. To save explanation Donald said, "The glass will break."

"No matter."

"An' you must decoy him to the side or he'll be a deid man."

"No deaths! I'll decoy him; he doesn't know this face. That gets us through the gate. Then we go through the dormitory

213

block where we shouldn't meet anyone, then through the recreation centre where there will be three or four for Donald to stun, and down a passage to the infirmary. Will should be there."

"An' if he is no' there?"

"We seize an attendant and shock the information out of him. I'll lead. Donald will stay with me, gun ready. Jim will come behind to help with Will; we don't know his condition." He grinned like a con man. "Easy pickings."

"Ay. Nae mair than forty things can gae wrang."

"You don't know the set-up; I do."

Donald shrugged; Lindley looked patient.

"Leave the van now, Donald, and walk to the Checkpoint Office—about eighty yards. We'll be there first with the van and I'll have the duty man in talk and out of your line of fire. Do your stuff when ready."

"Passers-by?"

"It isn't a commercial street. There won't be more than two or three, and what can they do except vid the Police? Joke! Questions? Then out with you!"

As Donald stepped to the footpath, feeling wickedly unprepared, Angus banged on the cabin wall and the van moved away. There were indeed only three people spread over two blocks. Surrounding the Complex, a low wall was broken only by the Checkpoint Office. He did not hurry but concentrated on a proper setting for removing the glass.

The gun could shatter it with a single burst of high-energy vibration, generating a high-pitched, split-second crack of generalized splintering, followed by the sound of twenty square yards of plate glass hitting concrete. The surge of power might possibly kill the duty man and the noise would be enough to bring personnel running from more directions than he could be sure of dealing with. What he had was a gun, not a magic wand. The alternative was to use a lower energy setting with wider aperture and take more time over it.

The van pulled up and Angus disappeared through the gate. He set the gun and hurried. At the Checkpoint Office he saw that Angus had the patrol man engaged at the inner courtyard window, back to Donald and well to the side. As he aimed the gun from the hip, keeping it concealed, Lindley slipped from the van and watched with irritable interest.

For perhaps twenty seconds nothing happened, then the pane cracked mildly as if a pebble had been tossed against it. The patrolman turned in time to see his office wall collapse in a faint tinkle of flinders and greyish dust. Donald dropped the gun to its lowest setting and knocked him out before he could start across the floor.

Lindley came across the footpath and with a short bray of approval Angus broke into a run. "Come on!"

The few people in the street seemed to have noticed nothing. At more than a short distance there had been nothing to notice.

Two wings, administrative and barracks, confronted each other at the Checkpoint. Angus led to the left, to the dormitory wing, into a long and silent corridor and said quietly, "Leave your boots here; it doesn't matter if we can't pick 'em up again. And pull this over your head." *This* was a fine-mesh, tight hood, transparent. "An old idea, but girls don't wear stockings any longer."

Lindley also produced a hood, and Angus led boldly down the corridor. A snore rasped from behind a door but they saw no one. Angus paused briefly at the door at the far end to whisper, "Rec area next; sure to be someone," and pushed through. Donald raised the gun and followed, nerves taut.

The recreation area was empty.

Angus went warily through all the lounges and games rooms without sighting a patrolman.

He said, "Nobody writing to mother or playing chess or porning over Gone Time comics stolen from Archives? I don't believe it. I almost feel we are expected." The thought did not slow him. "It's too late to go back, and if they know we're in we won't easily get out."

They went swiftly down the long corridor from the recreation area to the infirmary. Not a patrolman showed or sounded. They turned left into a corridor with a glass wall and were looking into the infirmary.

It was a ward of six beds, with not a patient or attendant in sight. Angus indicated a door at the far end of the ward, partly open. "Behind that door is a psychlinic, with an interrogation unit."

As soon as they entered the ward they heard voices. Parker's sounded clearly from the half-open door.

"If we accept Santley's story, there are thousands of those guns in Britain. There will be warehouses with crates of them still in armourer's grease."

A stranger's voice answered in accents weary with repetition, "Highly radioactive guns and grease."

"They can be scoured and neutralized. Their existence in quantity is a standing temptation to any hotheaded administration—think of the New York Soviet, the Kremlin Hegemony."

"They must be destroyed, not neutralized."

"True, but I'll not pretend I wouldn't like to strip and test one."

Donald kicked the door wide and strode in. "This one?"

A portion of his mind registered banks of electronic machinery whose leads converged in anonymous devices ringing a structure like a dental chair, and a white-gowned psychlinician leaning against a bench, but he kept his attention for Parker.

Who said, "That one—if I thought you'd surrender it."

He sat at ease in the interrogation chair, ankles crossed and knife-edge creases disposing the grey slacks just so.

"We're takin' Will oot o' here."

Parker shook his head. "Will is already out of here. I had him moved as soon as I was notified of your plan for—what romantic name would you give it? A commando raid? You may as well take those useless hoods off. Nursery stuff!"

He laughed aloud at the disgust revealed on Donald's face..

From a doorway Lindley said, "The double-cross was always a possibility." He did not seem disturbed. "Thing is, what did Ferendija stand to gain by it?"

Parker asked genially, "Ferendija? Why him?"

Angus pushed forward. "Then who?"

"Specialist White," Parker told them and ignored their dumbfoundedness. His interest was in the Campbell face and his tone of mock reprimand did not hide the fury beneath it. "The hands, Angus! Those corded claws identify you in any mask from clown to mannequin. Doctor Brown, here's Santley's

216

shapechanger that you couldn't believe in." The psychlinician took a pace forward, staring, doubtful. "A creator of legends down the ages, eh, Angus? What name do you wear for the Commissioner? Jones, Robinson? Does it matter while the face behind the mask is Thomson?"

Angus let his Campbell face relax and his own features show briefly and vanish.

The psychlinician muttered, "Holy Yeshua, but I believed it was Santley's delusion."

Parker had not doubted the possibility but the reality outran fantasy. He said, "I trusted you, Angus," in bitterness for the disorder brought to his orderly world.

"You don't know what trust means. Even your God is only Parker with a dictatorship."

"You can't bait me, Angus. You no longer matter; the nature of the operation has changed. Was this idiot raid really designed to recover Santley?" He leaned forward, eyes on the gun. "With that filthy thing in the hand of a trained larrikin it might have succeeded—if, that is, the Scottish larrikin had kept his hands off Specialist White, who took unkindly to being taken for bed meat by a Gone Timer." He flashed cruel sweetness at Lindley. "Once was apparently enough for her."

He lifted himself out of the chair. "But after ten years of Jeanie Deans, what's a minor betrayal, Mr Baird? Did sweet Alice think I would arrest you just to keep you out of mauling distance? Much spite there but no brain. I wouldn't arrest the Commissioner's pawns, though I don't imagine he loves a Gone Timer any more than she does."

He turned his back. "Put the gun away, larrikin. No one in the Complex would dream of preventing you going."

In the extended silence they might have gone, taking humiliation as their reward, but he spoke again with a hot, blistering fury.

"It is the practice to allow the younger teen groups some licence of aggression among their peers before settling to social responsibility. Today that aggression was not dissipated therapeutically against peers but turned deliberately against their elders. The ground has been laid for trauma in the rite of passage. Your work, Lindley?"

None of them spoke. Lindley preserved an expression of contemptuous interest.

"If I find that it was, I promise you the mental reconstruction Commissioner Beckett saved you from."

Lindley's answer, loaded with professional condescension, made Parker's slender frame tighten to the toes.

"You and your psychlinicians know nothing of rites of passage or of children. Melbourne Town's youngsters suffer from a lack of youth. The products of computer psychology can only be computers."

"Get out," Parker said. "Quickly."

16

With the arrival of the Police the riot had petered out (the little thugs knew enough to stop before tolerance evaporated), so she was back well before him.

Because he did not believe Parker or did not want to, because his humiliation was unbearable, because there had been in spite of failures of understanding a pulse of warmth—because, in fact, he was at the damn fool stage of beginning to want her—he went raging through the barracks after her.

He found her in the Law Library.

He stood shouting in the doorway, unintelligible with hurt. "Ah kenned the bitch in ye but Ah didna fear treachery!"

Heads rose from books and notes. Someone ssh'd. A girl asked, "What on earth is he saying? Is that the Scot?"

Alice piled her reference books, straightened her papers and went slowly to him; in her still face he read determination and anger, no shame. He stopped his own white-knuckled shaking because he must school himself or stand as the gutter-bred boor she thought him.

"Why? Why did you do it?"

She said, "Let us at least get out of the library," and before her coldness he retreated into the corridor. She had understood only "bitch" and "treachery", which were enough. She tried, but failed to see her action through his eyes.

He repeated, "Why? Did I offend so greatly?"

218

It seemed he thought, ridiculously, that their disagreements had swayed her actions. Too irritated to argue, she said, "I followed orders."

For any but a Gone Timer that would have ended misunderstanding, but he spat at her, "Whose orders?"

She did not have to answer, but his hurt was abominably plain and her ill-temper gave way before it. "The Commissioner's."

To her that said everything; to this unreachable man it said nothing. "*He* told you to betray us? To Parker?"

"That was plain. You *must* see you couldn't be told; you might not have acted your parts properly."

"An' you didna protest?"

"Against an order?" Surely an ex-soldier knew the meaning of unquestioning obedience.

It seemed not. "The damned Parker could ha' killed us a'—an' been in his right doin' it!"

She had known it and been deeply troubled by her duty, had suffered the agony of the dilemma-caught while waiting on news of their safety, though Ferendija had pooh-poohed danger. Now she said nothing. He searched her face and she gazed back at him, thinking in her rightness that he understood.

At last he said, "The great man promised a protection he didna mean to honour. He threw us to the grey dog."

"He said it was—a calculated chance."

"Did he say it didna matter if the calculatin' was wrang?"

She did not know, because her instruction had been relayed through Joe as the Gone Timers fled through the shop; it was Joe who had reasoned with her and been unsuccessful as a comforter because his own doubts shouted below his soothing. She could only retreat on a most brittle logic.

"A soldier knows any plan involves risk."

His obduracy was unending. "Our soldiers had leaders wi' hairts, no' bluidy computers!" He said contemptuously, "But you're a chiel o' your age, comprehendin' nothing beyond your ain babysuck lairnin'. Men may be taken an' slaughtered but the virtuous maiden needna greet over that. She's doin' her job!"

The unfairness broke her. She shrieked, "What would you have me do? Betray Security?"

She shocked herself with her own noise and to her surprise it brought him up short. He thought it over before he said, "Ay, given your trainin' an' your beliefs you could ha' done no other." His face changed. "An' there was another reason you could ha' seen us deid withoot a qualm. We—Angus an' Doctor Lindley an' mysel—are no' people. Especially me, that laid a haund frae the Gone Time on your pure indoctrinated elbow in the public street."

She retreated from the feelings that made his glare hideous and had no moment to identify pain, rage, shame and desolation because she turned and ran and did not stop until the door was locked and she shivering on her bed.

Lindley told him: "When *Columbus* came home this world did try to treat us as human beings, and all it got for its pains was trouble. There's nothing for us here now except to be occasionally used—used up. Like all people that have devoted themselves to a one-track ideal, these daren't stop to think that all their striving may be only another mistake."

"So here's you an' me an' a world o' folk wishin' us elsewhere. We don't count for much wi' Angus, either; to him we just live a day or twa an' gang, forgotten."

"I've become used to my position, in a grey fashion. Perhaps you will. What Angus thinks I can't guess. There's a schizoid nature at work there."

Ferendija called them to the private office and ignored their glumness. Alice's mute withdrawal and Sanders's careful blankness avoided the Gone Timers' eyes. Sanders, Donald thought, would be capable of shame. Lindley attempted indifference. Only Angus smiled back at Ferendija as if he knew the real game was still to be played.

The Commissioner was smug. "A success. There were minor casualties among Acolytes and patrolmen, which don't grieve me. A fourteen-year-old was beaten by an Acolyte, who will be dealt with by the proper authorities, but Parker's men behaved impeccably. A considerable success."

Donald asked, "What's failure? Will's still lost to us."

"The purpose of the operation was to discover whether and how he would become further lost."

Lindley murmured, "The double-double-cross."

In the end Ferendija had to explain it to them. "We did not know Parker's aims and motives. He stole our Gone Timers apparently in a fit of pique and only then discovered the value of his loot; he would have had no trouble draining Santley of information in a few hours, including the speculations about Angus. His withholding of Santley from Specialist White proved nothing; only a man with cold tea in his veins would have failed to follow the clues for the sheer wonder of them. Question: Did he react only with wonder, or did he plan dangerously? It was necessary to force him to a revealing action.

"Security could not move openly; confrontation could end only in public revelation—not to be thought of—but a raid concealed from public view would surely force his hand. Not a successful raid, just a dramatic threat of one to make him jump. He jumped. The moment Specialist White called him with her tale of emotional righteousness—which was as soon as you quitted the street riot—he showed himself fully prepared against a Security move. We saw Santley removed by flyer from the Complex roof before you nullified the Checkpoint; by the time you reached Parker he had clean hands and control of the situation.

"But—he had had a choice and made it. Declared himself. Declared that he knows the stakes and is prepared to play for them and that he thinks he has a chance of winning—against Security."

Angus asked at once, "Where's Will? Gangoil?"

"The obvious guess, but no. Some smart DNA-mapping would soon begin milking the prize—so Gangoil is closed to Parker, to everyone but Security. I talked with World Council as soon as I understood the situation and the PM has been informed that Gangoil is a Ward-of-Council, on the ground that an investigation bearing on world stability is to take place there—a genetic check on the mutations reported by Tech Sanders."

Angus snapped at him, "So now the PM knows!"

"Only that mutations exist. That's all he will know. Parker doesn't want you public knowledge any more than I do."

"And where's Will?"

"I don't know or care. Where Parker has him doesn't matter. What does matter is that in the last hour Parker has notified the PM that he will be taking his accrued recreational leave—five or six weeks, it seems—and taking it immediately."

Ferendija appeared pleased with his news and Donald thought Angus was about to cheer. Angus said, "The hell he has!"

"As you say. But where will he take his vacation? Any suggestion, Mr Thomson?"

"Scotland."

"My thought. From your knowledge of his organization, is the trip practicable?"

"*If* he can get the PM's approval for an orbiter or even a medium flyer—not too difficult—and *if* he can get anti-radiation gear—he can write requisitions for that, which will be unaccountably delayed between collection and auditing—then he'll be hell-bent for Glasgow for the lick of his holy life."

"To—how would you put it? Corner the mutant market?"

"It's the sanest move. He doesn't know we're spread round the world because Will doesn't know it. He'll think Glasgow the centre for the whole pack. Do we go after him?"

"We?" He let the question lie, to say, "He's not gone yet. No move is possible until we're sure what he'll do."

Angus said, "Bet on it!" and turned to Donald. "It won't be much of a homecoming, in a radiation suit."

Ferendija shook his head. "Assuming Glasgow is the target, no suits."

"What, then? A quick snatch and home for treatment before the symptoms grow serious?"

"No. There is something which Parker may or may not know. After the Collapse, investigators of the dusted areas reported them as uninhabitable for a century. Well, it was a time of great disruption and nobody had expertise to waste on assessment of garbage; the loose phrase, 'uninhabitable for a century', gained currency as truth because no one cared enough or had reason to challenge it. Aside from residual radiation, Britain is almost ready for rehabilitation, which Security has known for some time. It was not considered information of importance to a world which has plenty of living space, nor was it concealed; it appeared in some minor dispatch contexts for those who read with their brains open. Consensus is that radiation creams and injection of chelating agents will give enough protection. Will Parker know this, Mr Thomson?"

Angus, he thought, was unaccountably pleased.

The small man said, "Probably not, because I didn't know it. It was my job to keep him abreast of useful non-Service information, but nobody can keep up with all the junk on the chatter terminals."

"Quite so. And what's a dead Scotland to anybody?"

Angus said, in a sudden laughing assumption of a brogue as fine as Donald's, "Ah'm Campbell an' Ah'm Thomson an' Ah say Scotland's alive an' bonny while Donald Baird survives!"

Ferendija looked so closely at him that Angus feared he had allowed exuberance to overplay his hand. But perhaps the Commissioner thought he joked. He said only, "We can be spared the national rejoicing. That will be all for the moment."

Lindley stirred. "Not quite all. Parker thinks me responsible for the use of the young-teens, threatens me with psychological 'rehabilitation' if he can prove it—and I have no black uniform to protect me. What is my position?"

Lindley was afraid of Parker, with reason, and he feared the pragmatism of the dutybound Ferendija, but he spoke with a thin edge of contempt.

If there was guilt in the air, it touched Sanders rather than the Commissioner. The Tech said uneasily, "It was my idea, though I didn't expect it to be acted upon. If I'd thought twice I'd never have suggested it." Ferendija's glance of disgust steadied him. "Parker will have to be told."

"No!" A furious Ferendija turned from him to Lindley. "Why does he blame you?"

"He probably thinks social opportunism smells of the Gone Time touch. In my day we blamed communists and terrorists when we wanted a scapegoat; now you have Lindley."

Satire was wasted. Ferendija said slowly, "Let Parker think as he pleases, but there must be no *public* proof of Security involvement."

"And me?"

"Oh, we'll find some way to look after you."

Lindley sneered openly.

Donald said, "Twa days since, you promised me protection. Where was your protection in the Complex? What would it ha' signified if Parker had arranged a misfortune that saw the three o' us deid?"

Ferendija stood, dismissing them. "Nothing, Mr Baird. Nothing at all."

Angus had said that a metabolism geared to survival needs little doctoring; he might have added that it needs little psychiatric care. Survival cannot permit really crippling mental upheavals.

But even inbuilt survival traits have their operative limits. He had saved himself endless explanation by letting Lindley presume an amnesic episode, an erasure of the causes of breakdown, but he knew with sickening minuteness of detail what the Campbells meant to him, and General Murray, and Derby ... and Prince Charles Edward Louis Philip Casimir, long-legged in Stuart tartan ... and Scotland generally, what remained of it ... And that what remained of it was intensely concentrated in Donald Baird.

He could contemplate these things now with a weary gnawing of assimilated guilt. Battened-down memory had exploded in psychological discharge, but that was done with—for the moment. Though the facts remained, the immense repressions built up since Culloden and the Great Glen and the terrible Clearances had again plastered over the haunted basement of his mind. Guilt expressed itself now in a sense of driven obligation, to Donald. (And he knew himself well enough to admit that part of his new devotion revolved around playing the game for its own involuted sake.)

In Glasgow he had rejected The Company's reinforcement of forgetfulness and would reject it again. It was time to attempt ephemeral humanity's way of paying intolerable debts: expiation.

He needed, first, a legal mind to validate his conclusions concerning Donald. In the tight circle of secrecy he could turn only to Alice White . . . whose allegiance was to Security and whose indoctrination was formidable.

She could be managed, he decided. His psychology was empiric but soundly based in the vast stocks of data accumulated since Akhnaton and the misty millennia before him; she could be managed.

So he stopped her in the corridor as they dispersed from the private office. "I must talk to you, alone."

She had had little contact with him, nor wanted it. Strangeness lurking under a familiar form stoked distrust, and she faced him coldly. "Why?"

"To consider the payment of debts."

It was a shrewd gambit and he saw that she suffered. "I'm not to be taken again through stupid misunderstandings of treacheries and decencies."

"Treachery? Decency? Ferendija's methods leave a bad taste but they get results. I resent being duped but bow to necessity. So does Donald; his hurt is elsewhere."

"So?" Basic indifference is not easily assumed and she was no actress.

"For the payment of debts—yours and mine also—I need legal information."

She said sharply, "I acknowledge no debts. For yours, use the Law Library."

"I need *expert* information. Interpretation."

"Of what?"

"The Ruined Regions legislation."

International law; her area of expertise. Interesting. Probing, she jibed, "To safeguard your holdings in Scotland?"

He accepted the mockery and used it. "Just that."

She was intrigued; his need might uncover something of his strange and ancient soul. "Very well; come to the library."

"No. To the roof."

She was at once suspicious. "Why?"

"Because on the roof are no vidcoms with bugs incorporated in their shells and no building is high enough to overlook it with laser mikes."

She hesitated, but he had banked on curiosity for a hook to

draw her to the escalators. And she would tell herself it was her duty to satisfy curiosity where suspicion warned.

On the roof, in cool twilight, he asked, "Are you recording?" and she turned her lapel, showing the activating thumbslide in open position. "Thank you. This must be confidential."

She said at once, "I have an oath to Security."

"And an obligation to Donald Baird; it's his fate we have to settle."

The name cut away self-possession. "I owe him nothing! I am not interested! He is destestable—coarse and contemptuous and degraded!"

Her angry shouting surprised herself and him.

"Neither coarse nor degraded, Miss White. As for contempt, the signs are that he likes you very well."

"Likes!" A large and spiteful and petty part of her resentment slipped out before she could guard her tongue. "He called me 'sonsy'!"

He bit back laughter. So *that* was whence the bitching originated. "It was hardly a crime."

Seeing he thought her childish, she covered shame with fury. "It isn't in the dictionaries, but I traced it through the literary glossaries. It's guttermouth dialect! It means 'fat'!" She glared, daring his comment. "I am not fat!"

Hard put to it for control, he said seriously, "It can also mean generously built or pleasantly plump. It can be used with appreciation; not every man favours a beanpole in his bed. He's no vulgarian, whatever your opinion; I imagine he smiled when he said it."

"Who cares? There's a time and place for such things."

He wondered what the time and place had been. "It was a compliment."

She was silent.

"A compliment from a Gone Timer! Is that it?" He had her; the muscular stillness, her very silence betrayed her. "A tomcat mewed at a Persian pure? Do you imagine men weren't male last century, or that Gone Time couplings were inevitably degrading? That yesterday's scullion has no right to desire today's kitchen wench?"

"You make a fool of me."

"Your training does." He changed tack quickly, while she wavered. "Ferendija won't protect him, you know. He's of the old school who class the Gone Time with vermin and garbage. He'll let him be killed."

She said strongly, "He wouldn't do that." But she said it strongly to cover her doubt.

"His conditioning will do it for him. Donald will be used and put aside like a diseased animal. Lindley too, with no Beckett to protect him. In your heart you know it. What has Donald done wrong, except be born out of time? Or is he to be punished for paying a compliment to a heartless bitch?"

It was either too much or just enough.

She leaned on the parapet and refused to look at him.

When finally she asked, "What do you want to know?" he reflected on the ease with which these children of indoctrination were subverted, confused and tricked. There was much to be said for experience against a blind IQ.

17

The movement of a major transport vehicle, its records available to any curious terminal explorer, was unconcealable. Ferendija knew within minutes when Parker got his intercontinental flyer. Parker was a man of concentrated energy, not to be underestimated; it had taken him just three days after the backhanded raid to beg his flyer, assemble his team and vanish on his accumulated leave.

How he had managed it Ferendija did not care. His business was with Parker and if the PM were involved to the neck and higher, he could wait his turn.

He could not discover whether or not Parker had taken Santley with him, but thought it would have been strange if he had not—if only as bait to be thrown to The Company.

He did know that a group of Acolytes had gone with him— healthy young thugs devoted to whatever God Parker promised them—when he "vanished" across the Pacific, an unexpected direction in a time when transoceanic flights were rare because rarely programmed. Vidcom contacts were worldwide and it was not yet an age of tourism.

Perhaps he thought that avoidance of the land-hopping route to Europe, through Malaysia, India and Turkey, would divert attention from his true destination, but nothing diverted the attention of a forewarned Security satellite primed to track him from lift-off to landing.

Angus remarked that they could provide him with a welcoming committee; an orbiter could outstrip him easily.

"And do what? We will leave tonight and be there a few hours after him. I would prefer that he find your Company for us."

"So that you can take him as a plotter red-handed? Drama for the newscasts!"

Ferendija said reasonably, "If he attempts some sort of coup we will have a foolproof case."

"First he has to find them. Do you realize how big Glasgow is? Have you ever walked in one of the old cities?"

"Life leaves traces and Parker's no simpleton. He hasn't flown off without a method."

Probably not, but Angus had other ideas as to what might take place there and he judged it time to bring them forward.

He asked, "Who will you take?"

"Yourself and a squad of Techs with reconnaissance training. The Scot, too; his mercenary strategies could be useful if the Acolytes give trouble, which is what they are for. And he will know the city as well as you do."

"Better than I. And Lindley?"

"What use is he?"

Angus said carefully, "To control Donald."

Ferendija reacted frigidly to the change of tone. "The Gone Time is not directing this operation."

Angus thought, *The Cult God forgive me if I have overlooked anything here*, and said, "Doctor Lindley is employed by Security but not bound to service. He tendered his resignation, through acting-Commissioner Edwards, this morning. He has accepted a position as confidential aide to Donald Baird and should serve your interests as a useful brake on Baird's unfamiliarity with executive power."

For Angus the expression on Ferendija's face was a first down-payment for all he had done or might do. The Commissioner said wonderingly, "Executive?"

"Donald is naturally eager to use the opportunity to return home to claim his statutory right."

"What right?"

"As a Scottish citizen." He laid an envelope on the desk between them.

Ferendija stared, not touching it. "What's this?"

"A submission to World Council requiring that Donald Baird, as sole surviving Scottish national, be recognized under the provisions of legislation affecting minorities and ethnic nationals as the sole legal authority in the Ruined Region formerly known as Scotland."

With murder in his eyes Ferendija saw what had been done while his thought circled only round Parker. His hands shook with fury as he opened the envelope.

Angus continued, unawed by the raging of any short-lived man, "There are three fair copies, as legally required. One has been dispatched to World Council and one to Data Control for authentication and record; Donald holds the third. Copies-in-reproduction are available for all parties who require them; you have one in your hand. The formalities have been observed to the letter."

Ferendija did not need to read the long submission. He was intent on setting shock aside and trying to see what this might do to his intentions. Who, in the name of insanity, had alerted that ignorant bravo from the scrapheap of history to the legal loophole, little more than a quibble, which allowed him to stake a claim beyond the dreams of paranoia?

He growled, "What do you gain, gameplayer?"

"Mainly the protection of his life. He's no longer just a temporal by-blow to be used in violence and perhaps shot down by Parker's men to feed the world's contempt of his kind."

"Council has yet to ratify the claim. That may take weeks." Ferendija was recovering equilibrium.

Angus did not trouble to disguise hostility. "You wouldn't dare appear before Council when the case is tabled and admit that you lost him in a Glasgow street fight, knowing that his claim was in progress. And it would do your credit no good to leave him behind here, preventing him from proving his citizenship by search of the Scottish records."

"He shall go. And Lindley. As you say, he may be useful; more to the point, I need all of you where I can see you. Literally." He smiled thinly. "I don't imagine your concern for justice is selfless."

"It isn't. He is Scotland now—and I owe Scotland a debt."

Ferendija gazed uncomprehendingly after his retreating back.

He felt surrounded by gameplayers. He needed administrative bolstering, not knowing what traps might lie in the old and unused Ruined Regions legislation; his team needed a lawyer. He had not considered using the female Techs in what might turn out to be a physically demanding operation, but the White girl was the only Specialist in International Law in this HQ; her advice could be vital now.

On the thought *advice* he took up the papers and riffled through them, observing without surprise that Lindley and Thomson had signed the last page as witnesses to Baird's signature and—still without surprise but with another upsurge of his simmering anger—that the last line of all read: *Preparation and Legal Advice by Alicia Margaret White.*

So the Gone Timers had got to her. It was more than ever necessary to keep them, and the girl, where he could control them.

Not that anything they might do could alter the decision crystallizing in his mind; only Council-in-Session could do that.

He thought about loyalties, not having before considered that Gone Timers might side with The Company against their own kind. Meaning against himself.

Is this paranoid thinking? It might be, but the facts supported it. There was the psychlinician's joke, supposedly after some Gone Time original: being paranoid doesn't mean the bastards aren't out to get me.

They weren't out to get him, of course, but to cross his planning with schemes of their own. The only people who knew all the facts were operating against and in spite of Security.

All of them?

Paranoia or none, he needed to be sure.

He sent for Sanders.

With a copy of the submission spread on the desk, he asked, "Have you seen this?"

Sanders answered, with set expression, that he had.

"While it was in preparation?"

"Yes, sir."

"And did not inform me?" Meaning, declare yourself, Sanders—now!

The Tech made to speak and changed his mind twice before he said, "I couldn't see that it made any difference. It was a simple legal procedure, with no concerned person infringing law or Ethic. It did not occur to me—" and here his deliberateness verged on the offensive "—that it would matter whether you became aware then or later. They couldn't be prevented. *That* would have contravened both law and Ethic."

Ferendija was being paid, in the most insolently legal tender, for tergiversation and the young-teen riot.

Nor was he in a position to refuse the payment.

PART THREE

Glasgow, AD 2037 — Power and Fear

It is when power is wedded to chronic fear that it becomes formidable.

ERIC HOFFER, *The Passionate State of Mind* (1954)

I

The Security craft, faster than Parker's and flying a shorter route, was over southern France when the orbital satellite switched its tracing unit to Standby and the slave needle in Ferendija's map-room steadied—expectedly—on the Glasgow co-ordinates. Refinement of the figures gave the precise point of landing and Angus gave it a name.

"Abbotsinch airfield. It will be overgrown but the tarmac should be fairly clear. But you won't want to drop beside him."

In the tiny room Ferendija was discomforted by Angus's nearness; Angus, caring not a damn, treated distaste as if it did not exist. "I prefer to avoid him until a confrontation is useful." He adjusted a street map under the console light. "Are there other fields?"

"The old orbiter terminal is too close to Abbotsinch; he'd see us come in."

"A wide street?"

"Enclosure between buildings is poor tactics."

Ferendija stiffened. "You think he'd dare attack us?" The idea was an insult.

"It's possible. When he becomes aware of you he'll know he must win outright or lose everything—including possibly the life you all cling to as if there were more than minutes between sixty years and seventy."

Ferendija ignored the baiting while he stored every word of it. "You have a suggestion?"

"Take a hundred-mile swing round the city, low down out of sight, and move up the Clyde at water level. Settle on the water a few miles behind him so we have him between us and the centre of the city. We can tie up on the north bank—there are old shipyards and bridge pylons."

So, at midnight the flyer came to silent rest when Angus called a halt beneath the Erskine Bridge at Old Kilpatrick.

(Had they used Parker's direct entry across the centre of the city they would have observed a line of lights which Angus, after some thought, would have recognized as a beacon. It would have caused him immoderate but secret laughter. As it was, only Parker's crew saw them.)

The flyer's embarkation ladder could be angled to form a gangway of sorts and it was Donald who took a rope ashore and drove metal stakes to serve as bollards while the flyer, buoyant but clumsy in the water, rolled sluggishly against the current. Lindley watched the uncertain passage, knowing he would have risked a ducking had he tried it.

Returning, Donald halted over the water. Something palely phosphorescent, barely visible, moved just below the surface, wavering, thin-gutted and immensely long. A gigantic eel. Or a length of ribbon, waterlogged and about to sink. The slow writhing could have been an effect of tide and current but it gave an appearance of life. He knew of nothing like it in Scottish waters.

It bumped against the hull, nuzzled and curved and sank out of sight.

Lindley, at the hatch, pitied his bleak eyes and forbore any fool's remarks about homecoming. "It's cool."

"No' so bad. April in Scotland could freeze the balls off o' you at night. This is mild."

There had been, Lindley recalled, an attempt at control of the accelerating cooling of the northern hemisphere by bombardment of the Van Allen belts, to effect a small escalation in the low heat spectrum received from the sun. In the early nineties, He had thought it stupid and dangerous. *Did we actually leave behind us something that worked?*

In the map-room Ferendija was asking, "How quickly can you locate your people?"

"Starting now, I might find them by dawn—before they find us. I'll need Donald."

It was a demand. Ferendija asked coldly, "For what?"

"He will know where to find sonics, where the ordnance stores are. Also, if we run into Parker we would be better off with superior weapons that don't necessarily kill."

That was sense, but, "In view of Baird's legal situation I don't trust him out of my sight."

"Not to draw it too fine, he doesn't trust you out of sight or in it. Why should he?"

Ferendija declined the engagement. "Ideally, I'd like two pistols for each man."

"Shouldn't be difficult."

"You can take the jeep."

"No. We want to be individually manoeuvrable if we run into Acolytes. The power-bikes can outsmart mass transport in narrow streets and aren't much slower in the straight."

Ferendija could not think on such lines; the commonplaces of battle appreciation were foreign to him and he was less in command because of it. He said ungraciously, "Suit yourself. See Sanders for protective creams and injections." He added, as if in afterthought, "He will go with you."

"To keep an eye on us?" His tone said, poor Sanders.

"On Baird. It's too soon for him to conceive ideas above his station."

"And too late if he already has them."

Ferendija walked away, needing air. In this precarious situation of working together while at odds he accepted that he must bear with the independence of Angus and Donald—to a point. Later there would be opportunities for seizing; in the long run Security would hold all the options.

Once the unbearable question of The Company was satisfactorily answered—and it would be, it would be, if he could nerve himself to the obvious ...

That Scottish "laird" and his "confidential aide"—

That such relics of the gutters of history should raise barriers against reason and right ...

His venom surprised him. This was how the Gone Timers had thought of their blacks and Jews. But their hate had been irrational, without reason. He and his people had a whole shattered world of reason.

2

The cooling units in radiation suits had only a limited effectiveness; Parker had expected to be mildly too warm. In degrees of temperature he might have been but the fine sweat on his forehead was cold; the immensity of desolation and decay took his rigid personality with psychic shock.

This was no Melbourne, wrecked and rebuilt but always linked with life; Glasgow had died intact, moving from life to death without a stone dislodged.

Skeletons in the streets, hung with rotted scraps of cotton or wool, or obscenely decorous in enduring synthetics, in the attitudes of sleep as often as in the contortions of the stricken, grinned at silence. In places sheltered from wind and weather they sat upright against walls, strangely whole. Others shattered at a touch.

In this public square an assembly of death had formed to await the end; the red paving was layered with their bones. *Layered*. At first he had not recognized this as a charnel site; it was after midnight but the moon was not yet fully risen above the buildings and the bones hid in shadow, grey and dirty with age and weather. His boots had ploughed into them, snapping and rattling a passage, before he saw that he violated a tomb.

Melbourne Town Data Retrieval had located an old street map in the Library's pamphlet collection and made copies for him, so he knew this was George Square. In its centre a stone column soared towards the faint, clouded stars, commemorating a forgotten somebody or something. At the eastern end was a lower, white structure, streaked with neglect, whose grimed and eroded plaques allowed him, in the dim light of a masked torch, to identify it as a war memorial. That repellent century, heartless and cynical, had yet raised monuments to its deceived and wasted soldiery!

He trudged back to the centre through skeletons entwined in love or friendship as though they had dwelt calmly on their going out. (Not everywhere; there had been violence also and parts of the city had burned.) Could the square have possessed tribal genius, drawing them for some last revelation or recognition? There must, after all, have been more to that century than cold blood and the profit motive; the psychology of the Gone Time held mysteries as well as horrors.

The northern edge of the square had once been a gently

sloping lawn shaded by trees. In an eerie fashion it still was. The trees had died with those who walked under them but the defoliated trunks remained in their files, rotted but upright, and something like grass had survived in unpleasant manner, greyish, hard-bladed stuff crackling like splinters underfoot. An Acolyte, probably a biology student, had begun a whispered dissertation on mutation and selective ecology, and Parker had shut him up; the hand of his God had lain heavily here and the mighty imprint was not to be trivialized by tiny erudition.

The buildings surrounding the square were modest structures by Gone Time standards, four and five storeys high, mostly office blocks. Beyond the cenotaph squatted a heavy, ornate pile which the map noted as City Chambers, and on the north an ancient box of a building displayed almost obliterated lettering naming it the North Britain Hotel.

It was in this last that lights had gleamed as he swept in low from the south just after nightfall.

They gleamed still, warmly yellow, from a row of dormer windows in the slate roof and he wondered irrelevantly about the power source.

His flyer had set down at an airport the map called Abbotsinch, its tarmac broken and pierced by stiff pseudo-grass but at least free of the strange and tangled shrubbery covering the open area of the field.

Pinpointing the lights, he and a group of Acolytes had suited up and come to this open grave of a square. Their transport, hurriedly assembled, had been little more than a collapsible tray on wheels which shuddered over passably preserved macadam. They had lost themselves twice but arrived at length to find the lights shining still.

Parker disposed his little force tactically, hiding men as well as possible in the shadows of the dead trees and the scattered statues and artefacts, and waited.

Sooner or later someone would emerge from the building.

Someone may already have done so, unseen. In this crowded cemetery it was easy to imagine a company of dead stares hiding among them one living gaze. The aura of the moon was growing behind the City Chambers; shortly it would flood the square and he would see who or what moved.

In the dormers of the North Britain Hotel the lights went out.

Finished for the night? Desks or benches cleared prosaically amidst the hecatomb? Ready for home—or merely turning off the lights and settling for sleep?

He could wait. Sooner or later he or she or they must come out. Laborious methods could search out a handful of rabbits in a city-sized warren but here he could wait on certainty.

At last the moon heaved a slow crescent over City Chambers and drove a bright shaft to the lake of bones.

A woman's voice said clearly but from a distance, "I am here if you are waiting for me."

Across the front of the cenotaph, flanked by the stone effigies of couchant lions, stretched a low white wall. She sat atop it, outlined by the moonlight behind her.

Around the square fluttered the small sounds of alerted men.

Parker ordered harshly, "Be quiet! Be still! She's walked straight through you!"

"Not straight," the woman said, "I had to force a passage."

"Did you kill him?"

She laughed, not pleasantly; he heard contempt and a touch of incredulity. "Kill? Why? What had he done? I stunned him with a sonic pistol; he will recover in minutes. You wouldn't know about sonic pistols."

"I have seen one." That was incautious, he thought, showing too much too soon.

"You have?" She sounded wary, then changed her tone. "Are you going to stand under the column all night, shouting at me?"

He did not fancy facing a sonic pistol. Also, her pronunciation reminded him of Lindley's so-called English accent. Her kind could not be regarded as Gone Timers in the restrictive sense but the voice called up the same consciousness of the different and distasteful.

So he was angered when she took his hesitation for cowardice. "Man, I am surrounded! Eight men, all armed, and so I suppose are you. My little pistol isn't a kill-all against enemy on every side."

"In that case, *you* come to *me*."

"Ah, a dominant male! Well, why not?"

She came rapidly, kicking bones aside, swinging down to

240

him with a mannish stride, dressed in slacks and heavy work shirt, sleeves rolled. From five yards she said, "You must all be simmering in those absurd things—radiation suits? Surely you have simpler protection against low-dose fields?"

He had not dared trust the outside rad readings at Abbots-inch—low figures flying in the face of received understanding of the Ruined Regions—thinking them a local aberration. He had creams and chelating agents for emergencies but not enough to risk discarding the suits, which in any case he would not have dared until doubts were resolved.

She said idly, "Randal may have something you can use," and stopped before him, hands spread to show she did not heft the pistol, which was holstered at her belt.

He grunted through the speech relay, "Show your face."

Mockingly obedient, she turned to let the moonlight fall full on her.

Early twenties (well . . .), good looking, dark, impudent. Something should be different about such people, visibly different. Nothing was.

He asked, "Jeanie Deans?"

She smiled delightedly. "That was ages ago. Tonight I'm Diana of the Double-crossways." An in-joke, he gathered, with a hint of menace for good measure. "You don't know Meredith? No time for literature in all your busy do-gooding? Knowing of Jeanie, you must have met Angus—in Australia?"

He said with a force which caused her eyes to widen, "I have met Angus!"

Her smile returned. "He has that effect on people."

"I have also spoken to Will Santley."

"Is that nothing still alive?"

The disinterest could be a pose; he pressed, "Also your Donald."

"Old Sweetie! He must be doddering. Is he well?"

"So far. His behaviour is not always wise." She shrugged; subject covered and closed. "Your Angus also is in damnably good health."

"Why should I care about that hysterical exhibitionist? If the social amenities are complete, tell me what you want."

"To speak with the senior man of The Company."

" 'Take me to your leader'? I'll do for leader."

"No."

She summed him casually, amused. "Listen, mayfly-in-a-radiation-suit! Your kind rules the world by weight of numbers but no one rules the Children!" (*Children? Some alternative name for themselves?*) "You will tell me why you wish to see the—'senior man' will do—or turn round and go home. I will decide whether or not you see him. Like your Security, we delegate the man on the spot."

He was more impressed than she might guess by that item of knowledge indicating detailed information of the outer world. Britain had been less than isolated.

He temporized. "You realize that your existence is known? As yet to a few persons only."

"We have recognized that under present conditions it soon must be."

"Then you appreciate the unwisdom of making that existence *generally* known? Cultural shock—"

"We are more concerned about the probability of being used as laboratory animals. And we are not all agreed about the cultural shock."

Of course, of course—Dissident. He said rapidly, "Nor are we," and thought her eyes narrowed minutely. But that might have been a trick of moonlight. "Yet we feel that our continuity as a culture needs protection from you and that at the same time your welfare as a minority must be assured. I am empowered to make preliminary negotiation."

"Empowered by whom? Your World Council?"

He seized the opportunity to explode into propaganda. "By the Lord Yeshua, no! You'll find no mercy at the hands of that pack of ethical wolves. I am employed by Australia. Call me a secret agent. Australia owns Gangoil, the focus of the world's biology research; only Australia possesses the scientific weight to protect you."

"At a price."

"Would some co-operation be such an unreasonable request?"

"Yes, it probably would." She kicked idly at bones and at length said, "You have just told at least four lies, but they were interesting lies. I think John will see you on the strength of them."

He had not counted them, not really planned them, simply said what seemed most cautious and least complex, hardly aware where half-truth leaned one way or the other. Her penetration scarred his self-possession. Best to be non-committal. "I'm sorry you think that."

"I suppose you are; it puts you at a disadvantage. Planetary breakdown has taught your kind nothing; you play your power games as though world crises are to be manipulated like chess problems. We'll have to talk with you to extract the facts from your nonsense."

She looked through the faceplate directly into his eyes, smiling still, baring her teeth slightly and holding his gaze. Then without farewell she walked away, forgotten deaths crackling underfoot.

He called after her, "I have questions."

"Save them." As if she sensed his temptation she added, loudly enough to be heard everywhere in the silent square, "Don't order your men to hold me. They might be forced to kill me, which is not easy, and for that the Children might set about killing you. Which is very easy."

Swallowing pride, he shouted, "How do I find you?"

"When we need you we will let you know. Stay on your airfield and we won't have to search the city for you."

So they had already been reconnoitred.

She merged with the shadows of old, weathered buildings.

For the first time in his adult life Parker knew the nakedness of a failed authority.

3

While Parker encountered the stillness of history in George Square, Angus's team manhandled power-bikes across the rocking gangway to the foot of one of the huge concrete pylons of the Erskine Bridge. With the closing of the flyer's hatch they were alone with night and the river. No moon yet.

All three wore the camouflage of civilian dress. It was heavy cloth against the cold night of early spring but a sharp little wind penetrated.

For Sanders it was reason to get moving. "Where do we look for the guns?"

"In the nearest polis station. They were held there for issue to vigilantes."

"Is there one near here?"

"Maybe; I dinna ken every corner o' the toon. We'll look for a shop or hoose wi' a telephone an' search the book."

Sanders did not know what a telephone or its book might be but followed in hopeful ignorance as they walked the bikes across a hundred yards of treacherous river flat to a broad road, an unfamiliar grass crackling wickedly underfoot.

On the Dumbarton Road they stumbled across their first skeleton, collapsed in a shop doorway, feet protruding in the remnants of rotted shoes. Nylon socks clung to the bones, faded grey-white but still whole, but woollen trousers crumbled and shredded as Sanders tripped over the feet; the once white terylene shirt folded as the bones which had balanced through decades in shelter tumbled together at last.

He bent to take a small bottle from the collapsed finger bones. "Poison?" He shone his torch on the label's nearly vanished print. "Methylated spirit!"

"Ay. Liquor was scarce at the end an' there were always some would drink it anyway. I'd no' care to dee on it."

Angus said harshly, "Death by irradiation is protracted and painful. Any ending might be preferred." As they contemplated him silently he said, "We do know about death; not having to fear it, we understand it."

"Do you, noo; I'd wondered." Glancing up to the eaves he said, "There's a phone in here," assessed the panels of the door and splintered the wood with a driving kick. "The whole city will be rotten."

The telephone book had survived with cover mildewed but its inner leaves intact. He located a police station further down the road, in Dalmuir suburb.

Sanders pondered the close-printed volume. Reared on data-retrieval and a schooling which had emphasized the Gone Time as automated to the point of soullessness, he was uneasy before an artefact whose manual clumsiness contradicted the lore. He knew he was not alone in his generation in thinking that the historical teachings sometimes clouded truth, but . . .

It was not a thing he could readily discuss with the Gone Timers; he did not harbour the deep resentments of his elders but there was always a cultural restraint in personal contact.

They rode the bikes down the ghostly road.

The most silent hours of a living city cannot match the stillness of a dead one. No sense of the unearthly oppressed them but a sense of familiar things deserted by a people who rose from their occupations and went away, taking nothing. What remained—their homes, shops, parked cars, garbage tins and impotent street signs—spoke of no more than a thoughtless walk to the corner for a paper or a packet of cigarettes and an inexplicable failure to return. After the first they saw few skeletons in the streets.

"Folk gang hame to dee wi' their ain. Or they look for company in gatherin' places. Only the helpless an' the freendless dee alone." He would not pass to them the feeling that nobody had gone, that behind doors, round corners, in the shadows of their gardens they watched, appraising and resenting the living.

It was three miles to a shopping area and a police station.

The station smelt of decay, but the flooring, though it complained at their tread, held firm. The place had no ghosts; no skeletons filled posts of final duty; the last hours had not been wasted in grasping at straws of order.

The guns were in the back room, seventeen of them in an open crate and spaces where three had been issued long ago.

Sanders was disgusted. "Not even locked away!"

"So? At the end could a gun gie life?"

"I'm sorry. I was thoughtless."

"I dinna follow your world either, but I try." He had unwrapped a gun as he spoke. "Shit!"

He unrolled the mess on the floor; the weapon was completely stripped, each component embalmed in armourer's grease.

"No matter; I've assembled a hundred o' them." He laid the elements out in the torchlight; the thick yellow grease clung like river mud. "There's ainly nine parts, slidin' together wi' magnets; there's no recoil so magnets do well enough." He held up a unit the size of a large bead. "This is a whustle that blows a note you canna hear an' directs it into the wee crystal—here. An' the crystal—so my instructor had it—acts like the amplifyin' slug o' a laser. So he said, though maybe that was only by way o' example, but the wee sound o' the whustle comes through strang an' killin' frae the snoot."

Sanders said, "The grease is thick; we need rags."

"You're no' a soldier; that's the hard way. We'll boil them; only the wee crystals must be cleaned by haund. Then I'll show you the assemblin' drill an' we'll a' hae guns."

"Uncharged," Angus demurred.

"These are factory charged. The batteries are wrapped in insulation under the grease; the charge canna leak."

They found a stainless-steel boiler in a hardware store and broke up rotting wood for fuel; the bikes' lamps could be adapted for ignition. But for water they had to return to the river.

They found plastic buckets and improvised ropes from their belts to lower and haul from the low bank. Dragging up the final bucket, Donald caught sight of a ribbon of slime hanging over the lip and would have brushed it away if it had not moved sluggishly as he touched it.

In torchlight he glimpsed the whitish, flat segmented strip as broad as a man's wrist. The thickened section that moved from side to side in a lazy seeking motion might have been a head though no eyes showed, only a squarish and blunted end with four darker blotches, lifting itself blindly from the coils trapped in the bottom of the bucket. The free end of its tail stretched over the lip and down to the water.

Surprise ebbed in revulsion. In a delayed reflex he up-ended the bucket and let the thing splash into the river. It sank, writhing slowly.

Sanders asked, "What was that?"

"Nothing I know. A strange one."

From the darkness behind them a voice enlightened, pitched quietly for themselves alone to hear. "We suspect that its father was a tapeworm. Most extreme mutations are non-viable but this is an odd one that has survived. Don't swim in the

246

Clyde; it's brimming with the things. They're sluggish and brainless but also hungry and persistent."

Angus chuckled. "Always full of information, Alastair."

"Do you know you're being followed at a distance?"

"I had begun to suspect it. Some of yours?"

"No, yours; from that very beautiful flyer at Erskine Bridge. Do you feel they don't trust you?"

Angus asked, "Did you know about this, Corey?"

"No, but in Ferendija's place I'd have ordered it."

"Don't you trust me either?"

Sanders answered with exactness, "I trust you to keep your given word, and not an inch where it's not given."

To Donald it sounded as if Angus then put a question that trod treacherous ground.

"Whose side are you on, Corey?"

"Not yours, because I don't know what you want. Not Parker's because fanatics are unpredictable. If I were forced to a choice I'd back Donald. He's honest."

"Do you have a choice? Does Security have a policy?"

"If it has, the only man who knows it hasn't told me. But I will obey his orders, irrespective of questions of side."

"I hope it doesn't become difficult for you."

Sanders said nothing to that. Alastair asked politely, "Have you settled how little you trust each other? Is that really our Donald with you? He hasn't turned out to be one of us, has he?"

"It is. He hasn't. Explanations later. Where can we talk?"

"At the workshop, further up river. Your friends won't follow because they haven't a boat and I have."

First they had to complete boiling off the guns, while Angus, for curiosity's sake, went quietly to observe their tailing party—four hapless Techs whispering between themselves, unhappy in a necropolis. They, and Ferendija, were due for frustration.

The moon was high when they loaded the bikes aboard Alastair's dinghy and, with Donald at the second oar, rowed easily against the slow current. Only one word was spoken, when Alastair dipped his oar and brought it up—"Look!"—and a festoon of pale flesh slid gently back to the dark water.

Angus said there were sounds of pursuit along the bank but by the time they tied up at Alastair's jetty they had lost their

247

observers. Alastair told them now that he had not seen the Security flyer arrive but had seen a splash of light reflected on the bank, probably when the hatch opened to let them ashore; he had taken an hour to move close enough by water and land to identify Angus's voice.

Did they know that a flyer had streaked over the city in early evening and set down at Abbotsinch? He had word that Smith was preparing a reception for that, since there was no point in concealment once the human wolves had taken the scent. John's receptions could be disconcerting.

Angus explained the situation briefly, leaving Alastair thoughtful but silent.

For Donald, time repeated itself when they stepped on to concrete with a torch to guide their feet; a door opened in a looming surface and as they passed inside a light came on.

"I don't use many lights," Alastair said. "I'm on storage batteries."

"Still?" Donald asked.

"Still; we can run generators only when weather conditions blind those damned satellites, and we have to use storms as cover for recharging the batteries. They don't seem programmed to pick up tiny usages like lighting and heating but we use dispersion networks for safety."

The draughting office had been cleaned up and was in use again; work in progress showed on several boards.

"You've help the noo."

Alastair answered shortly, "Some," and glanced enquiringly at Sanders.

Angus said, "Corey's a friend—of a sort. A Security Tech. He knows the score because he's absorbed Will's brain tape. That's a mental—"

"I know what it is. So the Disses have their way and hiding's over for ever." Then, as if that were that, discussed and dismissed, "Come through and I'll make coffee."

Later, in the recreation room, Angus asked, "How do you get real coffee?"

"From old Tanzania, ferried from France and run north by ground car at night. We don't go short of much except TV and items that create more discharge than we can diffuse. We

248

keep up to date. You see, after the slaughter at Gangoil, John and Carlo made their way back here. It took them ten years of walking and island-hopping through Indonesia but on the way they opened up contacts and established Glasgow as the major focus for all of us. Isolation made the city ideal when the rad count began to fall and supplies were no problem once the continental chain had been set up. The first years were no holiday—long bouts of nausea and weakness—but we were able to keep abreast of what went on outside and we saw that technological civilization would be on us again in the space of a few long breaths. Once the planetwide data networks were formed we knew our separate existence was as good as over, so John started calling in the Children."

"Calling them here?"

"A safe place. He knew we'd eventually have to come to terms with the shorties, so he wanted to assess what we had to bargain with that might prevent them handing all of us over to the Gangoil ghouls."

"A census of heads and capacities. What of it?"

"You know what he found: a long-life population of about three hundred, most of whom decided to stay in Glasgow." He grinned at Donald. "Can you imagine them wanting to stay in your dreary old Glasgow?"

"Ay. I'm gettin' the hang o' your way o' thinkin'. You're a people who'll bear discomfort an' no' complain, but you canna abide disorder. Glesca gied little comfort but it was preferable to the nursery noises o' a world settlin' into ways that had no' been seen in history before."

Alastair was impressed. "Jeanie never did pick duds."

"That's no compliment. So you've counted heids, but what o' the capacities?"

Angus gave it harshly. "What capacities? John was hoping something would turn up because no survey had been attempted before. But nothing did, eh, Alastair?"

"A few like yourself and Jeanie, with talents better kept out of sight; a few athletic freaks of no use to anyone; a couple of flawed geniuses like old John, brilliant in spasms but without intellectual stamina; for the rest a catalogue of prehistoric memories tagged to IQs that rarely rise above a hundred and

249

thirty. We're ordinary to the point of uselessness. When you count our virtues all we have to offer the shorties is evolution's sourest joke—a useless mutation that doesn't die out." He put a sudden question to Sanders: "So what will your Council do with Methuselah's apes who have nothing to bargain with?"

Curious for Sanders's answer, Donald kept a straight face. Poor little Company, crying helplessness against the masters of the world! He did not think Sanders would be taken in; neither did he expect what came.

"I can't guess Council's mind. What answer fits a problem that persists as long as babies are born? It could outlast the human race. I'm glad the decision isn't mine."

"If it were?"

"You want me to talk treason? I won't."

Donald said, "He wants a Security man to tell how Security thinks. If you were man on the spot, Corey, how would you advise?"

Sanders made an unlikely gesture; he moved behind Donald's chair and placed his hands on the Scot's shoulders, not choosing sides but recognizing the existence of more than one right and obligation. "I would advise: play for time. Stand with Donald and see what comes of it. The gamble is worth taking."

Angus snorted, "Of course it is! Why else did I set it up?"

"And what," Alastair asked, "can Donald finally do with life, death and the odds for and against?"

"As a Security man it's my business to explain your rights, whether I favour them or not." His blank face told them nothing about his favour. "I'll spell it out. The loose wording of the Territorial Rights legislation gives Donald provisional title to the whole country down to the old English border. We call him the Laird of Scotland, and the joke's on us. He has the right to accept stateless persons—yourselves—as naturalized citizens. Take him for your chief administrator and you'll have somebody with legal power to guard your social rights and physical safety. At worst it will raise a legal and ethical smoke screen and buy time for argument to produce a workable solution to the question of your impact on humanity. If a workable solution exists."

Ferendija listened in impassive fury as a hapless Patrol Tech explained how he had lost his quarry :

They had climbed into a rowing boat, with their power-bikes, and stroked into the darkness . . .

Ferendija could have wept for such simplicity.

Yes, they had obtained sonic guns; the patrol had brought back the remaining contents of the plundered crate, but without Baird they felt unsure of assembling them correctly, simple as they seemed. Someone could be injured . . .

Ferendija felt useless and stalemated. The larrikin Scot did not matter; his juvenile title-gambit could be quibbled out of existence. It was Angus, insolent, confident, smug, who worried him. And sending Sanders had been an error of judgement; he should have sought out a man stolid enough to kill on suspicion of deviousness. He would protect such a man.

Sanders had not only not stopped them, he had gone with them.

Under compulsion? He did not think so.

What he thought was that every tool turned in his hand and that only his own, personal, unshared action could be depended on to do what he needed of it.

He was man on the spot.

4

Alastair was highly amused by what he at once dubbed the Clan Baird impertinence. "It's a neat piece of temporizing but it sidesteps the real issue. It could be useful but, with all respect, Donald, there's no need for a hurried decision."

Sanders's conception of common sense was outraged by the acceptance of time as the eternal ally. History no longer drifted by their deathless indifference; caught up in it, they must act with intelligent haste.

Augus seemed to think so. "Every need! Tonight! Shorties don't wait for patterns to form—they form them! With death waiting and no centuries on call, they're *fast*."

That was better, but Angus was not typical of Company attitudes. Alastair probably represented the norm and Alastair was being maddeningly reasonable. "Then Ferendija's victory is already prepared and any action is too late."

Angus would not have it. "Rubbish; Ferendija can't move. He came here, like Parker, to round up The Company, and was hoping to catch Parker in proceedings that would justify arresting him. My bet is that he plans to take the handful he thinks are here back to Australia. But how many are there in fact?"

"Close to three hundred, all armed with sonic guns. We rooted those out when discovery became inevitable. So he certainly won't arrest us." Alastair smiled with a boyishness Sanders found eerie. "We might arrest *him*."

Because these people might be capable of such prankishness, Sanders said quickly, "The last thing you want to do is make possible protectors hate your guts."

Angus said, "Possible protector Ferendija does that already, but thank for the advice. Is advice-giving covered in your instructions? Are you something more than a watchdog?"

Sanders's unready, "Do you think I'd tell you?" was less than a riposte.

"I don't know, Corey. The man who protected his Commissioner's killer isn't wholly predictable."

That was under his guard but now he had his proper answer. "I am Security's man on the spot to do whatever I think necessary. As when I aided you."

"Why, then," Angus said brightly, "we must study to retain your good will," but with Alastair he was sharp: "I want to see John, tonight."

"Then see him, if you can't sit still. He's in the transit house. Ten miles in the dark over unmaintained roads—and much good may it do you."

He was, Sanders thought, in a plain old-fashioned huff at having his good sense overruled in favour of melodrama. They left him with it.

Summers and winters, rains and snows, winds and tiny shiftings in the earth had pocked the surface of the Dumbarton Road with small cracks and potholes, like shadows in the beams of the power-bikes' lamps, and occasionally larger traps that could bring a rider down. They did not make good time.

The night air was bitter now, and for Sanders the grimness of night in an old industrial city, preserved in full ugliness, was an experience worth avoiding. The ancient area was close-crammed and black with pollutant grime, huddling with shattered windows over streets so narrow as to seem rathole alleys. He did not understand how a planet had conspired to live in squalor.

"The shipyards," Donald said, pointing. The tall gantries stood stark and slender in the moonlight, their travelling jibs outflung as though they guarded an ancient trust. They had rusted through half a century over their dead.

Sanders murmured, "As if they prayed."

For a sentence Donald's grief showed. "Ay—for work; the yards were silent years before the dust fell."

Angus said, "Alastair was building a ship of sorts there—an orbital factory. He seems to be at it still."

Sanders contradicted him. "Not now. My secondary rating is engineering design and I had a quick look at some of his boards —major axis cross-sections of what you people called O'Neill Colonies."

Angus did not comment and Donald muttered that the man had shown a talent for filling in time, but Sanders discovered a germ of thought: an O'Neill Colony with a monopole drive . . . Jerking over an unseen hollow returned him to the present. "Angus, why weren't you called back to Glasgow for census?"

"Why should I be? What had he to learn from me? He called the hundreds he didn't know. The thirty or forty he sometimes consorted with will still be loose around the world."

Ask a silly question . . .

At last Sanders recognized some false memories, streets excerpted from the Santley filament, an unsettling *déjà vu*. They stopped at a small house in an allotment between age-filthy shells of old warehouses, and leaned the bikes against the fence.

They were heard. The door opened, light flooded and Jeanie exclaimed, "Angus!" It was neither surprise nor welcome. "We must really be in trouble. Still setting the world to rights, Iscariot?"

He pushed past, ignoring her. Sanders, recognizing the name from Cultist texts, speculated.

Sight of Donald surprised her. "Glesca Donnie! Don't say it, let me guess—a Gangoil revenant! How's life in a pickle jar? Couldn't you keep away from me?"

Bright sexual curiosity was undisguised. Her excellent reflexes were not fast enough to evade the backhander that cracked her head against the wall. She straightened in a burst of venom. "How I could make you regret that!"

Angus spoke over his shoulder. "Leave him alone; he's more important than you will ever be. And you, Donald, leave *her* alone. You understand her less than you think."

Sanders surprised her in a stare of blind rage directed at Angus's back. Then, as if nothing had happened, she took stock of the Tech. "Who's this? One of ours?"

"Security."

"What have we done to earn a creeping Jesus? Have you a name, Handsome?"

"Yes," he said bluntly and plunged after the others, frankly afraid of her eyes on his.

To the left was what Sanders thought Gone Timers had called the "sitting-room" or just "front room". From it came a young voice chattering with a repellently un-young petulance.

"Who's there? Get them out of here, Jeanie! Affairs are in crisis! I will not be—" The complainant appeared—slender, fair-haired, much younger-seeming than Sanders and behaving with the testiness folklore said was endemic among the old. "Who's that? I know him! Angus? Angus who? Giles! Why didn't you say so? What are you doing here?"

Sanders had never seen a really old man and could not quite imagine one; in John Smith he observed only a healthy adult behaving like an ill-bred child, impossibly less than Will's awed portrait of authority.

The room was ascetic: comfortless chairs, a plain kitchen table, bookshelves stuffed with folders, papers and spools but no books. A monkish cell. Did extreme longevity divorce interest from comfortable vanities?

Without waiting for answer, the memory that had trouble with Angus fastened accurately on Donald. "Baird. Well preserved. Gangoil got to you, eh? Haven't come back for that damned woman of yours, have you? Stay away from her!"

"Ay. I've come to try to save your people."

Smith said lightly, "My, but that's a big order! The mind reels. You Scots are as bizarre as Gascons." Leaving Donald to untangle the comparison he turned to Sanders. "Who's this?"

Jeanie said disgustedly, "A nursemaid from Security."

"Don't underestimate them. They're preferable to the Orthodox Kremlin, for instance; they don't sermonize at the point of a knife. And what, young man—*very* young man, you understand?—are you doing here?"

"At the moment," Sanders said, "nothing."

"Surely some sort of official scurry?"

"Nothing useful, that is." Seeing an opening, he embroidered with imagination: "After all, of what use are you? To us? To anybody?"

It brought him Smith's full attention; even Jeanie listened with respect. Angus was openly delighted.

Smith suggested drily that the Gangoil biologists might have an answer for him, little as he favoured it.

"Those? Some of us would prefer them left ignorant."

"Admirable! And what of our useless selves?"

"Do as Donald wants."

Smith inspected Donald with fresh interest, but waited politely. Sanders continued with sudden woodenness. "In recommending it I may be stretching my responsibilities. I can't tell. Your very existence raises questions to make moral certainties seem like ideas gone to rot."

In their appraisal he knew he had made himself felt.

Jeanie spoke, smugly. "We Dissidents always said they'd think straightly about the problem."

"None of *you* think straightly about it." He spoke across her to Smith. "The real problem is that Santley is one of yours and that he can procreate."

Angus said, "No!" and Smith shook his head, smiling.

Jeanie looked bored until Sanders asked, "But why not?" Then she snapped, "Is genetics your subject?"

"No, but with millennia of background radiation, genetic

255

error and the laws of chance forever zeroing in, why not? Chance doesn't wait on eternity to bring off coincidence."

Smith returned to testiness. "Where's the proof? It would be a disaster. It needs proof."

Angus said, "It doesn't. It doesn't even have to be true. It only has to be rumoured and the whole planet will see us as monsters ready to breed them out of their birthright. Isn't that what you're telling us, Corey?"

Sanders answered only, "Do what Donald says; it may help." As they turned in expectation to the Scot, Sanders continued incredibly, "A man called Ferendija, a World Councillor, is here to talk to you. Don't trust him."

He sucked in his lips, petrified at his burning of bridges and loyalties in a strike of inner lightning. Perhaps only Angus who had summed and weighed for days past knew that the Tech had come to the parting of right and righteousness, intellect and feeling.

Smith surveyed them both intently before he said, "The Children appreciate advice, but what does Mr Baird offer? And why does he offer it?"

Donald became violently uncomfortable. "Angus is my freend. That may no' mean much to him—in a hundred years maybe no mair than an acquaintance he gied good day to once upon a time. But I've only the feelin's o' my few years, so when a freend asks, I gie what I have."

He ran down rather than stopped, in embarrassment.

Jeanie said, "Believe him; he's a sentimentalist. These people don't live long enough to see their world whole."

"It's a fault worth gratitude," Smith noted. "The offer, Mr Baird?"

"That all o' you accept Scottish nationality wi' mysel in authority until we work oot a fair form o' government."

Jeanie whooped with laughter. Her romantic Donald!

Smith, with centuries of observed human foolishness at call, asked mildly, "Autocrat, Mr Baird?"

"Ay. I am the yin livin' Scot an' my claim to my country is filed wi' World Council. If I am the law o' this land Security itsel canna lay hands on you withoot my say, so lang as you do nothin' to menace world order."

For once Jeanie lacked a ready jibe. Smith asked, "Angus, can this be right?"

"Yes. It's legal chicanery, of course. The law on territorial claim is a device for satisfying minorities and settling boundary disputes; it never allowed for the possibility of a Gone Timer living to claim anything, let alone an entire country. Council will fight, of course; a Gone Timer thumbing his nose is unforgivable. They'll amend the law and dispossess him, but that will take at least a year under Delay For Reconsideration and we'll gain time to talk Council into some understanding of the implications, because they daren't risk public revelation of our existence until they've decided how to deal with it. With Donald to say No we'll at least be safe from the biologists."

"An arranged accident might remove the claimant."

"No. A Gone Timer claiming a country is a number one scandal and every newscast in the world is carrying it by now. Doctor Lindley saw to that before we left Australia. Donald will be safe while the case is in progress because Ethic-breaking smells even worse than a Gone Timer, and the progressive youngsters who like seeing authority's nose out of joint won't let the story die. The Laird of Scotland may be the first Gone Timer to become a popular hero."

A furious Sanders had not guessed the extent of their planning. "You talk as if you could hold the planet to ransom!"

"Do you care? Your loyalties must be in an unenviable dilemma."

Smith snapped at him, "The dilemma of the Children is far less enviable. There is another offer. A man describing himself as a secret agent of the Australian Prime Minister has offered protection."

Sanders was scandalized. "Parker? An agent so secret his Prime Minister won't have heard of it! You've seen him?"

Jeanie giggled. "I have. When his machine came screaming in we decided to upset whoever it might be from the start, and we set a lamp in the window for him. His offer was at least partly genuine but I couldn't decide which part. Too many lies. We need to know what he really has in mind."

Angus warned, "He's devious."

She gave him a sidelong, wicked smile. "Spice! All that protective suiting couldn't hide attractive eyes."

"Those eyes could get you more than you bargain for. I hope you follow it up."

Smith crackled contempt. "Time has taught dignity to neither of you. Security man, what is the third offer?"

"The Commissioner's?"

"A figurehead! What will World Council do?"

Sanders hazarded, "Procrastinate."

"Jeanie, is this man honest?"

"So far. Procrastinate was an opinion with other possibilities behind it, but he hopes it is true."

Sanders demanded, "Is she telepathic?"

"No. It's a learned technique, not important. Don't you trust your Council?"

"I think they will welcome Donald as a diversion giving them legitimate deferment for thought."

"But?"

The Tech said heavily, "I no longer trust anyone to do what's right."

"Sensible of you." He continued briskly, "We should think in terms of blackmail and for that we need the eugenic truth about Santley. Where is he, Angus?"

"Surely in Parker's flyer. He's too vulnerable to be left in Australia for Security to find."

Jeanie said, "I can go out there and ask Parker. He can't lie; even in that outlandish suit little tensions betray him and he has no voice control worth the name."

Donald snarled at her, "For so ancient a bitch you're a bluidy silly yin! Parker couldna take you on your ain groond but you might get a beatin' on his. If he wants a hostage, can you deal wi' twenty men?"

"Can you?"

"Ay, wi' care an' plannin' an' a sonic gun—an' a lick o' Baird's luck. We'll gang wi' you—Angus to talk, you to catch the lies an' me to bring Will back wi' us."

She said sourly, "You haven't been crowned at Scone yet; you don't run the country."

"Dinna bet on that."

Smith intervened. "Jeanie, do as he says."

He was prepared to back the pawn who had jumped to royal status but he did not have the last word. Sanders said, "I'll do the talking with Parker."

Angus shook his head. "Keep out of it. Observe. Don't get tangled in Ferendija's web."

"Ferendija's not here; I'm man on the spot."

Angus conceded with a warning, "Make a mistake and Ferendija will crucify you."

"Then perhaps I should swear—what did they call it? Fealty?—to Donald while I can."

"That's no joke. You don't know where this may end."

Sanders raised his sonic gun like an offering in cupped palms. "When I saw a World Councillor prepared to use these things I knew we had come to the end of our run; Security is ready to turn on its trust. Do you know how we batten down violence across the planet? Not by the Ethic and example but by limiting the manufacture of arms. Not only is it too late to limit these but Security is the first to reach for them, so what am I to think? That a life's training and belief can be destroyed by sight of a gun and the temptation of power? The Commissioner has Gangoil now, remember." He holstered the gun. "You're right, Angus—I don't know where this may end. But I will do what has to be done."

Smith had listened closely. "You're another Angus, crusading with high motives and confused emotions. And I'm cynic enough to use you. Well, don't get yourself hurt unnecessarily. Would somebody make a pot of tea?"

He strolled across to Sanders and tapped the holster. "Ferendija has upset your comfortable philosophy by adopting this thing, but against whom do *you* carry it?"

He turned his back, knowing that Sanders-in-crisis had no answer.

5

Smith sent for transport. What arrived was a tracked prospector with plank seats bolted to the tray, better suited than a tyred vehicle to crumbling roads. From the cinema strip of Will's memories, Sanders placed the driver, tentatively, as Carlo, and turned out correct.

It seemed that when a Company decision was taken, action followed without ceremony; Smith did not look up from scrutiny of papers when they left.

Carlo had reconnoitred the airfield while Jeanie reconnoitred Parker, and told them that the flyer was in the middle stretch of the runway. Dropping them half a mile from the field he said, "I'll slip the exhaust baffles and run round the perimeter; the noise will distract them while you go in."

He roared off, a rowdy ghost in the dead suburb.

The field was waist deep in a lush growth of normal-seeming grass but the short-bladed mutant flourished at the roots and snapped underfoot; silence was impossible.

The windows of Parker's long-bodied flyer were shaded, but standard lamps had been sited about it, and under each one stood a suited figure with a riot gun—a slow-firing light calibre carbine whose actual use was nearly unheard of.

"Parker's maybe a guid polisman but he's no' a soldier. Sentries under lights!"

Angus told him quietly, "You are probably the only professional soldier alive. And he's not so badly off, with the grass to call every step we take."

"Dinna fash. We'll advance, noise an' a', to twenty yards frae the tarmac—ten yards apart in case some scairt boy lets fly wi' his popgun. If he does, gang on your guts quick but keep crawlin' forward; they'll no' hit whit they canna see. In close, I'll put them oot o' action."

"How?"

"Wi' the sonic; you've no' seen a' the tricks it can play. If some fule sentry comes searchin' in the grass, hit him wi' low power. Low power, mind! We'll no' kill silly boys. Noo—forward!"

He gave no special consideration to Jeanie, who did not need it and would not have thanked him for it.

With lamps, moonlight and the crackling underfoot Sanders reckoned himself a giant target, though he could not yet be heard and might be seen only by long chance; they were still a quarter of a mile from the runway. The knowledge was not enough to quiet the thought of being cut down by the reflex action of a jittery boy. Angus and Jeanie could lie wounded and wait for healing to begin; he could only lie while the blood ran out and his short years with it.

In all his life he had never been required to face an imminent and deliberate death. Few of his world ever had; street fights and kid-gang wars were surrogates hedged with unwritten rules and no physical risk that could not be cancelled by the clinics. They were dangerous *games*.

He understood, in a burst of insight, what had perverted Beckett—not the dream of endless continuance but its twin and correlative, avoidance of the hounding reality of death.

It was time to point out that there were other ways of claiming Santley. They didn't definitely know that he was in the flyer . . . It wasn't worth the chance of life spirting out for a gesture . . .

Donald's whisper to "Haud the line, man !" told him he had lagged. He hurried, struck with a mute surprise at having obeyed without question, *like a damned soldier*. Then with a dismaying shame—that a Gone Timer, no more protected than himself, could face with a calm decision what his civilized intelligence could manage only under coercion.

In the struggle to submerge fright and (though this did not consciously occur to him) to not earn Donald's contempt by abandoning the raid, he had not seen how far the little line had advanced. The first round whistled past his ear before he heard the crack of the gun and he stood paralysed until Donald bellowed, "Get doon, you stupid bastard !"

He dropped on his belly and began, surprised at his own sudden calm, to crawl forward while Donald urged and exhorted somewhere on his left. Random shots whipped overhead; then the useless carbine quit for lack of targets.

He heard shouting round the flyer, Acolytes questioning and blaming, and could picture the confusion. He knew how they felt. He raised his head above the level of the grass and nodded satisfaction at men disorganized by the unfamiliar.

He was not the first or last man to discover, in the whistle and crack of a death that did *not* stop to claim him, that he became his own man again, looking on action with the eye of orderly life.

The Acolytes froze as Parker's voice snapped through an amplifier, "Be still! Face front! Nobody told you to fire!"

Above the hull a thin mast lofted, opened umbrella arms and flung out a feathery substance which spread and thinned to a net, a mist, a vanishment. A sound screen.

Parker's voice came privately to each ear. "Who are you and what do you want?"

Waiting for Donald's answer, Sanders recalled that it was he who had insisted on the right to parley; Donald was waiting for him, man on the spot, to speak and speak rightly. He stood, saw the guns swing on him, prayed they would not again fire without orders, cupped his hands about his mouth and bellowed, "Security here!"

Silence. He had done well; a speechless Parker was a rattled Parker. Shocked Acolytes whispered and peered, unnerved by the unheralded presence of power.

Parker's silence persisted too long; he was not the man to succumb to surprise. Donald muttered, "Get doon again."

Without warning the lamps developed extra brightness, blazing up until the grass was flooded with brilliance.

Sanders found Donald beside him. "Lend me your sonic an' I'll show you a bonny trick wi' twa guns."

He handed it over without protest; he had no wish to use the unpleasant thing.

Parker's voice, grown gargantuan, roared, "Stand up!"

"Ay, do that! Whit he sees'll be the mair confusin'."

As they rose, Parker's mutter came clearly: "No protective gear!" He sounded furious at a simple oneupmanship. At speech level he ordered, "Come forward! The guards will shoot at a hostile move. Hands to your heads!"

Sanders saw Donald lift his guns to belt level, and glimpsed a power stud set fully forward. "Do what the polisman says."

As they lifted their hands in ragged obedience Donald took his only half way—then swung the guns in opposing arcs that must have skipped the Acolytes' heads by inches.

They did not get off a single answering shot.

Sanders caught the sidespill of full power as a soundless and shattering bellow; he could only guess at the ultrasonic agony of those directly below the beams. One man screamed so loudly that the screen filled the field with appalling torment; most dropped their weapons and clutched their heads; one collapsed.

"Bring him oot, Corey."

"PARKER, COME OUT!"

The hatch opened, framing a radiation-suited figure. Parker asked in softly raging helplessness, "What do you want?"

"Parade your men—all your men—outside with hands raised. All weapons on the tarmac."

Parker came down the steps. Men followed him. Guns clattered to the ground, their sound distanced as someone de-activated the screen. Sanders counted: "Twelve Acolytes and three crew. That's about right, but where's Santley?"

Donald decided, "We'll gang in. Angus, bide an' cover us. If you must shoot, only stun. No mair than that."

Angus laughed. "Yessir, boss!"

"Dinna kill, Angus. I'll no' hae it!"

They went forward, guns in sight. Parker stood before his men, his voice coming clearly through the suit grille: "The bloody woman . . . Baird . . . Thomson . . ." He changed to the professional jeering tone they recognized better, seeking advantage. "Plain clothes, Tech Sanders? That limits your powers of arrest. You need written authority. Show it!"

Sanders retrieved his gun from Donald. "My authority!"

"A Security *bandit*?"

"I want Santley. He's here, isn't he?"

He expected some token resistance and got it. "Here but not available."

Sanders asked patiently, "Under therapy still?"

"Still."

Jeanie said, "That's truth but it covers an evasion."

Parker's helmet turned ponderously towards her. "Another witch-woman attribute? Or blind guesswork?"

"It used to be called reading body English—a technique lost and rediscovered a dozen times. I learned it in Mohenjo-Daro, though the place had other names then."

Sanders interrupted the Company penchant for straying from

263

the point. "I want Santley, in no matter what condition. Get him!"

Parker hesitated, shrugged, gave the order. Two Acolytes climbed into the flyer.

Sanders said, "It is thought that you want—I quote—'to corner the mutant market'."

"No."

Jeanie said equably, "Liar."

Parker agreed. "Quite so, but the expert must be tested as rigorously as the charlatan. Yes, I had hoped to pick up all the long-living persons in Glasgow."

Sanders jerked a thumb at the flyer. "In that? There are three hundred of them here."

Despite the enclosing suit they saw him stunned by the information, so much so that shock emerged in a near-childish petulance. "It wasn't right that Security should have them."

"But right that you should? Do you want to live for ever? Or to have the power of giving and withholding life? Why?"

Parker astonished them with a furious, passionate shout: "For the glory of God!"

An answering murmur ran through the ranked Acolytes.

Sanders looked a question at Jeanie, who had her hands to her mouth between wonderment and laughter. "He means it! He doesn't want it for himself, only for his God! I've heard nothing like it since mad Luther. He means it!" She dropped her hands to say gravely, "Be careful, Security man; he'll do more for his faith than you for yours."

Sanders grunted, "He confuses God with Parker. Controller, you've broken no law yet, and you had better not." His dislike broke out in a needless cruelty: "You're Ferendija's whenever he likes to clench his fist."

The two Acolytes appeared, with a white-coated attendant, and manhandled Will, strapped to a stretcher, down the steps. He was grey, drawn, drugged, unable to speak.

Angus bent over him. "Amateurs! Witch doctors! Has hit-or-miss botching gained you a single word?" The psychlinician, whom they had seen in the Police Complex, shook his head. Parker turned his back. "How could it, you fumbling bastards? It isn't a synaptic block!"

The psychlinician said, "I learned that. What is it?" As Angus hesitated, "Don't you know either?"

"I don't know the mechanism but I know how to deal with it. We're taking him away for treatment."

"The Controller—"

"—is content that we have our way. God has his head in a cloud and can't hear the outrage of the righteous."

The psychlinician gave him contempt. "God makes better jokes, with the last laugh inbuilt."

Will was unable to stand. Donald carried him pickaback.

Parker, watching them fade beyond the ambit of his lights, counselled himself patience. *God is not mocked.*

Carlo cried, as Donald eased his burden on to the tray, "Our Willie! Born for disaster, that one."

With a common impulse they waited in the road for Sanders to say what was needed. Angus pressed, "Where to now? Do you want him?"

"Can you really rescue his memory?"

"You heard me say it."

"I can't read body English."

"Have you ever been wrong to trust me?"

"I haven't trusted you. If I say, 'To Ferendija', what then?"

"Then so be it, but unwillingly."

Jeanie muttered, "Shit!" but did not argue.

Sanders said, "Our skills are no better than Parker's." He kicked at the macadam. "Take him to your people."

He knew it was the right decision and that he would pay for it.

At the transit house Smith sent at once for Cooke, who examined Will with professional disgust. "Chemical shock! They must be desperate. Where their computers fail to diagnose, they're blind incompetents. Let him rest."

Angus asked if the drugs in Will's system could be nullified.

"Yes, but if he's ours he'll clear himself by midday. If he isn't—" he nodded at Donald and Sanders "—he's just another suffering human."

"If we're to open his mind, the physical weakness could be an advantage. Could he stand it tonight?"

"Give him twelve hours' rest."

"Smithy! Can we raise a probe team? Say, six?"

Smith said, "Easily," and continued thoughtfully, "We might make some tactical use of the procedure. Yes, I will arrange it. Laurel is available but not peyote at such short notice."

"Laurel will do."

"It should. In his mind it is only days since you relinquished him; you should take him again without resistance."

"That, yes. But I didn't plant this seal in him; if it's self-perpetuating, finding the key may take hours."

"You're doubtful?"

"Prudent. It won't be a quick job."

Smith smiled boyishly enough to shake Sanders's belief in his antiquity. "I'll put you on your mettle. You shall perform before an audience of all the parties concerned. Flaunt your ancient magic and much may come of the meeting of squabbling minds. Carlo can take a summons to the policeman. The rest of you get breakfast if you need it, then go back and annoy Commissioner Ferendija. Persuade him here for eleven tonight."

Sanders reminded him stubbornly, "What's to be said to Ferendija, I'll say."

Smith beamed, as at a bright child. "You are determined and quite vengeful. Whose side are you on?"

"Mine!" His mind gagged on the persistent question.

At mid-morning Carlo drove them back in the prospector and dropped them at the Erskine Bridge.

Donald was uneasy about the man's safety at the airfield but Angus said, "Parker knows violence will only bring him greater violence. And if he took a hostage, what could he bargain for? Nothing. If he had a prisoner he wouldn't even know what questions to ask."

6

Excepting the bored sentry at the water's edge, only Ferendija was in sight.

The Commissioner, out of uniform, sat alone on the narrow dorsal strip which did duty as a deck, poking with a swagger stick at the segmented worm coiled untidily at his feet, observing it intently. "Enjoying himself," Angus commented, "in his unhappy way."

In casual dress Ferendija was diminished; his shoulders lacked muscle, his legs tapered to a spindle point, his stockiness was illusory. He gave an unexpected smile, as if with the uniform he had cast a layer of rigidity, and called out to them, "Have you eaten? I'm told the Scots breakfasted on something called 'parritch'; did you?"

"No, sir. We had Irish Sea lobster, eggs from the Highlands and coffee from Tanzania. The Company eats well."

"Then fate cannot harm you, Tech Sanders, for you have dined today. Old saying—not to be depended on." The smile remained but a warning had been posted. As they crossed the makeshift gangway he lifted a sliver of worm on his stick and advised, "Don't fall in."

Angus said, "We have seen friends of your friend."

"This one is eighty feet long and could ingest your entire blood supply." With a subtextual menace that swelled and hardened his presence he added, "I hope, Sanders, that you spent the night usefully."

"I think so, sir. Will you take a verbal report?"

Ferendija nodded and listened but after a while produced a knife and began idly to chop the worm into short lengths and kick them overboard. They writhed as smoothly without head or tail as with them. He interrupted, as if unaware of Sanders's recital, "There's no reason why one of these, able to regrow head and tail and to retain something of learning procedures—which Biology Reference says is likely—shouldn't live for ever. Managing without any brain at all!"

He feigned shocked surprise at Angus's immediate willingness to kill him.

Sanders resumed his summary, cold-voiced. When he had done, Ferendija said nothing but banged on the deck with his stick and when a head appeared from the entry hatch, sent for Specialist White.

She came, in uniform, awkwardly on the rope ladder. She

observed the group with curiosity but avoided Donald's eye. She avoided him always but was never less than aware of him.

Ferendija greeted her with stiff anger. "His Lairdliness, Mr Baird, has anticipated his warrant by recruiting for his blighted demesne. Since Council has not yet approved his application, what is the legal situation?"

"Sound." He stirred slightly at the unhesitating affirmation. "They may make temporary arrangements, pleading the relevant statutes. It then becomes the business of World Council to disprove their interpretation."

"Law proves what it wishes to prove."

"In the wrong mouths. Here, there are precedents."

"You can cite them?"

"Several."

"Without reference to a data bank?"

She saw, too late, the trap she had dug for herself with rapped-out replies. "I—I would have to check reference numbers and dates."

"But you have familiarized yourself with Baird's dabble in international law?"

She said shakily, "It seemed advisable."

"Advisable also to discuss it with him? Or with the real intriguer, Mr Thomson? You did, didn't you?"

She whispered, frightened of him and of the closing trap of double-crossings, "Yes."

"In fact, from the start you provided the legal expertise for this move." She stood mute. "*Answer me!*"

"Yes."

"Sir!"

"Yes—sir."

"You will continue your duties as *my* adviser. In Australia the matter will be taken further. Conspiracy to obstruct, perhaps?" The threat drove colour from her face as he loosed an access of rage: "Why did you do it? For sweet intrigue's sake? Or for the sexual arrogance of a Gone Timer?"

She stared, petrified, with no idea what an honest answer might be. He told her, with a fury of loathing, "You disgrace your birth! Get below!"

Donald shouted at him, "An' how were you got? By a

268

mongrel oot o' a snufflin' sow? Your parents were Gone Timers, meester, an' may it grind your guts to remember it!"

Ferendija said simply, "It does. You and Thomson—get below, out of my sight." He watched with incandescent animosity as they went. "So, Tech Sanders, we are summoned to a midnight witching. What does this Smith hope to gain?"

Sanders had considered that. "To bring you and Parker together and balance your intentions against each other's. Or to set Security and Australia at odds. He could make capital of almost any difference between you."

"I suppose they do understand that in spite of the attractions of eternity they constitute a global menace?"

"They've known it for millennia."

"And what do they fear from us?"

"I get the impression there's little they fear; all discussion is flat, impersonal. I think that tonight they'll show us what we're up against—elements we may not have appreciated."

"There aren't any." Ferendija changed direction with an evil edge to his tone. "You gave them Santley. Why?"

"If Parker couldn't break his block, could we?"

"Why should I want to break it? I'm not interested; *they* are. So *you* gave them Santley who might have been a useful bargaining counter."

"Bargaining for what?"

He learned at once that Ferendija was not concerned with bargains. "What matters is that you had advantage and gave it away. Deliberately. Your conduct reeks of partisanship. Hand me your gun; you are relieved of duty. You will not leave the flyer; sentries will see to it. In Australia you will be given a psychlinical attitude test. Go below."

Sanders took his stripping—for it amounted to that—impassively. As he began to descend the rope ladder, Ferendija asked, perhaps of the river or the sky, "And what will be the scoring of the test?"

Between rung and rung Sanders took the last step through his indecision. "Most unsatisfactory," he said.

Alice was angry when, moving from the deck to the hatch, the men casually placed her between them to descend the ladder.

269

She had researched Gone Time social usages in all their point-lessnesses (could it matter who went first through a door?) and assumptions of female ineptitude. The hand on elbow to cross a street, and its aftermath, still rankled.

She saw that the conventions could be used tactically in the mating game and that Donald, stepping through the hatch and turning to assist her to a footing, was an opportunist player even in this crux of distress.

To push angrily past him would be childish. (That was the tactical trap.) She need only lean an instant on his arm and say a word of thanks. *I will not be outdone in ritual play.*

She regretted the gracious movement at once as his grip tightened, guiding her aside to let Angus through. And that little gameplayer extraordinary would chart evey nuance of pursuit and capture as he edged past with insultingly straight face. Their conventions were acts of war!

Donald said (and she could not deny the warmth), "You'll pay for lendin' your brains to a Gone Timer."

"That's to be seen; there are higher authorities than he." She tugged against his grip. "Let me go."

Instead, he took her breath away. "There's a place for you in Scotland. We'll need mair than Company here."

"Are you mad?" He hung on to her arm and she went on in a fluster, "I'm signed to Security for ten years. I can't just walk out. And why should I?"

"Because under Ferendija your future is nothing frae noo on. But there's a regulation—you can marry your way oot o' the service." To her wide-eyed astonishment he said doggedly, "I checked it."

"Regulation! Checked!" He was beyond belief. "Do you seriously mean that I should marry you?"

"Why no'? I'm no' such an unpresentable man an' you've the guts to make a bonny wife when times are dangerous."

She mocked, "There's romance for you!" but her laugh was not a success. "Or is this a business proposition?"

"Ay, the business o' survival. Oot there the world is boilin' to a heid, an' steadfast folk should find each other soon. Think aboot it. Think wi' your heid as well as your heart—an' there'll be time for a' the romantic courtin' your dreams ask for—withoot advice frae a computer."

He went off and left her to recover as she might, as if he had not just tried to push her over a cliff.

Ferendija kicked the worm's remains into the river. On the deck its leaked fluid stained and stank abominably.

Now we are plagued by all the centuries since life crawled from the sea. Thirty yards away, on shore, the sentry faced away from him, no doubt bored to inertia. *Or is he? I am cut off from the men's thoughts, but I know that Security crumbles from within—Sanders, the sex-silly White, how many more? If I erred in setting up that comic street fight and erred further in shuffling off reponsibility—which was necessary—is it so certain that ends never justify means? For right or wrong, the man on the spot must decide . . .*

He decided.

He went below, turned the Satellite Laser Communications Tech out of his electronic den, locked himself in, called on a Satellite link and encoded a message swaddled in secrecy techniques. Absolute secrecy was impossible, but he thought he did well enough. He fed his message to the encoder and sent it out in a single concentrated beep.

Last, he fed a single instruction chip into the Deferred Action circuit, to be sent at its proper time.

But first the midnight witching, in case some unguessably new thing came to light, changing the situation and his mind—and the Deferred Action chip.

He thought it unlikely.

7

In the twilight Parker did not at first fathom the change in George Square. When he saw that overnight the hecatomb of bones had crumbled into pale dust he trickled a handful through unsteady fingers and guessed that the last of yesterday had been shaken to a carpet of powder by sonic violence.

A practical move, since The Company wished to use the

Square for tonight's gathering, but the grotesque and terrible relic should have been preserved; not often could a garbage dump carry so cogent a warning. But what were warnings to ancient minds weary of history?

During the morning the surgeon, Cooke, had sent him ointments and sequestering agents and, although a totally anointed body was a sticky irritation, the gift of movement without suits was welcome. So, when he signalled the Acolytes to dismount from the tray-bodied truck which was the best transport he had been able to requisition in his hasty departure from Melbourne Town, they came in a youthful rush, eager for close sight of the condemned past. None of them had been out of Australia before.

Their hesitant course through the city on the previous night had been a creeping through mystery; the echoing canyons had roused only a sense of the strangeness of a soul's encounters on dark and deserted worlds. Now they exclaimed at the narrowness of streets, at architecture of a fashion over-florid in their austere teaching and at statues scattered as though the Gone Time had abounded in virtue for commemoration. They ridiculed while they gaped, not realizing that an intangible vitality had vanished from the world.

They would have spread like pecking hens if Parker had not ordered them to be still and be quiet.

At his shoulder Jeanie's voice asked, "Mayn't they discover that there is more to their past than ratrace and ruin?"

"They may discover what they like at a suitable time. I don't like being crept up on from behind."

She sidled round him, smiling up to his face; he noticed a slight baring of teeth and was reminded of something . . . he could not place it.

"It's history creeping up on you, that record of errors created by selfishness in the name of idealism."

He turned from the smile that lingered too long. "Errors can be recognized and avoided."

"That's what Angus believes, and his record of interference at critical moments is disastrous—Caesar, the Decembrists, Prince Charlie, Xerxes and a hundred more. The great double-crosser! Our clumsy Iscariot!" At his sharp intake of breath she explained hurriedly, "No, no—a Company joke; he wasn't involved in that. Poor, confused Judas made his own mistakes. Angus never dabbled with religion after he failed with Akhnaton. You've heard of Akhnaton?"

"No. What is Angus planning now?"

"You'll hear soon enough." She added, as one passing casual gossip, "He's insane, you know."

"I wish I could think so."

"Oh, not your kind of insane—all dribbling and exhibiting. Our kind. He just shouldn't be allowed to mix with people."

"A problem for you, too, is he?"

"Why for us? *You* are people; *we* are—what we are. *People* are bad for Angus, not he for them." She mused, happily insulting, "It isn't easy to realize that in your fashion you are a well-meaning race. I suppose it's the price of having to *struggle* for existence. The need simply to stay alive is used to justify any beastliness."

She left him abruptly, on a bemused thought: *It's true— death overtakes before we have time to overtake the brutishness.* She had justified, almost sanctified, his planning.

As she slipped into the shadows, a youngster of twenty or so moved in to say, "She heard me approach. Be advised: Keep away from her."

This one seemed astonishingly juvenile, barely full-grown. "Her hearing must be sharp."

"In her kind it is."

"Kind?"

"She, Angus and a few others—the face-makers. They are the shape-changers of Nordic legend, but fables of lycanthropy are exaggerations. I suppose she was as usual talking too freely."

"You have some authority over her?"

"Not as you use the word, Mr—Walker, is it?"

"Parker."

"Yes, the policeman. They call me Smith. They give me simple names, but I tend to forget recent happenings."

Parker tried a goad. "That's a symptom of senility."

"Yes, but don't take risks; you aren't on your home ground." The menace was as light as small talk. "You spoke of authority; what I command is respect and some deference. I am neither despot nor leader; I am a convenient focal point. If I give orders they are usually carried out, but—" he smiled with peculiarly vacant animation, like one doing his best to charm a bore, "—we are rarely under a necessity to get things done."

"You don't *struggle* for existence?"

"Did she say that?" He chuckled. "It's her intellectual *bon mot* for new acquaintances."

"It explains much about human history."

"Which indeed needs explaining as well as justifying. Did she smile and show her teeth to point philosophy?"

Parker's breath stopped half-taken as he made the connection between the girl and Angus. "She did."

"She's an opportunist. Avoid her eyes."

Parker said, "She's done it two or three times."

"Not often enough to effect a capture," Smith told him cheerfully, "though she might jar your self-control for a moment or two. What else did she tell you?"

"That Angus is insane."

Smith flew without transition to blind rage. "I swear I'll terminate her!" He put his hands to his face and when he dropped them was smiling vaguely again. "We rarely terminate our own, but that madwoman is incalculable."

"Do you mean it's she that is mad?"

"Since the cat's out—they both are. All face-makers are un-balanced; it is part of their genetic heritage. We do suffer disadvantages, we Children." Parker's frown seemed to cheer him. "Our insanities are not yours. Our systems take care of common mental disorders very quickly but there are psychic imbalances peculiar to the Children. They could mean nothing to you."

"Indeed? I'm not an idiot."

As though he had not spoken Smith continued, "We must exchange some honesties before we speak with the party now arriving. Come with me."

On the south side a long skimmer, monopole-powered to float and glide, more sophisticated than any machine Parker could command, had pulled in. Ferendija descended, wearing civilian dress (Parker wondered, did he fancy it defrosted him?) and followed by a dozen black-beetles, armed to the teeth no doubt and with uniforms activated to snare sight and sound. Then Thomson. And the White girl, the man-hungry upstart.

He flinched from Smith's hand lightly on his elbow, urging him away, "Racialist instincts, Controller?"

"I dislike contact. Why should I go with you?"

"So that the Commissioner shall not know your plans until we have decided how much is good for him."

He let Smith lead him, prosaically, to a park bench. Fifty yards away, at the edge of the square, Ferendija watched them while he gave orders to a uniformed Tech who fiddled with the buttons and flaps of his overall.

"We shall add a vulgar note to his listening." Smith produced a small box with a trailing wire which he hooked round one of the iron seat-bolts. At once the dark air shimmered around them and the outlines of trees, men and buildings rippled like reflections in stirred water.

"Alastair made this for me. It is inferior to your privacy scramblers but it will create atrocious noises in that man's directional microphone. Now, Controller! What do you want and what can you give? Do, please, be truthful."

Ferendija was not amused by a cursing Tech and an unbreachable colloquy; Parker was capable of the unexpected.

A woman's voice suggested, "You should learn lip-reading. Not all the old skills were despicable."

"No skill is despicable." He surveyed her without pleasure. "Jeanie Deans? Is that actually your name?"

"No—Messalina." She looked past him at the waiting Techs. "Where is Sanders?"

"Out of your reach. Is his presence, er, desirable?"

She replied without hostility, "This won't be an occasion for simple pleasures," and spoke past him: "Your team's ready, Angus."

Angus pushed through the group of Techs. "How many?"

"Five and yourself."

"Competent?"

"How should I know? Two women, trained at Delphi—if that matters."

"It does."

"The men all claim expertise. Cooke vouches for one."

"They'll do."

She nodded without interest and walked off.

Ferendija would have welcomed explanation, but Angus ignored him and went to join Donald and Lindley where they waited apart from the Security group. Ferendija had let them make their own way on power-bikes, giving the machines only because he knew their presence was obligatory but wanting it clear that they formed no part of his responsibility.

Angus drew them forward. "We'll use the memorial at the east end for a stage setting; nicely impressive."

"An' whit will you do there?"

"High psychiatry! It will look more like a witches' coven to you out here—rich cloaks, dramatic lighting, drugs smoking over a brazier, coloured fire at critical moments. Most of the ritual is bogus but it will help hook Will into a state approaching the transcendental but still open to delicate direction."

"A bluidy theatre turn? You'll no' use the memorial!"

At a loss, Angus asked, "Why not?"

"Because your witchcraft's puir if you canna do as well withoot it. The cenotaph belangs to deid men whose short lives owe no debt to yours, an' they can be left to keep whit's theirs withoot bluidy cantrips to debase them."

Angus shook his head in a small wonderment, said, "If that's what you wish," and went off to find his team.

Only feet away, Ferendija had heard, and remarked to Lindley, "I'm forever astonished at the reverence your hard-headed time paid the symbols of grief and death."

"Hard-headed and soft-hearted," Lindley told him. "Your time is neither."

Donald explained what a mercenary knew without telling: "Deid men are ainly deid men, but a livin' chief must be master o' his difficult clansmen. The wee Angus kenned that an' surrendered like the gentleman he isna." He wagged a finger at the fascinated Ferendija. "Or maybe it was just that I'll no' see my monuments pranced on by political mountebanks."

Twilight became night. Parker and Smith talked behind their

screen. Ferendija seemed absorbed, giving no orders, paying no attention either to his frightened Legist aide.

In the open space between the Scott column and the cenotaph, Angus conferred with his team. A brazier had been lit; red heat shone through its iron lattice. Beside it a metal dish held a pile of dried leaves. Laurel, Alice wondered? Corey had mentioned it and Pharmacy Data had informed her that the sibyls of Delphi were reputed to have used its smoke to induce heightened awareness. That was a mocking of computer psychology. Eerie.

So were the people eerie who gathered under the skeletal trees on the north lawn, their speech too soft to cross the central space. Three hundred of them, Corey (stripped of career and freedom for lurching into honourable truth) had said; indistinguishable from humanity but not of it.

Eerie, too, was Jeanie, lingering, assessing Techs with thoughtful eyes—striking, attractive but not beautiful in a Reconstruction woman's eyes. Not "sonsy".

Still, it was unfair of Jim Lindley to serpent-hiss in her ear, "What do you think of the competition?"

She refused to answer.

"All right; it isn't so. But they must have made a fine pair."

She said, aloofly (she thought), "I can understand what she saw in him."

He laughed at her incompetence. "Can you? The price of freedom from misconceptions is high."

It was comment, warning and challenge. Between her teeth she said, "You bastard!"

In bright starlight Smith and Parker crossed to Ferendija. Angus and his team had vanished, leaving the chair and hot brazier; the quiet Children were patient under the trees, not counting time as other than expendable.

Ferendija turned his head, ordered, "Out of earshot!" and the black uniforms retreated. "White!"

Not even "Specialist" White. She stepped up. "Sir."

"Record everything. Speak only if required."

She activated her uniform, relaying whatever transpired to the Communications Cabin on the flyer.

At their first physical meeting Parker and Ferendija examined

277

each other with mutual contempt. Smith hovered between them like an upstart imp with his sense of humour tickled. "Are you gentlemen not on speaking terms?"

Ferendija said, "There's a line drawn; we know where it is." He asked Parker, "Who's this brat?" He knew perfectly well.

Smith sniggered. Parker grinned darkly, diagnosing (wrongly) frayed nerves. "He calls himself John Smith and claims to be thirty thousand years old. I see no reason to doubt him. He is a leader of sorts. Their authority system is too fluid to be easily grasped, but it's him we must deal with."

Ferendija's laugh flickered over them. "It is me you both must deal with."

Smith was amenable. "Why not? You have extraordinary powers and we have, as used to be said, only what we stand up in." He mimed poverty. "And that may be a damned sight more than you think."

"Have the intelligence not to threaten."

"I never do; I act. I have already taken some action." He peered into the dark. "Where's that Scotsman?"

Parker bellowed with unexpected parade-ground power: "Baird! Donald Baird!"

Donald came lounging. "Och ay—whit?"

Smith said genially, "Now we're all face to face, are we protagonists or antagonists?"

"When the chips are doon we're a pack o' connivin' bastards withoot honour. Get on wi' the hagglin'."

"Plain speaking! I said, Commissioner, that some action had been taken. This: we have agreed to accept Mr Baird's offer of Scottish nationality. So Donald is laird of the Highlands, the Lowlands—and of the Children of Time. A comment, Commissioner?"

"White! The legal position?"

Unsettled by his animosity and as much again by Donald's eyes on her, she said shakily, "They can remain undisturbed while Council debates the submission already made. With Delay For Reconsideration they may have a year."

Donald was suspicious. "*May* have?"

"The Delay can be cancelled by a declaration of emergency."

"An' whit constitutes an emergency?"

Ferendija took over. "Whatever I deem to be one."

They considered that without comfort until Smith said, "I have not come up from the caves without surviving alarms and perils; and we, the Children, do not react to casual menace in the tense human fashion. So let us observe facts equably. Controller Parker, after treating me to some remarkable half-truths and fantasies, has a suggestion you may find less than credible but which interests me."

All round them a ripple of talk erupted and died as into the Square stepped six figures in fitted robes, which swept the ground, in brilliant electric green, to shimmer through crimson and cobalt in the brazier glow as they glided through the soft dust of a city's bones.

"Pantomime?" Ferendija asked. "Cries and weird music?"

Smith eyed him with distaste. "Hocus-pocus for a primitive purpose beyond psychlinical capability. Let us hear Controller Parker's ideas."

Parker looked directly at Ferendija with wintry dislike and said, "My concern is with God."

Ferendija sighed gently and listened.

"Mr Smith's people disagree as to whether or not they are human. Plainly they are not *homo sapiens*; biological variations rule them out. But this does not make them *un*human. Cro-Magnon man and the Neanderthaler were not *sapiens*, but they were human. They represent what *sapiens* once was, as the Children represent what *sapiens* one day will be. They are human." He searched their expressions. "Am I understood?"

Donald caught Alice's eye and winked. She thought angrily that he had no sense of occasion. But it was not easy to absorb Parker's pedantries with suitable respect.

Ferendija pointed out, suffering, that he had not come for a semantic juggling act, while Smith twinkled like a small boy who loved a good juggler. "But I'll concede technical humanity, if it helps."

"They call themselves the Children of Time. Fanciful but fair. As humans, they are also the children of God."

He paused, as if on a statement of power.

Ferendija interpreted, "So you say that they are members of

the community of man, and so the Ethic protects them while no law is broken or right infringed. White?"

It was an obvious point, one to which she had given sufficient attention to turn up an odd fact. "There is no precise definition in science or law of the word *human*."

Parker started; Smith snickered; Donald said, "So the wheels o' decision are obstructed until they make one. I foresee some bonny brawls in your corridors o' power."

Ferendija asked sourly of his Legist, "What else?"

She was frightened, unable to anticipate what humiliations he might contrive, but answered as stoutly as self-respect demanded. "A group awaiting definition may continue their group practices without let, so long as no rights of others are encroached upon."

"Well, Mr Smith," Ferendija admitted, "God and the law smile on you. But do you believe in God?"

"In a supreme being?"

"What else?"

"It seems naive, doesn't it? And it isn't what Mr Parker means, if I understand his explanation to me."

Parker said as if to a kindergarten, "God is a spirit."

Ferendija threw up his hands. "From the naive to the vacuous."

It was Donald who suggested, "The spirit o' Man, perhaps? The spirit o' what Man aspires to be?"

Parker shot him a glance of astonished approval.

"Quite so," Smith said. "The heresy of the Emerging God! Men have burned for it though it is no more amenable to proof or disproof than the iconic concept of a Semitic patriarch, but it might make a more respectable foundation for a philosophy. I accept the Controller's God—" he twinkled happily at them "—pro tem."

"You accept", Ferendija told him, "whatever protection such convenience may afford you. 'Conniving bastards' was your chosen leader's phrase."

Smith offered a thought, like one holding it up for inspection. "What can you care, Commissioner, when pragmatic atheism overrides all arguments and evasions?"

The damned man knew he would not admit that. "I'm listening to your ideas, aren't I? Might I hear the rest of the Controller's plan? Is there more to it than metaphysics?"

He contemplated the green robes in the square, iridescent where brazier light caught the folds. It made effective spectacle. Mystic stuff. The chair, almost a throne, behind the brazier would be Santley's venue of popular stardom. Was it worth waiting for? His resolution of the Gordian knot so finely tied by Angus and the White girl was as good as settled.

He was glad to hear Smith take over from Parker, who would have expounded morality as long as an audience remained awake.

"Briefly, the Controller proposes that the Children of Time, being also the children of God, should share their physiological advantages with the children of mortality."

"By way of the laboratories of Gangoil?"

"How else?"

"I thought that you objected to demotion to the status of laboratory rats."

Smith's smile became humourless. "We do, but some give-and-take seems unavoidable. If the matter is regulated to prevent a bargain-sale rush by frenzied biologists with longevity dangled before them like a spangled carrot, the experience may prove bearable. At any rate, the idea offers the first suggestion of a controlled solution."

"And when the short-lived world is promised heaven on a plate, what then? Even partisan Doctor Lindley quails at the thought of a world stripped of the ordinary considerations of mortality. So do I."

Smith's twinkle recovered its brightness. "Mr Parker assures me that intensive and intelligent religious teaching will avert extreme deterioration."

Parker intervened with infuriating tranquillity. "When we no longer *struggle* to live we will think beyond life and transient needs. Solutions now unthinkable will appear."

Ferendija's incredulity overflowed. "Are you both mad? Rampant greed for life will say to hell with religion and philosophy and training and every damned thing but the promise of an endless tomorrow!"

Parker would have raged at him but Smith signed to him to

hold still and, amazingly, the Controller subsided. Ferendija was impressed; he would not underestimate Smith.

And Smith proceeded to read him a lesson. "You are an upstart representative of an upstart culture that has forsaken all its fathers knew except their capacity for self-deception. You deride the idea of a religious brake on human passions, but I tell you that your people are so empty of everything but the complacency stuffed into them that they can be led in any direction a promise points. The Children have not your need for religious comfort against the unknown, but we have seen races and cultures rise and fall—and the millennia of anarchy, tyranny, blood and distress called always for the peace of some unattainable godhead. Belief, in no matter what, is not to be taken lightly. It has held the crumbling world together before this and may do it again. Think twice, Commissioner."

Ferendija made a small, flicking gesture. "Save it for the impressionable. Parker's promised life will fall to an elite of Cultists. A tyranny of gentle Jesus!"

"In which case the rush of converts might shake even your self-satisfaction."

Ferendija asked, as if it could only be a joke, "You surely won't throw in your lot with God-the-peacemaker?"

"I can't make such a decision alone, but I have more sense than to reject it unconsidered." He peered into the darkness across the square and breathed a quiet, "Ah!" as movement stirred in the shadows. "Your pantomime is about to begin."

He left them as if he had lost interest in their talk, without so much as a gesture. Ferendija stared after him, uncomprehending.

"Doesn't he want to know what we others think?"

A down-to-earth Parker, his visionary side withdrawn, jeered at him. "Don't you understand that he . . . *they* don't care what we do, what action we take? A temporary unpleasantness, is how they see all this. Some bother—and then back to whatever it is they do in the jungles of eternity. They stir a little at imminent discomfort but at bottom they don't *care*."

It made a kind of sense but Ferendija did not answer; he was thinking that a Cultist planet would finally be an abortive

282

alternative, all schism and bigotry. Such things must not happen and he would see to it that they did not.

He turned to the performance. It could hardly produce information to alter his determination, but the indoctrinated respect for justice demanded that he sit it out on the offchance.

The action had begun without announcement. Santley had appeared from the dark fringes, walking wearily to the brazier where his witches gathered in stillness.

Ferendija thought there might after all be little to see—when the brazier blazed whitely incandescent. Yellow and blue flames licked head high and the witch-robes answered with rainbow brilliance as they fell back from the spell-centre. As suddenly, the flames died, leaving the surface of the fuel white hot, shedding light harsh enough to render the faces as devil masks with knife-edge features and empty hollows.

It was exotic, eye-catching; he could not guess the nature of the fuel but supposed they had picked up a barrel or two of tricks down the ages.

The silence from the massed Children of Time (a brash conceit, that) made insect squeaks of the comments and questions of Techs and Acolytes—selfconsciously apart and watching each other with suspicion.

He asked quietly, "Parker, how much do your Acolytes know?"

"Nothing; I'm not an incompetent."

Ferendija's Techs also were ignorant, but how much might not everybody know by the night's end? The question had bearing on his plans. He moved away from the group, needing solitude; only his Legist waited near, silent, on call.

He heard Santley's voice raised, but no words. The man's shirt and trousers made shabby contrast with the robes. Some manipulation of these by the wearers created bands of colour leaping from figure to figure. Clever! He thought Santley's eyes followed the colours in tired fascination.

It was a *moiré* effect, of course, reminding him of the hypnopatterns used by psychlinicians to separate strata of consciousness. This was a primitive use of the principle.

Santley was protesting now, and Angus arguing. Santley covered his eyes against brightness (or against Angus?), stepped

283

backwards, collided with the chair and staggered. He vanished under a swirl of robes. When they brought him to his feet he was tractable; Angus had renewed control.

From the darkness Smith slipped in beside him. "He resented being taken again when Angus had formally freed him all those years ago. We don't approve of broken faith but there was no choice." Ferendija did not look at him or answer. "We know certainly that Santley is mutant flesh. In four hours he threw off the drugs that fool of Parker's had fed him."

Angus hovered behind the chair, face satanic with shadow, speaking, apparently a single word or short phrase at a time, into Santley's ear.

"All day, Commissioner, the group has been preparing lists of the keywords which may have been used to confine a section of Santley's mind in a closed synaptic circle, shutting out all other sections. This is not a hypnotic block, more of a self-sustaining quarantine."

"The possible number of keywords must be astronomical. I haven't a year to waste."

"Not so. There is a limit to the relevant themes and images. The number is not unmanageable."

Astonishingly, the robes were producing repetitive lateral and vertical patterns in staggered rhythms. Ferendija conceded more to it than simple *moiré*; no amount of practice could achieve such effects. His eyes followed, marvelling.

"Look away every half minute or so, Commissioner; it is easy to succumb, even to lose balance." Smith's voice changed as he came to the nub of his presence, "I broke off our conference because I thought it best that your contribution was not made at that time."

So it was a fishing expedition. Ferendija let the man stew—so he imagined—until he was ready to speak, then said, "I have no contribution to make."

Smith laughed delightedly. "Didn't Tech Sanders explain body-English to you? You can't lie to a reader. I'm no brilliant Jeanie but I'll not be gulled by you."

"As you like. If I'm lying, what's the truth?"

"We decided long ago what Security's truth must be. You have an insoluble problem : knowledge of the Children's existence can only destroy your culture, but as a recurrent mutation, we can't be eliminated. In any case, that human terror of death, which we do not share, wants us alive for biological research. You can't live with us or without us. So, Commissioner, you have decided to defer the problem until decades, perhaps generations of study have found an answer."

It was true; no comment would alter it.

"I could choose a more congenial ruin than Glasgow," Smith said regretfully, "for a quarantine station."

When Ferendija dared to look for him, the man had gone again. *Flibbertigibbet.* Which in the medieval era of Gone Time had been the name of a devil—food for Hellmouth.

8

Sanders was not under restraint, but three disappointed Techs had been left to man the duty watches. There had been an expectant air about Baird and Lindley and the town detachment, so they felt hard done by.

The sentry glooming on the river bank would have liked to ask Sanders about his unexplained house arrest, but Sanders paced the "deck" and spoke to no one. Also, hobnobbing might be imprudent, if the matter were really serious.

The thoughts circling behind Sanders's silence would have alerted Ferendija to dismay at an irrecoverable error. He knew the man smarted, and justifiably, at the treatment dealt him over the teen riot, but the threat of an attitude test had been a necessary shock tactic to encourage rethinking (he had no intention of enforcing it on so excellent a man), but he did not guess how much of himself he had revealed or the depth of Sanders's disillusionment. High echelons were to a degree deconditioned to allow room for creative thinking, but a Tech *belonged* to the Service that reared and cared for him. There had been odd cases (the Campion affair of five years ago had been most odd), and he knew that a lifetime's conditioning could sometimes be broken by an exactly applied mental savagery, but he did not understand that a savagery of inconsistent action-against-belief was what he had in fact applied.

So, in the starlight, Sanders thought about Ferendija's un-spoken intentions towards The Company.

From the first he had seen what the pragmatic solution should be, but it was one he could not bring himself to apply if the implementing were his. When Smith questioned him he had been evasive, because it was a barbaric solution which no Security man could carry out. It might just be possible to the ice-souled Parker.

Now, seeing from the uncluttered vantage of a liegeless man, he speculated on the possibility of an ice-souled Ferendija.

Ferendija, stripping and threatening and isolating him, had cut him off from the Service which was his only link with existence. Cutting another's lifeline was a demonic act. And after the attitude test—he was sure of this—he would be dememorized and reconditioned, and all his past would have been lived for nothing. Only cold wickedness condemned a man to that . . .

The two off-duty sentries would be, he knew, in the Recording Cabin, scanning the screen and tapes as the Techs in George Square transmitted what was said and done, trying to under-stand what they saw, but he was interested only in the message Ferendija had sent when he had turned the operator out of the Satellite and Laser Cabin and locked himself in.

The message would have been to Council or one of the Ancillary Offices; nothing less could call for such privacy. He had a shrewd idea of the content, and meant to be sure.

Decision made, he swung down the rope ladder to the hatch. Satellite and Laser, a separate system from the Recording unit, was located forward, behind the Flight Cabin. It would be untenanted because Ferendija, flaunting a stronger retinue against Parker's Acolytes, had taken the Specialists with him, leaving incoming messages to the automatic tape-and-hold.

The cabin was open. Doors in a Security establishment were rarely locked; in an emergency all capacities must be available to the man on the spot.

He knew the approximate time the Operator had been ejected, and searched the data bank for messages sent between eleven and midday—routine reports, a quartermaster's return, a batch of greetings . . . and one message on lock-and-block, retrieval-coded to the sender only. Most, most secret.

The only datum available was that it had been relayed via Satellite 3; its data bank would have the text of the message.

Checking, he looked in on the Recording Cabin for a few minutes, but the Techs were ill at ease with him, unsure of his standing; their non-committal reserve preferred his absence.

He said, with the diffidence of the out of favour, "I'm putting in some study time. I'll be in S and L with the coding manuals."

They nodded and waited for him to go, which he did, satisfied that if they knew where he was they would not disturb him. A Tech under discipline commonly sat it out in limbo.

They would not have understood that he did not suffer. He had passed through rage at injustice and leaped the whinings of self-pity to arrive at the half-hallucinated stage of suspecting enormities. And intending to uncover them. He was the wronged man who would, against power and authority, prove his rightness.

Back in S and L, he keyed the laser to Satellite 3, transmitted the time of Ferendija's message and demanded playback.

The Satellite replied that no message had been relayed from the flyer at the hour given.

From general training he had some idea of the tricks possible to a multi-purpose assembly, so he asked had the Satellite taken a message from any source at the time specified. The idiot machine assured him that it had.

From what source? The peculiar reply to that set him riffling through the Operators' Manual. From a welter of confusing symbols (confusing because the Satellite sent him a farrago of evasions in its effort to make what answer it could on a subject which an awkward order had told it to ignore but not to erase, and at the same time to deny to a seemingly legitimate questioner what should be freely available for playback scrutiny—it was a simple transfer station, not a logician) he deduced that Ferendija had tried to conceal the point of origin.

Because the point of origin would pinpoint Ferendija?

He asked the destination of any message sent by Ferendija at that time. Properly, the Satellite ignored him. He felt as stupid as the machine he was trying to outwit.

The lock-and-block could be released only by the call-signature of the originator—and World Councillors had coded signatures which would not be released to casual enquiry.

So—who was to be denied the knowledge? He knew of only one receiver Ferendija would contact on this affair: the only one with knowledge of it—Council.

No, said Satellite 3, no message had been relayed to Council at the time stated. But, Sanders knew, a copy of *any* message relayed under a Councillor's code would be passed automatically to Historical Archives Storage.

World HQ denied receipt of any Satellite-relay message at that time. So Ferendija had got round the data-bank trap and kept Historical ignorant of what he did. Why? The hair at his nape crawled.

He thought about it. To achieve action at the receiving end the signature would have to be authoritative. A personally signed, private message, for instance, would not go to Historical unless directed there. But the relaying bank would copy it; nobody could bypass that action-check procedure.

So Ferendija must have done the obvious—sent his name in clear, trusting to the lock-and-block to conceal him. As it would have done had Sanders not known that the message existed.

He transmitted a cancellation of the lock-and-block and signed it as Security Commissioner, Australasian Sector, Istvan Georg Ferendija. On the seventh variation of that combination he struck it correctly. The Satellite disgorged.

He requested playback in printout. Hard evidence.

In victory he knew himself at a point of no return. His hand shook as the tape snaked across the desk and he picked up the running end, knowing that this was the finish of him in Security or in any position of trust anywhere.

Then he forgot conscience, consequences, everything but rigid shock as he recognized the address of the receiver. The text itself was monstrous.

Moonrise wrought transformation. Clouds scudded, parted, evanesced; stars spiked the sky; light searched out the watchers beneath the skeleton trees; a loosening of tensions rippled round the square and something of mystery departed.

Only Ferendija seemed unmoved. To Donald, alert with distrust, the man seemed to have placed himself apart in spirit as he had done physically.

A robed figure threw leaves on a metal dish poised over the brazier; they crackled like tiny percussion caps and loosed a grey smoke. Will was lifted, and his head thrust forward into the fumes; Angus urged, and he breathed deeply until his lungs revolted and he began to choke. They guided him to sit again. An acrid aroma came faintly on the air.

Lindley sniffed. "Laurel and mystic herbs! It's crude, but there's still much to learn about these great-grandma concoctions. Angus swears this one helps to release the thought below thought—which is gobbledegook."

Smith joined them and watched without speaking until Donald asked, "Do you want something o' me?"

Smith's spirits seemed spritely still. "What should I want of you, you man of blood?"

"Your laird's good will, maybe."

"Oh, I'll knuckle the forehead to impress the groundlings, so long as you don't imagine I mean it."

Parker broke a long silence. "Why shouldn't you mean it? The man who keeps Security from your throat is no cipher." He addressed Donald, stiffly, striving not to confess desperation, "Mr Baird, I'd like to join forces with you; we have a common antagonist."

"Ay, so? This game makes unlikely partners."

"We should link advantages."

"Ay." Unenthusiastic but practical.

On a freakish note of rapture Will bayed suddenly at the sky, setting flesh crawling until the howl died in gabble.

Smith chuckled. "The sibyl in revelatory ecstasy!"

Whatever the sibyl told, Angus listened intently, and made signals to his cabal, whose robe manipulations ran down subtle gradations to a fireheart of deep rose.

Parker said with a harsh, disbelieving urgency, "This is a fine display, but what can Santley's genes mean to you, Mr Smith? What's your interest in procreation when mutation makes increase for you?"

Smith's veneer of amusement vanished. He snapped, "What is your need of a God?"

"To render existence meaningful."

"No God, no meaning? Can't your manipulation of the world make existence meaningful for you? How can you think otherwise when all your history is of mass movements towards greater and greater mass unities? You claim that man will develop until he is God; if he remains only Man, isn't that the same thing? The fact that you live *is* your meaning. What you do with life—" his voice took on an edge of irritation "—takes meaning away from it by insisting on individualism while you yearn towards a world soul."

Lindley spoke between them. "And you? Your people are solitary by nature, clustering only when you must. No world soul for you. What do life and genetics mean to you?"

Smith took time to answer, said at last, "The explanation may be unintelligible to you. How can I show life to one contaminated by the certainty of death? In allusive terms, perhaps? Have you ever thought like a running fox or an albatross in full glide or a bear at the honeycomb? Have you ever understood, as the thoughtless beasts understand, the excitement of being alive? Have you *enjoyed* frozen fingertips or thirst under a brass sun or the agony of a long fall—*enjoyed* them as elements of the splendour and infinite change of the universe? I have lived through ten million dawns, yet I rise early for a new sunrise because in all my life there have been no two alike and every miracle at dawn is a miracle of the universal life that transcends organisms of blood and flesh to encompass stars and the fabric of spacetime itself. These are the birthright of the Children of Time. We celebrate life. It *is* and we *are*! If tonight we receive the ultimate gift—the creation of new life, new celebrants—then the universe is ours. No greater joy remains to find."

Parker's turning away was eloquent; he might have accepted a new mysticism, never a simple hedonism. Lindley only sucked on his lips, foreseeing more terrifying changes than his fears had encompassed.

Donald said practically, "A man might learn, after years. But most wouldna. Because—" It was too complex an idea for a ready statement, seeming to involve a simplicity of mind and attitude which all his experience rejected. But he saw something of what frightened Lindley. "Your ain folk live as ordinary men till the years show them they are something else. Can they then throw off all their man-thinkin' an' become . . . become vessels o' livin'?"

The answer was short. "Many do not."

Lindley asked, "And those who do not?"

"Some, like Angus, like Jeanie, involve themselves in ceaseless activity. Insanity takes its toll there."

"And others?"

Smith turned on him a grin of sheer malevolence. "They kill themselves, Mr Lindley. Those who cannot face the universe remove themselves from it. I warn your greedy world that more have taken their useless lives than have lived through until today. The failure rate is formidable."

Lindley, his fears confirmed, said nothing.

Donald saw it otherwise. "I think I'd prefer Angus's insanity to your mental health."

"So you might—until you had suffered it. Still, without it you would surely be forty-five years dead."

"Is it so? Tell me aboot that."

"You're impetuous, Scottish laird. You won't care for the implications, not at all."

Sanders's mind centred on action, the only track it could follow without paralysis of thought.

He needed a special weapon, and must improvise.

In the galley he fingered a cleaver, but it lacked the psychological element; it was too ordinary a threat. But he took it, as a necessary tool, together with a three-pound lump of raw meat, a meathook and a bucket.

A portable source of naked flame was a more exotic need in a non-smoking, electrically-powered environment, until he remembered the compressed-gas burners in the sample-testing laboratory; self-contained, they could spirt a thousand-degree flame at medium aperture for a short period.

With his load he climbed to the deck. Under the bright moon every action would be seen by the sentry, but the man would prefer to ignore rather than query him while his activities were eccentric rather than culpable.

From the railless deck he peered into dark water until an undulating ribbon wavered into view. The river was alive with them. He undid his belt, passed one end of the meathook through the buckle and on the other hung the gobbet of meat. Flat on his face, he lowered the belt and bait at full stretch until the lower edge of the meat hung a couple of feet above the water. From what he had seen of the Techs' fascinated "fishing" during the day, that should be near enough.

The beast was at once aware of food. Scent? He did not know or care.

Its blind, squared club of a head, spotted with four purple suckers, emerged vertically from the water, slid back and reached again, and again, each time closer, until a sucker caught and the thing dragged itself to a firm hold. Suction and digestive acids began a furious feeding. (Gone Timers had harboured smaller versions of this brute in their intestines. A thought to vomit on.)

Rising to his knees, he dragged the bait and its load to the deck, the brainless length gorging as it clung.

"The ability of the face-makers to impose mental control", Smith said, "is one we don't understand any more than they do. It exists. Gangoil—" his voice flattened with resignation "—will no doubt locate the governing nucleotides and will discover that there is a correlative of mental instability—madness. They go together. In your Jeanie it takes the form of sexual appetite for muscular humans. She will hold a satisfactory mate for years, or several men, until he or they begin to—to *fray* under her attentions."

Donald said gently, "She's no' my Jeanie. Her sickness is a sair one, but it's no' insanity as I ken it."

"You *ken* insanity as violence and unpredictability—the scared-herd definition. Her mental violence is a cruelty of bondage, years long. Is that less abnormal?"

"It doesna affect her doin' an' thinkin'. She's evil, no' mad."

Smith sighed. "Mr Baird, I am about to insult you beyond bearing. Can you control yourself?"

"Maybe. It's you chancin' it, no' me."

"As you say. So tell me what you would think of a human who formed sexual liaisons, years long, with prize animals of the countryside."

Donald shuddered. "You get no thanks for remindin' me o' the human place in your esteem. I knew it already."

"Tut, Mr Baird! We don't really think in those terms; nobody can risk such contempt. I suggested only a strong biological parallel. We are different and the difference is crucial. Sex is not with us a major irritant, an eternal goad, as with you. When it pricks it must be relieved; we learn to live with this as a—peccadillo—a necessity, not an addiction. When, as with Jeanie, it develops into emotional dependence, it passes the socially bearable norm. That fits your definition of imbalance as well as ours."

"Angus! What's his indecency?"

"A sexual drive, but not so outrageous. His real trouble is more curious. Angus is, from our viewpoint, emotionally retarded. He wants to be taken to your human hearts, to give all his affection and sentimentality to a circle of loving friends. He yearns to bask in the esteem of you, his loving godchildren. He pretends to regard you as pets, but it is not so."

"An' that's daft? Wantin' to be a man an' no' a freak?"

"It is savagely dangerous—to humans. His need to identify with men rather than with a crippled minority—that's how he regards his own kind—is so great that throughout history he has interfered in human affairs for what he sees as the good of humanity but what is in fact the frenzied placation of a mind driven by private devils. I could site a dozen instances, but one will suffice to burn your romantic Highland heart."

"I'm no' a Hielander."

"But you are a romantic, so the Forty-five will mean something to you?"

"Ay, a disaster."

In the centre a change had occurred. The brilliant robes were still, frozen in moonlight. Angus kept his mouth to Will's ear, speaking a single syllable, waiting, speaking another . . . A relaxed Will, head slack against the chair-back, answered an occasional slow word.

Smith said, "Soon now, I think. Angus is tremendously talented—and for his errors he lives in a perpetual sickness of atonement. You, Mr Baird, are his atonement for that Bonnie Prince Charlie of romance and maudlin memory."

"I don't understand that an' I'm no' flattered. He was the ruin o' Scotland."

"Oh no, that was Angus. You'll recall that General Murray led Charles's rebel army south to Derby, outwitting English forces like quicksilver, with the king in London packed ready to run? And how Murray turned back from Derby though Charles wanted to make the dash for London, and that history wonders why Murray refused the chance?"

"It's thought that French Louis promised his support, then didna gie it, an' Murray felt his luck had run oot."

"A half-truth. Had Murray advanced, Louis's support would have arrived; he sent a secret agent to tell Murray so. The agent was Angus and Angus lied. He saw the Stuarts as a self-serving breed and a Stuart on the English throne as the ruin of a nation poised for greatness. So, not for the first time, arrogant Judas lied."

Donald said slowly, "Then the Hielanders deed four deep—literally—at Culloden, an' the English plundered an' murdered doon the Great Glen while the bairns starved an' the clans were broken. In time it led to the Clearances, when chiefs turned against the clansmen wha had revered them like godlings, an' ran them off the land to make room for sheep because sheep were the new source o' money."

"Some chieftains, Mr Baird, *sold* their landless men to the American plantations, *sold* them after centuries of loyalty. We've seen too much to think highly of humanity when its pocket is at risk."

"It was a *Company* falsehood destroyed the Hielanders."

Moonlight haloed Angus in his still pose of listening to Will, whose lips moved now in a flood of talk they could not hear. The robes closed in to catch his speech. Over the square a sense of climax gathered.

Donald thought of Angus at the Police Complex, small-boy excited, on edge with anticipation. Yes, he could imagine him making decisions, taking action . . . and regretting, regretting ever after.

"But yours is a biased story," Smith said. "The Highlands were overpopulated; historians agree that social forces would have produced the same result without the slaughter. Violence hastens history but rarely changes it. As for Angus, his fixation allows him to see only his blood-guilt. Periodically we clear his memory but the guilt seeps back and throws him into agonies of abasement and it's all to be done again. After three centuries his devotion to this particular misery has erupted to make the last Scot a gift of Scotland as a symbol of atonement. Ostensibly protecting us but in fact grovelling at your feet, begging absolution for his inadequate soul! Mad as the proverbial March Hare and Hatter."

"So we're all in debt to the braw wee loon—*clever* loon."

Smith actually stamped with vexation. "He's an hysterical gameplayer! And—" he placed a hand on Donald's elbow, to whisper, "—if Santley out there is confirming that the impossible has happened, your braw wee loon will have condemned you to life imprisonment. Do you understand that?"

"What sort o' warnin's that?"

"Will that silent statue of a Commissioner leave you free to tell what you know of the Children? Don't you know what he will do?"

The last Scot removed the offensive hand. "Ay, he'll haud us here, incommunicado. It's a chance I thought on, an' took."

Smith wrinkled his mouth in disgust, turned his back in ostentatious insult and left him.

Parker, at Donald's shoulder, breathed barely above a sigh, "Ferendija is not a man to be guessed at. We must be very watchful."

Thirty feet away, the Commissioner turned, as though some subtle vibration of his name had reached him. For three menacing seconds Donald met the scrutiny of a stone face and empty eyes.

With the cleaver Sanders severed the head behind the second segment of its body. The dough-white hose of the remainder slid back into Clyde water. To grow a new head, as the terminal printout had suggested?

The sucker-mouths clung to the meat. From the open tube of the rear segment seeped a trickle of dull fluid—digested food—mixed with thin, pink blood. It ate, oblivious of violence, too primitive to realize decapitation. *The purpose of life is to stay alive. Hence this thing—and Angus and his kind.*

After ten minutes it was still digesting its way into the meat, burying its disgusting head.

Revolted but determined, he took hold to tug it loose. Its grip defied him; the head stretched but did not let go, nor did feeding cease. Mindless reflexes did not permit interruption. Possibly, it was unaware of him.

Adjusting the gas burner to a fairly cool flame, he advanced it to the thing's severed end. It convulsed violently and dropped to the deck, writhing like a caterpillar under ants.

In time it quieted, lay still. Dead? He thought not. He pushed the lump of beef closer, and the head quested. It tried to move to the food on insufficient segments, one of them half roasted, unconscious of ruin. He pushed the meat against it. Feeding began at once.

He severed the piece of meat and dropped it, with its clinging diner, into the bucket.

He went back to fishing and when he had a second head serenely gorging, climbed back inside the flyer, where he took his catch to the Satellite and Laser Cabin and placed the bucket on the desk. The segments had stopped leaking and the open tubes of their bodies were closing slowly, like sphincters. He thought they were swelling with too good living, so with the burner he separated each from its chunk of meat. He did not want them gorged and somnolent.

He sat down to wait.

Around the brazier action erupted as Angus's probing found a mark in Will's abused mind. He surged out of the chair in a storm of wordless howling, bursting through the shining figures to seize the smoking herb dish in bare hands and with hysterical strength fling it discus-like across the square.

It struck the paving flat-sided and spinning, to skip like a stone on water into the ranks of Techs. A man yelled with pain as it struck him in its passage and passed on to ring like a gong when it struck a lamp standard and clattered to the ground.

The robes swarmed over Will in an iridescent mound, mutely restraining while he fought and squalled. They forced him back into the chair and held him till he quietened, which was not quickly. Behind him Angus stood, hand to mouth in the classic pose of uncertainty and indecision, troubled deeply.

The Senior reported to Ferendija. "Jones has bruised ribs, maybe one broken; Ballantyne has a burned hand and arm."

"Is first aid sufficient immediate attention?"

"We think so, sir."

"Thank you."

The words seemed scarcely to have disturbed his abstraction. The Senior Tech hesitated between discipline and mystification, and said, "Sir!"

"What is it?" Ferendija did not look at him.

"What is going on here? The men are uneasy."

"They—and you—will have to wait a while for explanation." He paused so long that the Tech was about to retire in snubbed anger, then said, "I understand little of what I see here, only that there must be an ending. Be alert."

The man rejoined his platoon, dissatisfied and scowling.

Ferendija was conscious of Smith squeezing softly out of shadow to play imp-of-mischief, wearing the bland smile the Commissioner suspected concealed nothing of importance.

He no longer wished to bother with the man and this endless display. It must, surely, be time for him to be moving . . .

He checked the time by his watch. It should be . . .

Smith asked, "Do we keep you from a more urgent appointment?"

"No."

"Ah! That had the ring and shape of truth. Perhaps someone is late for an appointment with you?"

Ferendija took refuge in simplicity. "No."

Smith was mildly upset, as if a quip had misfired. "That also was true!" He was admiring but pensive. "It is no mean feat to tell, at a moment's notice, exact truth in such fashion as to conceal truth. I asked the wrong questions."

Ferendija turned away, shaken, and so saw Will in fresh upheaval.

The brazier went over with a clatter of metal and a swishing flood of coals across the pavement, like white diamonds smoking and glaring. Will screeched in a high terror of sound, hard to couple with a human throat. Again the robes bore him down, barely able to handle his hysterical strength.

Angus came running to Smith. "I have the cue but I think there's a suicide reflex planted, to operate when it is spoken. We can't go on."

Smith's twinkle did not falter. "Thought of everything, didn't they? Well, now, Commissioner, shall we risk killing the man with our good intentions?"

Donald, Lindley and Parker loomed alongside, eyes questioning.

Ferendija spoke over his shoulder to Alice. "Join the platoon. I won't need you again."

She went unwillingly, but there was time for Donald to smile at her and for her to acknowledge it, involuntarily, before a weakening dignity remembered the gulf between. He understood and turned the smile to a victory grin.

To Smith, Ferendija observed, "I didn't think your kind would die so easily."

"We don't but—and this may be contrary to your surmise—we don't take much account of death and know how to meet it if it becomes necessary. Someone seems to have convinced Santley's subconscious that at a certain crux it will be necessary."

Ferendija jeered, "And we shall never know whether or not he fathered a son."

Smith glittered with special brightness. "But we've known for some time, haven't we? If Santley is not David's father the whole Gangoil charade makes no sense. David was young—in our terms—still gripped by human emotional ideas, and so he was dissident. Human attitudes persist for some time. A generation gap, would you say? He was foolish enough to let his father know that he proposed to use his biological training to bless humanity with long life; his father, older and wiser, threatened reprisals. So, in his certainty that the old are

298

reactionary and blind to eternal truths, he dealt direly with father, up to and including a death-wish implant. Sentimentality! Should have murdered him outright! But it took a whole team to construct that synaptic closed circuit and implant, and at this late date there is no point in seeking out their names. But too many heads make a poor secret, so a whisper came to me and I set Angus to work. The rest has been misfortune for all concerned. Hadn't you decided some such sequence?"

"Yes."

"But—?"

"There was always the chance of another sequence, one wherein Santley was not—not—"

"That he was just a simple Gone Timer? A poor enough organism in the eyes of your self-sufficient godlets, but preferable to a proliferating mutant."

To Ferendija he seemed to be talking at random, with his real attention on Angus. And Angus stood in listening pose, as if he detected music beyond common hearing. Ferendija recalled what he had experienced only on filament, the acuity of the man's senses, and glanced again at his watch.

Smith did not miss the movement. "Ah, that unkept appointment! Is there time for us to kill Santley for your pleasure? To make a dramatic end to this futile play?"

Ferendija gathered himself to project authority. "Stop the play and stop playing the fool! What difference does one man's fertility make while geneticists exist to create it?"

Smith said gently, "We would like to know. There are few fine and new things in our existence."

"Leave the man alone!"

Parker added a voice. "Knowledge was never worth killing for."

Smith said, "That's a matter of opinion," but his attention stayed with the listening Angus. Without warning he raised a trumpet voice that whipped clearly the length and breadth of the square. "You must understand, Commissioner and Controller, that love of life is not to be equated with fear of death. We don't give a damn for death—yours or ours. With death as your only counter you cannot bargain with us, or threaten or cajole."

From the area of lawn and trees came a rustle of sound between speech and applause; there was laughter in it.

Parker said softly, as if to himself, "Yet these also are God's creatures!"

Ferendija glanced at him in startled disapproval. Smith snickered and recovered himself to say, "Angus won't kill him for you, anyway. His pseudo-humanity has obstreperous quibbles over what he feels are unnecessary killings. So sentiment is preserved on all fronts, and Santley lives."

He lived at that moment with enormous vitality, heaving amongst his captors, tossing and striking, defying mastery.

Donald watched anxiously but was concerned, too, with Angus's absorption. "Whit do you hear, Angus?"

Angus only looked wolfishly at Ferendija and exaggeratedly consulted his watch.

From the dark behind them Jeanie said, "Jet engines. Very high up. Or lower and coasting on low power."

Angus corrected her. "High and circling. About thirty thousand feet, I'd say. Is it time, Commissioner?"

Ferendija could hear nothing but he knew he could trust Angus in this. "Time?" he asked. "We have wasted enough of it and I am leaving. Why was I brought here? What is Santley to me? Your silly comedy has come to nothing."

Smith said mildly, "We had hoped to learn what you propose to do with us. Or against us."

There was greater uproar, a shouting and dismay in the struggling group in the centre, but Ferendija and the inaudible aircraft took all attention now.

The Commissioner said distinctly, "I'm not in confessional mood."

He turned with formal smartness and moved away. And cannoned into a yelling, dishevelled, nearly mindless beast that grasped at him with clawed fingers. He dodged aside thinking he was attacked, but Santley rolled with him, clutching and weeping.

"Take me with you! Take me away ... I don't *want* memories ... take me away ..."

Ferendija grasped his wrists and could not dislodge a grip powered by terror, but he was not a man to flounder before the unexpected. He called coolly, "Angus, get your puppet off me."

Angus answered, as coolly, "Deal with your own problems," and fended away robed players who would have assisted. "Let the bastard rot."

Santley clung hysterically. Ferendija bellowed into his ear, "Listen! Santley, listen to me!" Whatever penetrated, authority or merely noise, Will stopped pleading but kept his desperate grip.

"Listen, these are your people. You must stay with them." Santley buried his face in the Commissioner's chest. "They are your people; they will look after you."

Santley lifted his face to scream, "They aren't. I'm human! They're killing me. Take me away from them."

Ferendija's patience broke; he yelled at Angus, "God's guts, but have you told him nothing! What sort of creatures are you? Santley, listen to me! You are Company!"

Santley cried with a noisy, snuffling horror, "No!"

"You are! You're one of them! You were born over a century ago. You aren't Will Santley. Your name is David; you are Edwin David's father!" Santley stirred against him and he heard vaguely that Angus shouted something furious and warning. "If a name means anything to your kind, yours is David. Now let go of me and join your own people!"

Will straightened, released him, stepped back and stood perfectly still, staring down at the pavement.

Ferendija was aware of the brilliant cloaks standing in touching distance, eyes on Will, of Angus and Smith coming towards him as Jeanie slid out of the shadows, and of Angus saying in tight rage, "We can't stop it. There's no way."

Will raised his head and stared at Ferendija with intense concentration. The Commissioner saw, even in the darkness, that his face was congested, black with blood. His fists clenched and he swayed slightly.

Ferendija, not understanding, reached to steady him and touched a frame whose every muscle was iron rigid. Will turned in his hands like an unbalanced doll and his features caught

301

the moonlight—a suffused mask, a rictus without even an expression of pain.

He made no sound. Ferendija was not sure of the moment of death, only of a creeping guilt and horror that set him backing away before the falling body should carry him down with it.

Instinctively he bent, feeling for a pulse, sure there would be none.

The only sound was of Angus, savagely mocking. "Not all Gangoil could put him together again. That's *our* kind of goodbye. Every capillary in his brain is burst. Hadn't you a brain of your own to tell you that his identity was the obvious suicide trigger?"

Ferendija straightened, his composure shattered, nodded minutely to Angus, admitting guilt, then quickly rejoined the Techs, as if glad to be hidden in the ranks that opened to receive him.

Tension took toll. Sanders was asleep, stiffly upright, when the recognition signal squealed the arrival of the aircraft. Unbalanced half off the chair, he acknowledged with scrambling speed.

The beep, analysed and reconstructed in the decoder, told him only that the ships circled on radio-alert, awaiting direction.

Uniform and personal radios could not be linked with the VHF aircraft channels, so Ferendija must return to the flyer. Soon, he hoped. Sleep was perilous.

He decided to keep moving, walking the three-pace length of the cabin, preserving total readiness.

His mind—he observed it like an onlooker—was dull, inert.

A cold-blooded man? He had never thought so, but now he felt only his intention and his readiness. Nothing else, nothing at all.

Standing over Will's body, Smith echoed a thought of Lindley's : "If only we had killed him in the first place—"

Jeanie finished for him "—it would have changed nothing. As soon as we touch human affairs we suffer the same idiot wastage as they." She looked to the sky. "What now?"

"Quarantine. Ferendija has called in his squadrons. We are

to be prisoners of Glasgow lest we contaminate the world." He brightened like a mischievous boy. "Ferendija could be in trouble. He will have summoned his men from the nearest Security barracks, the south of France—and what arms have they to control three hundred sonic pistols?" He smiled at the platoon of Techs. "The entertainment may begin here."

Donald said, "There could be bad news for the first yin to laugh."

"Our soldier speaks!"

"Ay. Ferendija's no soldier but he knows a sonic's range is short. Less than fifty yards. He'll arm his men wi' sportin' rifles and telescopic sights. Maybe you're hard to kill, but men loaded for deer will knock you doon as easy as another at three hundred yards. He'll cover the outlets o' the city—an' you'll stay where he says, wi' broken banes for anchors."

Smith answered, for once urgently, "Then we leave Glasgow at once! We have transport in plenty."

Angus objected, "They'd hunt us like rabbits—and catch us. Better to be bored here than chased through the hills and glens. Most of us can hibernate." Like Jeanie he glanced to the sky. "What are they waiting for? Why don't they come down?"

Nobody had an answer. With Will's death an expectant momentum had braked; they needed a fresh direction.

Parker provided it with a question in his edged, official voice. "Thomson, is your hearing super-audial?"

"No, only acute. Why?"

"Monopole engines have extremely small apertures; their note is beyond audible range. Only some dogs hear them. What are you hearing?"

Angus faced him blankly, then looked to Jeanie. "You hear them?"

She nodded, "Turbo-jets. They must be."

Parker said stolidly, "Security has no turbo-jets. They were scrapped some years ago. *Nobody* uses turbines, only monopole jets."

"Then who are they?"

Parker corrected grimly, "Not who, but what?" He raised his voice to parade-ground pitch. "I advise every person with transport to leave Glasgow at once! There are aircraft overhead.

They are remote-controlled bombs!" He shouted to his Acolytes, "Out of here! At once! Move!"

Before they could take in his intolerable meaning a hugely amplified voice came from the Security platoon.

"No one will leave this gathering! That is the order of the Security Commissioner, speaking for World Council."

The Techs had formed an arc, facing out, sonics raised.

Parker bellowed at them, "Don't be idiots! There are three hundred of those guns against you in this square! Do you want to die? Where's that lunatic, Ferendija?"

The amplifier said imperturbably, "The Commissioner has returned to his headquarters. I repeat, no one will leave the square."

"Returned, has he? Does nothing penetrate your skull? He's gone to the flyer to call down the bombs!"

The amplifier assumed a touch of asperity. "What are you talking about? There have been no operational bombing craft since the Gone Time."

"They are Gone Time craft."

"You're out of your mind!" Then a confusion of sounds came through the amplifier, among them a voice saying insistently, "The museum, the museum."

Parker shouted, "That's it—the museum. Gone Time weaponry, fully maintenanced and in armable condition, from the Cairo War Materials Museum!"

Across the square a murmur flooded like a rising sea. The Techs closed in, huddling, pointing their futile sonics but questioning and arguing over their shoulders.

The amplifier asked, in anger and doubt, "Where are these bombs? We have no information; how do you know?"

Parker improvised, leaping the impossible complexities of explanation, "These people have old spark-gap detectors as part of their alarm system."

He didn't know whether that made sense. Perhaps it did not, because the amplifier snorted.

He strained his lungs to their bawling limit. "I tell you those machines are above us with bombs waiting—with death ready to fall!" The intensity of belief gave him his Tech audience, that and the fact that they knew him and that he represented what they had been taught to regard as a responsible authority. "Why has Ferendija returned to the flyer if not to reach the remote-control equipment? Realize that he has left you—his own men—to die under the bombs! Because you have seen and heard things that Council will not allow to be spoken of outside this city! Stay here and you are dead men! Killed by your own commander!"

He turned his back on them, addressing the square. "Get out of the city! All of you! At once! Those black puppets won't stop you. Their own leader has betrayed them!"

He might have saved his voice, for his Acolytes were already stumbling over each other to reach the road and the north lawn was a shambles of retreat.

Parker bore down on the Senior Tech like an avenging demon. "Get your men out! Don't you understand yet? You are man on the spot and their lives are your concern. Don't be afraid of Ferendija. I'll come with you; I'll deal with him!"

He pushed at the uncertain man to start him moving. His noise and anger gnawed at the man's disbelief, together with the sight of his platoon edging into a mass that swayed almost unconsciously back towards their skimmer, ready to break and run.

"You're speaking of a Commissioner. It can't be so."

Parker slapped him on the shoulder with a switch to hearty good will. "So stay and burn, Casabianca!" He pushed past, running.

It was enough. The Techs ran for safety and their lives.

Donald was the last man on the Security skimmer, pouring indignation to a demoralized Alice. "The bastard took my power-bike!"

She clutched at him, not caring about his satisfied grin as her instinct betrayed her. "How can it be true? There can't be bombs any more!"

From behind her, Angus, an excited jack-in-the-box in his brilliant robe, exclaimed, "Oh, but there can! There are! Chemical, incendiary, biological, fission, fusion, neutron, you name it! And Cairo isn't the only museum. Your racial sense of history has betrayed you into preserving horrors to feed your hatred of the past—your disgraceful *terror* of the past. And you

305

can believe, Alice, that where a weapon exists, sooner or later it will be used."

She shuddered.

Donald asked how long a lead Ferendija had, and the Senior Tech thought about ten minutes. Too long. They would not catch him; the skimmer was designed for load-carrying rather than manoeuvrability or speed; the power-bike would hold its lead.

Angus was saying calmly, "A sensible murderer would use neutron bombs and preserve most of the city. Also they kill more certainly, within their range."

Alice, who had not heard Smith's confidences, screamed at him, "You're enjoying this, enjoying it! You're mad!"

He peered at her with a cold and lonely questioning, and became stonily quiet.

Lindley thought with pity: The punishment of the insane is that in their hearts they are aware of their insanity.

9

Sanders proposed an abominable action and felt only serene expectation. *I am a machine, making justice.*

In the era of computerized psychiatry "paranoia" was a rare word in the common man's vocabulary.

A step on the makeshift gangway sent a tiny shiver and a ghost of sound through the flyer's hull.

Ferendija? Alone? The broken trampling of the platoon would have rocked the craft perceptibly. So he had left them behind. And he had made good time on unfamiliar ways, this dedicated man racing to his supreme act of service.

In the Recording Cabin they would hear him coming, and be all over him with curiosity and questions.

He listened patiently. Yes—a Tech's voice. Then Ferendija's, in tearing fury: "*What is he doing in there?*"

Nerves, Commissioner? Doubt? Guilt? Fear?

He took the worms behind the heads, one in either hand, between finger and thumb. They writhed slowly (smelling his flesh?) but could not turn far enough to fasten on him; he

306

made sure of that. Hands behind his back, he kept them inches apart; given the chance, they would strike on each other.

In the corridor Ferendija had recovered poise, covering nerves with smoothness. "Code manuals? Did he say what he wanted? Never mind; I'll see him."

Yes, indeed.

The heads pursued their restless seeking and he tightened his grip against exuded slime.

Ferendija stopped on the threshold, and uttered the unexpected. "What's that stench? Have you brought one of those stinking worms aboard?"

Sanders had become accustomed to the smell, had not thought about it. No matter. "Yes," he said, "two."

Ferendija lost his temper again with the violence of naked relief. "Bringing that filth inside! Are you out of your mind?" The very sight of Sanders must have fuelled rage. He shouted, "Stand to attention when I address you!"

"Not for you."

In Ferendija a lifetime's training took over, recognizing a subordinate driven too far. To be soothed.

He stepped into the cabin. "What's on your mind, Corey?"

"This!" Sanders swept his right hand in a furious arc and the hungry head fastened across Ferendija's lips, sealing his mouth, clinging more firmly than teeth. Feeding began.

Ferendija clutched at the thing with both hands, tugging. Sanders watched closely, charting the change from rage and revulsion to puzzlement and at last a blazing fright as the digestive fluids ate his flesh, driving him to an anguished beating at the unheeding parasite. A horrified whining issued from his nose.

Sanders stepped past him and closed the cabin door.

Ferendija forced a finger into the exposed left corner of his mouth, opening his lips enough for the distorted sketch of a cry for help. Only a sketch, a grating gasp.

Sanders swung him about and pushed him into the operator's chair; he seemed scarcely aware of what was done to him as he clawed at his face and whined.

Sanders leaned close, considering his work, caring now to forget nothing he had planned. He brought the second worm within an inch of the contorted face, and the flat, square head distended in its effort to reach the food.

He said, "Be quiet, Istvan Georg, or I'll fix this one to your eyeball."

Holding the head steady, he opened the Commissioner's jacket and removed his sonic gun. That had been the first aim of the vicious performance, to obtain the weapon before it was used on him. Now that he had it, Ferendija's gambit was finished. With his thumb he set the control on low power.

"This can hurt, Istvan Georg, much more than a hungry tapeworm." A doubtful statement against the unremitting erosion of stomach acids, but it took Ferendija's labouring attention.

He fell silent. He dropped his hands to his lap, staring at Sanders through dark, horrified eyes. *Horrified*, Sanders noted, storing detail for some unimaginable thesis of terror, *not frightened. Ready to think. He could have been a great man.*

From the severed rear of the wormhead a drop of thick fluid emerged, swelled and dripped to the floor. With the damaged segment not yet completely closed, the thing fed and leaked.

Sanders moved the gun slightly to align it on Ferendija's stomach and tossed the second head back into the bucket. The Commissioner's face flickered with a desolate relief.

"Does it hurt, Istvan Georg, being eaten alive?"

The dark eyes, he thought, glowed with contempt. Rightly. It had not been a civilized taunt. Ferendija was, bloody-mindedness aside, a remarkable man. Some unpleasantness was needed to drown his reviving respect.

"I'll remove that thing, when you understand that your game is over and can't be restarted—that dedication isn't enough, that you're a failed hero."

Ferendija paid close heed. It was a powerful mind that could rise above the monster at his mouth.

Sanders released his urge to communicate, justify, explain. "I had nothing to do here but think about the plans and purposes played so close to your chest, with no one allowed to know them. And your message in secret."

Ferendija's head inclined in a slow, expressionless comprehension. Though he trembled and his eyes started from a shock-white face, intelligence ruled.

"I broke your message block. Tedious, not difficult. But difficult to credit the message—at first. When you clear your mind of the junk fed it from birth, you can credit anything. Did it seem so obvious, to wipe out the centre of contagion and then hunt down the rest by computer check? All that just to gain time! What sort of man murders three hundred people—just as a beginning?"

A voice chattered in his head that he was unbalanced by misery and despair, but he was intent on being understood. And he was wound up past stopping.

"You stripped me naked when you showed me Security's true purpose—to keep the world in Security's paternal clutch. Security will retire gracefully when it is no longer needed—we say that, don't we? And all the star-eyed Techs believe it. What *you* believe is that the world can't live without your hand at its back and that the Ethic is anything that turns the world the way you want it. Power confused with right, *Gone Timer*!" That hurt; he saw the flinch. "No honest man could do what you did with those kids in Melbourne Town, but you did it. And left me to wear the smell of it in my heart. Nursery games, Lindley calls our pat-and-lecture guardianship, and we hate him for it—so we've become big babies who play with loaded guns and pretend they won't be used for killing."

He had lost the thread; he didn't have to justify destiny to the damned. And he felt that Ferendija's stolid silence did not properly observe him as avenging Fate.

"You Gone Time founding father of Security, engrossed in the good of humanity! What threatens must be eliminated, even if it means the slaughter of some humans. Culling! So, away with the Children and all who know about them—except, of course, the Councillor trustees of the culture, with objective minds above suspicion! There'll be more Children next generation, but you'll have bought a breathing space, a few years to study the answerless problem—to save your nurselings having to face challenge and change. You were to be the folk hero of our time, weren't you? Man on the spot who acted while others confused themselves with seeing both sides of the question! The man strong enough to leave his Techs to die! Because they're back there, aren't they?"

Ferendija's face began a ragged, irregular twitching as his resistance ebbed, but his eyes held steady on an infinity wherein, Sanders was sure, he continued to plan.

"If knowledge of the Children was to be obliterated, then our Gone Timers must die with them. Small loss? Parker and his Acolytes must go, too; they'd seen too much for comfort. Small loss again, perhaps, but closer to the ethical bone. Then, slicing right to the bone, your Techs must go before they thought and deduced and understood. Dedication I know about, but not your kind."

Ferendija's eyes flickered to the console.

The man must try soon, Sanders reasoned, before failing strength made nonsense of courage.

"And we here in the flyer? Death by sonic gun, all burst skin and blood, never knowing why? Because you *could* get out before the missiles fell, couldn't you? It is just possible for one man to fly this ship home by locking on to the point-to-point beacons. But then, what of your reception by Council? You weren't sure, because you took decision and action alone, trusting them to see how right you were. If they did not, if in disgust they trampled you into the Chamber floor—then you'd be a martyr, blessed by History!"

He leaned close, "I have it right, haven't I, Hero of the Ages?"

He laughed, stood back, using the movement to allow the sonic casually to swing off target.

For Ferendija it must have been the supreme physical effort of his life, all spirit and courage amongst the dregs of pain and defeat, but he moved like a man possessed to beat a squeezing trigger by speed and surprise.

He flung his arm back and sideways across the console, opening the Satellite relay and continuing the downward swing to depress the beeper key just once.

The beep hieroglyph streaked to the Satellite with its operational instruction to the circling craft. Ferendija collapsed, eyes burning and waiting for death.

The trigger was unsqueezed. Sanders would have smiled but it seemed unfair. "I removed your message chip and encoded another. You have just sent an instruction to Cairo to call its nestlings home."

The dark light in Ferendija's eyes went out; purpose and spirit went with it.

Sanders reached for the burner and removed the wormhead from the man's mouth. He did not stir. Sanders tossed the thing into the bucket, where it seized on the other and clung; it did not know what it fed on, did not need to know.

After a while Ferendija lifted his hands to his raw and swollen mouth; the flesh was eaten out in red circles where the worm had clung. Huge, unregarded tears gathered on his eyelids. He could not speak past a thickened, protruding tongue, for a sucker had penetrated his mouth.

Sanders had not intended that; he shivered to a creeping horror of himself, the onset of shock. He launched again into condemnation, driven and urgent, holding his own punishment at bay.

"Six pilotless orbiters covering the city, each with a cluster-head of ten neutron bombs! Sixty of them! Not a bug in a hole or a worm in the river would have escaped. Or an enemy. Or your own men. Istvan Georg Ferendija, latest of the great destroyers in the name of righteousness! Our children's children would bawl your praises! You're worse than Parker's prayer-mongering God."

Ferendija gestured weakly, pleading, unable to speak. From his ruined mouth blood ran down to soak his jacket.

Sanders understood, said, "Yes, in a minute." He had not much time left because people were coming aboard. Several people; the vibration was distinct. The platoon, after all?

"You know you've killed Security? Council itself won't survive this revelation. Two successive Commissioners sunk in greed and moral vanity! Man on the spot will never wield unquestioned power again. If it means giving the world back to the Parkers and Davids and the Mediterranean vendetta groups and the crazy New York Soviet, then we'll have to bear it. The Big Daddy experiment is over. The Children are amongst us and nobody has an answer to them because there isn't any. They're our biological bomb, waiting since Adam to go off, and they'll blow us right out of history. What's the betting on a new Dark Age?"

311

Footsteps pounded the corridor. Donald's voice yelled, and Lindley's.

Then Angus called through the door, excited, elated, enjoying climax, careless of all those tomorrows he could take for granted. "What are you doing, Commissioner? Open up or we break in." Like a child at a party: *Coming, ready or not.*

Ferendija gave no sign of hearing.

Angus again, sharp, suspicious: "Do you hear me, Commissioner?"

Sanders said, "He does."

"Corey! What are you up to in there?"

Ferendija extended his hands, palms up, imploring.

"Yes," Sanders agreed, sulkily, as if the affair had turned unsatisfactory, as if this were anti-climax and there should be something more. Something of grandeur. A great and magic moment for Sanders, perhaps?

But he felt only cold and ill and lonely.

He pushed the power stud fully forward and blew Ferendija's head off.

The door was not very solid; Donald kicked the lock loose.

The cabin was a shambles of blood and brains and pale strips. He turned his back on what was left of Ferendija to examine an inert but breathing Sanders.

He knew what had happened there. The sonic spillage in the confined space had been more powerful than the man's inexperience had appreciated; in the corridor they had felt it through the wall.

"Jim, Angus! Get him to bed!"

Nobody questioned his right to command; the laird was on his home ground.

"You, Parker! Take your flyer an' gang to the Council an' make full report. In person. Everything. It's the hidin' an' plannin' that's brought us to this."

Parker inclined his head gravely and went. God, he noted, had preserved him with His usual exactness of manoeuvre. Emerging God, waiting for man to become Him, was in the meantime a practical politician.

AFTERTHOUGHTS

Excerpts from "The Lindley Memoir"

(Notebook 8—The Glasgow Fragments) 3 *May 2037*. Parker is almost unapproachable in his scarifying hatred of the Council. Thanking his God for Donald's choice of him, he raced off to Hawaii actually hoping to see his revivalist plan put into action by a Council grovellingly grateful for his perception and preparedness. Fanatics have no brains whatsoever when fanaticism is paramount.

Council knew better than to set that sort of detonator in the fuel store; they bundled him and his flight crew back to Glasgow —and this time there really was a Security guard armed with rifles, closing all exits from the city while a Satellite watched for ground movement.

Then they set the data networks to flush out the rest of the Children, and we think they are all in here now—three hundred and forty-seven all told.

21 *May 2037*. Council sits in plaintive session, counting its fingers and unable to make the sum other than ten; for once ethical mathematics won't supply a pragmatic answer. Two murdered Commissioners—and the reasons for their dying— have sapped their confidence in themselves. (I imagine them watching each other like hawks for the answering glint of greed-for-life in a colleague's eye.)

They are literally terrified that the news will leak out. Their first reaction, we're told, was panic—shoot first, then think. Only a bare majority of the rational humane prevented poor Ferendija's murder plan from being carried out. The philosophic culture, all ethics and goodwill, was nearly a dead dog before Parker had finished reporting.

23 *May 2037*. The Children have withdrawn; they stay away from us.

I saw Alastair one day, by chance, and asked him why. He looked *down* at me, though I am taller, from some height of the ego and said that for the first time in history they were no longer *obliged* to live cheek by jowl with us.

Celebration on leaving the slums! So much for Man who will one day be God.

Since they don't care much for each other's company and have no use for ours, in what isolation does each one of them live?

Is that the terrible price of longevity?

But is it so "terrible" to them? I see no signs of unhappiness amongst them—but would I recognize the signs peculiar to them?

Not all the Children ignore us. Angus and Jeanie and a dozen or so other emotional cripples haunt us for their human (quasi-human? pseudo-human?) needs.

Only the insane find us compatible.

We have agreed to keep this aspect of truth from the quarantined Acolytes and Security platoon; life in a tomb is dull enough for them without adding to its aspects of a lunatic asylum.

18 *June* 2037. The latest from Council—I'll say this for them, they keep us informed—is that they are seriously considering the Parker plan. There's desperation for you! (The news was received here with a hilarity which has driven the Acolytes into furious apartheid.) Council has reached the stage of considering anything at all that may leave them some vestige of control; they can't face up to their meaninglessness in a world where death will no longer be the most intrusive element in life.

Their unadmitted problem is how to ensure ten thousand years of *power*.

It hasn't occurred to them yet that, given ten thousand years, the power might seem unimportant.

28 *July* 2037. Three months of Council wrangling and no sign of a decision. I am reduced to retailing gossip:

Jeanie has a broken jaw. It seems she set her snare for Parker, only to have the manipulation broken immediately by his self-absorption which repelled intrusion and had frightened off the much more accomplished Angus. Parker fetched her a mighty crack which her own absorption failed to let her see coming.

Angus says the Children are laughing themselves sick over it. At least we pity our mental cases.

The laird of the Highlands, the Lowlands and the Islands is looking mighty pleased with himself. His Alice is regressing daily into a sonsy bit o' Glesca fluff and will cave in as soon as she feels her pride has held out decently long.

He talks of marriage, but who will conduct the service?

Given his imaginative approach to administration, I don't put it past him to create a bishop for the occasion.

2 *Sept* 2037. Sanders is improving. His breakdown was catastrophic; having murdered the symbol of all he believed in, he had nowhere to go save inwards to his own almost vacated soul.

I am piloting him through the guilt-reaction phase (it gives me something useful to do) and finding myself in some sympathy with his breast-beating cry that Ferendija was right and that he should have let the slaughter proceed, and that his interference has solved nothing.

Perhaps. But without it I would have been among the dead. It's a consideration that short-circuits really heartfelt agreement.

28 *Nov* 2037. I have completed my Memoir (seven fat exercise books mostly filled with scurrilous invective for posterity to raise its eyebrows over) and am struck with a wonder whether it is worth while expanding this book of notes on the same scale.

Do we matter? While Security continues to supply ointments and sequestering agents to keep us healthy we know that the debate of greed and fear continues.

But, after seven months, what in hell do they find still to discuss in that paradisal Hawaiian gabble-house?

I asked Jeanie what she thought they would eventually do (I don't have to be afraid of her; she won't bare her love-me-honey teeth at my fifty-one-year-old bag of bones), and she said, "Do you care? Since you don't believe in an afterlife and dead Glasgow is a poor version of this one, whatever they do can only be an improvement."

The logic of eternity gives me the everlasting shits.

317

1 *Dec* 2037. Alice and Donald are doing nicely. She is pregnant (without a bishop!) and worrying about the effect of background radiation on the child.

They routed out a resentful Randal Cooke who cursed her for being so stupid as to let it happen but said the dangers could be minimized and agreed to see her once a week.

What a time to be born into!

24 *Dec* 2037. The Acolytes are singing carols in George Square and singing them not too badly in a fine drift of snow.

If God exists he must be touched by this naive performance on the edge of eternal night. For that is what it is.

The Security craft flew in yesterday, three big personnel transports in full arrogance of power. Whoever they carried remained unseen, but swept through the city in closed vehicles. They did not come near us or Parker's youngsters or even their own bewildered and disheartened platoon, but went straight to the areas where the Children live.

A few hours later they left as they had come, behind shutters.

Angus came last night and told me about it. Unnecessarily; it was pretty plain that the humane objectors on Council had finally seen the obvious action as the only one.

There had been eight Gangoil bio-chemists, surgeons and geneticists in the party, one of them David, apparently still uninformed of his own ambiguous standing. They had selected a dozen of those they deemed the most suitable Children—those with age arrested at the peak of physiological development—and taken them away.

That was all.

"Study, experiment, select, introduce gradually over a century or so," Angus said, "with useful and important people getting first bite of the apple. It will choke more of them than they imagine but as they see it, it's a sensible and practicable programme."

"And we?"

"Well, Glasgow's too big a secret to keep for ever." He grinned and quoted Peter Pan: " 'To die will be an awfully big adventure.' "

Well, maybe. "They didn't hint?"

"Only by being there and doing as they did."

I was (and am) less frightened than resigned. It is all so expectable, has been from the beginning.

I had to ask, had to know, "How does the prospect of death affect you?"

"Not at all. I have no unfinished business."

We were strolling by the Clyde in the Christmas cold, with Angus skipping flat stones across the black water. "Do you know," he said abruptly, "that I have been doing this for thirty thousand years? Is it a habit or an obsession?"

"A compulsion. I thought you didn't recall much before Akhnaton."

"Some things stick; ducks and drakes is one. And Altamira. I helped with the cave paintings."

"Talent!"

"Never believe it. I ground the colours for the shaman types who did the painting. In return they developed my manipulative power. That isn't so rare a gift as you think; lots of you have the unrealized potential."

After a while he asked, "And you, Jim? Are you afraid?"

I had done all my thinking about that. "No. I would have thought it more distressing for you, after so long."

"Why?" When I couldn't answer intelligently he said, "The Children live in an eternal present, tomorrow no different from yesterday or today. For you, tomorrow has rarity value because it may never come; for us it is only an expectable instalment of the world-without-end that can never be fully explored by a finite mind. We have no time sense. An ending in time is not an ending with a particular meaning; mere duration is not a special virtue. A thing or a person *is*—then isn't. Where's the distress, the horror?"

"You make it sound as though losing the fear of death makes life static."

"Only as static as you allow it to be. Stagnation is the unbearable burden and not an uncommon one. I think Smithy told you about our suicide rate."

"What about those who elect to live?"

"Life is for us a challenge, sometimes an intolerable challenge,

319

to the mind. The joy of life lies in the acceptance of the challenge and in overcoming it, piece by piece, from one action to the next. Fear of life grinds smaller than fear of death, because it has no inbuilt finish to promise release. It takes courage to live indefinitely. We tried to tell this to your Gangoil wizards, but they only lectured us about psychological techniques. They think they can live for ever and still be human."

For the first, last, only time he lifted a corner of the veil over his own desperation: "Even poor, mad, human-loving Angus knows better than that."

Surprisingly he hugged my shoulders, rubbed his cheek against mine—and left me. I knew it was for final farewell when, from the top of the embankment, he shouted, "Merry Christmas in hell, heaven or oblivion!"

Do you hear the Acolytes, Angus, singing in the square?

> "Unto us a child is born!"
> Merry Christmas, Angus.
> Happy New Year, World!

2

Across the bottom of the page, in another, much later hand is written:

Glasgow was neutron-bombed on 25 December 2037. The city was searched as soon as radiation levels permitted and all documentation relevant to the Children removed.

Gangoil's work on the specimen Children began immediately.

3

A third hand squeezed in at the very bottom, in a script not developed until many centuries later and in a language forgotten everywhere save in very old books:

Timor vitae conturbat me.

Scarlet Discovers
True Strength

Scarlet Discovers
True Strength

Shana Muldoon Zappa and Ahmet Zappa
with Zelda Rose

𝒟ısɴᴇʏ Press

Los Angeles • New York

Printed in China
Reinforced Binding
First Boxed Set Edition, May 2016
1 3 5 7 9 10 8 6 4 2

FAC-025393-16137

ISBN 978-1-4847-8707-6

For more Disney Press fun, visit www.disneybooks.com

To our beautiful, sweet treasure,
Halo Violetta Zappa. You are pure light and joy
and our greatest inspiration. We love you soooo much.

May every step upon your path be blessed with positivity and
the understanding that you have the power within you to
manifest the most fulfilling life you can possibly imagine and
more. May you always remember that being different and true
to your highest self makes your inner star shine brighter.

Remember that you have the power of choice. . . . Choose thoughts
that feel good. Choose love and friendship that feed your spirit.
Choose actions for peace and nourishment. Choose boundaries
for the same. Choose what speaks to your creativity and unique
inner voice . . . what truly makes you happy. And always know
that no matter what you choose, you are unconditionally loved.

Look up to the stars and know you are never alone.
When in doubt, go within . . . the answers are all there.
Smiles light the world and laughter is the best medicine.
And NEVER EVER stop making wishes. . . .

Glow for it. . . .
Mommy and Daddy

And to everyone else here on "Wishworld":

May you realize that no matter where you are in life, no
matter what you look like or where you were born, you, too,
have the power within you to create the life of your dreams.
Through celebrating your own uniqueness, thinking positively,
and taking action, you can make your wishes come true.

Smile. The Star Darlings have your back.
We know how startastic you truly are.

Glow for it. . . .
Your friends,
Shana and Ahmet

Student Reports

NAME: Clover
BRIGHT DAY: January 5
FAVORITE COLOR: Purple
INTERESTS: Music, painting, studying
WISH: To be the best songwriter and DJ on Starland
WHY CHOSEN: Clover has great self-discipline, patience, and willpower. She is creative, responsible, dependable, and extremely loyal.
WATCH OUT FOR: Clover can be hard to read and she is reserved with those she doesn't know. She's afraid to take risks and can be a wisecracker at times.
SCHOOL YEAR: Second
POWER CRYSTAL: Panthera
WISH PENDANT: Barrette

NAME: Adora
BRIGHT DAY: February 14
FAVORITE COLOR: Sky blue
INTERESTS: Science, thinking about the future and how she can make it better
WISH: To be the top fashion designer on Starland
WHY CHOSEN: Adora is clever and popular and cares about the world around her. She's a deep thinker.
WATCH OUT FOR: Adora can have her head in the clouds and be thinking about other things.
SCHOOL YEAR: Third
POWER CRYSTAL: Azurica
WISH PENDANT: Watch

NAME: Piper
BRIGHT DAY: March 4
FAVORITE COLOR: Seafoam green
INTERESTS: Composing poetry and writing in her dream journal
WISH: To become the best version of herself she can possibly be and to share that by writing books
WHY CHOSEN: Piper is giving, kind, and sensitive. She is very intuitive and aware.
WATCH OUT FOR: Piper can be dreamy, absentminded, and wishy-washy. She can also be moody and easily swayed by the opinions of others.
SCHOOL YEAR: Second
POWER CRYSTAL: Dreamalite
WISH PENDANT: Bracelets

Starling Academy

NAME: Astra
BRIGHT DAY: April 9
FAVORITE COLOR: Red
INTERESTS: Individual sports
WISH: To be the best athlete on Starland—to win!
WHY CHOSEN: Astra is energetic, brave, clever, and confident. She has boundless energy and is always direct and to the point.
WATCH OUT FOR: Astra is sometimes cocky, self-centered, condescending, and brash.
SCHOOL YEAR: Second
POWER CRYSTAL: Quarrelite
WISH PENDANT: Wristbands

NAME: Tessa
BRIGHT DAY: May 18
FAVORITE COLOR: Emerald green
INTERESTS: Food, flowers, love
WISH: To be successful enough that she can enjoy a life of luxury
WHY CHOSEN: Tessa is warm, charming, affectionate, trustworthy, and dependable. She has incredible drive and commitment.
WATCH OUT FOR: Tessa does not like to be rushed. She can be quite stubborn and often says no. She does not deal well with change and is prone to exaggeration. She can be easily sidetracked.
SCHOOL YEAR: Third
POWER CRYSTAL: Gossamer
WISH PENDANT: Brooch

NAME: Gemma
BRIGHT DAY: June 2
FAVORITE COLOR: Orange
INTERESTS: Sharing her thoughts about almost anything
WISH: To be valued for her opinions on everything
WHY CHOSEN: Gemma is friendly, easygoing, funny, extroverted, and social. She knows a little bit about everything.
WATCH OUT FOR: Gemma talks—a lot—and can be a little too honest sometimes and offend others. She can have a short attention span and can be superficial.
SCHOOL YEAR: First
POWER CRYSTAL: Scatterite
WISH PENDANT: Earrings

Student Reports

NAME: Cassie
BRIGHT DAY: July 6
FAVORITE COLOR: White
INTERESTS: Reading, crafting
WISH: To be more independent and confident and less fearful
WHY CHOSEN: Cassie is extremely imaginative and artistic. She is a voracious reader and is loyal, caring, and a good friend. She is very intuitive.
WATCH OUT FOR: Cassie can be distrustful, jealous, moody, and brooding.
SCHOOL YEAR: First
POWER CRYSTAL: Lunalite
WISH PENDANT: Glasses

* * * * * * * * * * *

NAME: Leona
BRIGHT DAY: August 16
FAVORITE COLOR: Gold
INTERESTS: Acting, performing, dressing up
WISH: To be the most famous pop star on Starland
WHY CHOSEN: Leona is confident, hardworking, generous, open-minded, optimistic, caring, and a strong leader.
WATCH OUT FOR: Leona can be vain, opinionated, selfish, bossy, dramatic, and stubborn and is prone to losing her temper.
SCHOOL YEAR: Third
POWER CRYSTAL: Glisten paw
WISH PENDANT: Cuff

* * * * * * * * * * *

NAME: Vega
BRIGHT DAY: September 1
FAVORITE COLOR: Blue
INTERESTS: Exercising, analyzing, cleaning, solving puzzles
WISH: To be the top student at Starling Academy
WHY CHOSEN: Vega is reliable, observant, organized, and very focused.
WATCH OUT FOR: Vega can be opinionated about everything, and she can be fussy, uptight, critical, arrogant, and easily embarrassed.
SCHOOL YEAR: Second
POWER CRYSTAL: Queezle
WISH PENDANT: Belt

Starling Academy

NAME: Libby
BRIGHT DAY: October 12
FAVORITE COLOR: Pink
INTERESTS: Helping others, interior design, art, dancing
WISH: To give everyone what they need—both on Starland and through wish granting on Wishworld
WHY CHOSEN: Libby is generous, articulate, gracious, diplomatic, and kind.
WATCH OUT FOR: Libby can be indecisive and may try too hard to please everyone.
SCHOOL YEAR: First
POWER CRYSTAL: Charmelite
WISH PENDANT: Necklace

* * * * * ⭐ * * * * *

NAME: Scarlet
BRIGHT DAY: November 3
FAVORITE COLOR: Black
INTERESTS: Crystal climbing (and other extreme sports), magic, thrill seeking
WISH: To live on Wishworld
WHY CHOSEN: Scarlet is confident, intense, passionate, magnetic, curious, and very brave.
WATCH OUT FOR: Scarlet is a loner and can alienate others by being secretive, arrogant, stubborn, and jealous.
SCHOOL YEAR: Third
POWER CRYSTAL: Ravenstone
WISH PENDANT: Boots

* * * * * ⭐ * * * * *

NAME: Sage
BRIGHT DAY: December 1
FAVORITE COLOR: Lavender
INTERESTS: Travel, adventure, telling stories, nature, and philosophy
WISH: To become the best Wish-Granter Starland has ever seen
WHY CHOSEN: Sage is honest, adventurous, curious, optimistic, friendly, and relaxed.
WATCH OUT FOR: Sage has a quick temper! She can also be restless, irresponsible, and too trusting of others' opinions. She may jump to conclusions.
SCHOOL YEAR: First
POWER CRYSTAL: Lavenderite
WISH PENDANT: Necklace

Introduction

You take a deep breath, about to blow out the candles on your birthday cake. Clutching a coin in your fist, you get ready to toss it into the dancing waters of a fountain. You stare at your little brother as you each hold an end of a dried wishbone, about to pull. But what do you do first?

You make a wish, of course!

Ever wonder what happens right after you make that wish? *Not much*, you may be thinking.

Well, you'd be wrong.

Because something quite unexpected happens next. Each and every wish that is made becomes a glowing Wish Orb, invisible to the human eye. This undetectable orb zips through the air and into the heavens, on a one-way trip to the brightest star in the sky—a magnificent place called Starland. Starland is inhabited by Starlings, who look a lot like you and me, except they have a sparkly glow to their skin, and glittery hair in unique colors. And they have one more thing: magical powers. The Starlings use these powers to make good wishes come true, for when good wishes are granted, it results in positive energy. And the Starlings of Starland need this energy to keep their world running.

In case you are wondering, there are three kinds of Wish Orbs:

1) GOOD WISH ORBS. These wishes are positive and helpful and come from the heart. They are pretty and sparkly and are nurtured in climate-controlled Wish-Houses. They bloom into fantastical glowing orbs. When the time is right, they are presented to the appropriate Starling for wish fulfillment.

2) BAD WISH ORBS. These are for selfish, mean-spirited, or negative things. They don't sparkle

at all. They are immediately transported to a special containment center, as they are very dangerous and must not be granted.

3) IMPOSSIBLE WISH ORBS. These wishes are for things, like world peace and disease cures, that simply can't be granted by Starlings. These sparkle with an almost impossibly bright light and are taken to a special area of the Wish-House with tinted windows to contain the glare they produce. The hope is that one day they can be turned into good wishes the Starlings can help grant.

Starlings take their wish granting very seriously. There is a special school, called Starling Academy, that accepts only the best and brightest young Starling girls. They study hard for four years, and when they graduate, they are ready to start traveling to Wishworld to help grant wishes. For as long as anyone can remember, only graduates of wish-granting schools have ever been allowed to travel to Wishworld. But things have changed in a very big way.

Read on for the rest of the story. . . .

Prologue

"So you're saying Vega heard from her?"

"Cross my stars. A holo-text. She got it last night."

"Well, what did it say? Where has she been this whole time? Is she in Starland City? Did she run away?"

Scarlet recognized the Star Darlings' voices outside her window immediately. She didn't have to peer down, but she did. She could also tell right away that they were talking about her. *How dare they?* was all she could think.

Scarlet was perched up in the loft of her dorm room—her *new* dorm room—a place that, these stardays, she seldom left. It had all happened so fast it still felt like yesterday: Lady Stella's informing her that her being assigned to the Star Darlings was all a "starmendous and most unfortunate" mistake, and that, as a result, she would need to be reassigned to a new dorm room so her replacement—some meek-looking orange-haired first-year student—could move into hers. At first, Scarlet had looked at that, at least, as the silver lining, since she and her roommate, Leona, had been bickering. But it didn't take long for her to realize that there would never, in a moonium staryears, be any silver linings to the cloud she had found herself in.

"It didn't say where Scarlet's been, unfortunately." That tinkly voice belonged to Cassie. Scarlet gazed down at the top of the first-year student's silver-white pigtailed head. She and her roommate, Sage, were walking along the path between their Little Dipper Dorm building and the Big Dipper Dorm, where third and fourth years, like Scarlet, lived. Scarlet couldn't help smiling as she thought how clueless they were; she was right there, just two floors above them, and they had no idea. "All the holo-text said," Cassie went on, "was for Vega to meet her in the hedge maze . . . which makes me wonder if Scarlet's still here at school. . . ."

Sage tossed her long lavender hair dramatically from one shoulder to the other, a habit that had always made Scarlet roll her eyes. "I don't know," Sage said. "If Scarlet was at school, don't you think she'd go to classes? I mean, she's already been kicked out of the Star Darlings. Does she want to get kicked out of school, too?"

Kicked out! She nearly leaned out to yell, "I was not *kicked out!*"

"She wasn't kicked out . . ." said Cassie.

Thank you! thought Scarlet. Cassie always had seemed a little smarter than the rest.

". . . exactly. I mean, she didn't do anything wrong."

"Mistakes happen, I guess," Sage said. She shrugged and re-tossed her hair.

Mistakes . . . thought Scarlet. *Mistakes?* Accidently using your roommate's toothlight was a *mistake*. Being told that you, in fact, weren't Star Darlings material? That wasn't a *mistake*. It was just plain wrong!

"I don't know. . . ." Below, Cassie slowed to a stop, pulling Sage with her. Their arms were linked, as Starling arms usually were when they walked together.

"What?" said Sage.

"It's just . . . so many strange things are going on. There's poor Leona . . . ruining her Wish Pendant and not getting a Power Crystal when her mission was otherwise such a success."

"Well, wasn't that her fault? She never used her special powers."

"I know . . . but to ruin your Wish Pendant?" Cassie shook her head.

Above, Scarlet nodded sympathetically. Leona's ruined Wish Pendant didn't come close, of course, to Scarlet's losing her place as a Star Darling, but it had to hurt.

"And then, of course, there are those flowers," Cassie went on. "Have you noticed, by the way, that we aren't fighting anymore?"

"Oh, Cassie!" A laugh bubbled out of Sage as she started to pull Cassie forward. "You and your conspiracy theories. You are too cute! Really, you are."

CHAPTER
1

"Hellooooo?"

Scarlet turned from the window at the sound of a reedy, shrill voice calling from below. She slid from the window seat and peered down the stairs. "Who's there?" she said cautiously, not sure she wanted to know.

As she started down the curving ladder, a Starling came into view. It was a woman—an old woman, Scarlet could tell immediately—grinning and bent over a crystal-tipped cane.

"Hello?" Scarlet said. Her eyes swept the room uneasily for a glimpse of her roommate, Mira. "Er, excuse me," she said, not finding her, "but how did you get in?" Usually, Scarlet was the one sneaking up on people, not the other way around. Plus, as far as she knew, the only way to open the door was by using the palm scanner outside. Then it had to approve you. So how did the woman get in? "Er . . . can I help you?"

The little old Starling craned her neck to peer up at Scarlet. "Why, hello, and star salutations, dearie," she said sweetly. Her voice cracked with age. Wire-rimmed star-shaped glasses rested halfway down her nose, and silvery lilac curls framed her pinched but pleasant face. "As a matter of fact, you can. I'm looking for my grand-daughter, Mira. The Bot-Bot guard at the front told me this was her room?"

"Oh . . ." That made a little more sense. Scarlet guessed family members' hands must work on the palm scanners, too. Not that she would know. After two and a half staryears at Starling Academy, her own family had still never visited her, not once. The only time Scarlet saw her parents was when she met them on tour. They were classical musicians and composers, famous throughout Starland for their otherworldly sounds and scores. Scarlet's mother played the halo-harp, her father the violin, and they traveled staryear-round through-out Starland, recording holo-albums and selling out the most prestigious concert halls. Even when they played in

Starland City, Starland's capital and the home of Starling Academy, rehearsals and interviews kept them so busy that Scarlet always had to go to them. Their schedules were simply too full to fit in a visit to the school.

Growing up, Scarlet had toured Starland with her parents, living out of suitcases, staying in five-star hotels. In between shows, her mother or father—depending on whose turn it was—would tutor her backstage as they tuned their precious instruments. By the time she had reached the Age of Fulfillment, Scarlet had met every dignitary on Starland—but not many other kids.

Scarlet's parents were naturally proud and not surprised when she showed an interest in music. They were astonished, however, when she chose to play the *drums* and began to wear a lot of black. At first, she'd just wanted to shock and annoy them and rebel against their stodgy ways. And she succeeded—particularly when she started adding black streaks to her hot-pink hair. Soon, though, she found herself loving the drums and her adopted color, too. Both made her feel strong. Both let her show her feelings without having to say a single word.

Still, Scarlet needed more. She needed a life that was truly her own, which was why she had applied to Starling Academy. She was stunned when she got in and sure she would struggle in her classes, but she found they were easy for her. The only things that were hard were fitting in and making friends.

"What's the matter, dearie?" The elder Starling chuckled. "Glowfur got your tongue?"

"Oh . . . star apologies," Scarlet said quickly. She was suddenly aware that she probably seemed rude. "Uh, yes. Yes, this is Mira's room. But, well . . ." She looked around and shrugged. "She's not here."

"Oh, what a pity!" The woman's face folded into a pained expression, like one of those comedy/tragedy masks that hung over Mira's bed. She sighed and shook her head slowly. "Well. I suppose I'll just wait for her, then. I should have told her I was coming. Hopefully she won't be long." She shuffled across the room, smiling sweetly and looking ever so slightly confused. "Please do forgive me for surprising you. I didn't realize she had a roommate, you see. I could have sworn the last time she wrote to me she said she lived alone."

"She did," said Scarlet. "I just moved in." She tried to sound less bitter than she felt.

"Ah, good!" said the old woman. "Glad to know I wasn't wrong." She tapped her head just above her ear. "Two thousand and three and still sharp as a prism. So what's your name, my dear?"

"It's, um, Scarlet."

"Scarlet! How lovely! We had a glowsow on the farm with that name when I was a girl. So!" She crossed the star-trimmed corners of her shawl. "Just moved in, you say. Does that mean you're new?"

"No, ma'am . . ." Scarlet shook her head and turned back to her loft, longing to climb back up. She was usually so glad her new roommate, Mira, was always at "play rehearsal," or whatever that drama stuff she loved so much was. For once, though, Scarlet wished she would hurry back to their room so her grandmother would have someone else to talk to.

The old woman, meanwhile, settled onto the bench in front of Mira's dressing table with a frail yet eager sigh. She took a moment to catch her breath and take in Scarlet's side of the wide, softly lit room. Her eyes lingered on the hot-pink drum set perched on a raised platform across from Scarlet's black-and-fuschia-covered bed. Scarlet's things had been moved for her the same starday Lady Stella had broken the news. When her Star-Zap finally led her to her newly assigned room on the other side of the Big Dipper Dorm, it wasn't clear who was more put out: Mira, who'd been quite content having a single, or Scarlet herself.

"Are those drums?" asked the old woman, pointing.

Scarlet nodded. What else would they be?

"Ooh! What fun! Can I try them?" She was already out of her seat. She hobbled over to the platform, raised her cane, and gave the cymbal a powerful smack.

CRASHHH!

"Don't! *Stop!*" Scarlet cried, hurrying over. "I mean, I'd rather you didn't, um, please." Scarlet didn't want to be rude, but nobody—not even a little old Starling—was touching her precious drums. "Maybe you'd be more comfortable waiting for Mira in the Illumination Library. I'm sure a Bot-Bot guide could show you the way."

"Oh, starry nights, no." The old woman grinned and set her cane back on the polished star-studded floor. "I'm just as comfortable as can be. Where is my lovely grand-daughter, though, do you know? I'm just as eager to see her as I can be."

Scarlet didn't know, though she wanted to be help-ful. If Mira had ever said anything to her about where she was going, Scarlet was too focused on her Star Darlings problem to care. Besides, Scarlet preferred for other Starlings to keep their noses out of her business, so she tried to set an example by keeping her nose to her-self, too.

"I'm not sure . . . maybe play rehearsal?"

"Oh, yes, you're right, I'm sure!" crowed the old woman. "That Mira is quite an actor! Destined for stardom! Don't you think?"

"Is she? I don't know," Scarlet confessed. "I've never seen her act." Since leaving her parents to attend Starling Academy, she'd tried to steer clear of theaters and auditoriums. Quite frankly, she also had yet to see the appeal in running around, dressed up like a fool, pretending to be somebody else.

"Moon and stars!" Mira's grandmother gasped. "Never? What a shame. Oh, but surely you've seen her act *sometime.* . . ."

Scarlet shook her head. "Star apologies. No."

"Never?" The old woman leaned forward, twisting slightly. The corners of her mouth twitched, one at a time. A bluish star-shaped freckle on her cheek began to sparkle. Scarlet watched it closely, the familiarity clicking at last. How hadn't she noticed it before?

"All right, I'll admit it." Scarlet sighed to hold back a groan. "I saw her once."

"Really? You did see her? When?"

"The Time of Shadows production. Our first year at school."

"Oh, that was a good one!"

Scarlet stifled a smile as she clicked her tongue and slowly shook her head.

"It wasn't?" The woman's blue eyes grew round. "You really don't think so? Why not?"

"Well, some parts were good . . . like the scenery. . . . And the props could have been worse."

"What about the acting?" croaked the old woman.

Scarlet looked down and smiled.

"*Well?*" Mira's "grandmother" waited, tapping her cane against the floor, sending sparks into the air. "Wasn't it good? Of course it was! We got a standing ovation at the end!"

"*We?*" Scarlet glanced back up, raising one eyebrow in a sharp arch.

The old woman threw back her head. "*Starf!* You knew it was me!" she groaned. Then she laughed and tossed off her shawl so it dangled behind her. "Tell me I had you going there for a while, though," Mira said as she pulled off her wig. Her long indigo hair spilled down her back in shimmering waves. Beneath a thick layer of stage makeup, a whole galaxy of bright blue freckles flashed like sunlight on a lake.

"For a starmin," muttered Scarlet. She did have to live with her, after all.

"Really? Is that all?" Mira sighed. "Sunspots. I guess that's why you're not in that remedial group anymore." She grinned at Scarlet—then blanched in the heat of Scarlet's simmering glare. "No offense!" she said quickly. Like everyone at Starling Academy, it seemed, Mira assumed the special class the Star Darlings went to last period was for extra help so they didn't fail out of school. "Star apologies. I just thought . . . you know . . . since it was a mistake and all . . ."

"It was a mistake, all right," hissed Scarlet.

"Are you mad?"

Am I mad? thought Scarlet. Did a glowfur eat green globules? She was mad, all right. Madder than Leona when she'd had to try out for her own band!

Suddenly, Scarlet's Star-Zap beeped. A holo-text was coming in.

She read it: IN THE HEDGE MAZE. R U STILL COMING?

It was Vega, waiting to meet.

"Forget about it. I'll be fine," Scarlet snapped as she climbed off her bed.

She'd be perfectly *startacular* . . . just as soon as she set everything straight again.

CHAPTER
2

Scarlet burst out of the Big Dipper Dorm and hopped onto the Cosmic transporter. She passed the dancing fountain as she headed to the hedge maze, ignoring the water's friendly wave. She knew all too well that once encouraged, the fountain would only work harder to try to keep a Starling there.

The campus was quiet, as it often was after dinner, when most students flocked to the Lightning Lounge. That was a place, though, that Scarlet usually avoided. Everyone was far too sociable and eager to hang out and chat. One couldn't even lie back and gaze at the stars from underneath the retractable roof without some shiny Starling leaning over and saying, "Ooh! Aren't they pretty?" or "Do you think they look the same from Wishworld?" Scarlet's jaw ached from holding back rude responses, like "*No*, they look like globerbeems from Wishworld. What a startacularly silly question! Of course they look the same!"

Scarlet didn't care much for the hedge maze, either— for a different reason. The hedge maze drove her crazy, the way its pattern constantly changed. No sooner would she think she'd found a way out than a path would turn, a wall would shift, or a leafy new hedge would suddenly appear. Where the fun in *that* was, Scarlet had no idea. She thanked her stars for the single red blossom in every hedge wall that would open a door when plucked. She plucked one every time. Vega, on the other hand, would never have dreamed of doing such a thing. She loved the maze and spent more time there than all the other Star Darlings combined, so it was the best place Scarlet could think of to get a few words with her—alone.

Even before she spotted Vega, Scarlet saw her sapphire aura. The constantly changing maze, however, made actually reaching her hard.

"Vega!" Scarlet finally shouted through the glittery hedge wall. "I'm over here! Come! Hurry up!"

Vega was beside her in a starsec, only slightly out of breath.

"How did you get here so fast?" asked Scarlet as a new wall of hedge popped up behind Vega.

"Easy," Vega said. "I waited for the hedge to shift left, then ran south ten degrees, then doubled back through the—"

Scarlet held up her hands. "That's all right. Never mind. I don't care." At the same time, though, it was exactly this love of puzzle solving that gave Scarlet hope that Vega could help.

"So what did you want to talk about—*finally*? It's good to see you, by the way. Where in the universe have you *been*? We've been worried about you for star-days. So . . . did you want to hear about my mission?" Vega smiled proudly, ignoring Scarlet's immediate sneer. "You'll be happy to know that—unlike Leona's . . ." Vega sighed. "Poor thing. Anyway, unlike Leona's mission, mine was a *great* success. Another Power Crystal collected! Not that I didn't have a little issue—but everyone does, it seems. I found my Wisher fairly easily. It's the wish *identifying* that's so tricky. I know they always tell us that, but you don't really know until you try. Luckily, Clover came down and helped me figure it out in plenty of time. It was actually quite an interesting wish. . . ." She paused, finally noticing Scarlet's pained expression.

"Really, Vega? Do you truly think I wanted to meet to hear all about a Star Darlings mission when I can't go on one anymore?" Scarlet shook her head and her black hair swung back and forth across her eyes. "I thought you were smarter than that. That's about the *last* thing I want to talk about."

"Of course!" said Vega. "What was I thinking? Star apologies." She reached out to pat Scarlet's shoulder, but Scarlet shrank away. "So then . . . what is it? Oh!" Vega nodded. "It's the *band*! You want to come back. That's startastic!" She clapped. "We need you! We really do! Clover was filling in, but she couldn't take Leona anymore. Not that *you* should worry about her. Yes, she's mad that you dropped out, but she also knows what a starmendous drummer you are."

"Freakin' fireballs," Scarlet groaned. "The band is the *second*-to-last thing on my mind!" Sure, she missed the band—well, she missed playing the drums—but she definitely wasn't ready to go back to it, and she wasn't sure she ever would be. Of course Vega, who played the bass, was fine. And Sage and Libby were okay, too. Sage wasn't the best guitarist, but she had good instincts and worked to improve. Libby tried way too hard to make everyone happy, in Scarlet's opinion, but she was startastic on the keytar. It was Leona who drove every-one crazy by bossing them around. Frankly, Scarlet was surprised she didn't try to play every instrument herself.

"Then *what*?" said Vega. Under her bangs her fore-head wrinkled. For Vega, the only feeling worse than having the incorrect answer was not having an answer at all.

"Something's wrong. Very wrong," said Scarlet.

"Ah." Vega nodded. "I see. I know. You're right. It's so unfair. It really is. And I'd feel exactly the same if I were you, I'm sure."

"What? *No!*" Scarlet scooted out from under Vega's hand again. "I mean, yes. It's unfair. Of course. But it's unfair because it's a huge mistake. That new girl—Oph-elia, or whatever her name is—should never have been picked to take my place!"

"You don't think so?"

"I do not!"

Vega sighed and crossed her arms. "Truth be told, you could be right. I've been wondering about her myself."

"You have?"

Vega nodded. "She's so far behind in Star Darlings class—which made sense in the beginning. No one expected her to know anything yet. But she's just not catching up. Do you know she still can't manipulate a watt of energy? Not a single watt! Ooh!" She suddenly jumped as a branch reached out to tickle her ribs. "Come on, we should keep moving," she told Scarlet. "The maze doesn't like it when you stop."

Vega moved to link her arm with Scarlet's. But Scarlet had never been the touchy-feely, arm-linking, hand-holding type. Instead, she put her hands behind her back as they moved along the ever-twisting starlit path.

"You know," said Vega, sensing Scarlet's impatience with their route, "if you just focus and look for a pattern, you have a much better chance of making it out. It's when you try to fight it that you end up feeling trapped."

"Whatever," said Scarlet. "Just get me out of here."

So Vega linked arms with Scarlet (despite her protests) and they quickly made their way out of the maze.

"Star apologies," said Scarlet, "but I just can't play peekaboo with a bush and think at the same time. You're good at solving puzzles, Vega. I've never had patience for them. So think: why would someone so new and totally unprepared to grant wishes be picked to take my place when my wish-granting potential's so starmendously high?"

"You're right. I do like puzzles . . ." said Vega. "At the same time, though, this was Lady Stella's decision, and we have to trust her, don't you think? Still . . ." She paused. "It is strange." Scarlet could sense that an idea was being born in Vega's mind. "And if you talked to Cassie, she'd tell you that's not the only strange thing going on."

"I know," said Scarlet.

"You do?"

Scarlet shrugged and scowled. "I might have . . . overheard her . . . talking about me, and Leona's Wish Pendant."

"And the whole flower thing?" Vega's bright blue eyebrows shot up.

"She did say something about flowers . . . but I didn't actually get that part. What flowers was she talking about?"

"The bouquets," said Vega. "You know. The ones we all—all the Star Darlings, I mean—had delivered to our rooms?"

"Oh, those." Scarlet nodded. She did remember, though she hadn't thought it strange at the time. "So you still don't know who they're from?"

"No," Vega said, "but that's not even it. Cassie has this crazy idea that they were making us fight with each other over the littlest things. In fact, she's so sure, she took my bouquet to the botany lab to be evaluated. She'd already thrown hers and Sage's away."

"What do *you* think?" Scarlet asked. "Do you think Cassie might be right?"

Vega smoothed her hair back. "No, I don't. In fact, we made a bet. If I was right, she would do a puzzle with me every day for a double starweek."

"And if she was right?"

"I'd help her study for her Astral Accounting test."

Scarlet frowned.

Vega winked. "I know. Win-win. But I'm not too concerned about helping her study. Piper's still annoying me as much as ever. She makes these sounds when she's meditating. . . ." Vega closed her eyes and cringed. "Ugh! I can hear them all the way from upstairs in her part of the room. It sounds like a Bot-Bot on the fritz. Like this high, whiny *ohmmmm*." She winced. "How about you and Leona?" she asked Scarlet. "How were you getting along? Before you switched rooms, I mean."

"Oh, I don't know. Leona and I had our testy moments. . . ." Scarlet shrugged. "But I'm sure we would have anyway. So what did the botany lab say?"

"Nothing . . . *yet*. But we should probably hear soon."

"Promise to tell me when you do."

Vega drew an X over her heart. "Cross my stars—and moons. But . . . how? I mean, when will I see you again? Where have you been all this time?"

"I've been . . . around," said Scarlet vaguely. "They gave me a new roommate. Her name's Mira."

"I don't know her," said Vega.

"Neither did I."

"Is she nice?"

"She's fine," said Scarlet. "We don't really know each other yet. She isn't around that much, and I pretty much stay in my loft all the time, so maybe we never will. . . ."

"Have you been to any classes since . . ."

"No," said Scarlet bitterly.

"Don't you think you should?" Vega gently asked. "I mean, I can understand dropping out of Leona's band. No one—well, except Leona maybe—blames you for that. But even if you're not in the Star Darlings anymore, you're still a student at the school, and you can still go to Wishworld and grant wishes one day . . . but only if you graduate, of course."

Scarlet looked over her shoulder, past the hedge maze, toward the majestic Crystal Mountains, which glimmered across Luminous Lake. Vega was right, she guessed. Not that Scarlet was worried about falling

behind in any subjects. Her classes seemed to get easier for her every year. But hiding from everyone and
everything, while it made life simpler right then, wasn't
helping her solve her problem, either.

"You can't hide forever," Vega went on, almost as if
she'd peeked into Scarlet's mind. "How about I make you
a deal like I made with Cassie?"

"I don't make deals," muttered Scarlet. "But what?"

"You start going to your classes, and I'll do whatever
I can to help you get to the bottom of what went wrong."

CHAPTER
3

The next day, Scarlet went through the motions of going to morning assembly, classes, meals . . . all the things she was *supposed* to do. But the more she tried to act like everything was normal, the surer she was that everything was wrong.

She didn't even try to move all the desks in Wishful Thinking class, and yet with a single eyebrow raise she did exactly that. She was just as surprised as everyone else when it happened but was determined as always not to let her emotions show.

Even Professor Dolores Raye's mouth fell open. "Who did that?" she gasped.

In the far corner of the room, Scarlet slowly raised her hand.

"Oh, my stars!" said Professor Raye. "I didn't even see you back there, Scarlet. Welcome back to class, by the way. I must say, I've never seen such control in a third year. Those are very special powers. Er . . . now, if you don't mind, would you be so kind as to move the desks back to where they were?"

This only confirmed something Scarlet had already begun to sense: somehow, instead of feeling less special since leaving the Star Darlings, she felt as if her wish energy powers were stronger than ever before.

At lunch, Scarlet managed to sit by herself: no small feat in the Celestial Café. The tables were large and round and designed to encourage Starlings to linger and talk for starhours. Scarlet sequestered herself at an empty corner table, where she promptly spilled her mug of Zing. "Forget it," she told the Bot-Bot waiter who appeared instantly with another as the puddle disappeared. Instead, she ordered a steaming bowl of stewed garble greens—the smell of which was guaranteed to keep other Starlings far away.

Rather than eating, though—she *hated* garble greens—Scarlet observed the Star Darlings from afar. They sat together, as they had since they'd been summoned, at the middle table near the window overlooking Luminous Lake. Astra was dressed in her neon-trimmed fiery-red star ball uniform. It could have been a game day or not. With her, you never knew. Cassie was nose-deep in a holo-book, and Gemma was giggling and prattling away. Listening to Gemma was one thing Scarlet did not miss in the least.

Vega noticed her and waved so that the others couldn't see. She flashed Scarlet a sparkly smile of friendly encouragement, which Scarlet accepted reluctantly.

As she watched them all, Scarlet couldn't help remembering what Vega had told her in the maze about roommates bickering. And, indeed, they were. If they weren't barking at or arguing with each other, they were sitting far enough apart that they didn't have to talk. Cassie and Sage were the only roommates who appeared to be enjoying each other's company—and Leona and Ophelia, who were sharing a glimmerberry shake.

What a dud, thought Scarlet as she studied Ophelia. There was nothing at all best or brightest or star-charmed about her—at least from what Scarlet could see. While the Starlings around her radiated confidence, brilliance, and power, Ophelia gave off an awkward, muddled aura of confusion and fear.

So why was she there instead of Scarlet? Instead of *anyone*, really . . . but especially Scarlet.

Scarlet remembered the explanation Lady Stella had given when the headmistress had delivered the shocking news.

"I'm truly sorry, Scarlet. Star apologies don't begin to express how I feel. But accidents happen, even on Starland, and I'm afraid one has occurred here. As you know, I chose the twelve Star Darlings myself, using an intricate algorithm comprising numerous factors, including grades and test scores and energy records."

"Yes?" Scarlet had said. She could tell something grave was coming, but she had no idea what on Starland it could be.

"Naturally, great care was taken with the data, and yet . . . somehow, somewhere, a glitch occurred along the way . . . and your name, most unfortunately, was given to me in error."

"I don't understand . . ." Scarlet had whispered with what little breath she could find in her chest.

"I must say, I don't, either. And yet the holo-records Lady Cordial has shown me are as clear as the night sky. Your scores and those of another Starling, Ophelia, were mixed up in the holo-files. Therefore, *she* is the rightful twelfth Star Darling—something you, Scarlet, were never truly meant to be."

Naturally, Scarlet had argued—vehemently. But the energy had been spent in vain. She left Lady Stella's office stinging, as if a hive of angry glitterbees had attacked her, and the feeling still hadn't gone away. The black hole Scarlet had felt in her stomach at that moment was still there, just as deep. In fact, sitting in the Celestial Café, watching Ophelia in her place among the other Star Darlings, only made the feeling worse. Scarlet knew her grades and scores were strong, so the whole thing already made no sense. But in what crazy parallel universe could a starling such as Ophelia have one score higher than Scarlet's, let alone a whole file's worth?

Scarlet blinked and slid her now cold bowl of garble greens across the table before standing up and leaving the café. She had Lighterature next period, but she didn't care. The thought of sitting in a class full of happy, carefree Starlings made her want to zap something. Besides, they were reading a tragedy by Shakestar that she had read hydrongs of times—*Romea and Jupiter*. The whole star-crossed romance thing made her want to hurl. So when she left the Celestial Café, she turned away from Halo Hall and headed across the Star Quad, straight back to the Big Dipper Dorm.

The building was empty except for the Bot-Bot guard inside the front door. "Star greetings, Scarlet," it welcomed her.

"Star greetings," she muttered back.

Scarlet stepped onto the Cosmic Transporter as it rolled through the halls.

Outside her door, Scarlet placed her hand on the palm scanner. The door opened with a gentle *whoosh*. As she walked in, the door slid smoothly closed. Scarlet scrunched her eyes to dim the lights and gazed around the room. Her eyes fell on her drum kit on its platform. *Yes!* That was just what she needed to do! Bang out a few dark and angry riffs . . . or maybe a few hydrong.

Scarlet hadn't played the drums much at all since she'd left the Star Darlings. Before that, she'd played hours every day—either with Leona's band or in their old room while Leona sang. They found it was the one thing they could do together without getting on each other's nerves. As soon as Lady Stella told her she was out of the Star Darlings, however, Scarlet stopped going to band practice, too. Every other member was still a Star Darling, and the last thing she needed was to hear them talk about their missions—or deal with their pity or, worse, their phony good cheer. The only place she could play was her room, but lately the inspiration just hadn't been there.

That day, she felt different, though. The drums seemed to be calling to her. She grabbed her sticks and climbed the platform and sat down. She waited a moogle for the stool to adjust itself beneath her, then gave her bass drum pedal three fierce stomps: *BAM! BAM! BAM!* The energy in the room flickered and rolled away from the star-shaped drum pad in powerful glittery waves. Scarlet smiled and whacked the cymbals—*CRASH! BANG!*—one at a time. She did it again . . . and again . . . and again . . . and again. *CRASH! BANG! CRASH! BANG-A-DEE-BANG! CRASH! BANG! CRASH! BANG-A-DEE! BANG-A-DEE! BOOM!*

With her eyes closed, she let her arms fly in a series of rolls and riffs, wherever they wanted to go. If her eyes had been open, she would have seen the energy aura surrounding her glow brighter and brighter pink. But the light grew so blinding she would have soon had to close them again.

Scarlet had never played her drums so hard before or felt so energized. All her frustration, her bitterness, her confusion dissolved with every beat. Finally, after what felt like a moogle but could have been a staryear, Scarlet had to stop. Exhausted, she let go of her drumsticks and let them twirl in the air above the tom-tom while her head fell back. As her eyes opened, she let out a gasp at the dazzling sight of pure sparkling energy pulsing throughout the room.

Did I do that? Scarlet wondered. There was no other source she could see.

Gradually, the energy faded, but Scarlet's clarity did not. From the beginning, she had suspected there was something not right about Ophelia's replacing her. Now she was sure. And if *she* didn't get to the bottom of it, who else on Starland would? Maybe Vega could help her. But maybe not. Who knew? *And why wait to see,* Scarlet thought as her eyes fell on her roommate's jam-packed costume closet, *when I have all I need to do it on my own?*

CHAPTER
4

The door to Scarlet's dorm room slid open and a small, distinguished-looking man stepped into the hall. He wore a long silver topcoat with a wide forest-green collar and half-moon-shaped buttons as big as ears. His own ears were covered by a burnt-orange fedora tilted so far forward it concealed his face. The only feature not hidden, in fact, was the very tip of his emerald beard. Pausing, he stroked the bright green whiskers as his head swiveled right and left. Satisfied that the hall was empty, he raised a star-studded shiny black combat boot and boarded the Cosmic Transporter as it rolled past him.

Scarlet hoped her disguise (courtesy of her roommate's closet) was convincing. The first test was the Bot-Bot guard at the front door.

She brushed past it, keeping her head down and her velvet collar up.

"Star greetings, Scarlet," the Bot-Bot guard said cheerfully.

Scarlet sighed. "Star greetings," she mumbled without turning. Bot-Bot guards were a useless gauge, she guessed. They could read an aura a floozel away. Hopefully, the Starling adults where she was going would be easier to trick.

Once outside, Scarlet headed directly for the enormous star-shaped building between the hedge maze and the Celestial Café. Although it wasn't geographically at the center of campus, it was the hub in every other way. Halo Hall, as it was called, housed all the Starling Academy classrooms, as well as the Astral Auditorium, where assemblies and performances were held. In the hall, too, were various offices, including that of Lady Stella, the headmistress. Its most spectacular feature was the gleaming lone white tower attached to the Wish-House. At the very top sat the Wishworld Surveillance Deck, the platform where Starlings could observe

Wishworld and its Wishlings through telescopes and where they waited to catch a shooting star when their day for a Wish Mission came at last.

Normally, a Starling walked up the white starmarble stairs and entered through the front doors. Since this starday was far from normal, however, Scarlet hurried around the Bot-Bot guard at the front and made her way into Halo Hall through the back. After all, she wasn't going to some old class in Stellation four or five. She was on a mission to right what was wrong.

If only she knew exactly where she needed to go.

As far as offices went, Scarlet was familiar with only two: that of the perky guidance counselor, Lady Solara, who had made it her mission to "light Scarlet up," and Lady Stella's. Both were offices Scarlet hoped to stay well clear of, since she didn't want to see either administrator just then. Fortunately, they were clustered with other faculty offices in Stellation one and she was fairly certain that the office she was looking for was in Stellation two . . . or maybe three.

She decided to try the second wing first, since it was closest. Like every hall, its walls and floor were made of gleaming rainbow-hued starmarble. In that wing, they gave off a pink-tinged glow. Up near the ceiling ran a series of windows, letting light from outside shine in.

Scarlet hurried down the hall, passing door after door. As she did, she lifted her hat brim ever so slightly to read the holo-signs outside of each.

SUPPLY ROOM, read one star-shaped plaque. STAR-ZAP REPAIR AND MAINTENANCE, announced the next, followed by TECHNOLOGY, SWIFT-TRANSPORTATION SERVICES, and WISH ENERGY MANAGEMENT. Then Scarlet read the holo-sign by the door at the end: BOT-BOT SECURITY.

Freakin' fireballs, she thought. *Security! Time to turn around!*

Heart thumping, she scurried back down the hall and rounded the corner into the safety, she hoped, of Stellation three. *Please let me find what I'm looking for here,* she wished.

That hall looked basically the same, except the glow given off by the marble walls was a bit aquamarine. These doors, too, had holo-signs, and Scarlet read the first one on her right: ADMISSIONS. Lady Cordial's office. Of course. Scarlet remembered it now from her own Time of Applying, when she had first visited the school. She'd come alone, since her parents had been on tour and unable to take the time off. Lady Cordial, the head of admissions, had been pleasant in their interview but not as welcoming as one might have hoped—especially one with test scores such as Scarlet's, which were practically off the charts.

But that was Lady Cordial, Scarlet now realized: stiff and skittish and often at a loss for words. Scarlet had eventually learned, like every Starling Academy student, not to take things too personally with her.

On the other hand, Scarlet's next interview with Lady Stella had been one of the best starhours of her whole life. There was something about the headmistress that made every Starling feel as if she'd known her for staryears. Scarlet had already *thought* she wanted to go to Starling Academy, but meeting Lady Stella had sealed the deal. The headmistress didn't care if Scarlet didn't like rainbows as much as rain clouds or loved the most unloved of Starling colors—black. She seemed to know, too, that Scarlet wasn't half as interested in learning to grant wishes as she was in living on her own. And yet she welcomed Scarlet into Starling Academy with warm and open arms. Lady Stella had always seen Scarlet for who she was and admired her for being herself, which only made Scarlet feel worse about having to leave the Star Darlings—and more determined to get back in.

With that in mind, she moved on, shifting her hat to continue reading each star-shaped sign.

ATTENDANCE, ACCOUNTING, ALUMNI RELATIONS, STU-DENT LIFE, FACULTY LOUNGE . . .

"'Faculty lounge'?" *Hmmm.* Scarlet paused. So *this*

was where their professors hung out when they weren't teaching the finer points of Wishful Thinking or giving a pop quiz on wish identification. She could only imagine what they did in there. Compare lesson plans? Share grading tips? Complain about students, such as Scarlet, who liked to bark out answers instead of politely raising their hands? She pictured them gathered around a table, sharing sighs and cups of Zing.

"Are you going in?"

Scarlet froze.

The person behind her spoke again. "Star apologies. I don't mean to rush you." A hand reached over Scarlet's shoulder to cover the scanner in the middle of the door. "It's just, well, my class ran a few moogles over and I'm late for my massage."

The scanner glowed bright blue. "Welcome, Professor Nicola Cecelia," a Bot-Bot voice greeted the teacher—her Astral Accounting teacher, Scarlet realized—as the door to the faculty lounge opened wide.

Starf! thought Scarlet as her eyes took in the scene. She was careful to keep her hat low, but she could still make out much of the room—everything from the frozen cocomoon yogurt bar to the manicure/pedicure stations to the hot tub *and* swimming pool! Most classes were still in session, so the lounge was far from full.

Nevertheless, there were plenty of teachers already enjoying themselves. Professor Elara Ursa, the Wishers 101 teacher, was having her hair done by a Bot-Bot stylist as she read a holo-magazine. Professor Eugenia Bright, meanwhile, was playing a rather intense spark-filled game of star-pong with Professor Dolores Raye. Giggles spilled out of a holo–photo booth, but Scarlet couldn't see who was inside. She sniffed. Was that zoomberry trifle she smelled? She sniffed again. *Mmm* . . . yes, it was . . . and glorange meringue pie, as well. Scarlet's mouth was already watering by the time her eyes found the buffet.

"Come on in!" By now, Professor Nicola Cecelia had slipped around Scarlet and stood inside. Reaching up, she pulled a silver-star-topped comb out of each side of her tight plum-colored bun. With a shake, she let her hair tumble down loose over her shoulders, and it stopped well below her waist. "Don't be shy. Substitutes are welcome. More than welcome, in fact!" She flashed a smile far sunnier than Scarlet had ever seen on her normally dour face. "You could probably use a break the most. These students are bright, but give them half a chance and they'll wear your glow away. Whose class did you have, by the way? I didn't realize anyone was out. I hope you didn't wear that hat and coat all day. You know, there are Bot-Bot valets to see to things like that."

For a moogle, Scarlet was actually tempted to play along and follow her teacher inside. Before, she had thought that the students' Lightning Lounge had everything a Starling could ever desire. But its cozy fireplaces, pillows, and walls of holo-screens were nothing compared with the faculty's giant lounge. The only problem was Scarlet knew that as soon as she took her hat off, she would give herself away. Frankly, she was surprised—*star*tled, even—that Professor Nicola Cecelia hadn't raised a single violet eyebrow at her beard, which was steadily shifting sideways.

"*Ahem.*" Scarlet cleared her throat as deeply as she could. "Star salutations," she said gruffly. She gave the brim of her hat a dapper tap, the way she'd seen her father do. "But, *ahem*, I'm looking for another, *ahem*, room. *Ahem.*"

"Oh." The teacher's grin faded. "I see. And what room is that?"

"*Ahem.* Er, holo-records."

"You mean the holo-records room right there?" Professor Nicola Cecelia pointed a delicate sparkly purple-polished fingernail at the next door down the hall.

Scarlet turned and squinted to read the sign. STUDENT HOLO-RECORDS. There it was!

"Star salutations!" Scarlet said—too quickly, she

feared. But then Professor Nicola Cecelia's head suddenly snapped around. Her Bot-Bot masseuse was summoning her, rather impatiently by then.

"*Starf!* Got to go. So there it is. Glad I could help. Oh! And so you know, Lunadays we always play astro-poker in the lounge. I almost always win, but still, keep it in mind."

Scarlet let out a long sigh as the door slid shut between them. She hadn't even realized she'd been holding her breath. She checked to make sure no other teachers were coming. They weren't. She sighed again.

It took just a starmin to reach the door of the holo-records room. Then the only question left was, how was she going to get inside?

CHAPTER
5

Scarlet knew better than to try the hand scanner. That would only give her away. There were other ways to get into a room, though, especially now that Professor Nicola Cecelia had confirmed the strength of her disguise.

Scarlet checked her reflection in the mirrorlike surface of the polished marble wall. She slid her beard back to the center and gave it a fluff. She tugged her hat down even farther and propped her collar higher. Satisfied, she raised her fist and rapped on the door . . . once . . . twice . . . three times.

While she waited for the door to open, she went over the story she'd already rehearsed a hydrong times in her mind:

"Hello, my name is Sir Copernicus, and I am here on behalf of Sir Andromedus and Lady Melodia, the famous musicians, as I'm sure you're well aware. Apparently, they've sent numerous holo-requests for their daughter's records, none of which has received a reply. You can imagine what an eclipse they're having. One would think a school like this would have all its stars in a straighter row. But since they're clearly not, the family has sent me to retrieve Scarlet's records, as they're on an extended tour across the Star-Belt region and so could not do it themselves. It's crystal clear, of course, that you're very busy, so I wouldn't dream of taking up your valuable time. Rather, if you'll just point me in the direction of the third-year holo-files . . . Star salutations for understanding. I'll take it from here, if you don't mind."

Scarlet would be free to compare all her scores to Ophelia's—and anyone else's she chose. Leona's, for one . . . Gemma's maybe, too . . . Then she would at least understand why *they* were all Star Darlings and she suddenly was not.

It had to work. It just had to. Otherwise, Scarlet didn't know how she was going to go on. She couldn't keep avoiding everyone and everything forever. Her grades would suffer, and so would she. But until she had some real answers, she would never, in a hydrong star-years, be able to relax.

The only problem was the door wasn't opening. So Scarlet took another breath and knocked again. She tapped the toe of her thick-soled boot. Sparks bounced up from the floor. Did she have to *keep* knocking? She raised her fist. She guessed she did. That was when she noticed, for the first time, the hand scanner—or not the scanner, but what it said.

Scarlet groaned.

She should have looked at it sooner, but she'd been too focused on the door. Instead of displaying a hand outline along with the unnecessary PALM HERE message, the scanner scrolled a series of words: OFFICE HOURS: SUNRISE TO APEX. PLEASE COME BACK. STATUS: CLOSED.

On the way back to the dorm Scarlet shed her disguise behind a lumilac bush about halfway to the building. Classes had ended and Starlings were wandering about, and if one more student had pleasantly waved and called, "Star greetings! Welcome to Starling Academy!" Scarlet would have exploded into a moonium bitter, red-hot stars right there in front of them. When she wasn't in disguise, the other students knew better than to try to talk to her or even share a smile. After Scarlet's more than two staryears at Starling Academy, her reliably antisocial reputation preceded her.

Thankfully, Scarlet made it back to her room before Mira, so she had time to put everything away. The floppy orange hat went back on the hat rack, and the coat went into Mira's costume closet, along with the itchy beard. Scarlet had just sat down at her drums and picked up her drumsticks when the door slid open and Mira breezed in.

"There you are!" Mira pointed one long glittery finger at Scarlet. The other hand perched on her hip. She was dressed as a regular Starling student for a change, even if she had a cobalt blue scarf the size of a bedsheet around her neck. "*Starf!*" she exclaimed. "*So* many Starlings have been asking me about you! Especially all those remedial Starlings, like Leona and Adora—and Ophelia now. 'Where's Scarlet?' 'Have you seen her?' 'Could you please give her a holo-message for me?' I'm like, 'Send her your own holo-message.' And they're like, 'We do, but she won't reply.'" Mira cocked her head and frowned. "Did you lose your Star-Zap or something? We could literally find it in a moogle with my Zap-locate app, you know."

"I didn't lose it," mumbled Scarlet. "I've just been busy."

"Oh." Mira's eyes skimmed Scarlet's drum kit. "Right. Okay. I see. Well, don't let me stop you." She shrugged and tossed a long triangle of scarf over her shoulder. It took three tries before it stayed. "I'm zipping right back out again, anyway. I just popped in to get my holo-script before rehearsal. Now . . . where did I leave it do you think . . . ?"

"Why don't you just memorize your lines over-night?" asked Scarlet. Wasn't that what sleep and headphones were for, after all? So Starlings could play back and absorb class lectures and textbooks and any-thing else they needed to learn?

Mira sighed. "You don't know anything about act-ing, do you?" She tossed her head to show that *she* did.

Scarlet lowered her own head to hide the smile she couldn't keep from springing up. Oh, after her day, she knew about acting. . . . Too bad Mira hadn't seen her. She would have been impressed.

"A script," Mira went on, "is just the beginning. Like a supernova!" She held her fists out and flashed open her fingers. "It's merely the raw matter from which superstars are born. In rehearsal, we're taking notes con-stantly and making changes. It's not just memorizing a hydrong lines," she said, scoffing. "It's a *process*. A *jour-ney*. You know?"

Scarlet nodded, hoping to satisfy Mira, though she'd stopped listening at "beginning."

"Is that your script?" Scarlet pointed to a holo-book near the edge of Mira's makeup-crowded table, behind a long sparkly teal wig on a tall silver stand.

"Is it?" Mira picked up the holo-book and brought it close enough to read. "Star salutations! It is! Okay, I'm off. Again." She paused then, leaning toward Scarlet. "Are you sure you're okay? You know, you look a little green. . . ."

"I do?"

"Mmm-hmm. Around here." Mira stroked her cheeks and chin.

The beard! Scarlet realized. Quickly, she rubbed her face to brush off whatever green glitter was stuck to it. "I'm fine," she said. "Don't worry about me. Just go do your script journey . . . process . . . whatever you call it."

Scarlet had lowered the window shades and blinked off the lights by the time Mira returned. The room had a soft, dreamy violet glow. Dinner was over, as was star-gazing hour, though lights-down had yet to come. Except for the secret Star Caves, of course, no place ever got truly dark on Starland, the way places on Wishworld did. In fact, it actually got brighter as the sun went down and all the wish energy stored in every atom on Starland approached its maximum glow potential.

Scarlet "acted" again, this time as if she was sleeping, in case Mira had more questions to ask her or, worse, offered unwanted advice. She lay as quiet and still as a moonbeam and waited for Mira to take her nightly sparkle shower and slip into bed herself. Actually falling asleep, however, was impossible. The thoughts whizzing through Scarlet's mind simply would not let her rest.

At last, Scarlet had no choice but to get out of bed. She couldn't lie there for a moogle more. Mira was fast asleep, though restlessly muttering something like "Wait! Where's my mark? Somebody moved it from stage left!"

Scarlet slid out from her silky black sheets and scooped her combat boots off the floor. As light as a flutterfocus, she tiptoed past Mira, blinked open the door, and, still wearing her pink-and-black polka-starred pajamas, slipped out into the hall.

To save energy, the hallway Cosmic Transporter ceased flowing after lights-down, but Scarlet was happy to walk. She left her feet bare on the off chance that some other wakeful Starling might hear the *clomp-clomp* of her boots through their chamber doors. Starlings slept exceptionally soundly . . . still, "better safe than lost in space," as Scarlet's father sometimes said.

It wasn't Scarlet's first venture out after lights-down. She'd been taking walks on restless nights since the beginning of the year, when she'd literally stumbled upon the entrance to the mysterious Star Caves. That was before Lady Stella had taken the Star Darlings there, via a secret door in her office, to show them the Wish Cavern she'd had built in the deepest chamber for them and them alone. It was there that the headmistress kept their Wish Orbs. Scarlet knew she had looked as awed and surprised by the caves as everyone else at the time. That was yet another example of her acting talents, she supposed, since she had already discovered the caves herself more than a starweek earlier.

She had arrived at school, as usual, stardays before everyone else. She'd had quite enough of her parents and living out of a suitcase for one Time of Lumiere break. She had checked out her room and was aimlessly riding the Cosmic Transporter around the dorm when she noticed the neon sign on the door in front of her. STARLING ACADEMY STAFF ONLY, it temptingly flashed.

Naturally, she got off and opened it (after peeking over each of her shoulders to make sure she was alone). But it was just a plain old supply closet full of baskets of star-pong balls, sparkle-shower gel, and stuff like that. Because nothing on Starland ever got truly dirty, there were no cleaning supplies, of course. There were, however, a few dust mops and feather dusters for adding an extra layer of stardust to anything that might need shining up. Scarlet had never actually used one, since Bot-Bot maids were always there to shine her hotel rooms. Curious, she took a step into the closet to pull a duster down and see exactly how it worked. "Freakin' fireballs!" she exclaimed as the toe of her boot caught on something and sent her stumbling into a wall of shelves. The next thing she knew, glo-pong balls were raining down on her head like the Perseid meteor shower.

Scarlet looked down as the balls bounced and flashed around her, and that was when she saw the trapdoor. A rogue glo-pong paddle had kept it from closing completely, and that was what had tripped her up. Without thinking twice, she raised the panel and waited as a bunch of glo-pong balls spilled through the hole. She listened to them bounce down a long winding set of metal stairs for several moogles, until they hit a distant floor . . . then, flipping her Star-Zap to flashlight mode, she climbed in to see for herself exactly what was down there.

Since then, not counting her trips with the Star Darlings, Scarlet had been down to explore the Star

Caves more than a dozen times. She'd covered only a tiny fraction, she knew, but on each visit she tried to delve a little deeper than before. This night, without really thinking, she headed due north, down a wide winding tunnel, roughly in the direction of Halo Hall.

As ever, the cave air was cool, like at the top of the Crystal Mountains, but also damp and slightly musty, like her boots before they dried out after a day in Starland snow. The air clung to Scarlet as she moved. Without a doubt, the energy was different down there. What Scarlet liked best of all about the caves was the light that came from glowing rocks set in the walls. It gave her the feeling of being in outer space, where the only light came from distant twinkling stars. Every now and then, as Scarlet walked, a big cold drop of water would splash somewhere on her hair or face. One time, she'd caught one on her tongue. She couldn't say it had much taste.

Suddenly, she heard a high *squeak,* followed by the rustling of wings, and sensed a bitbat swooping down. Scarlet lifted her arm and held out her hand. A starsec later, a silvery-white creature the size of a glowfur settled onto her finger and dangled upside down.

"Star greetings," said Scarlet.

The bitbat blinked its wide fluorescent green eyes

and squeaked twice more, as if in reply. Why bitbats made the other Star Darlings nervous, Scarlet would never know. They were as gentle as any flutterfocus, she thought, just not as hyperactive and ostentatious. Unlike every creature that lived on the surface of Starland, Star Cave creatures did not show off.

The creatures were her second favorite thing about the caves. She envied their solitude, their privacy, their freedom to be themselves and to be alone.

As quickly as it had appeared, the bitbat took off again. Scarlet watched it fly deeper into the cave.

"What's down there?" she called out, following it.

She tried to keep up, but the bitbat was too fast. By the time she rounded a tight corner, Scarlet had lost it in the darkness.

But she had found something else. . . .

CHAPTER
6

Scarlet was dressed and out of her room the next morning before Mira was even awake. Scarlet hadn't slept a wink. She'd spent most of the night in the room at the top of the stairs she'd discovered in the Star Caves, after losing sight of the bitbat. Was it luck that those stairs had led to a trapdoor into the Office of Student Holo-Records? Or was it somehow fate?

Halo Hall would not open officially for another hour but she couldn't see waiting around. She raced across campus to the entrance and begged the Bot-Bot guard to let her in.

"I have to see Lady Stella!" she said. "It's urgent! It can't wait!"

"Star apologies, Scarlet," the Bot-Bot guard replied

mechanically. "Halo Hall is not open, nor is Lady Stella in. Would you like to make an appointment? I can help you with that, if you wish. Lady Stella's office hours are eleven to thirteen starhours. She has another meeting scheduled from twelve to twelve-eighty. What time do you request?"

Scarlet's energy sizzled. That was exactly the problem with thickheaded Bot-Bots. They didn't *understand*. She didn't need an *appointment*. She needed to see the headmistress right *then*!

"Sc-sc-scarlet! Er, st-st-star greetings."

Scarlet turned to see the head of admissions, Lady Cordial, walking briskly toward the door with a stack of files and a mug of Zing.

"Star greetings, Lady Cordial," said Scarlet, bowing.

"You're up early. Feeling better?" She stood before Scarlet, smiling in an awkward but sweet way. Scarlet realized she hadn't seen the head of admissions since learning that her being a Star Darling was a mistake.

"I know what *happened* . . ." Lady Cordial paused and cut her eyes to the Bot-Bot guard, who, like everyone else, knew nothing about the top secret group. "If you don't mind, I'm going to turn off your hearing for a star-sec," she told it.

"Yes, Lady Cordial. As you wish."

Lady Cordial fixed her eyes on its head and narrowed them. "Can you hear me now?" she asked.

She waited.

"Very good. So, er, I was s-saying . . ." She turned
back to Scarlet. "I know this mix-up with Ophelia was,
well, quite a . . . quite a blow, I'm s-s-sure. Of course,
I take full responsibility for everything." She lowered
her head and shook it. "How it happened, I'll never
know."

"But that's why I'm here! I don't think it *did* happen!"

Lady Cordial's head rose slowly, as Starland's sun
was doing just then. "St-st-star excuse me? You don't
think *what* happened?"

"I don't think there's been a mix-up!" blurted
Scarlet. "I mean, yes, there's been a mix-up—but it's the
mix-up that's a mistake! I looked at my holo-records and
there's no way in the Milky Way that the scores recorded
in them are mine! On the other hand, Ophelia, whose
records I also checked, has exactly the scores that I
should have. And that's why I'm here—to tell Lady Stella
that our scores were switched somehow!"

"*What?*" Lady Cordial gasped. Her cup of Zing
slipped out of her hand. Scarlet jumped back and used
her energy to catch the cup in midair, but not without hot liquid splashing over her tights and boots.

Of course, it all disappeared in a starsec, as spills on Starland always did.

"St-st-star apologies," said Lady Cordial. She blinked her cup back into her hand and clutched both it and her folders to her chest. "Clearly, you've taken me by star-prise here. Moon and st-st-stars . . ." She took a breath. "If this is true, why . . . er . . . we have more problems than we thought. . . . I must look into this immediately. And inform Lady St-st-stella, of course."

"I'll go with you!" Scarlet told her.

"No, no. St-st-star s-s-salutations, but you've done your part—and more." Lady Cordial's smile slowly returned. "Please, Sc-sc-scarlet, let me take this from here. It's, er, the least I can do."

Scarlet was so excited she couldn't eat breakfast. And no way could she go to class. How could she sit through another lecture on energy manipulation when her whole life was about to change? About to get back on track, at last!

She had to find some way to pass the time, though, while she waited for Lady Cordial to set everything straight. She flipped open her Star-Zap, tapped Vega's icon, and dictated a holo-text.

MYSTERY SOLVED! MEET ME IN THE ORCHARD.

Within a starmin another message came through: NO WAY! ★MENDOUS NEWS!

When Vega arrived, she was not alone to Scarlet's surprise. Cassie, with her pinkish white pigtail buns and her star-shaped glasses, was arm in arm with her.

Scarlet knew Cassie, of course, from the Star Darlings class but not very well beyond that. The first-year Starling had become particularly close to Scarlet's old roommate, Leona—something Scarlet could never understand, since Leona was, without a doubt, the most self-centered, self-absorbed Starling Scarlet had ever met.

Still, besides that, Scarlet had to admit that what she did know of Cassie, she admired. Cassie was never too loud or bubbly or bossy, and it was clear that behind her glasses, a very intelligent mind was hard at work.

"You don't mind that I brought Cassie, do you?" said Vega. Something about Scarlet's expression must have prompted her to ask. "I promised her I'd tell her the next time we met. I told her about your . . . theories, and of course—"

"I think you're right!" Cassie cut in. She leaned forward and pushed up her glasses. Her normally soft pink glow flashed bright, almost blindingly white. "I don't care what Leona says. There is no way in the galaxy that Ophelia could grant a wish. Tell us everything!" she said. "What have you found out?"

So Scarlet told them everything. . . .

"Moon and stars!" Cassie gasped at the end. "So when will you hear back from Lady Cordial?"

"Soon," Scarlet said. "I'm sure."

"Oh, I hope it's all a mistake, the way you say!"

"Does that mean you'll come back to the band?" Vega asked. "You know, there was just an announcement this morning—did you hear?—that this year for Starshine Day there's going to be a battle of the bands. We could win with you playing, Scarlet. I really think we could. In fact . . . maybe you should come back, no matter what, even if it turns out no mistake was made."

"First of all"—Scarlet's eyes narrowed—"there *was* a mistake. A starmendous one. That's just a fact. Second, as I've said a hydrong times now, the band is about the last thing on my mind."

Vega and Cassie lowered their eyes and traded glances.

"Star apologies," said Vega. "Of course. We can talk about the band later. One thing at a time. So . . . if there was a mistake . . . how in the stars did it happen? How did your and Ophelia's scores get switched?"

Scarlet shook her head. "That's what I don't know." Her eyes flashed and flickered between Vega and Cassie. "You're the puzzle solvers. Any thoughts?"

"These things happen, I suppose," said Vega.

Cassie frowned. "Not here. Not at Starling Academy. All these 'mistakes,' 'coincidences,' 'mysteries'—they don't just *happen* here."

Vega nodded reluctantly. "Agreed."

"So do you think somebody switched our records?" said Scarlet. "On purpose? But those things don't happen here, either . . . do they?"

The three Starlings traded worried looks. They were all thinking the same thing, but no one was quite ready to put such a dark thought into words. Then, suddenly, Cassie's lacy silver sweater pocket beeped. She pulled out her Star-Zap and read the holo-text. Behind her glasses her eyes grew big and round.

"It's the botany lab!" she exclaimed. "They've finished testing the flowers and have the results!"

"Well? What did they find?" asked Vega.

"They don't say. They just say to come."

"That's one connection I still don't see," Vega told her. "And it's not just because I want to win our bet. I was hoping Piper and I would get along better when the flowers were out of our room. . . ."

"And did you?"

"No. Nothing changed. In fact, you should have heard how she went on about my letting you take them to the lab to be studied. You would have thought I'd stolen her bed."

"Really . . ." Cassie's nearly translucent eyebrows slid together as she frowned.

"But then suddenly yesterday," Vega went on, "she gave me this sweet holo-poem she'd written . . . and this morning we meditated together." She smiled at Cassie's and Scarlet's dumbfounded expressions. "Cross my stars! I know!"

"There might still be a connection . . ." said Cassie.

Vega shrugged. "There's only one way to find out." She slipped one arm through Cassie's, then the other through Scarlet's.

"You want me to come, too?" Scarlet eyed Vega's elbow and gingerly unhooked her arm.

"Of course," said Vega. "Right, Cassie?" She tried not to look too hurt by Scarlet's initial response.

"Moon and stars, yes," said Cassie, smiling warmly. "We're in this together now."

CHAPTER 7

The botany lab was in Halo Hall in the science stellation, where the Starlings' Wishology and Astrophysics classes—among dozens of others—were held. Those labs, though, were on the lower floors. The botany lab took up most of the top floor and had a ceiling made of glass so the hydrongs of plants and flowers growing there had all the sunlight or starlight or moonlight they could want.

Naturally, there were specimens from all over Starland: featherjabbers, mellomallows, even nomadic druderwomps—shrublike knots of glittery branches that were constantly uprooting themselves and lazily rolling around the lab until they got bored and decided to stop and spread their roots, inevitably tripping someone up.

The lab was best known, though, for its extensive collection of flora samples from Wishworld. It was the largest collection on Starland, in fact. Generations of Wish-Granters had brought back everything from Spanish moss to buttercups to fragrant evergreen trees. Scientists were still working to get those to bloom ornaments the way they did on Wishworld . . . but so far, they'd had no luck. Scarlet's personal favorites were the dandelions, which were like two flowers in one, the second better than the first: a starburst of yellow petals followed by tickly cloud-white fluff. And best of all Wishers used them to make wishes! Plus they didn't overwhelm you with that cloying flower smell, which was always such overkill, Scarlet thought.

The three Starlings—Scarlet, Vega, and Cassie—entered and were met by a pair of turquoise-haired technicians in sturdy star-covered overalls under long shimmery white lab coats.

"Ah! Star greetings, Cassie," said one, a short woman with a blue holo–name tag reading GLADIOLUS ROSE. "Oh, my stars, you got here quickly! You must have ridden a laser beam!"

She clasped her hands and bowed, as was Starland custom. Her partner did the same. He was taller by a moonstone and wore a hard-to-miss star-shaped bandage on his nose.

Cassie bowed in return, as did Vega and Scarlet.

"We couldn't wait to hear the results of your tests!" Cassie told the lab technicians. She nodded to the man. "What happened to you, by the way?"

"What? Oh, this?" The man patted his bandaged nose, then turned to his flickering silver-tinged partner, who guiltily sucked in her cheeks. "Flying flowerpot . . . Funny story . . ." He sighed. "Or at least it will be, I hope, one starday."

"Why don't we show them those flowers?" said his partner.

He nodded. "Good idea."

"After you. Please." She waved him past.

"Star salutations, but please, no, after you."

They went on like that, back and forth, until Scarlet couldn't take one more exchange.

"Why don't you show us *together*?"

"Great idea!" they said in unison. "To the back of the lab. This way."

The Starlings followed them down a winding aisle between empty workstations.

"Where is everyone?" Vega asked.

Gladiolus Rose picked up an uprooted kaleidoscope

tree sapling and set it on a counter between a broken beaker and an upside-down microscope. "Most of the botanists decided to go home early yesterday. We stayed to finish this job. The energy in the air was rather . . . *tense*, you might say. Lots of name-calling, flowerpot flinging, energy sapping, I'm afraid."

"Not much work getting done," said her partner. "Not safely, anyway."

Scarlet gazed around at the mess and couldn't help cracking a smile. She could only imagine the scene that must have made it.

"That sounds like Piper and me," said Vega. "Until yesterday afternoon." Suddenly, her expression began to change. "When exactly did your fighting stop?"

"Almost as soon as we put them behind glass," Gladiolus Rose answered. "When was that?" She turned to her partner. "In the afternoon?"

"Indeed, it was."

Cassie's eyes grew round, and so did Vega's. Scarlet's jaw dropped slightly, too.

"Are you saying you think the flowers made you bicker and fight?" asked Vega.

"I'm afraid so," the techs said together. "Star apologies!" They bowed and laughed.

"As you can see," said Gladiolus Rose, "arguing is

not in our nature. So as soon as it started, we knew that something was starmendously wrong."

"The moment we put them behind glass, however," the man said, "the fiery tempers cooled."

He pointed to a glass case at the end of the lab. Inside, the Starlings could see Vega and Piper's lavish coral-colored bouquet.

Scarlet instantly remembered the flowers, though she'd given them little thought when they showed up in her room. Not surprisingly, Leona had claimed them for her half of the room almost immediately, so Scarlet paid even less attention to them after that.

"You were absolutely correct in suspecting those flowers of negative energy," Gladiolus Rose told Cassie as they moved toward the case. "The things are full of it, in fact. The measurements we recorded were frankly *floozels* off the charts. It's as if each and every flower was grown in negative-energy-infused soil."

Scarlet scowled and spoke up. "But isn't that impossible? Every Bad Wish Orb is destroyed immediately. That's one of the first things we learn when we get to this school."

"Moon and stars! We didn't think negative energy even *existed* on Starland," said Cassie with a gulp.

Scarlet hadn't thought Cassie could look any paler—and yet, somehow, she did.

Gladiolus Rose shook her head. "It doesn't. Technically," she said.

"What do you mean?" Vega asked.

The two lab technicians exchanged grim glances.

The tall one cleared his throat. "There have been leaks in the past . . . from the Bad Wish Containment Center."

"*But* that was *hydrongs* of staryears ago," his partner assured the Starlings. "There have been mix-ups, too . . . bad wishes mistaken for good ones at first. . . . But such a thing is exceedingly rare, and by the time the mistake is corrected, almost all the potential negative energy has yet to be released."

"'Almost'?" Vega said.

"Almost." The woman nodded. "So, yes, it's not beyond the spectrum of possibility for there to be a microjoule in the air. But nowhere near enough to account for the concentrations we're seeing here. It's unprecedented, frankly." She turned to peer into the case. "Never before, at least in this lab, have we seen negative plant life half as powerful—or *negative*—as this."

"So . . . what you're saying, then," said Scarlet, "is

that this mystery still isn't solved. You don't know where the flowers came from."

"Not yet. No. But our tests aren't finished. There are a few more we can do. Hopefully, we can identify the exact source of the negative energy and even pinpoint where the flowers were grown."

"How long will it take, do you think?" asked Vega.

"I'd say a starday . . . maybe two . . . three at most." Gladiolus Rose shrugged. "It's difficult to say until the rest of the staff returns to work."

Her partner gazed around the overturned lab. "We were also hoping to straighten things up a little first. That's one thing about this Wishworld dirt . . . it doesn't seem to clean itself up. It just sits there when it's spilled."

"Well, we can help you with *that*," said Vega matter-of-factly. She looked down at the loose Wishworld dirt scattered across the floor. Her eyes narrowed as she focused her energy on gathering the dirt into a pile. As soon as she collected it all, Vega flicked her wrist and lifted it in a steady stream, using her finger to steer it into the nearest flowerpot.

Scarlet looked over to see Cassie starting to use her energy, as well. One by one, on the counter in front of Cassie, overturned plants were popping upright.

"Star salutations!" said the lab technicians.

Vega beamed. "It's the least we can do! Scarlet . . . ? What are you waiting for over there? The faster we clean up this lab, the faster they can run more tests."

"Why don't we just zap up some Bot-Bot maids?" said Scarlet, looking bleakly around the room. She would rather have linked arms with Leona than do that job, even with the help of her energy manipulation.

"And where would be the fun in that?" asked Vega brightly, adjusting a trayful of laser-bean seedlings just so.

Suddenly, she jumped, and so did Cassie. Both Starlings pulled out their Star-Zaps.

"Moon and stars!" gasped Cassie. She looked at Vega, who was just closing her device and slipping it back into her fitted coat.

"What is it?" asked Scarlet.

Cassie hurried over to Scarlet and whispered so the lab technicians wouldn't hear: "Another Wish Orb's been identified." Only a few faculty besides Lady Stella and Lady Cordial knew of the existence of the Star Darlings, and it was imperative it stay that way. "We have to go to Lady Stella's office. Immediately. To find out whose wish this will be."

"I'm coming, too!" Scarlet moved toward the lab door.

"Did your Star-Zap go off?" Cassie asked.

Scarlet stopped and put her hand on the pocket of her hooded vest. She hadn't felt any vibration. She looked, but she knew the answer was no before she saw the screen. "I'm going anyway."

"I don't know. . . ." Cassie shook her head. "Lady Stella knows best, and if she didn't summon you, I don't think that you *can* go."

"But I'm a Star Darling!"

"*Shhh!*" Cassie quickly glanced over her shoulder. Luckily, the lab technicians were in the far corner, straightening some crooked holo-screens.

"But I *am* a Star Darling!" Scarlet hissed. "If there's a wish assignment, I should be there!"

Vega had come over, too. Both she and Cassie took Scarlet's hands. "Patience, Scarlet. If you truly are a Star Darling—and I certainly don't doubt it—then the stars will realign for you, all in due time," Vega said.

Scarlet yanked her hands away and squeezed her lips together tightly. She was close to saying something she just might regret.

"We'll let you know what happens," Cassie assured her.

"Whatever." Scarlet raised her chin and looked away.

She would have liked to see how much patience Vega or Cassie or any other Star Darling would have were she to trade places with one of them.

High above, over the ceiling skylight, a pink cloud the shape of a galliope's head slowly drifted past. She closed her eyes and thought of Wishworld, somewhere beyond it, orbiting through space full of wishes.

"Keep your stars up," said Vega. She reached out and gave Scarlet's arm a squeeze. "If we see Lady Cordial, we'll ask her about your reports. . . . I'm sure we'll have some good news for you by the time you're done helping here!"

"*Well?*"

"*Starf!*"

"*Scarlet!* Moon and *stars*!"

"You scared the light out of us!" Vega gasped.

"Star apologies." Scarlet stepped all the way around the column she'd been standing behind and pulled her hood back from her face. They were in the hall outside Lady Stella's office, where Scarlet had been lurking for a starhour, or quite possibly longer. She could have waited for Vega and Cassie to holo-call or text her, but waiting had never been Scarlet's style.

"Why were you hiding?" asked Cassie.

"I wasn't *hiding*. I was just trying to stay out of sight . . ." Scarlet explained.

Cassie and Vega wrinkled their glittery foreheads.

"Anyway," Scarlet went on. "What happened? Who got the mission? And what did Lady Stella have to say about *me*? I didn't see Ophelia come out. Have they already told her about the mistake?"

Vega's cheeks flashed ever so faintly. Cassie's lip slid beneath her teeth. Scarlet couldn't tell if they looked more like they'd eaten too much zoomberry cake or like someone had stolen cake from them.

"What's wrong?"

Vega's and Cassie's eyes met and something passed between them. Scarlet felt her glow dim as it did.

"Tell me."

Vega took a deep breath. "The Wish Orb was Ophelia's."

"The Wish Orb . . . the Wish Orb was *what*?"

"The Wish Orb was Ophelia's," Vega said again, letting her breath out as she did.

"Wait . . . so what are you saying?"

"The Wish Orb was Ophelia's," Cassie patiently repeated.

Scarlet's glow returned in a flash, this time hot pink. "I get that," she muttered. "But are you saying . . . Are you saying a *Star Darling* Wish Orb chose Ophelia? Are you saying the next Star Darling mission is *hers*? Are you saying . . ." Scarlet closed her eyes and opened them slowly. "Are you saying Ophelia is going to go to Wishworld to grant a wish instead of *me*?"

Vega nodded.

"Or at least almost there," Cassie said.

"Star apologies, Scarlet. For what it's worth, we believed you . . . but you were wrong, I guess." Vega reached out to touch Scarlet's shoulder, but Scarlet stepped away.

"I wasn't *wrong*," she snapped. "There was nothing to be wrong about. Scores are scores. I saw what I saw. Tell me . . . Lady Cordial . . . what did she have to say?"

Vega and Cassie responded with shrugs.

"Not much," said Vega, "as usual. She just wished Ophelia lucky stars."

"That's all? She didn't mention the holo-records? Did she at least look starprised?"

"*Everyone* looked starprised," said Vega.

"Especially Ophelia," Cassie agreed.

"Actually, Lady Cordial probably looked the least

starprised," added Vega. "Maybe she'd already looked into your theory, Scarlet, and all the holo-records, and didn't see what you think you saw."

"No one's saying you're lying, Scarlet—or that we were happy to see you go. . . . And we're definitely not saying there aren't weird things going on. . . ."

"But I don't think your leaving the Star Darlings is one," added Vega.

"You can still help us get to the bottom of the flower mystery!" said Cassie brightly.

"*Flowers?* Are you shooting my stars? I don't give a crater about your flower mystery," Scarlet fired back. "I hope whoever sent them sends you a hydrong more, in fact!"

CHAPTER
8

The rest of the day passed in a haze of bitter disappointment for Scarlet. She skipped lunch in the Celestial Café and filled her stomach with cocomoons and gloranges from the Starling Academy orchard instead. Since Starland fruit grew back, full and ripe, as soon as it was picked, Scarlet didn't have to worry about taking too much—or getting in trouble for it.

Skipping class was another story. That wasn't as easy to do. So Scarlet sat through hers, hood pulled down, in the farthest back corner of each room. She barely listened to the lessons, though, since what did they matter to her now? Did she even want to go to Wishworld to grant wishes? The more she thought about it . . . who *cared*?

So as Professor Andromedus Galapas droned on about the Enlightenment and the lighterature of the day, Scarlet drafted a holo-message to her parents, begging them to take her . . . *somewhere*, since they didn't exactly have a home.

Dear Mom and Dad,

Wherever you are, please come and get me. As soon as you possibly can. Or if you're too busy, feel free to send a Starcar and I will come to you. It's taken me almost three staryears, but I finally see that I was wrong and you were right. I was lucky to be able to travel all around Starland with you, having tutors instead of teachers who think they're so shiny and bright at some silly snooty school full of Starlings who act like they're the center of the whole universe. I made a starmendous mistake applying to Starling Academy. I wasn't meant to grant Wishling wishes. Never mind what I said about hating the idea of a family trio. I was wrong. Take me back, please, so I can play the drums with you.

Love and stars,
Scarlet

She read it over . . . raised her finger . . .
She sighed and hit DELETE.

"You'd like to go, Scarlet?"

"Huh?" Scarlet heard her name and looked up.

Professor Galapas was staring at her. So was the rest of the class. Open holo-books hovered in front of everyone but Scarlet, their text projected into the air.

"You raised your hand? You'd like to read aloud next?"

"What? No, sir. I mean, I didn't mean to." Scarlet looked at her finger, which was still in the air, then back at the teacher in the front of the room.

His bald head gleamed like the ice-covered summit of the Crystal Mountains. His face was as round as a star ball and just as bright. When he wore dark robes, as he usually did, it was almost as if the moon was up there teaching the class.

"'*Mean* to.' A mere technicality. Some things are written in the stars. Please, Scarlet, *enlighten* us. Just pick up where Leona concluded, if you don't mind."

Scarlet panicked slightly, and her eyes cut to her old roommate, whose seat was always front and center in every room, like she was a curly-haired sun for the world to orbit.

"Um . . ." She opened her holo-book and projected a page. She had no idea if it was the *right* one. Before she could read, though, and know for certain, the image in front of her blinked. The page changed, and Scarlet sensed Leona looking at her with a half smile on her bright gold-flecked face.

"You owe me."

Scarlet had barely escaped from Constellation Classroom 315 when a voice behind her made her stop.

"What?" She knew the voice before she turned. Still, she hadn't expected Leona's expression, which was somewhere between "Please, don't leave me" and "Gotcha!"

"You owe me," Leona repeated.

"Uh . . . star salutations . . . ?" Scarlet said. Leona had been unexpectedly generous in giving Scarlet the correct page number, she supposed. She bowed and reluctantly worked to soften her permanent frown.

But Leona shook her head. "I don't want your salutations."

"Then what do you want?"

Leona crossed her tawny, sparkling arms over her gold mesh tunic. "I want you to come back to the band."

"Oh." Scarlet jammed her hands in the pockets of her hoodie. "Star apologies. No can do. Besides, have you

happened to notice you have a new roommate? *Ophelia?*"
She could feel her cheeks glowing hotter and hotter. "I'm
not a Star Darling anymore."

Leona shrugged. "Who said you had to be one?"

"Uh, you did, I'm pretty sure."

"Did I?" Leona squeezed one eye shut, trying to
remember. "Well, if I did, then I changed my mind."

"Great. Then find one of the other hydrongs of
students here to be your drummer, because I'm not
interested," Scarlet said.

"Oh, come *on*," Leona groaned. "Stop *pouting* already
and just come *back*. At least until Starshine Day, so we
can win the battle of the bands."

Scarlet laughed. "You're hystarical, you know that,
Leona?" She shook her head in disbelief. "Do you
honestly think I care one proton about some Starling
Academy battle of the bands? Or if the Star Darlings
win? *Especially* after the way you wrote me off the
moogle you found out I wasn't a Star Darling anymore?
How about I put this in your own words, the ones you
said when I came to you then: 'I don't give a star.' How's
that? Hmmm? Now you know how it feels."

Leona stood there, her glow visibly faded. She clearly
didn't know what to say. Scarlet would have been happy

with a simple "star apologies," but that was a lot to ask, she guessed.

Or was it?

Leona's golden lips slowly opened and a word began to form.

Beep!

She jumped at the sudden sound of her Star-Zap and quickly pulled it out. Whatever the holo-text said, it made her eyes pop, and whatever word she'd had primed disappeared.

"Gotta fly!"

"What happened?" asked Scarlet.

Leona paused. "It's Ophelia . . ." she began. Then she checked herself and turned away.

"What about her?" Scarlet went on.

But by then, Leona was gone.

If Leona had any idea Scarlet was following her, she didn't let on. When it was clear that she was heading to Lady Stella's office, Scarlet hung back a little more. She hugged the cool marble wall at the end of the corridor and watched Leona and the other Star Darlings file over the threshold. . . . Then, just as the door started closing, Scarlet silently slipped through.

The Star Darlings were all so excited no one took notice of the pink-tinged shadow making its way to the back of the room. Scarlet slid into the corner, behind a potted boingtree. The branches were far enough apart for Scarlet to peek through but full enough of bright color-changing leaves to serve as an excellent screen.

She looked for Lady Stella but couldn't see her. The Star Darlings seemed starprised by her absence, as well, and stood chattering anxiously instead of taking seats around the large full moon–shaped table in the center of the room, as they'd normally do.

When Lady Stella finally entered through the hidden door in the back of her office, which led to the Star Darlings' secret Star Caves, her face wore uncharacteristic lines. She paused to consider every Star Darling, gazing deeply into each pair of eyes.

"What's up?" Gemma blurted.

"*Gemma!*" Her sister, Tessa, elbowed her in the ribs.

"I'm afraid," Lady Stella began, "that something quite troublesome is up. There are problems with this latest mission."

"What kind of problems?" Sage asked with a flash. "The same kind of problems we've had before?"

"I'm afraid not," said Lady Stella. "These are far graver. . . . Ophelia's Wish Orb has gone black."

A unified gasp whooshed through the room, as if every air molecule was sucked out. From the shadows, Scarlet watched the stunned Star Darlings grab and squeeze one another's hands. A black Wish Orb meant not only a failing mission but the potential loss of a Starling, as well.

"So . . . what do we *do*?" said Leona. "Someone has to *help* her!"

"Yes, someone does," Lady Stella agreed.

"I'll go!" said Leona. "I'm ready right now. I can do it this time! Send me!" She moved toward Lady Stella, but the headmistress motioned her back.

"Star salutations, Leona, for your generous offer, but—"

"But what? I can't go because I failed my mission? But I thought you said that wasn't my fault!"

"No, it's not that, Leona," Lady Stella assured her. Calmly she waved away the sparks that were sputtering out of Leona's ears. "I'm afraid only a Wish Orb can pick who goes, as on every other mission when help is required. This situation, of course, is far more dire. But the same procedure is required." Then Lady Stella reached into the folds of the long silver robe she wore. In her hand sat Ophelia's Wish Orb. Each time before, when Lady Stella had gathered them to see who the Wish Orb would choose to help grant the wish, the orb had lost some of its glow. But this orb smoldered dully like a lump of crater coal. It was the ugliest thing Scarlet, or any other Starling, had ever seen in her life.

Lady Stella spread her fingers and let the orb rise and hover between her and the Star Darlings. After a moogle, it began to move . . . slowly drifting past each glittery, worried face in search of the one it would choose.

"Where is it going?" asked Vega as it floated up to her last, then swerved. "It's not choosing any of us? It's flying away. It's trying to get out of the room."

"No . . . it's not," said Cassie, pointing. "Look. It's heading into the corner over there, toward that kaleidoscope tree."

Sure enough, it was. Scarlet watched it approach, just as confused as everyone else. As it reached the tree and stopped, however, she understood at once.

"It chose me!"

Scarlet stepped out from behind the tree, beaming. It was the first smile she'd worn in stardays. She'd almost forgotten how smiling felt. In her palm rested the Wish Orb, which had firmly settled there as soon as she had held her hand out.

"*What the stars?*" exclaimed Gemma.

Tessa was too shocked to respond to her sister with her usual reproach.

"That's impossible!" said Leona. "She's not a Star Darling anymore!"

"And yet . . ." Lady Stella glided toward Scarlet, wearing an expression of not unhappy starprise. "Scarlet, I do not know how you got here, but Ophelia's Wish Orb has indeed chosen you. And it is you who must go help Ophelia—and hopefully make the wish come true."

CHAPTER
9

By the time Scarlet's shooting star delivered her to Wishworld, she had fully transformed from a Starling into as convincing a Wishling as a Starling could be. Her skin was flat and freckled, without a hint of sparkle or a tinge of pink. Her eyes were brown instead of rose-colored. She had even toned down her hair so it was black with a single streak of bright pink.

Scarlet was pretty sure, too, that the outfit she'd ultimately chosen would convince any Wishling she might encounter that she'd lived there all her life. First she'd picked those pants Wishlings adored—according to Professor Margaret Dumarre, who knew the ways of Wishlings inside and out. Dungarees, she called them, though most Starlings who'd been to Wishworld seemed to refer to them as jeans. Scarlet also wore a deep burgundy hoodie made of a dense, rather stiff Wishling fabric, with a puffy black vest over that. Finally, on her feet were brand-new boots from Lady Stella, which would be her Wish Pendant from then on. One day, on her own mission, the rows of star-shaped energy-absorbing jewel buckles would light up when she met her Wisher and absorb all the wish energy produced when that Wisher's wish came true. For now, however, Scarlet was careful to pull her jeans down to cover as many of the jewels as she could.

Scarlet stood where she'd landed, in a Wishworld meadow filled with green grass and yellow flowers, canopied by a bright blue sky. In the distance, she could see a sharp steeple and the starkly angled rooftops of what looked like a small town.

So strange . . . she thought as she looked around. *And so . . . uncomfortable, as well.*

She sensed it first on her back . . . then on the top of her head, under her hood: a deep, inescapable feeling unlike any other she'd ever had. It didn't take away from the excitement of being on Wishworld at last . . . it just distracted her a bit.

Scarlet pulled down her hood and that helped a little, especially when a light breeze swept through her hair.

But the uncomfortable feeling soon returned, stronger than before. Scarlet slipped off her vest and began to fan herself. That made a big difference, she discovered with relief.

Curious, she checked her Star-Zap to see what the temperature was. *Solar flare!* she thought as she realized how much warmer it was there than on Starland. Quickly, she reactivated her Wishworld Outfit Selector and dialed up a tank top.

Ah, much better, she thought.

She wasn't there to worry about her comfort, though, Scarlet reminded herself. She was there to do a job—and, even more important, to prove what she could do! She needed to fix whatever mess Ophelia had made and get a wish granted and wish energy collected as soon as Starlingly possible. Ophelia had already squandered half the time the Wish Orb gave her, so there wasn't a moogle left to waste.

Quickly, she folded up her star and slipped it into her pocket. Then she switched her Star-Zap to locator mode.

"Take me to Ophelia!" she told it, and directions appeared instantly.

To Scarlet's starprise, the directions led her away from the town and into a vast field. It appeared to be full of some kind of crop, from what Scarlet had learned of Wishling ways of growing food. The plants stood in straight rows and were tall—much taller than she—with long, pointy, floppy green leaves. Near each stalk bloomed tight tubelike flowers nearly the size of Scarlet's arm, each with dark silky threads spilling from its top.

They gave off a distinct sweetish scent, too, which made Scarlet's nose begin to twitch. . . .

She stepped forward and bumped right into something. "*Starf!*" she said, stepping back. She stepped forward again. Same thing. As she reached out into the air in front of her, Scarlet's hand encountered a smooth surface. Aha! A smile spread across her face. It was the smooth surface of an invisible tent!

"Ophelia?"

Scarlet knelt down and cautiously parted the flaps of the glitter-covered tent—Ophelia's glitter-covered invis-ibility-cloaked tent, to be exact. As she did, a glittery, wide-eyed, freckled face peered out with a tiny panicked squeal.

"*Eeh!* Oh! *Oh,* thank *stars* you're here!" Ophelia gasped, bursting out of the tent and into Scarlet's arms.

Scarlet fell backward onto the star-studded back pockets of her jeans.

"Star apologies!" said Ophelia, clambering off her.

"It's just so good to see a friendly—oh . . . um . . . to see a familiar face, at least."

Indeed, Scarlet's face was far from friendly then. She could feel the irritation hot beneath her sneer. "What in the stars are you doing in your tent, Ophelia? And please tell me you've changed your appearance and you don't still look like *that* to everyone here. . . ." Scarlet knew Starlings always looked glittery to each other, no matter where they were or what form they assumed. Something, though, about the way Ophelia was flashing and hiding made Scarlet think she just might look glittery to Wishlings, too.

Ophelia looked down at her shimmering skin and wrung her hands, which only amplified their glow. "Those answers go together, I guess." She looked up miserably and gulped.

"You were supposed to change your appearance and find your Wisher!" Scarlet said, disgusted. "Did you try to do *either* of those things?"

Ophelia nodded meekly. "I tried. But I don't know . . . nothing seemed to work. . . ." She pulled out her Star-Zap and showed it to Scarlet. "This was supposed to help me change my appearance, right?"

Scarlet nodded.

"Well, nothing happened. . . ."

"What do you mean 'nothing'? It's so easy. . . . No Wishworld Outfit Selector, either?"

Ophelia shook her head. "And when I asked it to take me to my Wisher . . ."

"What? What did it say?"

"It said, 'Reply hazy. Ask again.'"

"So did you?"

"Only a hydrong times," Ophelia groaned. "Finally, I just tried to go and find her in that little town on my own."

"Like *that*?" Scarlet asked, looking Ophelia up and down.

"Well . . . what else could I do?" she said meekly. "But I didn't try for very long. Everyone was staring and asking me questions like 'Is there a circus in town?' and 'Are you a clown?' What's a circus and what's a clown, anyway?"

"Um, they're like royalty," Scarlet guessed, since she didn't know.

"Oh." Ophelia nodded. "So, anyway, I gave up because of that. And because of this thing, too." She held her hand out toward Scarlet. On her wrist was a thick yellow bracelet studded with star-shaped jewels.

"Is that your Wish Pendant?"

Ophelia nodded. "Pretty, isn't it?" She sighed.

"Did it ever glow?"

Ophelia shook her head. "Not even a little," she replied. "I thought it was because I couldn't find my Wisher, but now I'm not so sure that it's not broken, too. . . . But anyway, that's why I'm here." She gazed at the field around her tent. "I didn't know where else to go, and at least my Star-Zap could do this. I really wanted to make this mission succeed. Truly, Scarlet, I did." She sniffed. "I didn't mean to fail." Her glittery orange eyelashes fluttered as glittery orange tears welled in her eyes. "I'm just so happy to see you, Scarlet! Truly, I am! How in the stars did you know to come?" She paused as another question suddenly popped into her head. "But why . . . how is it *you*, Scarlet? I thought . . ." She stopped and bit her thumb.

"It's okay. Go ahead and say it," said Scarlet. "You thought I'd been kicked out of the group for good? You're right. I was. But I never should have been. It was all a big mistake."

"So you're back in?" exclaimed Ophelia. She wiped her tears and began to grin. "That's starmendous! I'm so happy for you! And so relieved . . ." She sighed. "So. Shall I wait here while you go find the Wisher and grant her wish so we can go home?"

"I wish," Scarlet muttered.

Ophelia looked confused.

"It's still your wish," Scarlet told her. She shrugged as Ophelia's smile of relief collapsed. "Hey, don't blame me. I don't make the rules. According to Lady Stella, I'm here to help. That's all."

Ophelia gestured toward her Starling garments, then to her fluorescent-orange pigtails.

"Here." Scarlet dialed up APPEARANCE TRANSFORMATION on her Star-Zap and placed it in Ophelia's hand. "Try mine and see what happens."

Ophelia clutched it tightly, holding her breath.

"Recite the mantra!" Scarlet reminded her. "And put one hand on your bracelet!"

"Oh, right . . . Star light, star bright, first star I . . ."

"See tonight."

"See tonight. I wish I may, I wish I might, have this wish I . . ."

"Wish!"

"Wish . . . tonight."

Scarlet watched with more irritation than relief as the sparkle finally drained from Ophelia's skin and hair like sand through an hourglass.

She noticed a bit of loose glitter clinging to her arms and the frizzy ends of her dull orange pigtails.

"Shake," Scarlet told Ophelia.

She did.

"How do I look?" Ophelia asked, rubbing her newly green eyes and inspecting her pale pink fingernails.

"Dull," Scarlet replied approvingly. "Now dial up the Wishworld Outfit Selector and let's get out of here. See that?" She pointed to the steadily counting-down timer in the Star-Zap's upper left corner. "That's how much time we have left to grant this wish. One moogle longer and the mission fails."

Ophelia gasped. "But . . . isn't that less than a Wishworld week?"

Scarlet shook her head. "More like less than a Wishworld day."

"Oh, I hope we can grant it," said Ophelia. "It will be so hard to go back if we don't. . . ."

Scarlet laughed. She couldn't help it. Ophelia had so much still to learn.

"What's so funny?"

"Don't be silly," said Scarlet. "You'll just use your star." Scarlet sighed. This was way worse than she had imagined.

"My star?" Before, Ophelia had looked anxious. Now she simply looked confused.

"Your star," said Scarlet. "The one that you came on.

The one you have folded up in your backpack . . . Wait. What? No! Don't tell me you don't!"

Ophelia shook her head slowly—once in each direction. Her mouth trembled, but no sound came out.

"Well, where is it? What did you do with it?" asked Scarlet. She groaned. "Oh, don't tell me you let it fizzle out!"

"I didn't mean to . . ." said Ophelia, sniffling back tears. "Nobody told me about folding it up. . . ."

CHAPTER
18

No working Star-Zap . . . No shooting star . . .
Was it even possible for Ophelia to get back to Starland,
Scarlet wondered, even if they found Ophelia's Wisher
and somehow she granted her wish in time? They could
use Scarlet's Star-Zap to lead them in the right direction,
at least, which Scarlet quickly had them do. But how, if
every other Star Darling so far had collected less energy
than she'd hoped to on her mission, could an incompetent Starling like Ophelia ever collect enough to enable
Scarlet's star and Star-Zap to take them both home?

The answer, Scarlet realized, was that it wasn't her
problem! And she couldn't help smiling as she thought
about it more. Sure, it would be too bad if a wish didn't
get granted. Scarlet valued the energy wishes produced

as much as anyone else. And yet . . . if it meant Ophelia was stuck on Wishworld and out of the cosmos at least for a little while, that would also mean Scarlet's Star Darling status would return and her reputation would undoubtedly be redeemed. And Scarlet would just make up for the energy loss on her own mission, when the next Wish Orb chose her!

The thought burned so brightly in Scarlet's mind she couldn't think about anything else, including the quaint, quiet Wishworld town she and Ophelia soon found themselves in.

"Moon and stars . . ." Ophelia murmured as she hung close by Scarlet's side. She'd tried to link arms with Scarlet but had instantly sensed her mistake. "Wishworld is so much different than Starland City. Somehow, I thought they'd be more alike."

"This *town* is different," Scarlet agreed as she, too, took in the scene. Unlike the gleaming high-rise-filled Starland capital that went on for floozels—not including the suburbs, which stretched beyond that for floozels more—the Wishworld town appeared to be built around a single two-way street lined with tidy little stores. Scarlet read some of the signs in the windows and above the rectangular glass doors: LEE'S HARDWARE, GRANNY'S TOYS AND GAMES, MARVIN'S LUNCHEONETTE, ANNIE'S FUDGE

AND ICE CREAM SHOPPE. She wasn't sure what every word meant, but she felt like she got the idea.

A few dull yet cheerful adult Wishlings strolled along the sidewalks, greeting one another as they passed. "Hey, there," a man said warmly to Scarlet and Ophelia. He was pushing a cart full of folded papers and rectangular packages. Those were covered with paper, too. He stopped at the corner by a large blue boxy container with a slightly dented rounded lid. The Starlings watched him reach into the pocket of his short blue pants and pull out a key on a cord. He used it to open a door in the side of the box, where he found *more* paper.

"He's one of the Wishlings who asked me about the circus," whispered Ophelia. But he didn't seem too curious about her anymore. If he or any of the Wishlings in the town thought Ophelia or Scarlet looked out of place, they were not letting on.

"This seems like a small town," Scarlet told Ophelia. "I don't think all cities on Wishworld are this size. Just like on Starland, there are all different kinds. Have you ever been to Solar Springs?"

"Solar Springs?"

"You know, where Gemma and Tessa are from?"

Ophelia shook her head.

Scarlet shrugged. "You're not missing much. It's a lot

like this place. So where *have* you been?" she asked.

Ophelia tapped her fingers together. "Nowhere," she replied. "I've never been outside of Starland City before. I mean, until now."

"Not even Old Prism?" Old Prism was the original Starland settlement and the most popular tourist destination on Starland. Nearly every family took at least one vacation there.

But not Ophelia's family, evidently. She looked down and shook her head in reply.

"I didn't mean to make you feel bad," Scarlet assured her. "Star apologies. I'm just starprised. You know, you're lucky you don't have parents like mine who dragged you all over Starland with them."

"Do you really think? I think you're lucky to *have* parents," said Ophelia. She added, "I never actually got to know mine."

Scarlet caught a breath and swallowed it. Those were not words she'd expected to hear. She instantly wished she could take her own words back. But it was too late. *Now what?* she thought. How was she supposed to respond to something like that? *So you're an orphan? You need parents? Feel free to take mine!* Scarlet had never been good at finding the right thing to say. That kind of stuff was hard.

Luckily, she didn't have to say anything, because Ophelia said something first.

"Stars! Look! Palm scanners!" Ophelia pointed across the street at a square yellow box set on top of a pole. Inside, a big red hand flashed on and off. There was another one, they noticed, on their own corner, high above their heads. And they did resemble palm scanners—in some ways, Scarlet thought—but something about them wasn't quite right. First of all, yes, they were much, much too high for a Wishling palm to reach. Plus, there were no doors to be opened that Scarlet could see.

"I wonder how you reach them," said Ophelia. She stood on her toes and stretched her hand as far up to the one on their corner as it would go. Still, there was more than an arm's length between her hand and the red one, even when she jumped.

"Let's figure that out later," said Scarlet, "when we have to."

"Right," said Ophelia. "Of course."

Just then, a large yellow Wishling vehicle rolled past them on those round black things that Wishlings called . . . whorls? Wools? Whirls?

"That's a school bus!" said Scarlet. "And look! Here come some more."

"What's a school bus?" asked Ophelia.

"Are you serious?" said Scarlet.

She was.

"They're like starbuses, but they roll along on the ground instead of hovering above it. They take Wishling students to school when they don't already live there."

"Oh! So we're getting close to a school?"

"Very close," said Scarlet. She looked down the street at a large tan building with a tall gray pole planted in front of it.

"Look, Scarlet! Stars!" said Ophelia, pointing to the flag up at the top.

There wasn't enough breeze to keep the tricolored banner flying, but now and then it caught a gust. Scarlet saw the stars and instantly counted half a hydrong.

"So is that a school?" Ophelia asked as they watched the first yellow bus and several more exactly like it turn in and pull to a stop in front of the building.

Scarlet nodded and checked her Star-Zap. It was precisely where their directions led.

"It's so quiet. Where are all the Wishlings?" said Ophelia.

That was when they heard the bell. It came from inside the school, but even from that far away the ringing hurt their ears.

"What was that?" Ophelia asked Scarlet just as the doors to the school burst open and a flood of young Wishlings came pouring out.

Scarlet and Ophelia stood and watched lines form beside each school bus while other Wishlings simply walked away. . . .

"Oh, stars! Did we miss the school day?" Ophelia said with a gasp. "Is everyone going home? What are we going to do? I'll never find my Wishling now!"

"Not if you stand here like that, you won't," muttered Scarlet, grabbing her by the arm. She dragged Ophelia toward the school and pointed to her bracelet. "Keep an eye on your Wish Pendant!" she reminded her, sure that she'd forget. "We'll know we've found your Wishling as soon as it starts to glow."

Scarlet eyed Ophelia's bracelet, too, as they hurried past each bus. The lines outside the vehicles had all but disappeared. Engines were revving and drivers were calling, "All right! Find a seat and sit in it back there!"

"Superstar! There it goes!" said Scarlet as the bracelet blinked. "Your Wisher must be on this bus!" A moogle later she sighed. "Oh . . . no . . . The sun just caught a facet. It isn't glowing. Never mind."

She turned as a group of girls brushed past them, then paused by the closest bus. One girl was quite tall by Wishling standards, with laser-straight rows of tight black braids. The others were of average Wishling height. One had straight fair hair that hung smoothly down her back. The other's hair was dark and thick and curly and seemed to defy the basic rules of Wishworld gravity that Scarlet had learned in school.

"So you're sure you can't come home with us?" that girl was saying.

"Sorry. I really am," the tall girl said. "I have . . . all these chores to do today."

The fair-haired girl sighed heavily.

"You know this project is due on Friday," the first girl said. "And we're *all* supposed to contribute. This is a big part of our grade."

"Yeah. A *big* part." The other girl flipped her pale hair back with a toss of her head. "And we're doing *all* the work. I mean, I wish you'd said something about all these doctors' appointments and your piano recital—and today's chores—when we started on this."

"I . . . I . . ."

"If it's just chores, can't you do them later?" said the curly-haired girl. "Won't your mom understand if you just explain?"

The tall girl chewed on either side of her bottom lip.

"Well, you see . . . it's my *step*mom . . . and, well, she's, like, *soooo* mean."

"Oh . . ."

"Sorry . . ."

The two girls nodded sympathetically.

The tall girl heaved a heavy sigh, as if that was the story of her life.

"So what about *tomorrow*?" The girl with the fair hair asked more gently. "Can you at least come home with us then? If the chrysalises start hatching today, like I think they will, we'll have our butterflies and that'll be it."

"Oh, I hope they hatch today!" said the curly-haired girl.

"I know, right? I can't *wait*!" Her blond friend clapped quickly, as if beating a snare drum. "*Ooh!* You know what we should do? We should have a big butterfly party and celebrate!"

"Yes!"

The two traded *aha* grins while the third girl looked down at her shoes.

"Your stepmom would let you do that, wouldn't she?" the blond girl asked.

The tall girl shrugged. "I don't know. . . . She's so mean, like I said. . . ."

"All aboard!" the bus driver called down through the door just then. Both girls looked up and waved.

"Coming." The curly-haired girl turned back to the tall girl. "See you tomorrow, I guess, Arden."

"See you tomorrow, Chloe. Bye, Sydney."

"If the butterflies hatch, we'll text you."

"Great. Yes, definitely do."

"Um . . . sorry . . . about your stepmom and all. . . ."

"Thanks . . ." the girl murmured. "It's kind of hard."

"It's her!" Scarlet leaned over and hissed to Ophelia, more into her pigtail than her ear.

"Do you really think so? How do you know?" Ophelia turned to her. "Are you sure?"

Scarlet twisted her mouth in irritation. "Check your Wish Pendant and you'll see. I'll bet my stars it's that *stepmother*." Her eyes narrowed at the thought. "It's a classic Wishworld wish! She's probably been wishing to get rid of her . . . once and for all. But that's an impossible wish. *Well?*" She nodded toward Ophelia's wrist. "What are you waiting for? Check your bracelet!" Why she was so eager for Ophelia to find her Wisher, Scarlet didn't know. Just a few moogles earlier, she had wanted desperately for Ophelia to fail—but now, oddly, not so much.

She was as sure as a sundial the bracelet would be glowing like a fiery flare. But no . . . the star-shaped jewels on the bracelet were as lifeless as they had been before.

"I thought we'd found her. Didn't you?" Scarlet looked over her shoulder at the tall girl, still so close to them, watching her friends' bus pull away.

"Maybe she is my Wisher," said Ophelia. "Maybe, just like my Star-Zap, my Wish Pendant is powerless, too. . . ." She looked down at her wrist in frustration. Then, suddenly, her head bent farther down. "Did you bring a glowworm here with you from Starland?" she asked, pointing toward the ground.

"What?"

"You're glowing. There, on your ankle. Under your . . . what do you call those again?"

"Jeans," said Scarlet, distracted, as she followed Ophelia's eyes. Her ankle *was* glowing . . . even through the heavy pants!

She yanked up her cuff to discover the hot-pink star-buckles on her own Wish Pendant boots shining like quasars on her feet.

She looked up at Ophelia. "It's not a glowworm, it's my Wish Pendant."

Ophelia's eyes were as round as moons. "Why is *your* Wish Pendant glowing?"

"Don't ask *me*! *How should I know?*"

CHAPTER
11

The next thing Scarlet knew, her Wish Pendant faded from twinkling star to flat pink stone.

"What happened?" gasped Ophelia.

"I don't know. . . ." Could it have been some sort of false alarm? Then she looked up to see the tall girl had moved and was walking down the street. The Wisher just wasn't close. That was how Wish Pendants behaved.

"Come on. You've got to catch her!" Scarlet snapped at Ophelia as she hurried to follow the girl.

"Star greetings, Wishling."

The tall girl stopped midstride on the chalky gray sidewalk. "Excuse me?" she said, slowly turning, with a stiff note of dread in her voice.

Ophelia, who'd offered the greeting, covered her mouth with one hand. "Sorry! Forgot!" she whispered to Scarlet.

"*Hi.*" Scarlet looked back up and smiled at the Wishling. "Sorry." She pointed her thumb toward Ophelia. "My friend here thinks she's so funny when she says weird things like that."

The girl's eyes skipped back and forth between Scarlet and Ophelia. "Sorry, but do I know you? Do you go to this school?"

"No," said Ophelia innocently before Scarlet could stop her.

Scarlet smiled as she gritted her teeth. Had they been on Starland, sparks would have been shooting straight out of her ears.

"What she means is no, this isn't our regular school," Scarlet explained hurriedly. "But *temporarily*, yes, we go here." She checked to make sure Ophelia was listening carefully. "We're *exchange* students, you see."

"Really? That's so cool. Where are you from?" the girl asked.

"Where are we from?" *Good question*, thought Scarlet as her mind suddenly went blank. She tried to remember some of the names of places she'd learned in Wishworld Relations, names she'd imagined using on missions just like this hydrongs and hydrong of times. . . .

"Orion!" Ophelia blurted, lifting her chin and looking proud.

"Orion? Where is that?" asked the girl.

"It's just up there in the—"

Scarlet pulled Ophelia's arm down from above her head and put her other hand over Ophelia's startled mouth. "Did you think she said *Orion*? She said *Ohio*!" Scarlet laughed.

"Oh." The girl nodded, then grinned with a friendly shrug. "Well, welcome to Florida, I guess. I'm Arden. Nice to meet you."

"Hi. I'm Scarlet, and this is Ophelia. Nice to meet you, too," Scarlet replied before Ophelia could speak. She wasn't quite sure how Ophelia would have answered that introduction. She only knew somehow it would have been wrong.

"If you like, I could show you around," Arden offered.

"Really? That would be startastic!" exclaimed Ophelia.

Scarlet swallowed a groan and closed her eyes.

"Would you excuse us for just a minute?" Scarlet asked the girl, who shrugged.

Scarlet dragged Ophelia away from Arden by her backpack. "Ophelia!" she muttered. "You have to stop saying things like 'startastic' and 'star greetings.' Those are Starland phrases. Wishlings say things like 'awesome' and 'sick.' It's one of the first things we learned. Remember? Back in Wishers 101. What have you been learning at Starling Academy, anyway?"

"Star apologies . . ." mumbled Ophelia. "I guess I just forgot."

"Well, start remembering!" hissed Scarlet. "Or better yet, don't say anything else. Just let me do the talking. Okay? You worry about focusing all your energy on granting Arden's wish." She quickly checked her Star-Zap. "This clock is counting down very fast!"

"Yes. Okay." Ophelia nodded, and Scarlet hoped she understood. Scarlet wasn't sure how she'd gone from thinking it might be all right if Ophelia failed to being determined to see her succeed. It was almost as if she had no choice but to make the mission work.

"Is everything okay?" Arden asked when Scarlet and Ophelia returned.

"Everything is great."

"So, what do you think? Do you want to hang out? Do you want me to show you around? What haven't you seen yet?" asked Arden. "I know it's a pretty small town, but we have a really nice park. It's kind of famous for its butterfly attraction . . . er, um . . . but we can skip that part. It's not really all that great."

"Thanks," said Scarlet. "That sounds really nice. Really, it does. But . . ."

"But what?" Arden asked.

Scarlet tried to assume the expression she'd seen the other girls give Arden before—the one that seemed to say, "I feel so sorry for you, poor girl."

"You probably have to go straight home," said Scarlet.

"No," said Arden. "Not really." She smiled and shook her head. "I mean, I have to go home eventually, but later on—by dinnertime—not, like, right away."

Scarlet was confused and could tell that her face showed it. "Are you *sure*? I'd hate for you to get in trouble with your stepmother."

"How did you know I have a stepmother?"

"Er . . . I guessed, I guess?"

"Wow. Good guess," said Arden, who looked surprised but not upset.

"You probably wish you didn't have one," Scarlet went on, nodding. "Or at least that she wasn't so mean." She snuck a wink at Ophelia, then watched as Arden's expression slowly changed.

"No, my stepmother's great. She's not at all mean. In

fact—don't tell my mom this—but she's nicer than her sometimes."

Now it was Scarlet's turn to flip expressions. "But doesn't she make you stay home? And do all the chores? You know, and work all day and night?"

Arden's nose wrinkled and she started to giggle. "What are you talking about?" She looked down at her red ruffled skirt and sleeveless yellow tee. "Do I look like Cinderella? The only chores my stepmom makes me do are the dishes, sometimes, and make my bed . . . not that I ever do."

"But . . ."

Arden waited for Scarlet to finish, but Scarlet wasn't sure how to go on. Why had this Wishling told those others that she had a mean stepmother if she didn't? And most important, what was her wish, then? To have a *mean* stepmother? No, of course not. Why would any Wishling want that?

So then what could it be? Scarlet tried to think. She glanced at Ophelia, who was blank-faced, clearly trying to catch up. She wasn't going to be much help in figuring this out; Scarlet could tell from her frown. Then something else that Scarlet had heard before suddenly popped into her head—something about doctors' appointments. . . .

Of course! That had to be it!

There were no doctors on Starland, of course. There simply was no need. All the positive wish energy on Starland kept Starlings healthy throughout their Cycle of Life, until they began their afterglow. But Scarlet had learned in school about Wishworld doctors and all they did for Wishlings whenever they got sick. She'd also learned about the kinds of wishes that Wishlings often made when doctors couldn't help. Of course, those were impossible wishes, and maybe that was why Ophelia was having so much trouble. But Scarlet was sure they could help her make a more appropriate one.

"You're not well, are you?"

"Excuse me?"

"You're sick. Well, don't worry. We'll find a way . . ."

"But I'm *not* sick. I'm fine. Really. Why?" the girl asked, touching her cheeks. "Do I look bad or something?"

"No, no. You look good. It's not that," Scarlet said. What could she say now? If the Wisher wasn't sick and her stepmother wasn't mean, what wishes were left? Had she also said something about a piano recital?

Or . . . could it be that she wasn't their Wisher at all?

What a starmendous waste of time!

Scarlet looked down to check her Wish Pendant. It

was still glowing . . . which was odd. But it wasn't like this was *her* mission, so maybe it didn't mean anything.

"Omigosh," the girl said suddenly, as if a holo-text had just come through. "I get it." She turned to Ophelia. "You must have heard me talking to Chloe and Sydney."

Ophelia's cheeks filled like balloons as she worked to keep the words in.

"Yeah," Arden went on, not needing a reply. "Some of those things I said back there . . . they weren't exactly true."

"But *why*?" Ophelia blurted. "It sounded like they needed your help."

That was actually a good question, Scarlet thought, so that time she let it go.

"Oh . . . it's complicated," said Arden. She sighed and looked away.

"They're mean girls," said Scarlet knowingly. It was a common basis for wishes, unfortunately, but those weren't too hard to grant.

"No," said Arden. "They're fine. They're really nice and fun. And I want to be their friend. That's why I *wanted* to be in their lab group for this science project."

"Oh," Scarlet said, confused. Was this something Wishlings often did, she wondered—fail to make any sense?

"I didn't know they'd want to study butterflies. . . ." As she said that, Arden winced.

"What's wrong with butterflies?" said Scarlet.

"Are you afraid of them?" Ophelia asked.

Scarlet turned to Ophelia and did all she could not to roll her eyes. "Of course she's not afraid of *butterflies*!" she muttered. Could a Starling be more dim?

"I know," said Arden. "It's ridiculous, isn't it? But I can't help it. Do you know, I can't even look at pictures of butterflies without wanting to throw up? I tried to suggest other topics, but they were so into the idea. And they'd already ordered the caterpillar kit and everything. There was nothing I could say or do. Their minds were totally set."

"Did you tell them you were scared?" asked Scarlet. That seemed easy enough to do.

Arden nodded. "I tried to. But they thought it was a joke. They just laughed and said stuff like 'Can you imagine? Afraid of butterflies!'"

"So . . . they *are* mean," said Scarlet.

"No, they weren't being mean at all. They thought I was being funny. They thought it had to be a joke." Arden kicked a rock and sent it bouncing off the curb and into the street. "I guess I could have told them I was serious . . . except then, instead of laughing at the idea, they would have laughed at me."

"So what are you going to do?" Scarlet asked. She reached for Ophelia and pulled her near. She could sense a wish a breath away and wanted to make sure Ophelia heard it.

"What I've been doing, I guess: making up excuses to stay away. So I'll get an F on the project and Chloe and Sydney will never talk to me again. But what else *can* I do? I *wish* I wasn't afraid of butterflies . . . but we all know wishing doesn't help." She took a few steps away to kick another rock while Scarlet hung back and pumped her fist.

Yes! she thought as a sharp but not unpleasant jolt ran up and down her spine.

Scarlet turned to wink at Ophelia, but Ophelia's eyes were on the ground.

"Ophelia!" Scarlet nudged her with an elbow. "Your Wisher just voiced her wish! She doesn't want to be afraid of butterflies!" she hissed.

"Really? Oh! Sorry," Ophelia said. She glanced over her shoulder at Arden. "What do I do now? Oh . . . and what are butterflies? Are they, like, wings or something you can put on toasted Wishling bread?"

CHAPTER 12

After a quick explanation of what butterflies were ("They're basically like flutterfocuses, only they don't change color or light up."), Scarlet told Ophelia her plan.

"It's easy. We learned about these kinds of fear wishes in Wish Fulfillment, remember? No? Right. Of course you don't. Never mind. Basically, we have to get her to talk more about her fear and where it comes from. Then we have to reassure her that butterflies mean her no harm. Then we need to introduce her to butterflies. It's supposed to be little by little . . . but of course we don't have a lot of time. Luckily, there's that butterfly attraction she talked about—which is perfect! We just take her there! *Zap!* Done!"

"Talk, reassure, introduce," said Ophelia. She nodded

so her pigtails bounced like springs. "Star salutations, Scarlet. I'll try. I really will." Ophelia's chin was trembling, but she managed a smile. And somehow, before Scarlet could help herself, she was returning a grin.

Scarlet could feel it inside her. . . . *Ew!* Something was warming up and softening, like stars melting into thick molten glass. Scarlet tried to will it all back into sharp jagged crystals, but no—it was too late.

It was easy to be mad at Ophelia for taking her place, and even easier to scold her for making so many mistakes. And yet this whole situation wasn't Ophelia's fault any more than it was Scarlet's. The most important thing, whether Scarlet liked it or not, was to help Ophelia as much as she could to make Arden's wish come true.

"No," Scarlet told Ophelia sternly. "You're a Star Darling. You need to do more than try. You need to grant this wish. So go!" She pointed to Arden, who was walking away. "What are you waiting for?"

They caught up to Arden at the corner. She grinned at them warily. "So now you know my secret. You probably think I'm super weird."

"What are you talking about?" said Scarlet. "Everyone's scared of something. Take Ophelia here." She shot a quick nod at her partner.

"Me? Oh, yes! *Me!* I'm afraid of everything!" Ophelia

said. "Black holes . . . asteroids . . . gamma radiation . . . and even those energy bunnies that collect under the bed."

Scarlet and Arden both stared at her, speechless.

"Anyway," Scarlet said. "Being scared is nothing to be ashamed of. But it is something you can try to change."

"How?"

"Why don't we go to that park you were talking about," said Scarlet, "and talk about it there?"

The park was a short walk from the school, away from downtown. A dark metal arch marked the entrance at a corner where two roads crossed.

"Wait!" Arden grabbed Scarlet's and Ophelia's arms as they reached the corner across from it, just before they stepped off the curb. She pointed to the palm scanner across the street and the big bright red hand that was flashing at them.

"Right. The palm scanners," said Ophelia. "But I couldn't reach it. Can you?"

She started to jump as she'd done before in town, to reach the box above them. Scarlet almost joined her. But then she saw Arden laughing—not meanly, just as if they were all in on a joke. Clearly, Ophelia was way off. That wasn't a palm scanner at all. But if Ophelia was helping lift Arden's mood, why not play along?

"*Very* funny," said Scarlet. She chuckled and grabbed for Ophelia's arm. Just then, the hand stopped blinking and began to glow a steady red. As it did, a car whizzed past them, followed by another and more after that.

Scarlet watched Arden press a button on the side of the post on their corner, then read the small sign next to it: PUSH BUTTON TO WALK. A moogle later, the hand disappeared and was replaced by a white symbol of a walking man.

"Are you coming?" said Arden as she stepped off the sidewalk and into the street. "The light's going to change back if we don't hurry up."

"So . . . it's not a palm scanner?" Ophelia whispered to Scarlet as they followed. "I'm sorry. I messed up again."

"Hey, she's smiling," said Scarlet, nodding ahead. "I think you might actually have done something right."

"So this is our park," Arden said as they walked through the arch. She lifted her arms and stretched them out to her sides, turning slightly left and right. "It's small, but it's pretty nice."

It *was* nice, Scarlet had to agree, in an overly green Wishworld way. It was strange, and almost refreshing, to see grass so singular in color—and such straight paths that refused to move. It was actually nice to get away from all the glitter and sparkle of Starland and appreciate not just how colorful and brilliant things were but other qualities, as well. Like how the little brown creature on the branch high above them sounded, whistling its curious tune.

And the way the grass smelled. Scarlet took a deep whiff, which Arden noticed. She nodded as if she understood.

"They must have just mowed."

Ah, thought Scarlet. So that was what that sharp tangy scent was. Scarlet didn't even know how the grass on Starland smelled, she realized, or if it smelled at all. Starland grass always stayed the perfect length, so it never had to be cut.

Ophelia, meanwhile, was pointing at a large dull but colorful, oddly shaped structure behind a green metal fence. At the center was an elevated platform sheltered by a yellow roof. Along with a ladder, there appeared to be several other means by which to reach the platform: a winding blue ramp; a slick yellow pole; a thick knotted rope; and, last but not least, a long sloping red tube, out of which a small Wishling boy abruptly popped.

"What's that?" Ophelia asked.

"What's what?" Arden replied. Her eyes darted from

pole to ramp to tube, not quite sure what Ophelia could mean.

Scarlet pulled Ophelia close. "It's a playground. *A Wishling* playground," she clarified. She had seen them before from the Wishworld Surveillance Deck, but Ophelia obviously had not. If she had, she would have known that Wishling playgrounds were nothing like those on Starland, with their gyro-seesaws and anti-gravity slides and energy trampolines. There was one apparatus Starland and Wishworld shared, however, and Scarlet pointed it out to Ophelia. "See?"

Ophelia's eyes followed Scarlet's away from the platform, along a track of evenly spaced metal bars to a triangular frame from which hung three rubber slings on chunky black chains.

"Lucky stars! *Swings!*" Ophelia exclaimed. "Can we?" She turned to Arden first, then Scarlet. "I love swings so much!"

"*Now?*" Scarlet said. "*Really?* We came here to *talk*, Ophelia, remember? *Not* play."

"Star a—So sorry. Yes. Of course."

"We could do both," Arden said, shrugging. "I mean, why not? I haven't been on a swing in years." She grinned, suddenly looking happier than she had since they had met. "No one else is using them. It'll be fun.

C'mon! Let's go!" She left Ophelia and Scarlet to follow as she headed toward the playground gate.

"Star apologies. Truly," Ophelia murmured to Scarlet. She scrunched her freckled nose. "I didn't mean to delay the mission further. Don't worry. I won't do it again."

Ophelia dropped her backpack next to Arden's just inside the fence.

"Oh, no . . ." said Scarlet, eyeing it.

"What now?" Ophelia moaned. "What did I do?"

"You lost your key chain. I don't know what it's for. But I'm sure we'll find out now." Each Star Darling had received a glittery stuffed star attached to her backpack. Wishers called them "key chains."

"What key chain?" said Ophelia. "I don't know what you mean."

"Didn't you get one right before takeoff?"

"Nooo . . ." Ophelia said slowly. "No," she repeated, more surely.

"Oh . . ." said Scarlet. "Good," she declared. One less thing to worry about, at least.

They turned to watch Arden skip up to the middle swing and fall into the hard rubber seat with a smile.

"Well," Scarlet whispered to Ophelia with the barest of smiles, "what are you waiting for? Let's go."

By the time they joined Arden, the Wishling was flying back and forth, her feet nearly extending past the bar overhead.

Excited, Ophelia took the swing on Arden's right, gripping the chains extra tight in each hand. "*Wheeee!*" she cried as she leaned her head back and eagerly kicked out her feet. After a moogle, however, she sat back up. "Aw . . . mine's broken," she said.

"Mine, too," said Scarlet. It hadn't moved a shortsnip since she'd sat down. She raised her feet once more, just to be extra sure . . . but no, it did not want to move.

Between them, Arden slowed until her own swing was barely swaying. "What do you mean they're broken?" She gave Scarlet's chain a little tug, then peered behind her at the seat. "It looks okay to me."

"Oh, that part's fine, yes. It's the swinger," explained Scarlet. "It's not working." She lifted her feet again. "See? It doesn't fly like yours. It just sits here. Whatever." She shrugged. "It's no big . . . what do they say . . . deal?"

"You know, you have to *pump* to swing," said Arden. "You know . . . like this. . . ."

Scarlet watched Arden lean back and kick her legs out, exactly as Ophelia had done. But unlike Ophelia, Arden didn't stop there. That was only the first step, it seemed. Arden next swung her body forward and sharply bent her knees. Scarlet watched the swing respond by gliding backward, at which point Arden leaned back again. As she kept going like that, whipping herself back and forth, she made her swing fly higher . . . and higher . . . and higher still!

Who would have ever thought that Wishlings had to power their own swings? thought Scarlet.

Fortunately, this "pumping" wasn't half as difficult as it looked. Even Ophelia was successful almost immediately, much to her delight. Scarlet could have used a push to start, but after a few rough kicks and bends, she quickly began to catch up.

They all stopped at just about the same time but for different reasons: Ophelia because her Star-Zap fell out of her pocket when she practically flew upside down; Arden because she saw it fall and wanted to stop and help; Scarlet because as soon as she saw Arden reach for the Star-Zap, she knew she had to grab it—fast!

"Cool phone!" said Arden, who was already out of her swing and running her finger along the Star-Zap. Instantly, the top flipped up.

Scarlet's heart nearly stopped as she stared at it, terrified that a holo-something would suddenly appear. Only after a moogle did she remember that it had no energy. *Lucky stars!* she thought with a sigh of relief.

"It's actually a Star-Z—" Ophelia started to correct her.

"A Star-Zee?" Scarlet cut in, laughing. "Honestly, Ophelia. You make up the funniest names." She took the Star-Zap from Arden and handed it to Ophelia with a tight, open-eyed smile. "Here you go. Maybe put that in your backpack, why don't you. And keep it there. You'd hate for your *phone* here to break."

"Right . . ." said Ophelia. "Right! My *phone*!" She ran over to her backpack and dropped it in. She returned to the swing set, out of breath. "Better?" she asked with a grin.

Scarlet nodded. "Much better. Now." She sighed. "I think it's time we *talked*, don't you?" She turned to Arden and put her hands on her shoulders. "Here," she said. "Have a seat." Gently, she guided her back into her swing, then sank into her own. She didn't have to look at the Countdown Clock on her Star-Zap to know that there wasn't much time left in their mission. She could see the sun drifting steadily down toward the treetops. That meant there wasn't a moogle to waste.

"We're going to help you get over this fear of yours," she told Arden. "But first you need to talk."

"Talk about what?"

"Your fear," said Scarlet. "When it started. Where it

came from. All that good stuff. So go ahead. Fire away."

Arden's face, which had been so warm and open, seemed all of a sudden to hang a CLOSED sign. "My fear of butterflies . . . oh, no . . . I don't want to. It's too hard to talk about. I just can't."

"But . . ." Scarlet paused to check the sun again. "But you *have* to talk about it," she blurted.

Scarlet could feel her own face getting hot and probably red—especially when Ophelia spoke up from the next swing: "That's okay. We understand."

"Thanks." Arden twisted her swing toward Ophelia.

"I know what it's like not to want to talk about something," Ophelia continued. "You probably do, too, Scarlet. Right?"

"No." Scarlet frowned impatiently. "Well . . . okay . . . yes, maybe. Sometimes."

"It's just so embarrassing," said Arden.

Ophelia nodded. "You don't want to be reminded of it. I know."

"It was literally the worst day of my life," said Arden.

"I can only imagine," said Ophelia gently as she rocked her swing from side to side.

Scarlet's eyes, meanwhile, flashed from Ophelia to Arden, as she observed their exchange of trusting smiles.

Arden was actually about to talk, Scarlet realized—thanks to Ophelia, no less!

"I was at my grandparents' house—they live on a big farm. And I was little. I'd only just turned five. It was before dinner. I was playing hide-and-seek with my older cousins out in the fields around the barn. We used to do that all the time. So I see this big tree out at the edge of the meadow, and I decide to go hide behind that. The trunk was literally *this* thick." Arden held her arms out wide. "I mean *huge*. Big enough to hide three or four kids . . . I don't know, maybe more. And so tall that when you stood under it and looked up, you couldn't see the top at all. My grandmother says it was a big tree even when she was a kid, so you can imagine how old it must be now.

"Anyway, I ran up and stood there, hiding behind it—all by myself—while my cousin Jason ran around with no idea, busy finding everyone else. And then . . . I started hearing this kind of *rustling* sound all around me . . . kind of like a cat purring, only *really* loud. And the next thing I knew I was covered, I mean literally *covered*, in all these"—Arden shuddered—"all these *butterflies*! Evidently, they were roosting there—thousands of them—on their way to Mexico for the winter. My grandmother says they migrate through her farm every year. Which is why I refuse to go back there, by the way."

"But the butterflies aren't there all the time, are they?" asked Scarlet.

"No. Just the fall, when they're flying south. But just the thought of being there . . ." She winced and shivered again. "I love my grandparents . . . but it's just too hard. I get nauseous just thinking about it."

"So what did you do when the flutterfo—I mean butterflies landed on you?" asked Ophelia.

"I screamed. Like crazy," Arden said. "I mean, I was five and all alone. Sure, I realized pretty quickly that they were butterflies, but I still thought they were going to eat me alive. I couldn't get them off. It was like they were stuck to me with pins. They wouldn't let go with their little"—she cringed—"*feet*. I tried to brush them and shake them and knock them off, but they were in my hair, my clothes, everything, refusing to let go. Then, finally, I tried to run. But of course I couldn't see. So I tripped . . . and fell . . . and landed on the ground, on, like, a hundred of them." She paused to take a breath. "Basically killing them all. So there I am, lying on all these dead butterflies, covered with hundreds more. All by myself. Screaming. Crying. Oh—and I wet my pants, I was so scared. Did I happen to mention that?"

"*Aw* . . ." Ophelia patted her shoulder.

Scarlet leaned forward. "So what happened next?"

"Finally—after what literally felt like forever—my cousins and my grandma found me. By then, the butterflies had gone back up in the tree—except for the ones I murdered, of course. When they found out what happened, my cousins laughed and called me 'butterfly bait' for the rest of the weekend. In fact, they still call me that today. It's become a little family joke, that nickname."

"That's terrible!" said Scarlet.

Arden nodded. "Yeah, it is."

"I hope you call them something back!" Scarlet said. "I know some good names, by the way, if you need any suggestions."

"Oh, but I'm sure they don't mean to be mean," said Ophelia. "They probably just don't understand."

Arden hung her head, shaking it slowly. "They sure don't. Nobody does."

"We do," Ophelia said softly. "We know exactly how you feel." She glanced over Arden's shoulder at Scarlet. *What should I do next?* she mouthed.

Scarlet tried to think. . . .

Just keep going! she told Ophelia—not with words but by rolling her arm.

"You know what I think?" said Ophelia.

Arden waited to hear.

"I think . . . I think anybody would be scared of butterflies after that happened to them."

"Thanks," said Arden. She smiled a little. "And thanks for this. . . ."

"For what?"

"For letting me talk about it. To be honest, it feels kind of good. Do you know, I don't think I've ever told anyone that story before? Never, in all these years. And in a way, I think the story I actually remember was a little better than the one I was trying to forget."

"What do you mean?"

"Well, I mean, the butterflies were scary—for sure. But for some reason I'd remembered them biting me, like they had little teeth. Now, though, I realize that they didn't do much more than tickle me."

"Hey! It's our turn!"

Scarlet turned, along with the others, to find a long line of young Wishling children standing behind them, looking as if *they* might bite.

"You can't hog the swings!" said the first one.

"Yeah! No hogging!" chirped another. "Besides, you're too old. My mom said."

"Swings are for kids!" they started chanting. "Swings are for kids! Swings are for kids!"

Ophelia shuffled her swing toward Arden's. "Um, can we get out of here? They scare me."

Arden laughed. "Yeah, sure. Let's go."

CHAPTER
13

"I can't believe I'm doing this," said Arden.

Behind her back, Scarlet and Ophelia leaned in to share a smile of so-close-they-could-taste-it success. They were standing on the path that led to the butterfly exhibit, in front of a sign that read BUTTERFLIES! 200 FEET AHEAD.

"My stars," Ophelia whispered to Scarlet. "Did you know butterflies had two hundred legs?"

Scarlet studied the sign. "I didn't," she whispered back. "It's kind of starmazing that they can fly. . . ."

The wooden sign also had a carving of a butterfly, which Arden was regarding with an anxious expression.

"Don't worry," said Ophelia. "Like we said, if you don't want to go in, you don't have to."

"No, of course not. . . . But let's keep going," Scarlet said.

The path turned, and as it did, the exhibit itself came into view.

"Ooh! It's such a pretty structure!" said Ophelia.

Scarlet had to agree. The side they could see had multiple rising and falling arches, almost like the curves of a cloud. The walls appeared to be made of some kind of netting and were decorated with large colorful pictures of butterflies. No two were the same. Through the net, it was easy to see a veritable jungle of trees, vines, and blooming bushes growing inside. What they couldn't yet see—from such a distance, Scarlet figured—was any butterflies.

"Just imagine if that place glittered!" said Ophelia. "How stunning it would be!"

"I think they might light it up at night on the weekends," said Arden.

"*Really?*" Ophelia's face brightened at the thought (as much as a face on Wishworld could).

"Yeah, but I'm not sure. I've never actually seen it. It's just something I've heard."

"Ooh! I'd love to stay and see it. Scarlet, do you think we can?"

"Why couldn't you?" asked Arden.

"Let's just keep going," said Scarlet. "Shall we? I mean, if that's okay?"

Arden nodded. She took a deep breath and moved forward, ever so slowly. Her feet seemed to fight her for every step. Scarlet could hear Arden telling herself, "I can do this. I can . . ." between rapid shallow breaths.

Yes, Scarlet thought. She *was* going to do this. She was going to overcome her fear. Scarlet looked at Ophelia and pointed to her bracelet. *Be ready!* she mouthed. What was crazier, Scarlet wondered: that Ophelia's mission just might be successful or that Scarlet just might be happy for her?

As they got closer to the exhibit, they found themselves walking among dense vibrant flower gardens dotted with butterfly-shaped signs bearing various facts.

One showed the process a caterpillar went through to become a butterfly.

"'Metamorphosis,'" read Arden. "That's what our project is about."

"Wait? Is that really how butterflies are made? They start out as *those*?" Ophelia pointed to a caterpillar, then to a butterfly. "You'd think something that delicate and pretty would be made of flower petals and stardust."

"You're funny," Arden said. She suddenly looked more relaxed.

Scarlet could see how Ophelia had taken Arden's mind off her fear—without even meaning to—so she decided to try it herself. After all, she *was* there to help.

"This is interesting," she said. "Did you know butterflies don't eat? They can only drink. And they taste with their feet. That's uncommon, right?"

Arden laughed again.

It worked! Scarlet could practically feel the wish energy ready to come out of this Wisher, and she could tell that Ophelia was sensing it, too.

"Oh," Ophelia went on, not really getting the humor in anything but still happy to play along. "And look here. This says that they have four wings, two on each side, and only *six* legs. Not two hundred?" She paused to frown, seriously confused.

"Two *hundred*! You're so funny!" Arden giggled. "Both of you." She stopped in front of another sign. "Ooh," she said. "Check this out. According to this, butterflies can see ultraviolet colors. It helps them know which flowers have the nectar they want. *Hmmm*. What's so special about seeing ultraviolet colors?" She grinned. "I mean, can't everyone?"

"I don't get it," Ophelia whispered to Scarlet.

"You don't have to," Scarlet murmured back. "Just so it works. How about this one?" she said more loudly, pointing to another sign. "This is also about what butter-flies see. It says butterflies are attracted to bright colors, especially yellow and red. *Hee-hee!*"

She waited for Arden to laugh . . . or chuckle . . . or at least smile. Instead, though, she looked over to see Arden staring down at her bright yellow T-shirt. She touched the hem of her ruby red skirt.

"Er, what's wrong?" Scarlet asked.

"I can't do this."

"But you have to—I mean . . . yes, you *can.*"

"Maybe. But not today. Not dressed like this. What if they land on me? Uh, I thought I was ready. I did. But I'm not. I'm really not." She held out her hands. "Look." They were trembling like leaves in a solar storm.

Scarlet looked over at Ophelia. Did she have an idea? Any idea at all? Scarlet had done everything she could think of to help grant this wish in time, but it just wasn't enough in the end.

With the tiniest nod, Ophelia lowered her eyes back to Arden's hands and gently picked one up. "You know, you're not alone. We're here for you. Whatever you need. Would it help at all if Scarlet and I stayed right by your side and maybe held your hands?" She looked back at Scarlet warmly, clearly expecting her to reach out and take Arden's other hand. "Scarlet?"

"Well . . . I don't know. Here's the thing. *Would* it help?" Scarlet was skeptical at best. She'd never bought into that whole Starland hand-holding-all-the-time thing. What was the point? She didn't know. To other Starlings, linking arms and holding hands came as naturally as glowing, but to Scarlet it always felt forced. In fact, getting that close to others just made her feel more alone.

But Ophelia wasn't letting go, and neither was Arden.

Oh, why not? Scarlet finally thought.

She reached out and put her hand lightly on Arden's, surprised at how warm and soft it felt. Arden squeezed, and Scarlet nearly jumped. Instead, though, without even thinking about it, she flashed Arden a smile and squeezed back.

"You know . . . it's so weird how I met you today," Arden said with a small but grateful smile. "It's almost like a fairy godmother sent you or something."

"Well, *that* sure didn't happen," Scarlet said.

"Close, though." Ophelia grinned, then caught Scarlet's *"Really?"* face. "What? Oh. That's a *joke*."

"So, shall we try this again?" Scarlet said. "Together?"

"Okay." Arden took a deep breath. "Just . . . don't let go."

Hand in hand, they walked down the last bit of path toward the butterfly building and up to the wide glass door. Inside, they could see the stars of the exhibit: hydrongs and hydrongs of butterflies. Some were tiny, no bigger than a pinky. Others were almost as big as a hand. Some were yellow and black, some were orange, and some were all white. And some were the exact same blue as Vega's hair!

"Now, just so we're clear, if I start to scream or faint or anything like that, we're coming right back out."

"Of course," said Ophelia.

"We've got you," said Scarlet. She placed her other hand on Arden's, as well.

"Okay." Arden took a long and slow breath in, held it, then let it out quickly. "I think I'm ready."

"Wait . . . what? Oh, no . . ." groaned Scarlet.

"What's wrong?"

"We have a problem, I'm afraid." Scarlet nodded toward the door—to the sign hanging in the middle, right over the handle, where it was impossible to miss. In the most unsparkly black block letters, it read very simply CLOSED.

"What? What does that mean?" said Ophelia as she read it. "Does that mean we can't go in?"

"That's totally what it means," said Arden. "Look." She pointed to another sign to the side of the door that listed the operating hours. "They're closed every

Thursday. Oh, well. I guess this fear just wasn't meant to be conquered all in a day. But at least I got a little closer to facing it, right?"

"Right," Scarlet sighed.

A little closer. Great, she thought. If only energy could be captured from that.

But no. They needed a wish to be fully granted. And they needed it granted soon. Not the next day or that weekend, when Arden suggested they return.

"We're going in today. Right now," said Scarlet as she worked to unlock the entrance with her mind. She clasped Arden's hand more tightly and pulled her toward the door. "We've come this far. We can't stop now. C'mon, Ophelia. You too."

"What? How? But we can't. It's closed!" said Arden, confused but stubbornly holding her ground.

"Um, Scarlet. Scarlet." On the other side of Arden, Ophelia tried to get Scarlet's attention by waving wildly with her hand. "*Scarlet!*"

"What? It's no big deal. We'll go in and come right back out."

"But that's just it. I don't think we have to," said Ophelia, pointing.

Scarlet followed her finger to Arden's shoulder. . . .

"Freakin' fireballs!" she gasped.

Ophelia grinned. "I know! Right?"

"What? What is it?" Arden asked. She started to turn her head.

"No, no. Don't move," Scarlet calmly warned her.

Arden froze. "What is it? Tell me, please."

"Okay . . . there's a . . . there's a *butterfly* on your shoulder," Scarlet said as gently as she knew how.

"What?"

"It's very small."

"How small?" asked Arden.

Scarlet held up her first finger and thumb two inches apart. "It's kind of light gold," she said, "with black outlines. . . . There's even some orange and a little blue."

"It sounds kind of pretty," said Arden.

"Oh, it is!" said Ophelia.

"I think . . . I don't know. . . . Should I look?"

"Yes!" said Scarlet and Ophelia together.

"But slowly," said Scarlet. "Don't scare it away."

Slowly, very slowly, Arden swiveled her head to the right, until she could just barely see the butterfly out of the corner of her eye. Her heart must have been racing, Scarlet thought, if her own fluttering heart was any gauge. And Ophelia . . . Scarlet glanced at her and saw she was smiling at Arden. How excited she must be. . . .

"How do you feel?" asked Ophelia gently.

"I feel okay. . . ." Arden's eyes left her shoulder for just an instant to flit from Ophelia to Scarlet. "And you know what's even better? What I don't feel is afraid!"

Scarlet was ready for the wish energy to flow out of Arden, but she wasn't prepared for such an intense and powerful stream. It burst forth with such force that Scarlet staggered back, and Ophelia did, as well. Arden just stood there, oblivious, as Wishlings always were. She could only assume it was the butterfly they were reacting to, so she smiled and said, "Don't worry. It won't hurt you."

Of course, that was the last thing Scarlet was worried about. The first thing was making sure every drop of energy made it into Ophelia's Wish Pendant, which Ophelia seemed to have forgotten all about. Scarlet held her own hand out and pointed to her wrist to try to remind her, but Ophelia replied by shaking her head. That was when Scarlet realized the wish energy was already flowing into a Wish Pendant.

Not Ophelia's at all—but Scarlet's.

CHAPTER
14

Scarlet was so happy about all the wish energy she had collected that she didn't even mind giving Ophelia a ride back home on her star. Scarlet hadn't planned on holding Ophelia's hand the whole time, but somehow it turned out that way, and they were still holding hands when Lady Stella's door opened to welcome the returning Starlings in.

Maybe that was why every jaw in the room seemed to drop. Or maybe it was Scarlet's smile, which she couldn't hold back and for once didn't even try to.

"Scarlet . . ." Lady Stella walked forward, her stardust-flecked silver robe flowing behind her in a shimmering diaphanous cloud. "I owe you star salutations and, more importantly, star apologies." She stood before Scarlet and humbly bowed. "Clearly, you always were—and always will be—meant to be a Star Darling. If there was any doubt whatsoever left, this resolves it once and for all."

With that, the headmistress extended her arm. In her upturned palm was the Wish Orb, which she handed to Scarlet. It felt heavy and warm and then began to transform into a flower. "It's a punkypow," said Scarlet with a smile. The burgundy star-shaped petals were aglow.

And then her Power Crystal, the ravenstone, emerged. It was so beautiful and made Scarlet feel very special, indeed. "Take it, and hold it dear," said Lady Stella.

"Oh, I will. I will," said Scarlet. Her own heart seemed to stop as she received the gem and felt the pulse of its energy through her hands.

Meanwhile, Lady Stella, still smiling, but more sadly, turned to Ophelia. As she spoke, she shook her head. "To you, Ophelia, I must also offer star apologies. It is clear you are not a Star Darling, as we had believed."

Scarlet looked down. She remembered how those words had crushed her, and she could only imagine they'd wound Ophelia the same way. When Scarlet finally made herself look at the Starling, however, the words seemed instead to have lifted a great weight off Ophelia. Her whole aura had changed. Not only was she brighter and more sparkly, she looked almost happy—content and relieved. Her eyes skipped from Lady Stella to Scarlet, then around to each of the dumbstruck Star Darlings, who hadn't moved since the two Starlings had glided in.

"*What the stars?* Who's next?" Gemma suddenly blurted. "*Starf!* Hey!" she cried as Tessa elbowed her ribs.

Lady Stella clasped her now empty hands tightly in front of her, as if in prayer. "I know this is quite a lot for you to take in, particularly on such an . . . intensely emotional day. We've all been through quite a lot—especially, of course, Scarlet and Ophelia—which is why I think it's best to retire for now. Rest assured that Lady Cordial and I will work diligently to ensure that nothing like this happens again." She turned her head respectfully toward the admissions director, who'd stood off to the side in semi-shadow throughout the whole Wish Blossom presentation.

Lady Cordial took a step forward and bowed to the headmistress. Her deep purple bun looked especially tight. "We most c-c-certainly will," she said, her eyes still on the floor. "No mis-s-stakes like this. Ever again."

As fast as Scarlet had fled from the other Star Darlings when she'd learned she'd been dismissed from the group, she fled even faster now that she was back in. She could see everyone waiting to congratulate her and *embrace* her (*ugh!*) outside Lady Stella's office, and suddenly, it all seemed too much for her to bear. She would deal with them all later—be sociable—Scarlet thought as she rushed past them, but right then, more than anything, she needed to be by herself. She'd already hugged and held hands more in one day than she had in the whole rest of her time at Starling Academy. She was overwhelmed. She needed to breathe.

The holo-text came as she was descending the spiral staircase into the Star Caves.

WHERE DID YOU GO? it flashed as Vega's picture appeared in the upper corner of the screen.

Scarlet almost didn't answer, but then another line came through . . . and another after that:

WE HAVE TO TALK!

YOU WERE RIGHT!

AND SO WAS CASSIE!

THE LAB RESULTS CAME IN WHILE YOU WERE GONE!

And . . . ? Scarlet waited. *Well?* she thought. What had they found out?

Finally, she texted back:

WHAT DID THEY SAY?!

She realized she was holding her breath as she stared at her Star-Zap, waiting for Vega's reply. At last, the screen flashed again, this time with both Cassie's and Vega's faces, one in each corner. Cassie's picture coyly winked.

HERE'S A HINT: ISLE OF MISERA.

FOR MORE, MEET US IN THE HEDGE MAZE.

ASAP!

So as fast as possible, Scarlet spun and ran back up the stairs.

The Isle of Misera? That sad, barren, negative-energy dumping ground? Could it be that the Star Darlings' flowers had come from there?

Glossary

Afterglow: The Starling afterlife. When Starlings die, it is said that they have "begun their afterglow."

Age of fulfillment: The age when a Starling is considered mature enough to begin to study wish granting.

Bad Wish Orbs: Orbs that are the result of bad or selfish wishes made on Wishworld. These grow dark and warped and are quickly sent to the Negative Energy Facility.

Big Dipper Dormitory: Where third- and fourth-year students live.

Boingtree: A shrublike tree with tickly aromatic needles.

Booshel Bay: A vacation destination.

Bot-Bot: A Starland robot. There are Bot-Bot guards, waiters, deliverers, and guides on Starland.

Bright Day: The date a Starling is born, celebrated each year like a Wishling birthday.

Celestial Café: Starling Academy's outstanding cafeteria.

Cocomoon: A sweet and creamy fruit with an iridescent glow.

Cosmic Transporter: The moving sidewalk system that transports students through dorms and across the Starling Academy campus.

Countdown Clock: A timing device on a Starling's Star-Zap. It lets them know how much time is left on a Wish Mission, which coincides with when the Wish Orb will fade.

Crystal Mountains: The most beautiful mountains on Starland. They are located across the lake from Starling Academy.

Cycle of Life: A Starling's life span. When Starlings die, they are said to have "completed their Cycle of Life."

Druderwomp: An edible barrel-like bush capable of pulling up its own roots and rolling like a tumbleweed, then planting itself again.

Floozel: The Starland equivalent of a Wishworld mile.

Flutterfocus: A Starland creature similar to a Wishworld butterfly but with illuminated wings.

Galliope: A sparkly Starland creature similar to a Wishworld horse.

Garble greens: A Starland vegetable similar to spinach.

Glitterbees: Blue-and-orange-striped bugs that pollinate Starland flowers and produce a sweet substance called gossamer.

Globerbeem: Large, friendly lightning bug–type insects that are sparkly and lay eggs.

Glorange: A glowing orange fruit. Its juice is often enjoyed at breakfast time.

Glowfur: A small, furry Starland creature with gossamer wings that eats flowers and glows.

Glowsow: A large farm animal that is prized for the light it emits at night—perfect for working after dark.

Good Wish Orbs: Orbs that are the result of positive wishes made on Wishworld. They are planted in Wish-Houses.

Green globules: Green pellets that are fed to pet glowfurs. They don't taste very good to Starlings.

Halo Hall: The building where Starling Academy classes are held.

Halo-harp: A melodious stringed instrument played by striking its strings with a small mallet.

Holo-text: A message sent or received on a Star-Zap and projected into the air. There are also holo-albums, holo-billboards, holo-books, holo-cards, holo-communications, holo-diaries, holo-flyers, holo-letters, holo-papers, holo-pictures, and holo–place cards. Anything that would be made of paper or contain writing or images on Wishworld is a hologram on Starland.

Hydrong: The equivalent of a Wishworld hundred.

Illumination Library: The impressive library at Starling Academy.

Impossible Wish Orbs: Orbs that are the result of wishes made on Wishworld that are beyond the power of Starlings to grant.

Isle of Misera: A barren rocky island off the coast of New Prism.

Kaleidoscope tree: A rare and beautiful tree whose blossoms continuously change color.

Keytar: An instrument that is held like a guitar but has keys instead of strings.

Lightning Lounge: A place on the Starling Academy campus where students relax and socialize.

Little Dipper Dormitory: Where first- and second-year students live.

Luminous Lake: A serene and lovely lake next to the Starling Academy campus.

Microjoule: A tiny amount.

Mirror Mantra: A saying specific to each Star Darling that when recited gives her (and her Wisher) reassurance and strength. When a Starling recites her Mirror Mantra while looking in a mirror, she will see her true appearance reflected.

Moonium: An amount similar to a Wishworld million.

Old Prism: A medium-sized historical city about an hour from Starling Academy.

Power Crystal: The powerful stone that each Star Darling receives once she has granted her first wish.

Shooting stars: Speeding stars that Starlings can latch on to and ride to Wishworld.

Shortsnip: A tiny unit of measurement, generally referring to distance.

Silver Blossom: The final manifestation of a Good Wish Orb. This glimmering metallic bloom is placed in the Hall of Granted Wishes.

Solar Springs: A hilly small town in the countryside where Tessa and Gemma are from.

Sparkle shower: An energy shower Starlings take every day to get clean and refresh their sparkling glow.

Star ball: An intramural sport that shares similarities with soccer on Wishworld. But star ball players use energy manipulation to control the ball.

Starcar: The primary mode of transportation for most Starlings. These ultrasafe vehicles drive themselves on cushions of wish energy.

Star Caves: The caverns underneath Starling Academy where the Star Darlings' secret Wish-Cavern is located.

Starf!: A Starling expression of dismay.

Star flash: News bulletin, often used starcastically.

Starland City: The largest city on Starland, also its capital.

Starlicious: Tasty, delicious.

Starlings: The glowing beings with sparkly skin who live on Starland.

Star Quad: The center of the Starling Academy campus. The dancing fountain, band shell, and hedge maze are located here.

Star salutations: The Starling way to say "thank you."

Staryear: A period of 365 days on Starland, the equivalent of a Wishworld year.

Star-Zap: The ultimate smartphone that Starlings use for all communications. It has myriad features.

Stellation: The point of a star. Halo Hall has five stellations, each housing a different department.

Supernova: A stellar explosion. Also used colloquially, meaning "really angry," as in "She went supernova when she found out the bad news."

Time of Applying: The very busy time of year when Starlings work on and send out applications to schools.

Time of Letting Go: One of the four seasons on Starland. It falls between the warmest season and the coldest, similar to fall on Wishworld.

Time of Lumiere: The warmest season on Starland, similar to summer on Wishworld.

Time of Shadows: The coldest season of the year on Starland, similar to winter on Wishworld.

Toothlight: A high-tech gadget that Starlings use to clean their teeth.

Wish Blossom: The bloom that appears from a Wish Orb after its wish is granted.

Wish energy: The positive energy that is released when a wish is granted. Wish energy powers everything on Starland.

Wisher: The Wishling who has made the wish that is being granted.

Wish-Granters: Starlings whose job is to travel down to Wishworld to help make wishes come true and collect wish energy.

Wish-House: The place where Wish Orbs are planted and cared for until they sparkle. Once the orb's wish is granted, it becomes a Wish Blossom.

Wishlings: The inhabitants of Wishworld.

Wish Mission: The task a Starling undertakes when she travels to Wishworld to help grant a wish.

Wish Orb: The form a wish takes on Wishworld before traveling to Starland. There it will grow and sparkle when it's time to grant the wish.

Wish Pendant: A gadget that absorbs and transports wish energy, helps Starlings locate their Wishers, and changes a Starling's appearance. Each Wish Pendant holds a different special power for its Star Darling.

Wishworld: The planet Starland relies on for wish energy. The beings on Wishworld know it by another name—Earth.

Wishworld Outfit Selector: A program on each Star-Zap that accesses Wishworld fashions for Starlings to wear to blend in on their Wish Missions.

Wishworld Surveillance Deck: Located high above the campus, it is where Starling Academy students go to observe Wishlings through high-powered telescopes.

Zing: A traditional Starling breakfast drink. It can be enjoyed hot or iced.

Acknowledgments

It is impossible to list all of our gratitude, but we will try.

Our most precious gift and greatest teacher, Halo; we love you more than there are stars in the sky . . . punashaku. To the rest of our crazy, awesome, unique tribe—thank you for teaching us to go for our dreams. Integrity. Strength. Love. Foundation. Family. Grateful. Mimi Muldoon—from your star doodling to naming our Star Darlings, your artistry, unconditional love, and inspiration is infinite. Didi Muldoon—your belief and support in us is only matched by your fierce protection and massive-hearted guidance. Gail. Queen G. Your business sense and witchy wisdom are legendary. Frank—you are missed and we know you are watching over us all. Along with Tutu, Nana, and Deda, who are always present, gently guiding us in spirit. To our colorful, totally genius, and bananas siblings—Patrick, Moon, Diva, and Dweezil—there is more creativity and humor in those four names than most people experience in a lifetime. Blessed. To our magical nieces—Mathilda, Zola, Ceylon, and Mia—the Star Darlings adore you and so do we. Our witchy cuzzie fairy godmothers—Ane and Gina. Our fairy fashion godfather, Paris. Our sweet Panay. Teeta and Freddy—we love you all so much. And our four-legged fur babies—Sandwich, Luna, Figgy, and Pinky Star.

The incredible Barry Waldo, our SD partner. Sent to us from above in perfect timing. Your expertise and friendship are beyond words. We love you and Gary to the moon and back. Long live the manifestation room!

Catherine Daly—the stars shined brightly upon us the day we aligned with you. Your talent and inspiration are otherworldly; our appreciation cannot be expressed in words. Many heartfelt hugs for you and the adorable Oonagh.

To our beloved Disney family. Thank you for believing in us. Wendy Lefkon, our master guide and friend through this entire journey. Stephanie Lurie, for being the first to believe in Star Darlings. Suzanne Murphy, who helped every step of the way. Jeanne Mosure, we fell in love with you the first time we met, and Star Darlings wouldn't be what it is without you. Andrew Sugerman, thank you so much for all your support.

Our team . . . Devon (pony pants) and our Monsterfoot crew—so grateful. Richard Scheltinga—our angel and protector. Chris Abramson—thank you! Special appreciation to Richard Thompson, John LaViolette, Swanna, Mario, and Sam.

To our friends old and new—we are so grateful to be on this rad journey that is life with you all. Fay. Jorja. Chandra. Sananda. Sandy. Kathryn. Louise. What wisdom and strength you share. Ruth, Mike, and the rest of our magical Wagon Wheel bunch—how lucky we are. How inspiring you are. We love you.

Last—we have immeasurable gratitude for every person we've met along our journey, for all the good and the bad; it is all a gift. From the bottom of our hearts we thank you for touching our lives.

Shana Muldoon Zappa is a jewelry designer and writer who was born and raised in Los Angeles. She has an endless imagination and a passion to inspire positivity through her many artistic endeavors. She and her husband, Ahmet Zappa, collaborated on Star Darlings especially for their magical little girl and biggest inspiration, Halo Violetta Zappa.

Ahmet Zappa is the *New York Times* best-selling author of *Because I'm Your Dad* and *The Monstrous Memoirs of a Mighty McFearless*. He writes and produces films and television shows and loves pancakes, unicorns, and making funny faces for Halo and Shana.

Cassie
Comes Through

"Well, there you are, Itty!" Cassie cooed as her pet glowfur landed on her shoulder and gave her pale cheek a nuzzle. Itty's soft fur tickled her face and made the girl giggle. Cassie finished twisting her long, glimmering pinkish-white hair into a second pigtail bun, fastened it in place with a starpin, and reached over to give the creature a quick pat. She was rewarded with Itty's Song of Contentment, and Cassie, who had heard it many times before, hummed along.

"That's really pretty," someone said. Cassie turned around to find her roommate smiling at her. Sage was freshly gleaming from her sparkle shower, wrapped in a soft lavender towel that matched her hair and eyes.

Cassie nodded in agreement. "Did you know that glowfurs have twenty-six distinct songs?" she asked. "And that each glowfur has her own version of each tune? This is one of my favorites. After the Song of Joy and Song of Enchantment, of course."

"I can't believe it," said Sage. Then she laughed. "Actually, I'm pretty sure you've told me that before."

Not letting go of her towel, Sage opened her closet door with her wish energy manipulation skills and quickly got dressed behind it. Cassie, who was a private person herself, was grateful to have a similarly modest roommate. When Sage emerged, she was wearing a loosely woven, shimmery sweater over a long sleeveless dress that flickered and changed color as she moved—exhibiting more shades of purple than Cassie knew even existed.

Sage shook her head in mock seriousness. "Actually, what I really can't believe is you still haven't gotten caught with that thing," she said with a laugh.

Itty gave a squeak of indignation and Cassie said, "She's just kidding, Itty." To Sage she said, "This *thing* is my pride and joy." Itty gave another squeak, this time of approval. Cassie knew Sage was just teasing. She was actually quite fond of Itty, and even smuggled dessert leftovers out of the Celestial Café with the intent to entice the little creature to eat out of her hand. Plus, of course, she willingly kept Cassie's secret to herself.

"That's because Itty and I are very careful," said Cassie, smoothing her silver tunic with the ruffled hem. Itty took off from Cassie's shoulder and circled the room, still singing her song. Cassie smiled at Sage. "And because I have a very discreet roommate."

Sage nodded as she crouched to buckle her sandals. "I *am* discreet, aren't I?"

"You are," said Cassie. She had read the Starling Academy Student Manual from cover to cover and knew quite well that pets were expressly forbidden in the student dormitories. She told herself that she had taken Itty to school with her because the creature would have been lonely back at her uncle's mansion. He was away on book tours more often than he was home. But the truth was that Cassie simply couldn't part with her pet, who had once belonged to her dear departed mother. When Itty sang her evening song, Cassie knew that her mother had fallen asleep to the very same tune many staryears before. It wasn't much, in the grand scheme of things, but it brought her great comfort. So Cassie had packed up Itty and a case of green globules and successfully smuggled her past the Bot-Bot guards on the first day of school.

Sage stood and walked over to the door, her lavender braids gleaming.

"Ready to start the starday?" she asked Cassie.

"Ready!" said Cassie. Itty zoomed in for a kiss on her furry head and began her good-bye song, but it was the shortened version, not the one she'd sing if Cassie ever left her behind to go on a long voyage. She knew Cassie would be back in mere starhours.

Cassie hurried to the door. "Oh, let me," she begged, so Sage stepped aside. Cassie concentrated on opening the door with her wish energy manipulation skills and the door began to tremble, almost imperceptibly, as if it were trying to decide whether it wanted to be opened or stay closed. A starmin or so later, after Cassie's pale face got quite pink from the effort, the door slid open fluidly.

Cassie grinned and turned to Sage. "You're like my good luck charm, Sage," she said. "I wish I was as good in Wishful Thinking class as I am in our room." She shrugged. "I guess I get stage fright or something."

Sage nodded and for a starsec Cassie thought she caught a flicker of a smile on her roommate's face. But it disappeared as they stepped into the hallway and onto the Cosmic Transporter, and soon the observation slipped from Cassie's mind.

Cassie's stomach grumbled. "I wonder what to order for break—"

"Stop right there!" someone barked.

Cassie rolled her eyes and shook her head. They were standing on the Cosmic Transporter and couldn't stop even if they wanted to, for stars' sake.

But Sage laughed merrily. "Hurry up, Mojo!" she cried.

The Bot-Bot guard zoomed after them eagerly. His official name was MO-J4, but Sage thought that was too formal and had settled on the nickname, which he had embraced wholeheartedly. Mojo had taken an instant starshine to Sage during her orientation tour and had been delighted by everything Sage did and said ever since. Cassie later discovered that Bot-Bots generally acted by the holo-book, with a preset vocabulary and a limited range of programmed reactions. But Mojo was special. He had a personality that was silly and fun, and he often greeted Sage with special jokes and occasionally left a gift on her doorstep.

Cassie couldn't help feeling a small stab of jealousy as Mojo excitedly told Sage about the morning's star-rise and showed her the holo-video he had taken just for her. Sometimes Cassie wished that she and Itty could talk like Sage and Mojo did. Though she wasn't quite sure what Itty would say. Most likely, "More green globules, please." Or maybe, "Rub my glowbelly for another star-hour if you don't mind." The only present (besides the gift of music) that Itty had ever given Cassie was a half-eaten green globule, left in the toe of her silver slipper. And by the time Cassie had found it, it was as hard as a meteorite. Cassie had tossed it into the vanishing garbage can. She knew exactly what green globules tasted like, even at the peak of freshness. Horrible.

Still, she wouldn't trade Itty for all the wish energy on Starland. She half-listened to Sage and Mojo chat away. She smiled, remembering that Sage had initially confided in her that she found MO-J4's slavish devotion a bit annoying. But then the silvery creature had started to grow on her. Sage was used to small annoying creatures, she had told Cassie, who laughed, knowing she was referring to her younger twin brothers, who could be quite a handful. As an only child, and an orphaned one at that, Cassie had nodded along in apparent sympathy. But Cassie would have liked nothing more than an annoying sibling (or two or even three) to liven things up around her uncle's quiet home. That's why she liked it there at Starling Academy so much, she realized. It was lively and there was always something going on to keep her entertained. Like that time when Astra had bet everyone that she could do a triple flip off the starbounce—while eating a half-moon pie. It had looked like she was going to win the wager, too, when Leona had—

Just then she realized Sage was trying to get her attention. "Cassie!" she was saying, snapping her fingers in Cassie's face. Cassie blinked. "We haven't even discussed Scarlet's return yet! I mean, that was so unexpected. So what do you think about—"

Cassie held up her hand. She turned to MO-J4. "I'm going to shut off your hearing," she told the Bot-Bot. Even though he was extremely devoted to Sage, the Star Darlings couldn't take any chances with anyone—or anything—learning about their secret missions.

MO-J4's eyes flashed as if he was annoyed by the request, but he politely acquiesced. "Certainly, Cassie," he said smoothly.

Sage nodded her thanks. "Though I'm sure he wouldn't say a word," she hurriedly said.

"I know," said Cassie. "But as loyal as he is, we really can't take any chances. Lady Stella would want it this way."

Sage nodded solemnly. "So what do you think about Scarlet's return?" she asked. "What does it mean?"